MASTERWORKS OF
CRIME & MYSTERY

SIR ARTHUR CONAN DOYLE

MASTERWORKS
OF
CRIME & MYSTERY

Edited by Jack Tracy

The Dial Press
New York

mys

For

PETER E. BLAU

with all thanks for
his suggestions, encouragement and practical advice
in the preparation of this volume

Published by
The Dial Press
1 Dag Hammarskjold Plaza
New York, New York 10017

Manufactured in the United States of America
First printing

Library of Congress Cataloging in Publication Data

Doyle, Arthur Conan, Sir, 1859–1930.
Masterworks of crime and mystery.

1. Crime and criminals—Fiction.   2. Mystery and
detective stories, English.   I. Tracy, Jack, 1945–
II. Title.
PR4621.T7   1982   823'.8   82-10312
ISBN 0-385-27688-5

8-29-83

Contents

Introduction

"**B**EING a medical man," says the narrator of "The Recollections of Captain Wilkie," one of the stories in this collection, "I had none of that shrinking from crime and criminals which many men possess. I could make allowances for congenital influence and the force of circumstances."

It is no coincidence that the inventor of the modern detective story was, for the first ten years of his professional life, a physician in active practice. That Sherlock Holmes was in large part modeled after Prof. Joseph Bell, the diagnostic wizard of the Edinburgh medical school, is a well-known story which needs no retelling here. That the good Watson, Holmes's biographer, is himself a doctor is a natural outgrowth of his creator's background and the literary trends to be seen in the early stories of the present volume.

For Sir Arthur Conan Doyle's interest in crime and criminals, in mystery and deduction, was not limited to Sherlock Holmes. Both before and after the invention of Holmes, he wrote many fine tales of the type, most of which remain obscure and many altogether forgotten. His 1890 novel *The Firm of Girdlestone*, for instance, is a striking example of the psychological crime story, written decades before the likes of Cornell Woolrich and Francis Iles. The better specimens of his shorter crime and mystery fiction are collected here, many for the first time anywhere — and the most casual reader will perceive a remarkable prevalence of doctors and medical students in the leading roles.

A certain caution has to be exercised in assembling such a collection. The expectations of mystery readers in those days were not nearly as sophisticated as they are today, and Doyle, like his contemporaries, was at all times more concerned with character and incident than with plot. The result is that most nineteenth-century mystery stories, Doyle's included, are

curiously disappointing to us today. Having presented his
mystery and gauged his characters' reactions to it, the writer
then had no compunctions about revealing the solution through
the chance discovery of a letter or a secret passage, or through
the sudden, unmotivated confession of the culprit. There was
seldom any thought of the protagonist's unraveling the puzzle
through his own efforts, nor, oddly enough, of bringing the
criminal to justice, of seeing to the triumph of right. The idea of
finding clues and deducing from them the facts of the case was
left to a doctor-turned-writer who had the imagination to turn
the diagnostic technique of one profession to the purpose of the
other. But even then, the baffled victim had to resort to the
expertise of Sherlock Holmes rather than to his own resources.
Few of the Holmes tales are "fair" mysteries in the modern
sense, and the villain still gets away as often as not.

As a result, some of Conan Doyle's most powerful stories will
not be found in these pages. Among them may be mentioned the
two famous semi-Holmesian tales "The Man with the Watches"
and "The Lost Special," as well as "The Japanned Box," "B.24"
and "The Fiend of the Cooperage," all of which may be found in
the 1908 *Round the Fire Stories,* and "The Prisoner's Defence,"
which appears in *Danger! and Other Stories* (1918) — fine
narratives all, but omitted here because they are too well known
and because they do not present satisfying examples of the self-
reliant hero.

On the other hand, one or two of Conan Doyle's better-known
efforts have been included precisely because their protagonists'
resourcefulness reveals the author's best talents. A couple of
others are here for balance and variety, so that the volume may
lay some small claim to being as representative as one of its
limited size and scope may be. But the emphasis here is mainly
on those stories which have lain long enough in the shadow of
Sherlock Holmes and which deserve the attention both of the
reader who is looking for a good yarn and of the serious student
of Sir Arthur's work.

The tales in this collection were written between 1879 and
1898, and their publication neatly brackets the creation, phe-
nomenal success, and death of Sherlock Holmes during 1887–93.
Many of them could just as easily have been presented as
Holmes's cases, but they were not, which supports the notion
that Doyle preferred not to write of Holmes if he could avoid it.

"The Brazilian Cat" has strong parallels with Holmes's adventure of "The Engineer's Thumb." "The Case of Lady Sannox" might just as easily have been told to the great detective in the manner of "The Cardboard Box" or "The Veiled Lodger." Certainly Doyle's statement in his autobiography of his vow never to write a Holmes story which was not as good as he could possibly make it is suspect in this context, for "The Brazilian Cat" and "Lady Sannox" are both superior to the Holmesian tales with which they are to be compared. Some of these pieces, such as "Uncle Jeremy's Household," "The Parasite" or "The Winning Shot," in which the slow perception of impending tragedy provides the interest of the narrative, would not be successful as Holmes's cases. Some, the "caper" tales in particular, depend on humor for their success, and the Baker Street sleuth was a notoriously humorless fellow. Others deal too explicitly with the supernatural, as in "The Parasite" and "Lot No. 249," for Holmes firmly rejected any possibility of other than mundane influences, and his attitude was borne out even in the most macabre of his investigations. Still others can be seen actually to have foreshadowed the great detective — "The Mystery of Sasassa Valley" and especially "The Recollections of Captain Wilkie" are uncannily Sherlockian, even if they predate his creation.

So even though the stories collected here were largely contemporaneous with Sherlock Holmes, for one reason or another they did not become part of the Holmes saga. They are not numerous — to be sure, the quantity of Doyle's non-Holmes mysteries does not begin to compare with the number of cases narrated by Dr. Watson. And, after 1899, they pretty much cease altogether. Once he had brought Holmes back to life in 1901, Doyle wrote no more than two or three non-Holmes crime stories during all the rest of his career, and none of them is very distinguished.

Here then is the cream of Sir Arthur Conan Doyle's short mystery and crime fiction. Holmes and Moriarty may be lacking, but they abound nonetheless with memorable heroes and equally memorable villains. They display their author's typically suspenseful plots, vivid detail, and effortless narrative. They provide *dénouements* calculated to please the most demanding reader. And, while they are brimming with medical men of every description, they feature not a single detective. Sherlock Holmes was the only one Doyle ever invented.

MASTERWORKS OF CRIME & MYSTERY

The Mystery of
Sasassa Valley

*Young A. Conan Doyle was writing before he was practicing.
"The Mystery of Sasassa Valley," his first story, was published
anonymously in September 1879, when he was still a twenty-
year-old medical student at Edinburgh. He was paid £3 for it. It
was an auspicious beginning. Not only did it appear in the
prestigious* CHAMBERS'S JOURNAL, *but it is a tale of deduction,
in which the distinctive Doyle approach is already thoroughly
developed.*

Do I know why Tom Donahue is called "Lucky Tom"? Yes;
I do; and that is more than one in ten of those who call
him so can say. I have knocked about a deal in my time, and
seen some strange sights, but none stranger than the way in
which Tom gained that sobriquet and his fortune with it. For I
was with him at the time. — Tell it? Oh, certainly; but it is a
longish story and a very strange one; so fill up your glass again,
and light another cigar while I try to reel it off. Yes; a very
strange one; beats some fairy stories I have heard; but it's true,
sir, every word of it. There are men alive at Cape Colony now
who'll remember it and confirm what I say. Many a time has the
tale been told round the fire in Boers' cabins from Orange State
to Griqualand; yes, and out in the Bush and at the Diamond
Fields too.

I'm roughish now, sir; but I was entered at the Middle Temple
once, and studied for the Bar. Tom — worse luck! — was one of
my fellow-students; and a wildish time we had of it, until at last
our finances ran short, and we were compelled to give up our so-
called studies, and look about for some part of the world where
two young fellows with strong arms and sound constitutions
might make their mark. In those days the tide of emigration had
scarcely begun to set in towards Africa, and so we thought our

3

best chance would be down at Cape Colony. Well—to make a long story short—we set sail, and were deposited in Cape Town with less than five pounds in our pockets; and there we parted. We each tried our hands at many things, and had ups and downs; but when, at the end of three years, chance led each of us up-country and we met again, we were, I regret to say, in almost as bad a plight as when we started.

Well, this was not much of a commencement; and very disheartened we were, so disheartened that Tom spoke of going back to England and getting a clerkship. For you see we didn't know that we had played out all our small cards, and that the trumps were going to turn up. No; we thought our "hands" were bad all through. It was a very lonely part of the country that we were in, inhabited by a few scattered farmers, whose houses were stockaded and fenced in to defend them against the Kaffirs. Tom Donahue and I had a little hut right out in the Bush; but we were known to possess nothing, and to be handy with our revolvers, so we had little to fear. There we waited, doing odd jobs, and hoping that something would turn up. Well, after we had been there about a month something did turn up upon a certain night, something which was the making of both of us; and it's about that night, sir, that I'm going to tell you. I remember it well. The wind was howling past our cabin, and the rain threatened to burst in our rude window. We had a great wood-fire crackling and sputtering on the hearth, by which I was sitting mending a whip, while Tom was lying in his bunk groaning disconsolately at the chance which had led him to such a place.

"Cheer up, Tom—cheer up," said I. "No man ever knows what may be awaiting him."

"Ill-luck, ill-luck, Jack," he answered. "I always was an unlucky dog. Here have I been three years in this abominable country; and I see lads fresh from England jingling the money in their pockets, while I am as poor as when I landed. Ah, Jack, if you want to keep your head above water, old friend, you must try your fortune away from me."

"Nonsense, Tom; you're down in your luck to-night. But hark! Here's some one coming outside. Dick Wharton, by the tread; he'll rouse you, if any man can."

Even as I spoke the door was flung open, and honest Dick Wharton, with the water pouring from him, stepped in, his hearty red face looming through the haze like a harvest-moon. He shook himself, and after greeting us sat down by the fire to warm himself.

"Whereaway, Dick, on such a night as this?" said I. "You'll find the rheumatism a worse foe than the Kaffirs, unless you keep more regular hours."

Dick was looking unusually serious, almost frightened, one would say, if one did not know the man. "Had to go," he replied —"had to go. One of Madison's cattle was seen straying down Sasassa Valley, and of course none of our blacks would go down *that* valley at night; and if we had waited till morning, the brute would have been in Kaffirland."

"Why wouldn't they go down Sasassa Valley at night?" asked Tom.

"Kaffirs, I suppose," said I.

"Ghosts," said Dick.

We both laughed.

"I suppose they didn't give such a matter-of-fact fellow as you a sight of their charms?" said Tom from the bunk.

"Yes," said Dick seriously—"yes; I saw what the niggers talk about; and I promise you, lads, I don't want ever to see it again."

Tom sat up in his bed. "Nonsense, Dick; you're joking, man! Come, tell us all about it. The legend first, and your own experience afterwards. — Pass him over the bottle, Jack."

"Well, as to the legend," began Dick—"it seems that the niggers have had it handed down to them that the Sasassa Valley is haunted by a frightful fiend. Hunters and wanderers passing down the defile have seen its glowing eyes under the shadows of the cliff; and the story goes that whoever has chanced to en-counter that baleful glare, has had his after-life blighted by the malignant power of this creature. Whether that be true or not," continued Dick ruefully, "I may have an opportunity of judging for myself."

"Go on, Dick — go on," cried Tom. "Let's hear about what you saw."

"Well, I was groping down the valley, looking for that cow of Madison's, and I had, I suppose, got half-way down, where a black craggy cliff juts into the ravine on the right, when I halted to have a pull at my flask. I had my eye at the time upon the projecting cliff I have mentioned, and noticed nothing unusual about it. I then put up my flask and took a step or two forward, when in a moment there burst apparently from the base of the rock, about eight feet from the ground and a hundred yards from me, a strange lurid glare, flickering and oscillating, gradually dying away and then reappearing again. — No, no; I've seen many a glow-worm and firefly — nothing of that sort. There it was burning away, and I suppose I gazed at it, trembling in every limb, for fully ten minutes. Then I took a step forwards, when instantly it vanished, vanished like a candle blown out. I stepped back again; but it was some time before I could find the exact spot and position from which it was visible. At last, there it was, the weird reddish light, flickering away as before. Then I screwed up my courage, and made for the rock; but the ground was so uneven that it was impossible to steer straight; and, though I walked along the whole base of the cliff, I could see nothing. Then I made tracks for home; and I can tell you, boys, that until you remarked it, I never knew it was raining, the whole way along. — But hello! what's the matter with Tom?"

What indeed? Tom was now sitting with his legs over the side of the bunk, and his whole face betraying excitement so intense as to be almost painful. "The fiend would have two eyes. How many lights did you see, Dick? Speak out!"

"Only one."

"Hurrah!" cried Tom — "that's better!" Whereupon he kicked the blankets into the middle of the room, and began pacing up and down with long feverish strides. Suddenly he stopped opposite Dick, and laid his hand upon his shoulder: "I say, Dick, could we get to Sasassa Valley before sunrise?"

"Scarcely," said Dick.

"Well, look here; we are old friends, Dick Wharton, you and I. Now, don't you tell any other man what you have told us, for a week. You'll promise that; won't you?"

I could see by the look on Dick's face as he acquiesced that he considered poor Tom to be mad; and indeed I was myself completely mystified by his conduct. I had, however, seen so many proofs of my friend's good sense and quickness of apprehension, that I thought it quite possible that Wharton's story had had a meaning in his eyes which I was too obtuse to take in.

All night Tom Donahue was greatly excited, and when

Wharton left he begged him to remember his promise, and also elicited from him a description of the exact spot at which he had seen the apparition, as well as the hour at which it appeared. After his departure, which must have been about four in the morning, I turned into my bunk and watched Tom sitting by the fire splicing two sticks together, until I fell asleep. I suppose I must have slept about two hours; but when I awoke, Tom was still sitting working away in almost the same position. He had fixed the one stick across the top of the other so as to form a rough T, and was now busy in fitting a smaller stick into the angle between them, by manipulating which, the cross one could be either cocked up or depressed to any extent. He had cut notches too in the perpendicular stick, so that by the aid of the small prop, the cross one could be kept in any position for an indefinite time.

"Look here, Jack!" he cried, whenever he saw that I was awake. "Come, and give me your opinion. Suppose I put this cross-stick pointing straight at a thing, and arranged this small one so as to keep it so, and left it, I could find that thing again if I wanted it — don't you think I could, Jack — don't you think so?" he continued nervously, clutching me by the arm.

"Well," I answered, "it would depend on how far off the thing was, and how accurately it was pointed. If it were any distance, I'd cut sights on your cross-stick; then a string tied to the end of it, and held in a plumb-line forwards, would lead you pretty near what you wanted. But surely, Tom, you don't intend to localize the ghost in that way?"

"You'll see to-night, old friend — you'll see to-night. I'll carry this to the Sasassa Valley. You get the loan of Madison's crowbar, and come with me; but mind you tell no man where you are going, or what you want it for."

All day Tom was walking up and down the room, or working hard at the apparatus. His eyes were glistening, his cheek hectic, and he had all the symptoms of high fever. "Heaven grant that Dick's diagnosis be not correct!" I thought as I returned with the crowbar; and yet, as evening drew near, I found myself imperceptibly sharing the excitement.

About six o'clock Tom sprang to his feet and seized his sticks. "I can stand it no longer, Jack," he cried; "up with your crowbar, and hey for Sasassa Valley! To-night's work, my lad, will either make us or mar us! Take your six-shooter, in case we meet the Kaffirs. I daren't take mine, Jack," he continued, putting his hands upon my shoulders—"I daren't take mine; for if my ill-luck sticks to me to-night, I don't know what I might not do with it."

Well, having filled our pockets with provisions, we set out, and as we took our wearisome way towards the Sasassa Valley, I frequently attempted to elicit from my companion some clue as to his intentions. But his only answer was: "Let us hurry on, Jack. Who knows how many have heard of Wharton's adventure by this time! Let us hurry on, or we may not be first in the field!"

Well, sir, we struggled on through the hills for a matter of ten miles; till at last, after descending a crag, we saw opening out in front of us a ravine so sombre and dark that it might have been the gate of Hades itself; cliffs many hundred feet high shut in on every side the gloomy boulder-studded passage which led through the haunted defile into Kaffirland. The moon rising above the crags, threw into strong relief the rough irregular pinnacles of rock by which they were topped, while all below was dark as Erebus.

"The Sasassa Valley?" said I.

"Yes," said Tom.

I looked at him. He was calm now; the flush and feverishness had passed away; his actions were deliberate and slow. Yet there was a certain rigidity in his face and glitter in his eye which showed that a crisis had come.

We entered the pass, stumbling along amid the great boulders. Suddenly I heard a short quick exclamation from Tom. "That's the crag!" he cried, pointing to a great mass looming before us in the darkness. "Now, Jack, for any favour use your eyes! We're about a hundred yards from that cliff, I take it; so you move slowly towards one side, and I'll do the same towards the other. When you see anything, stop, and call out. Don't take more than twelve inches in a step, and keep your eye fixed on the cliff about eight feet from the ground. Are you ready?"

"Yes." I was even more excited than Tom by this time. What his intention or object was, I could not conjecture, beyond that he wanted to examine by daylight the part of the cliff from which the light came. Yet the influence of the romantic situation and of my companion's suppressed excitement was so great   that I could feel the blood coursing through my veins and count the pulses throbbing at my temples.

"Start!" cried Tom; and we moved off, he to the right, I to the left, each with our eyes fixed intently on the base of the crag. I had moved perhaps twenty feet, when in a moment it burst upon me. Through the growing darkness there shone a small ruddy glowing point, the light from which waned and increased, flickered and oscillated, each change producing a more weird effect than the last. The old Kaffir superstition came into my mind, and I felt a cold shudder pass over me. In my excitement, I stepped a pace backwards, when instantly the light went out, leaving utter darkness in its place; but when I advanced again, there was the ruddy glare glowing from the base of the cliff. "Tom, Tom!" I cried.

"Ay, ay!" I heard him exclaim, as he hurried over towards me.

"There it is — there, up against the cliff!"

Tom was at my elbow. "I see nothing," said he.

"Why, there, there, man, in front of you!" I stepped to the right as I spoke, when the light instantly vanished from my eyes.

But from Tom's ejaculations of delight it was clear that from my former position it was visible to him also. "Jack," he cried, as he turned and wrung my hand — "Jack, you and I can never complain of our luck again. Now heap up a few stones where we are standing. — That's right. Now we must fix my sign-post firmly in at the top. There! It would take a strong wind to blow that down; and we only need it to hold out till morning. Oh Jack, my boy, to think that only yesterday we were talking of becoming clerks, and you saying that no man knew what was awaiting him too! By Jove, Jack, it would make a good story!"

By this time we had firmly fixed the perpendicular stick in between two large stones; and Tom bent down and peered along the horizontal one. For fully a quarter of an hour he was alternately raising and depressing it, until at last, with a sigh of satisfaction, he fixed the prop into the angle, and stood up. "Look along, Jack," he said. "You have as straight an eye to take a sight as any man I know of."

I looked along. There, beyond the further sight was the ruddy scintillating speck, apparently at the end of the stick itself, so accurately had it been adjusted.

"And now, my boy," said Tom, "let's have some supper, and a

sleep. There's nothing more to be done to-night; but we'll need all our wits and strength to-morrow. Get some sticks, and kindle a fire here, and then we'll be able to keep an eye on our signal-post, and see that nothing happens to it during the night."

Well, sir, we kindled a fire, and had supper with the Sasassa demon's eye rolling and glowing in front of us the whole night through. Not always in the same place, though; for after supper, when I glanced along the sights to have another look at it, it was nowhere to be seen. The information did not, however, seem to disturb Tom in any way. He merely remarked: "It's the moon, not the thing, that has shifted"; and coiling himself up, went to sleep.

By early dawn we were both up, and gazing along our pointer at the cliff; but we could make out nothing save the one dead monotonous slaty surface, rougher perhaps at the part we were examining than elsewhere, but otherwise presenting nothing remarkable.

"Now for your idea, Jack!" said Tom Donahue, unwinding a long thin cord from round his waist. "You fasten it, and guide me while I take the other end." So saying he walked off to the base of the cliff, holding one end of the cord, while I drew the other taut, and wound it round the middle of the horizontal stick, passing it through the sight at the end. By this means I could direct Tom to the right or left, until we had our string stretching from the point of attachment, through the sight, and on to the rock, which it struck about eight feet from the ground. Tom drew a chalk circle of about three feet diameter round the spot, and then called to me to come and join him. "We've managed this business together, Jack," he said, "and we'll find what we are to find, together." The circle he had drawn embraced a part of the rock smoother than the rest, save that about the centre there were a few rough protuberances or knobs. One of these Tom pointed to with a cry of delight. It was a roughish brownish mass about the size of a man's closed fist, and looking like a bit of dirty glass let into the wall of the cliff. "That's it!" he cried—"that's it!"

"That's what?"

"Why, man, *a diamond,* and such a one as there isn't a monarch in Europe but would envy Tom Donahue the possession of. Up with your crowbar, and we'll soon exorcise the demon of Sasassa Valley!"

I was so astounded that for a moment I stood speechless with surprise, gazing at the treasure which had so unexpectedly fallen into our hands.

"Here, hand me the crowbar," said Tom. "Now, by using this little round knob which projects from the cliff here, as a fulcrum, we may be able to lever it off. — Yes; there it goes. I never thought it could come so easily. Now, Jack, the sooner we get back to our hut and then down to Cape Town, the better."

We wrapped up our treasure, and made our way across the hills, towards home. On the way, Tom told me how, while a law student in the Middle Temple, he had come upon a dusty pamphlet in the library, by one Jans van Hounym, which told of an experience very similar to ours, which had befallen that worthy Dutchman in the latter part of the seventeenth century, and which resulted in the discovery of a luminous diamond. This tale it was which had come into Tom's head as he listened to honest Dick Wharton's ghost story; while the means which he had adopted to verify his supposition sprang from his own fertile Irish brain.

"We'll take it down to Cape Town," continued Tom, "and if we can't dispose of it with advantage there, it will be worth our while to ship for London with it. Let us go along to Madison's first, though; he knows something of these things, and can perhaps give us some idea of what we may consider a fair price for our treasure."

We turned off from the track accordingly, before reaching our hut, and kept along the narrow path leading to Madison's farm. He was at lunch when we entered; and in a minute we were seated at each side of him, enjoying South African hospitality.

"Well," he said, after the servants were gone, "what's in the wind now? I see you have something to say to me. What is it?"

Tom produced his packet, and solemnly untied the handkerchiefs which enveloped it. "There!" he said, putting his crystal on the table; "what would you say was a fair price for that?"

Madison took it up and examined it critically. "Well," he said, laying it down again, "in its crude state about twelve shillings per ton."

"Twelve shillings!" cried Tom, starting to his feet. "Don't you see what it is?"

"Rock-salt!"

"Rock fiddle; a diamond."

"Taste it!" said Madison.

Tom put it to his lips, dashed it down with a dreadful exclamation, and rushed out of the room.

I felt sad and disappointed enough myself; but presently remembering what Tom had said about the pistol, I, too, left the house, and made for the hut, leaving Madison open-mouthed with astonishment. When I got in, I found Tom lying in his bunk with his face to the wall, too dispirited apparently to answer my consolations. Anathematizing Dick and Madison, the Sasassa demon, and everything else, I strolled out of the hut, and refreshed myself with a pipe after our wearisome adventure. I was about fifty yards away from the hut, when I heard issuing from it the sound which of all others I least expected to hear. Had it been a groan or an oath, I should have taken it as a matter of course; but the sound which caused me to stop and take the pipe out of my mouth was a hearty roar of laughter! Next moment, Tom himself emerged from the door, his whole face radiant with delight. "Game for another ten-mile walk, old fellow?"

"What! for another lump of rock-salt, at twelve shillings a ton?"

"'No more of that, Hal, an you love me,'" grinned Tom. "Now look here, Jack. What blessed fools we are to be so floored by a trifle! Just sit on this stump for five minutes, and I'll make it as clear as daylight. You've seen many a lump of rock-salt stuck in a crag, and so have I, though we did make such a mull of this one. Now, Jack, did any of the pieces you have ever seen shine in the darkness brighter than any firefly?"

"Well, I can't say they ever did."

"I'd venture to prophecy that if we waited until night, which we won't do, we would see that light still glimmering among the rocks. Therefore, Jack, when we took away this worthless salt, we took the wrong crystal. It is no very strange thing in these hills that a piece of rock-salt should be lying within a foot of a diamond. It caught our eyes, and we were excited, and so we made fools of ourselves, and *left the real stone behind.* Depend upon it, Jack, the Sasassa gem is lying within that magic circle of chalk upon the face of yonder cliff. Come, old fellow, light your pipe and stow your revolver, and we'll be off before that fellow Madison has time to put two and two together."

I don't know that I was very sanguine this time. I had begun in fact to look upon the diamond as a most unmitigated nuisance. However, rather than throw a damper on Tom's expectations, I announced myself eager to start. What a walk it was! Tom was always a good mountaineer, but his excitement seemed to lend him wings that day, while I scrambled along after him as best I could. When we got within half a mile he broke into the "double," and never pulled up until he reached the round white circle upon the cliff. Poor old Tom! When I came up, his mood had changed, and he was standing with his hands in his pockets, gazing vacantly before him with a rueful countenance.

"Look!" he said—"look!" and he pointed at the cliff. Not a sign of anything in the least resembling a diamond there. The circle included nothing but flat slate-coloured stone, with one large hole, where we had extracted the rock-salt, and one or two smaller depressions. No sign of the gem.

"I've been over every inch of it," said poor Tom. "It's not there. Some one has been here and noticed the chalk, and taken it. Come home, Jack; I feel sick and tired. Oh! had any man ever luck like mine!"

I turned to go, but took one last look at the cliff first. Tom was already ten paces off.

"Hollo!" I cried, "don't you see any change in that circle since yesterday?"

"What d'ye mean?" said Tom.

"Don't you miss a thing that was there before?"

"The rock-salt?" said Tom.

"No; but the little round knob that we used for a fulcrum. I suppose we must have wrenched it off in using the lever. Let's have a look at what it's made of."

Accordingly, at the foot of the cliff we searched about among the loose stones.

"Here you are, Jack! We've done it at last! We're made men!"

I turned round, and there was Tom radiant with delight, and with a little corner of black rock in his hand. At first sight it seemed to be merely a chip from the cliff; but near the base there was projecting from it an object which Tom was now exultingly pointing out. It looked at first something like a glass eye; but there was a depth and brilliancy about it such as glass never exhibited. There was no mistake this time; we had certainly got possession of a jewel of great value; and with light hearts we turned from the valley, bearing away with us the "fiend" which had so long reigned there.

There, sir; I've spun my story out too long, and tired you perhaps. You see, when I get talking of those rough old days, I kind of see the little cabin again, and the brook beside it, and the bush around, and seem to hear Tom's honest voice once more. There's little for me to say now. We prospered on the gem. Tom Donahue, as you know, has set up here, and is well known about town. I have done well, farming and ostrich-raising in Africa. We set old Dick Wharton up in business, and he is one of our nearest neighbours. If you should ever be coming up our way, sir, you'll not forget to ask for Jack Turnbull — Jack Turnbull of Sasassa Farm.

Bones

In "Bones," as in "The Mystery of Sasassa Valley," Doyle was still feeling the influence of Bret Harte, whom he admired enough to emulate in a series of tales he wrote for the magazine LONDON SOCIETY *between 1879 and 1885. They all deal with the gold-mining communities of Australia, and the majority are unalloyed adventure yarns, though already displaying the deft characterizations which always distinguish his work. "Bones," subtitled "The April Fool of Harvey's Sluice" and appearing in the issue of April 1882, gives a broader picture of Australian frontier society and concerns itself with more than the gold robberies and personal violence which characterize the other stories in the group. It features, too, the kind of mild sentimentality at which Doyle excelled and which is too little in evidence in those works for which he is best known to readers today.*

ABE DURTON'S CABIN was not beautiful. People have been heard to assert that it was ugly, and, even after the fashion of Harvey's Sluice, have gone the length of prefixing their adjective with a forcible expletive which emphasized their criticism. Abe, however, was a stolid and easy-going man, on whose mind the remarks of an unappreciative public made but little impression. He had built the house himself, and it suited his partner and him, and what more did they want? Indeed he was rather touchy upon the subject. "Though I says it as raised it," he remarked, "it'll lay over any shanty in the valley. Holes? Well, of course there are holes. You wouldn't get fresh air without holes. There's nothing stuffy about *my* house. Rain? Well, if it does let the rain in, ain't it an advantage to know it's rainin' without gettin' up to unbar the door. I wouldn't own a house that didn't leak some. As to its bein' off the perpendic'lar, I like a house with a bit of a tilt. Anyways it pleases my pard,

Boss Morgan, and what's good enough for him is good enough for you, I suppose." At which approach to personalities his antagonist usually sheered off, and left the honours of the field to the indignant architect.

But whatever difference of opinion might exist as to the beauty of the establishment, there could be no question as to its utility. To the tired wayfarer, plodding along the Buckhurst road in the direction of the Sluice, the warm glow upon the summit of the hill was a beacon of hope and of comfort. Those very holes at which the neighbours sneered helped to diffuse a cheery atmosphere of light around, which was doubly acceptable on such a night as the present.

There was only one man inside the hut, and that was the proprietor, Abe Durton himself, or "Bones," as he had been christened with the rude heraldry of the camp. He was sitting in front of the great wood fire, gazing moodily into its glowing depths, and occasionally giving a faggot a kick of remonstrance when it showed any indication of dying into a smoulder. His fair Saxon face, with its bold simple eyes and crisp yellow beard, stood out sharp and clear against the darkness as the flickering light played over it. It was a manly resolute countenance, and yet the physiognomist might have detected something in the lines of the mouth which showed a weakness somewhere, an indecision which contrasted strangely with his herculean shoulders and massive limbs. Abe's was one of those trusting simple natures which are as easy to lead as they are impossible to drive; and it was this happy pliability of disposition which made him at once the butt and the favourite of the dwellers in the Sluice. Badinage in that primitive settlement was of a somewhat ponderous character, yet no amount of chaff had ever brought a dark look on Bones's face, or an unkind thought into his honest heart. It was only when his aristocratic partner was, as he thought, being put upon, that an ominous tightness about his lower lip and an angry light in his blue eyes caused even the most irrepressible humorist in the colony to nip his favourite joke in the bud, in order to diverge into an earnest and all-absorbing dissertation upon the state of the weather.

"The Boss is late to-night," he muttered as he rose from his chair and stretched himself in a colossal yawn. "My stars, how it does rain and blow! Don't it, Blinky?" Blinky was a demure and meditative owl, whose comfort and welfare was a chronic subject of solicitude to its master, and who at present contemplated him gravely from one of the rafters. "Pity you can't speak, Blinky," continued Abe, glancing up at his feathered companion. "There's a powerful deal of sense in your face. Kinder melancholy too. Crossed in love, maybe, when you was young. Talkin' of love," he added, "I've not seen Susan to-day"; and lighting the candle which stood in a black bottle upon the table, he walked across the room and peered earnestly at one of the many pictures from stray illustrated papers, which had been cut out by the occupants and posted up upon the walls.

The particular picture which attracted him was one which represented a very tawdrily-dressed actress simpering over a bouquet at an imaginary audience. This sketch had, for some inscrutable reason, made a deep impression upon the susceptible heart of the miner. He had invested the young lady with a human interest by solemnly, and without the slightest warrant, christening her as Susan Banks, and had then installed her as his standard of female beauty.

"You see my Susan," he would say, when some wanderer from Buckhurst, or even from Melbourne, would describe some fair Circe whom he had left behind him. "There ain't a girl like my Sue. If ever you go to the old country again, just you ask to see her. Susan Banks is her name, and I've got her picture up at the shanty."

Abe was still gazing at his charmer when the rough door was flung open, and a blinding cloud of sleet and rain came driving into the cabin, almost obscuring for the moment a young man who sprang in and proceeded to bar the entrance behind him, an operation which the force of the wind rendered no easy matter. He might have passed for the genius of the storm, with the water dripping from his long hair and running down his pale refined face.

"Well," he said, in a slightly peevish voice, "haven't you got any supper?"

"Waiting and ready," said his companion cheerily, pointing to a large pot which bubbled by the side of the fire. "You seem sort of damp."

"Damp be hanged! I'm soaked, man, thoroughly saturated. It's a night that I wouldn't have a dog out, at least not a dog that I had any respect for. Hand over that dry coat from the peg."

Jack Morgan, or Boss, as he was usually called, belonged to a type which was commoner in the mines during the flush times of the first great rush than would be supposed. He was a man of good blood, liberally educated, and a graduate of an English university. Boss should, in the natural course of things, have been an energetic curate, or struggling professional man, had not some latent traits cropped out in his character, inherited possibly from old Sir Henry Morgan, who had founded the family with Spanish pieces of eight gallantly won upon the high seas. It was this wild strain of blood no doubt which had caused him to drop from the bedroom window of the ivy-clad English parsonage, and leave home and friends behind him, to try his luck with pick and shovel in the Australian fields. In spite of his effeminate face and dainty manners, the rough dwellers in Harvey's Sluice had gradually learned that the little man was possessed of a cool courage and unflinching resolution, which won respect in a community where pluck was looked upon as the highest of human attributes. No one ever knew how it was that Bones and he had become partners; yet partners they were, and the large simple nature of the stronger man looked with an almost superstitious reverence upon the clear decisive mind of his companion.

"That's better," said the Boss, as he dropped into the vacant chair before the fire and watched Abe laying out the two metal plates, with the horn-handled knives and abnormally pronged forks. "Take your mining boots off, Bones; there's no use filling the cabin with red clay. Come here and sit down."

His gigantic partner came meekly over and perched himself upon the top of a barrel.

"What's up?" he asked.

"Shares are up," said his companion. "That's what's up. Look here," and he extracted a crumpled paper from the pocket of the steaming coat. "Here's the *Buckhurst Sentinel.* Read this article —this one here about a paying lead in the Conemara mine. We hold pretty heavily in that concern, my boy. We might sell out to-day and clear something—but I think we'll hold on."

Abe Durton in the mean time was laboriously spelling out the article in question, following the lines with his great forefinger, and muttering under his tawny moustache.

"Two hundred dollars a foot," he said, looking up. "Why, pard, we hold a hundred feet each. It would give us twenty thousand dollars! We might go home on that."

"Nonsense!" said his companion; "we've come out here for something better than a beggarly couple of thousand pounds. The thing is bound to pay. Sinclair the assayer has been over there, and says there's a ledge of the richest quartz he ever set eyes on. It is just a case of getting the machinery to crush it. By the way, what was to-day's take like?"

Abe extracted a small wooden box from his pocket and handed it to his comrade. It contained what appeared to be about a teaspoonful of sand and one or two little metallic granules not larger than a pea. Boss Morgan laughed, and returned it to his companion.

"We sha'n't make our fortune at that rate, Bones," he remarked; and there was a pause in the conversation as the two men listened to the wind as it screamed and whistled past the little cabin.

"Any news from Buckhurst?" asked Abe, rising and proceeding to extract their supper from the pot.

"Nothing much," said his companion. "Cock-eyed Joe has been shot by Billy Reid in McFarlane's Store."

"Ah," said Abe, with listless interest.

"Bushrangers have been around and stuck up the Rochdale station. They say they are coming over here."

The miner whistled as he poured some whisky into a jug.

"Anything more?" he asked.

"Nothing of importance except that the blacks have been showing a bit down New Sterling way, and that the assayer has bought a piano and is going to have his daughter out from Melbourne to live in the new house opposite on the other side of the road. So you see we are going to have something to look at, my boy," he added as he sat down, and began attacking the food set before him. "They say she is a beauty, Bones."

"She won't be a patch on my Sue," returned the other decisively.

His partner smiled as he glanced round at the flaring print upon the wall. Suddenly he dropped his knife and seemed to listen. Amid the wild uproar of the wind and the rain there was a low rumbling sound which was evidently not dependent upon the elements.

"What's that?"

"Darned if I know."

The two men made for the door and peered out earnestly into the darkness. Far away along the Buckhurst road they could see a moving light, and the dull sound was louder than before.

"It's a buggy coming down," said Abe.

"Where is it going to?"

"Don't know. Across the ford, I s'pose."

"Why, man, the ford will be six feet deep to-night, and running like a mill-stream."

The light was nearer now, coming rapidly round the curve of the road. There was a wild sound of galloping with the rattle of the wheels.

"Horses have bolted, by thunder!"

"Bad job for the man inside."

There was a rough individuality about the inhabitants of Harvey's Sluice, in virtue of which every man bore his misfortunes upon his own shoulders, and had very little sympathy for those of his neighbours. The predominant feeling of the two men was one of pure curiosity as they watched the swinging swaying lanterns coming down the winding road.

"If he don't pull 'em up before they reach the ford he's a goner," remarked Abe Durton resignedly.

Suddenly there came a lull in the sullen splash of the rain. It was but for a moment, but in that moment there came down on the breeze a long cry which caused the two men to start and stare at each other, and then to rush frantically down the steep incline towards the road below.

"A woman, by Heaven!" gasped Abe, as he sprang across the gaping shaft of a mine in the recklessness of his haste.

Morgan was the lighter and more active man. He drew away rapidly from his stalwart companion. Within a minute he was standing panting and bare-headed in the middle of the soft muddy road, while his partner was still toiling down the side of the declivity.

The carriage was close on him now. He could see in the light of the lamps the raw-boned Australian horse as, terrified by the

storm and by its own clatter, it came tearing down the declivity
which led to the ford. The man who was driving seemed to see
the pale set face in the pathway in front of him, for he yelled out
some incoherent words of warning, and made a last desperate
attempt to pull up. There was a shout, an oath, and a jarring
crash, and Abe, hurrying down, saw a wild infuriated horse
rearing madly in the air with a slim dark figure hanging on to its
bridle. Boss, with the keen power of calculation which had made
him the finest cricketer at Rugby in his day, had caught the rein
immediately below the bit, and clung to it with silent concentration. Once he was down with a heavy thud in the roadway as the
horse jerked its head violently forwards, but when, with a snort
of exultation, the animal pressed on, it was only to find that the
prostrate man beneath its fore-hoofs still maintained his un-
yielding grasp.

"Hold it, Bones," he said as a tall figure hurled itself into the
road and seized the other rein.

"All right, old man, I've got him"; and the horse, cowed by the
sight of a fresh assailant, quieted down, and stood shivering
with terror. "Get up, Boss, it's safe now."

But poor Boss lay groaning in the mud.

"I can't do it, Bones." There was a catch in the voice as of
pain. "There's something wrong, old chap, but don't make a
fuss. It's only a shake; give me a lift up."

Abe bent tenderly over his prostrate companion. He could see
that he was very white, and breathing with difficulty.

"Cheer up, old Boss," he murmured. "Hullo! my stars!"

The last two exclamations were shot out of the honest miner's
bosom as if they were impelled by some irresistible force, and he
took a couple of steps backward in sheer amazement. There at
the other side of the fallen man, and half shrouded in the
darkness, stood what appeared to Abe's simple soul to be the
most beautiful vision that ever had appeared upon earth. To
eyes accustomed to rest upon nothing more captivating than the
ruddy faces and rough beards of the miners in the Sluice, it
seemed that that fair delicate countenance must belong to a
wanderer from some better world. Abe gazed at it with a
wondering reverence, oblivious for the moment even of his
injured friend upon the ground.

"Oh papa," said the apparition, in great distress, "he is hurt, the gentleman is hurt"; and with a quick feminine gesture of sympathy, she bent her lithe figure over Boss Morgan's prostrate figure.

"Why, it's Abe Durton and his partner," said the driver of the buggy, coming forward and disclosing the grizzled features of Mr. Joshua Sinclair, the assayer to the mines. "I don't know how to thank you, boys. The infernal brute got the bit between his teeth, and I should have had to have thrown Carrie out and chanced it in another minute. That's right," he continued, as Morgan staggered to his feet. "Not much hurt, I hope."

"I can get up to the hut now," said the young man, steadying himself upon his partner's shoulder. "How are you going to get Miss Sinclair home?"

"O, we can walk," said that young lady, shaking off the effects of her fright with all the elasticity of youth.

"We can drive and take the road round the bank so as to avoid the ford," said her father. "The horse seems cowed enough now; you need not be afraid of it, Carrie. I hope we shall see you at the house, both of you. Neither of us can easily forget this night's work."

Miss Carrie said nothing, but she managed to shoot a little demure glance of gratitude from under her long lashes, to have won which honest Abe felt that he would have cheerfully undertaken to stop a runaway locomotive.

There was a cheery shout of "Good-night," a crack of the whip, and the buggy rattled away in the darkness.

"You told me the men were rough and nasty, pa," said Miss Carrie Sinclair, after a long silence, when the two dark shadows had died away in the distance, and the carriage was speeding along by the turbulent stream. "I don't think so. I think they are very nice." And Carrie was unusually quiet for the remainder of her journey, and seemed more reconciled to the hardship of leaving her dear friend Amelia in the far-off boarding school at Melbourne.

That did not prevent her from writing a full, true, and particular account of their little adventure to the same young lady upon that very night.

"They stopped the horse, darling, and one poor fellow was hurt. And O, Amy, if you had seen the other one in a red shirt, with a pistol at his waist! I couldn't help thinking of you, dear.

He was just your idea. You remember, a yellow moustache and great blue eyes. And how he did stare at poor me! You never see such men in Burke Street, Amy"; and so on, for four pages of pretty feminine gossip.

In the mean time poor Boss, badly shaken, had been helped up the hill by his partner and regained the shelter of the shanty. Abe doctored him out of the rude pharmacopoeia of the camp, and bandaged up his strained arm. Both were men of few words, and neither made any allusion to what had taken place. It was noticed, however, by Blinky that his master failed to pay his usual nightly orisons before the shrine of Susan Banks. Whether this sagacious fowl drew any deductions from this, and from the fact that Bones sat long and earnestly smoking by the smouldering fire, I know not. Suffice it that as the candle died away and the miner rose from his chair, his feathered friend flew down upon his shoulder, and was only prevented from giving vent to a sympathetic hoot by Abe's warning finger, and its own strong inherent sense of propriety.

A casual visitor dropping into the straggling township of Harvey's Sluice shortly after Miss Carrie Sinclair's arrival would have noticed a considerable alteration in the manners and customs of its inhabitants. Whether it was the refining influence of a woman's presence, or whether it sprang from an emulation excited by the brilliant appearance of Abe Durton, it is hard to say—probably from a blending of the two. Certain it is that that young man had suddenly developed an affection for cleanliness and a regard for the conventionalities of civilization, which aroused the astonishment and ridicule of his companions. That Boss Morgan should pay attention to his personal appearance had long been set down as a curious and inexplicable phenomenon, depending upon early education; but that loose-limbed easy-going Bones should flaunt about in a clean shirt was regarded by every grimy denizen of the Sluice as a direct and premeditated insult. In self-defense, therefore, there was a general cleaning up after working hours, and such a run upon the grocery establishment, that soap went up to an unprecedented figure, and a fresh consignment had to be ordered from McFarlane's store in Buckhurst.

"Is this here a free minin' camp, or is it a darned Sunday-

school?" had been the indignant query of Long McCoy, a
prominent member of the reactionary party, who had failed to
advance with the times, having been absent during the period of
regeneration. But his remonstrance met with but little sympathy;
and at the end of a couple of days a general turbidity of the creek
announced his surrender, which was confirmed by his appearance in the Colonial Bar with a shining and bashful face, and
hair which was redolent of bear's grease.

"I felt kinder lonesome," he remarked apologetically, "so I
thought as I'd have a look what was under the clay"; and he
viewed himself approvingly in the cracked mirror which graced
the select room of the establishment.

Our casual visitor would have noticed a remarkable change
also in the conversation of the community. Somehow, when a
certain dainty little bonnet with a sweet girlish figure beneath it
was seen in the distance among the disused shafts and mounds of
red earth which disfigured the sides of the valley, there was a
warning murmur, and a general clearing off of the cloud of
blasphemy, which was, I regret to state, an habitual characteristic of the working population of Harvey's Sluice. Such things
only need a beginning; and it was noticeable that long after Miss
Sinclair had vanished from sight there was a decided rise in the
moral barometer of the gulches. Men found by experience that
their stock of adjectives was less limited than they had been
accustomed to suppose, and that the less forcible were sometimes even more adapted for conveying their meaning.

Abe had formerly been considered one of the most experienced valuators of an ore in the settlement. It had been commonly supposed that he was able to estimate the amount of gold
in a fragment of quartz with remarkable exactness. This,
however, was evidently a mistake, otherwise he would never
have incurred the useless expense of having so many worthless
specimens assayed as he now did. Mr. Joshua Sinclair found
himself inundated with such a flood of fragments of mica, and
lumps of rock containing decimal percentages of the precious
metals, that he began to form a very low opinion of the young
man's mining capabilities. It is even asserted that Abe shuffled
up to the house one morning with a hopeful smile, and, after
some fumbling, produced half a brick from the bosom of his
jersey, with the stereotyped remark "that he thought he'd struck

it at last, and so had dropped in to ask him to cipher out an estimate." As this anecdote rests, however, upon the unsupported evidence of Jim Struggles, the humorist of the camp, there may be some slight inaccuracy of detail.

It is certain that what with professional business in the morning and social visits at night, the tall figure of the miner was a familiar object in the little drawing room of Azalea Villa, as the new house of the assayer had been magniloquently named. He seldom ventured upon a remark in the presence of its female occupant; but would sit on the extreme edge of his chair in a state of speechless admiration while she rattled off some lively air upon the newly-imported piano. Many were the strange and unexpected places in which his feet turned up. Miss Carrie had gradually come to the conclusion that they were entirely independent of his body, and had ceased to speculate upon the manner in which she would trip over them on one side of the table while the blushing owner was apologizing from the other. There was only one cloud on honest Bones's mental horizon, and that was the periodical appearance of Black Tom Ferguson, of Rochdale Ferry. This clever young scamp had managed to ingratiate himself with old Joshua, and was a constant visitor at the villa. There were evil rumours abroad about Black Tom. He was known to be a gambler, and shrewdly suspected to be worse. Harvey's Sluice was not censorious, and yet there was a general feeling that Ferguson was a man to be avoided. There was a reckless *élan* about his bearing, however, and a sparkle in his conversation, which had an indescribable charm, and even induced the Boss, who was particular in such matters, to cultivate his acquaintance while forming a correct estimate of his character. Miss Carrie seemed to hail his appearance as a relief, and chattered away for hours about books and music and the gaieties of Melbourne. It was on these occasions that poor simple Bones would sink into the very lowest depths of despondency, and either slink away, or sit glaring at his rival with an earnest malignancy which seemed to cause that gentleman no small amusement.

The miner made no secret to his partner of the admiration which he entertained for Miss Sinclair. If he was silent in her company, he was voluble enough when she was the subject of discourse. Loiterers upon the Buckhurst road might have heard

a stentorian voice upon the hill-side bellowing forth a vocabulary
of female charms. He submitted his difficulties to the superior
intelligence of the Boss.

"That loafer from Rochdale," he said, "he seems to reel it off
kinder nat'ral, while for the life of me I can't say a word. Tell
me, Boss, what would *you* say to a girl like that?"

"Why, talk about what would interest her," said his companion.

"Ah, that's where it lies."

"Talk about the customs of the place and the country," said
the Boss, pulling meditatively at his pipe. "Tell her stories of
what you have seen in the mines, and that sort of thing."

"Eh? You'd do that, would you?" responded his comrade
more hopefully. "If that's the hang of it I am right. I'll go up
now and tell her about Chicago Bill, an' how he put them two
bullets in the man from the bend the night of the dance."

Boss Morgan laughed.

"That's hardly the thing," he said. "You'd frighten her if you
told her that. Tell her something lighter, you know; something
to amuse her, something funny."

"Funny?" said the anxious lover, with less confidence in his
voice. "How you and me made Mat Houlahan drunk and put
him in the pulpit of the Baptist church, and he wouldn't let the
preacher in in the morning. How would that do, eh?"

"For heaven's sake don't say anything of the sort," said his
Mentor, in great consternation. "She'd never speak to either of
us again. No, what I mean is that you should tell about the
habits of the mines, how men live and work and die there. If she
is a sensible girl that ought to interest her."

"How they live at the mines? Pard, you are good to me. How
they live? There's a thing I can talk of as glib as Black Tom or
any man. I'll try it on her when I see her."

"By the way," said his partner listlessly, "just keep an eye on
that man Ferguson. His hands aren't very clean, you know, and
he's not scrupulous when he is aiming for anything. You
remember how Dick Williams, of English Town, was found
dead in the bush. Of course it was rangers that did it. They do
say, however, that Black Tom owed him a deal more money than
he could ever have paid. There's been one or two queer things
about him. Keep your eye on him, Abe. Watch what he does."

"I will," said his companion.

And he did. He watched him that very night. Watched him stride out of the house of the assayer with anger and baffled pride on every feature of his handsome swarthy face. Watched him clear the garden paling at a bound, pass in long rapid strides down the side of the valley, gesticulating wildly with his hands, and vanish into the bushland beyond. All this Abe Durton watched, and with a thoughtful look upon his face he relit his pipe and strolled slowly backward to the hut upon the hill.

March was drawing to a close in Harvey's Sluice, and the glare and heat of the antipodean summer had toned down into the rich mellow hues of autumn. It was never a lovely place to look upon. There was something hopelessly prosaic in the two bare rugged ridges, seamed and scarred by the hand of man, with iron arms of windlasses, and broken buckets projecting everywhere through the endless little hillocks of red earth. Down the middle ran the deeply rutted road from Buckhurst, winding along and crossing the sluggish tide of Harper's Creek by a crumbling wooden bridge. Beyond the bridge lay the cluster of little huts with the Colonial Bar and the Grocery towering in all the dignity of whitewash among the humble dwellings around. The assayer's verandah-lined house lay above the gulches on the side of the slope nearly opposite the dilapidated specimen of architecture of which our friend Abe was so unreasonably proud.

There was one other building which might have come under the category of what an inhabitant of the Sluice would have described as a "public edifice" with a comprehensive wave of his pipe which conjured up images of an endless vista of colonnades and minarets. This was the Baptist chapel, a modest little shingle-roofed erection on the bend of the river about a mile above the settlement. It was from this that the town looked at its best, when the harsh outlines and crude colours were somewhat softened by distance. On that particular morning the stream looked pretty as it meandered down the valley; pretty, too, was the long rising upland beyond, with its luxuriant green covering; and prettiest of all was Miss Carrie Sinclair, as she laid down the basket of ferns which she was carrying, and stopped upon the summit of the rising ground.

Something seemed to be amiss with that young lady. There was a look of anxiety upon her face which contrasted strangely

with her usual appearance of piquant insouciance. Some recent
annoyance had left its traces upon her. Perhaps it was to walk it
off that she had rambled down the valley; certain it is that she
inhaled the fresh breezes of the woodlands as if their resinous
fragrance bore with them some antidote for human sorrow.

She stood for some time gazing at the view before her. She
could see her father's house, like a white dot upon the hillside,
though strangely enough it was a blue reek of smoke upon the
opposite slope which seemed to attract the greater part of her
attention. She lingered there, watching it with a wistful look in
her hazel eyes. Then the loneliness of her situation seemed to
strike her, and she felt one of those spasmodic fits of unreasoning terror to which the bravest women are subject. Tales of
natives and of bushrangers, their daring and their cruelty,
flashed across her. She glanced at the mysterious stretch of silent
bushland beside her, and stooped to pick up her basket with the
intention of hurrying along the road in the direction of the
gulches. She started round, and hardly suppressed a scream as a
long red-flannelled arm shot out from behind her and withdrew
the basket from her very grasp.

The figure which met her eye would to some have seemed little
calculated to allay her fears. The high boots, the rough shirt,
and the broad girdle with its weapons of death were, however,
too familiar to Miss Carrie to be objects of terror; and when
above them all she saw a pair of tender blue eyes looking down
upon her, and a half-abashed smile lurking under a thick yellow
moustache, she knew that for the remainder of that walk ranger
and black would be equally powerless to harm her.

"O Mr. Durton," she said, "how you did startle me!"

"I'm sorry, miss," said Abe, in great trepidation at having
caused his idol one moment's uneasiness. "You see," he continued, with simple cunning, "the weather bein' fine and my
partner gone prospectin', I thought I'd walk up to Hagley's Hill
and round back by the bend, and there I sees you accidental-like
and promiscuous a-standin' on a hillock." This astounding
falsehood was reeled off by the miner with great fluency, and an
artificial sincerity which at once stamped it as a fabrication.
Bones had concocted and rehearsed it while tracking the little
footsteps in the clay, and looked upon it as the very depth of
human guile. Miss Carrie did not venture upon a remark but

there was a gleam of amusement in her eyes which puzzled her lover.

Abe was in good spirits this morning. It may have been the sunshine, or it may have been the rapid rise of shares in the Conemara, which lightened his heart. I am inclined to think, however, that it was referable to neither of these causes. Simple as he was, the scene which he had witnessed the night before could only lead to one conclusion. He pictured himself walking as wildly down the valley under similar circumstances, and his heart was touched with pity for his rival. He felt very certain that the ill-omened face of Mr. Thomas Ferguson of Rochdale Ferry would never more be seen within the walls of Azalea Villa. Then why did she refuse him? He was handsome, he was fairly rich. Could it — ? no, it couldn't; of course it couldn't; how could it! The idea was ridiculous — so very ridiculous that it had fermented in the young man's brain all night, and that he could do nothing but ponder over it in the morning, and cherish it in his perturbed bosom.

They passed down the red pathway together, and along by the river's bank. Abe had relapsed into his normal condition of taciturnity. He had made one gallant effort to hold forth upon the subject of ferns, stimulated by the basket which he held in his hand, but the theme was not a thrilling one, and after a spasmodic flicker he had abandoned the attempt. While coming along he had been full of racy anecdotes and humorous observations. He had rehearsed innumerable remarks which were to be poured into Miss Sinclair's appreciative ear. But now his brain seemed of a sudden to have become a vacuum, and utterly devoid of any idea save an insane and overpowering impulse to comment upon the heat of the sun. No astronomer who ever reckoned a parallax was so entirely absorbed in the condition of the celestial bodies as honest Bones while he trudged along by the slow-flowing Australian river.

Suddenly his conversation with his partner came back into his mind. What was it Boss had said upon the subject? "Tell her how they live at the mines." He revolved it in his brain. It seemed a curious thing to talk about; but Boss had said it, and Boss was always right. He would take the plunge; so with a premonitory hem he blurted out,

"They live mostly on bacon and beans in the valley."

He could not see what effect this communication had upon his companion. He was too tall to be able to peer under the little straw bonnet. She did not answer. He would try again.

"Mutton on Sundays," he said.

Even this failed to arouse any enthusiasm. In fact she seemed to be laughing. Boss was evidently wrong. The young man was in despair. The sight of a ruined hut beside the pathway conjured up a fresh idea. He grasped at it as a drowning man to a straw.

"Cockney Jack built that," he remarked. "Lived there till he died."

"What did he die of?" asked his companion.

"Three star brandy," said Abe decisively. "I used to come over of a night when he was bad and sit by him. Poor chap! he had a wife and two children in Putney. He'd rave, and call me Polly, by the hour. He was cleaned out, hadn't a red cent; but the boys collected rough gold enough to see him through. He's buried there in that shaft; that was his claim, so we just dropped him down it an' filled it up. Put down his pick too, an' a spade an' a bucket, so's he'd feel kinder perky and at home."

Miss Carrie seemed more interested now.

"Do they often die like that?" she asked.

"Well, brandy kills many; but there's more gets dropped—shot, you know."

"I don't mean that. Do many men die alone and miserable down there, with no one to care for them?" and she pointed to the cluster of houses beneath them. "Is there any one dying now? It is awful to think of."

"There's none as I knows of likely to throw up their hand."

"I wish you wouldn't use so much slang, Mr. Durton," said Carrie, looking up at him reprovingly out of her violet eyes. It was strange what an air of proprietorship this young lady was gradually assuming towards her gigantic companion. "You know it isn't polite. You should get a dictionary and learn the proper words."

"Ah, that's it," said Bones apologetically. "It's gettin' your hand on the proper one. When you've not got a steam drill, you've got to put up with a pick."

"Yes, but it's easy if you really try. You could say that a man was 'dying,' or 'moribund,' if you like."

"That's it," said the miner enthusiastically. " 'Moribund!'

That's a word. Why, you could lay over Boss Morgan in the matter of words. 'Moribund!' There's some sound about that!"

Carrie laughed.

"It's not the sound you must think of, but whether it will express your meaning. Seriously, Mr. Durton, if any one should be ill in the camp you must let me know. I can nurse, and I might be of use. You will, won't you?"

Abe readily acquiesced, and relapsed into silence as he pondered over the possibility of inoculating himself with some long and tedious disease. There was a mad dog reported from Buckhurst. Perhaps something might be done with that.

"And now I must say good-morning," said Carrie, as they came to the spot where a crooked pathway branched off from the track and wound up to Azalea Villa. "Thank you ever so much for escorting me."

In vain Abe pleaded for the additional hundred yards, and adduced the overwhelming weight of the diminutive basket as a cogent reason. The young lady was inexorable. She had taken him too far out of his way already. She was ashamed of herself; she wouldn't hear of it.

So poor Bones departed in a mixture of many opposite feelings. He had interested her. She had spoken kindly to him. But then she had sent him away before there was any necessity; she couldn't care much about him if she would do that. I think he might have felt a little more cheerful, however, had he seen Miss Carrie Sinclair as she watched his retiring figure from the garden gate with a loving look upon her saucy face, and a mischievous smile at his bent head and desponding appearance.

The Colonial Bar was the favourite haunt of the inhabitants of Harvey's Sluice in their hours of relaxation. There had been a fierce competition between it and the rival establishment termed the Grocery, which, in spite of its innocent appellation, aspired also to dispense spirituous refreshments. The importation of chairs into the latter had led to the appearance of a settee in the former. Spittoons appeared in the Grocery against a picture in the Bar, and, as the frequenters expressed it, the honours were even. When, however, the Grocery led a window-curtain, and its opponent returned a snuggery and a mirror, the game was declared to be in favour of the latter, and Harvey's Sluice

showed its sense of the spirit of the proprietor by withdrawing
their custom from his opponent.

Though every man was at liberty to swagger into the Bar
itself, and bask in the shimmer of its many coloured bottles,
there was a general feeling that the snuggery, or special apartment, should be reserved for the use of the more prominent
citizens. It was in this room that committees met, that opulent
companies were conceived and born, and that inquests were
generally held. The latter, I regret to state, was, in 1861, a pretty
frequent ceremony at the Sluice; and the findings of the coroner
were sometimes characterized by a fine breezy originality.
Witness when Bully Burke, a notorious desperado, was shot
down by a quiet young medical man, and a sympathetic jury
brought in that "the deceased had met his death in an ill-advised
attempt to stop a pistol-ball while in motion," a verdict which
was looked upon as a triumph of jurisprudence in the camp, as
simultaneously exonerating the culprit, and adhering to the rigid
and undeniable truth.

On this particular evening there was an assemblage of notabil-
ities in the snuggery, though no such pathological ceremony had
called them together. Many changes had occurred of late which
merited discussion; and it was in this chamber, gorgeous in all
the effete luxury of the mirror and settee, that Harvey's Sluice
was wont to exchange ideas. The recent cleansing of the population was still causing some ferment in men's minds. Then there
was Miss Sinclair and her movements to be commented on, and
the paying lead in the Conemara, and the recent rumours of
bushrangers. It was no wonder that the leading men in the
township had come together in the Colonial Bar.

The rangers were the present subject of discussion. For some
few days rumours of their presence had been flying about, and
an uneasy feeling had pervaded the colony. Physical fear was a
thing little known in Harvey's Sluice. The miners would have
turned out to hunt down the desperadoes with as much zest as if
they had been so many kangaroos. It was the presence of a large
quantity of gold in the town which caused anxiety. It was felt
that the fruits of their labour must be secured at any cost.
Messages had been sent over to Buckhurst for as many troopers
as could be spared, and in the mean time the main street of the
Sluice was paraded at night by volunteer sentinels.

A fresh impetus had been given to the panic by the report brought in to-day by Jim Struggles. Jim was of an ambitious and aspiring turn of mind, and after gazing in silent disgust at his last week's clean up, he had metaphorically shaken the clay of Harvey's Sluice from his feet, and had started off into the woods with the intention of prospecting round until he could hit upon some likely piece of ground for himself. Jim's story was that he was sitting upon a fallen trunk eating his mid-day damper and rusty bacon, when his trained ear had caught the clink of horses' hoofs. He had hardly time to take the precaution of rolling off the tree and crouching down behind it, before a troop of men came riding down through the bush, and passed within a stone-throw of him.

"There was Bill Smeaton and Murphy Duff," said Struggles, naming two notorious ruffians; "and there was three more that I couldn't rightly see. And they took the trail to the right, and looked like business all over, with their guns in their hands."

Jim was submitted to a searching cross-examination that evening; but nothing could shake his testimony or throw a further light upon what he had seen. He told the story several times and at long intervals; and though there might be a pleasing variety in the minor incidents, the main facts were always identically the same. The matter began to look serious.

There were a few, however, who were loudly sceptical as to the existence of the rangers, and the most prominent of these was a young man who was perched on a barrel in the centre of the room, and was evidently one of the leading spirits in the community. We have already seen that dark curling hair, lacklustre eye, and thin cruel lip, in the person of Black Tom Ferguson, the rejected suitor of Miss Sinclair. He was easily distinguishable from the rest of the party by a tweed coat, and other symptoms of effeminacy in his dress, which might have brought him into disrepute had he not, like Abe Durton's partner, early established the reputation of being a quietly desperate man. On the present occasion he seemed somewhat under the influence of liquor, a rare occurrence with him, and probably to be ascribed to his recent disappointment. He was almost fierce in his denunciation of Jim Struggles and his story.

"It's always the same," he said; "if a man meets a few travellers in the bush, he's bound to come back raving about rangers. If they'd seen Struggles there, they would have gone off with a long yarn about a ranger crouching behind a tree. As to recognizing people riding fast among tree trunks—it is an impossibility."

Struggles, however, stoutly maintained his original assertion, and all the sarcasms and arguments of his opponent were thrown away upon his stolid complacency. It was noticed that Ferguson seemed unaccountably put out about the whole matter. Something seemed to be on his mind, too; for occasionally he would spring off his perch and pace up and down the room with an abstracted and very forbidding look upon his swarthy face. It was a relief to every one when suddenly catching up his hat, and wishing the company a curt "Good-night," he walked off through the bar, and into the street beyond.

"Seems kinder put out," remarked Long McCoy.

"He can't be afeard of the rangers, surely," said Joe Shamus, another man of consequence, and principal shareholder of the El Dorado.

"No, he's not the man to be afraid," answered another. "There's something queer about him the last day or two. He's been long trips in the woods without any tools. They do say that the assayer's daughter has chucked him over."

"Quite right too. A darned sight too good for him," remarked several voices.

"It's odds but he has another try," said Shamus. "He's a hard man to beat when he's set his mind on a thing."

"Abe Durton's the horse to win," remarked Houlahan, a little bearded Irishman. "It's sivin to four I'd be willin' to lay on him."

"And you'd be afther losing your money, a-vich," said a young man with a laugh. "She'll want more brains than ever Bones had in his skull, you bet."

"Who's seen Bones to-day?" asked McCoy.

"I've seen him," said the young miner. "He came round all through the camp asking for a dictionary—wanted to write a letter likely."

"I saw him readin' it," said Shamus. "He came over to me an' told me he'd struck something good at the first show. Showed me a word about as long as your arm—'abdicate,' or something."

"It's a rich man he is now, I suppose," said the Irishman.

"Well, he's about made his pile. He holds a hundred feet of

the Conemara, and the shares go up every hour. If he'd sell out
he'd be about fit to go home."

"Guess he wants to take somebody home with him," said
another. "Old Joshua wouldn't object, seein' that the money is
there."

I think it has been already recorded in this narrative that Jim
Struggles, the wandering prospector, had gained the reputation
of being the wit of the camp. It was not only in airy badinage,
but in the conception and execution of more pretentious practical
pleasantries that Jim had earned his reputation. His adventure in
the morning had caused a certain stagnation in his usual flow of
humour; but the company and his potations were gradually
restoring him to a more cheerful state of mind. He had been
brooding in silence over some idea since the departure of
Ferguson, and he now proceeded to evolve it to his expectant
companions.

"Say, boys," he began. "What day's this?"

"Friday, ain't it?"

"No, not that. What day of the month?"

"Darned if I know."

"Well, I'll tell you now. It's the first o' April. I've got a
calendar in the hut as says so."

"What if it is?" said several voices.

"Well, don't you see, it's All Fools' day. Couldn't we fix up
some little joke on some one, eh? Couldn't we get a laugh out of
it? Now there's old Bones, for instance; he'll never smell a rat.
Couldn't we send him off somewhere and watch him go maybe?
We'd have something to chaff him on for a month to come, eh?"

There was a general murmur of assent. A joke, however poor,
was always welcome to the Sluice. The broader the point, the
more thoroughly was it appreciated. There was no morbid
delicacy of feeling in the gulches.

"Where shall we send him?" was the query.

Jim Struggles was buried in thought for a moment. Then an
unhallowed inspiration seemed to come over him, and he
laughed uproariously, rubbing his hands between his knees in
the excess of his delight.

"Well, what is it?" asked the eager audience.

"See here, boys. There's Miss Sinclair. You was saying as

Abe's gone on her. She don't fancy him much you think. Suppose we write him a note — send it him to-night, you know."

"Well, what then?" said McCoy.

"Well, pretend the note is from her, d'ye see? Put her name at the bottom. Let on as she wants him to come up an' meet her in the garden at twelve. He's bound to go. He'll think she wants to go off with him. It'll be the biggest thing played this year."

There was a roar of laughter. The idea conjured up of honest Bones mooning about in the garden, and of old Joshua coming out to remonstrate with a double-barrelled shot-gun, was irresistibly comic. The plan was approved of unanimously.

"Here's pencil and here's paper," said the humorist. "Who's goin' to write the letter?"

"Write it yourself, Jim," said Shamus.

"Well, what shall I say?"

"Say what you think right."

"I don't know how she'd put it," said Jim, scratching his head in great perplexity. "However, Bones will never know the differ. How will this do? 'Dear old man. Come to the garden at twelve to-night, else I'll never speak to you again,' eh?"

"No, that's not the style," said the young miner. "Mind, she's a lass of eddication. She'd put it kinder flowery and soft."

"Well, write it yourself," said Jim sulkily, handing him over the pencil.

"This is the sort of thing," said the miner, moistening the point of it in his mouth. " 'When the moon is in the sky — ' "

"There it is. That's bully," from the company.

" 'And the stars a-shinin' bright, meet, O meet me, Adelphus, by the garden gate at twelve.' "

"His name ain't Adolphus," objected a critic.

"That's how the poetry comes in," said the miner. "It's kinder fanciful, d'ye see. Sounds a darned sight better than Abe. Trust him for guessing who she means. I'll sign it Carrie. There!"

This epistle was gravely passed round the room from hand to hand, and reverentially gazed upon as being a remarkable production of the human brain. It was then folded up and committed to the care of a small boy, who was solemnly charged under dire threats to deliver it at the shanty, and to make off before any awkward questions were asked him. It was only after he had disappeared in the darkness that some slight compunction visited one or two of the company.

"Ain't it playing it rather low on the girl?" said Shamus.

"And rough on old Bones?" suggested another.

However, these objections were overruled by the majority, and disappeared entirely upon the appearance of a second jorum of whisky. The matter had almost been forgotten by the time that Abe had received his note, and was spelling it out with a palpitating heart under the light of his solitary candle.

That night has long been remembered in Harvey's Sluice. A fitful breeze was sweeping down from the distant mountains, moaning and sighing among the deserted claims. Dark clouds were hurrying across the moon, one moment throwing a shadow over the landscape, and the next allowing the silvery radiance to shine down, cold and clear, upon the little valley, and bathe in a weird mysterious light the great stretch of bushland on either side of it. A great loneliness seemed to rest on the face of Nature. Men remarked afterwards on the strange eerie atmosphere which hung over the little town.

It was in the darkness that Abe Durton sallied out from his little shanty. His partner, Boss Morgan, was still absent in the bush, so that beyond the ever-watchful Blinky there was no living being to observe his movements. A feeling of mild surprise filled his simple soul that his angel's delicate fingers could have formed those great straggling hieroglyphics; however, there was the name at the foot, and that was enough for him. She wanted him, no matter for what, and with a heart as pure and as heroic as any knight-errant, this rough miner went forth at the summons of his love.

He groped his way up the steep winding track which led to Azalea Villa. There was a little clump of small trees and shrubs about fifty yards from the entrance of the garden. Abe stopped for a moment when he had reached them in order to collect himself. It was hardly twelve yet, so that he had a few minutes to spare. He stood under their dark canopy peering at the white house vaguely outlined in front of him. A plain enough little dwelling-place to any prosaic mortal, but girt with reverence and awe in the eyes of the lover.

The miner paused under the shade of the trees, and then moved on to the garden gate. There was no one there. He was evidently rather early. The moon was shining brightly now, and the country round was as clear as day. Abe looked past the little villa at the road which ran like a white winding streak over the brow of the hill. A watcher behind could have seen his square athletic figure standing out sharp and clear. Then he gave a start, as if he had been shot, and staggered up against the little gate beside him.

He had seen something which caused even his sunburned face to become a shade paler as he thought of the girl so near him. Just at the bend of the road, not two hundred yards away, he saw a dark moving mass coming round the curve, and lost in the shadow of the hill. It was but for a moment; yet in that moment the quick perception of the practiced woodman had realized the whole situation. It was a band of horsemen bound for the villa; and what horsemen would ride so by night save the terror of the woodlands—the dreaded rangers of the bush?

It is true that on ordinary occasions Abe was as sluggish in his intellect as he was heavy in his movements. In the hour of danger, however, he was as remarkable for cool deliberation as for prompt and decisive action. As he advanced up the garden he rapidly reckoned up the chances against him. There were half a dozen of the assailants at the most moderate computation, all desperate and fearless men. The question was whether he could keep them at bay for a short time and prevent their forcing a passage into the house. We have already mentioned that sentinels had been placed in the main street of the town. Abe reckoned that help would be at hand within ten minutes of the firing of the first shot.

Were he inside the house he could confidently reckon on holding his own for a longer period than that. Before he could rouse the sleepers and gain admission, however, the rangers would be upon him. He must content himself with doing his utmost. At any rate he would show Carrie that if he could not talk to her he could at least die for her. The thought gave him quite a glow of pleasure, as he crept under the shadow of the house. He cocked his revolver. Experience had taught him the advantage of the first shot.

The road along which the rangers were coming ended at a

wooden gate opening into the upper part of the assayer's little garden. This gate had a high acacia hedge on either side of it, and opened into a short walk also lined by impassable thorny walls. Abe knew the place well. One resolute man might, he thought, hold the passage for a few minutes until the assailants broke through elsewhere and took him in the rear. At any rate, it was his best chance. He passed the front door, but forbore to give any alarm. Sinclair was an elderly man, and would be of little assistance in such a desperate struggle as was before him, and the appearance of lights in the house would warn the rangers of the resistance awaiting them. O for his partner the Boss, for Chicago Bill, for any one of twenty gallant men who would have come at his call and stood by him in such a quarrel! He turned into the narrow pathway. There was the well-remembered wooden gate; and there, perched upon the gate, languidly swinging his legs backwards and forwards, and peering down the road in front of him, was Mr. John Morgan, the very man for whom Abe had been longing from the bottom of his heart.

There was a short time for explanations. A few hurried words announced that the Boss, returning from his little tour, had come across the rangers riding on their mission of darkness, and overhearing their destination, had managed by hard running and knowledge of the country to arrive before them. "No time to alarm any one," he explained, still panting from his exertions; "must stop them ourselves — not come for swag — come for your girl. Only over our bodies, Bones"; and with these few broken words the strangely assorted friends shook hands and looked lovingly into each other's eyes, while the tramp of the horses came down to them on the fragrant breeze of the woods.

There were six rangers in all. One who appeared to be the leader rode in front, while the others followed in a body. They flung themselves off their horses when they were opposite the house, and after a few muttered words from their captain, tethered the animals to a small tree, and walked confidently towards the gate.

Boss Morgan and Abe were crouching down under the shadow of the hedge, at the extreme end of the narrow passage. They were invisible to the rangers, who evidently reckoned on meeting little resistance in this isolated house. As the first man came forwards and half turned to give some order to his comrades both the friends recognized the stern profile and heavy moustache of Black Ferguson, the rejected suitor of Miss Carrie Sinclair. Honest Abe made a mental vow that he at least should never reach the door alive.

The ruffian stepped up to the gate and put his hand upon the latch. He started as a stentorian "Stand back!" came thundering out from among the bushes. In war, as in love, the miner was a man of few words.

"There's no road this way," explained another voice with an infinite sadness and gentleness about it which was characteristic of its owner when the devil was rampant in his soul. The ranger recognized it. He remembered the soft languid address which he had listened to in the billiard room of the Buckhurst Arms, and which had wound up by the mild orator putting his back against the door, drawing a derringer, and asking to see the sharper who would dare to force a passage. "It's that infernal fool Durton," he said, "and his white-faced friend."

Both were well-known names in the country round. But the rangers were reckless and desperate men. They drew up to the gate in a body.

"Clear out of that!" said their leader in a grim whisper; "you can't save the girl. Go off with whole skins while you have the chance."

The partners laughed.

"Then curse you, come on!"

The gate was flung open and the party fired a straggling volley, and made a fierce rush towards the gravelled walk.

The revolvers cracked merrily in the silence of the night from the bushes at the other end. It was hard to aim with precision in the darkness. The second man sprang convulsively into the air, and fell upon his face with his arms extended, writhing horribly in the moonlight. The third was grazed in the leg and stopped. The others stopped out of sympathy. After all, the girl was not for them, and their heart was hardly in the work. Their captain rushed madly on, like a valiant blackguard as he was, but was met by a crashing blow from the butt of Abe Durton's pistol, delivered with a fierce energy which sent him reeling back among his comrades with the blood streaming from his shattered jaw, and his capacity for cursing cut short at the very moment when he needed to draw upon it most.

"Don't go yet," said the voice in the darkness.

However, they had no intention of going yet. A few minutes must elapse, they knew, before Harvey's Sluice could be upon them. There was still time to force the door if they could succeed in mastering the defenders. What Abe had feared came to pass. Black Ferguson knew the ground as well as he did. He ran rapidly along the hedge, and the five crashed through it where there was some appearance of a gap. The two friends glanced at each other. Their flank was turned. They stood up like men who knew their fate and did not fear to meet it.

There was a wild medley of dark figures in the moonlight, and a ringing cheer from well-known voices. The humorists of Harvey's Sluice had found something even more practical than the joke which they had come to witness. The partners saw the faces of friends beside them—Shamus, Struggles, McCoy. There was a desperate rally, a sweeping fiery rush, a cloud of smoke, with pistol-shots and fierce oaths ringing out of it, and when it lifted, a single dark shadow flying for dear life to the shelter of the broken hedge was the only ranger upon his feet within the little garden. But there was no sound of triumph among the victors; a strange hush had come over them, and a murmur as of grief—for there, lying across the threshold which he had fought so gallantly to defend, lay poor Abe, the loyal and simple hearted, breathing heavily with a bullet through his lungs.

He was carried inside with all the rough tenderness of the mines. There were men there, I think, who would have borne his hurt to have had the love of that white girlish figure, which bent over the blood-stained bed and whispered so softly and so tenderly in his ear. Her voice seemed to rouse him. He opened his dreamy blue eyes and looked about him. They rested on her face.

"Played out," he murmured; "pardon, Carrie, morib—" and with a faint smile he sank back upon the pillow.

However, Abe failed for once to be as good as his word. His hardy constitution asserted itself, and he shook off what might in a weaker man have proved a deadly wound. Whether it was the balmy air of the woodlands which came sweeping over a thousand miles of forest into the sick man's room, or whether it was the little nurse who tended him so gently, certain it is that within two months we heard that he had realized his shares in the

Conemara, and gone from Harvey's Sluice and the little shanty upon the hill for ever.

I had the advantage a short time afterwards of seeing an extract from the letter of a young lady named Amelia, to whom we have made a casual allusion in the course of our narrative. We have already broken the privacy of one feminine epistle, so we shall have fewer scruples in glancing at another. "I was bridesmaid," she remarks, "and Carrie looked charming" (underlined) "in the veil and orange blossoms. Such a man, he is, twice as big as your Jack, and he was so funny, and blushed, and dropped the prayer-book. And when they asked the question you could have heard him roar 'I do!' at the other end of George Street. His best man was a darling" (twice underlined). "So quiet and handsome and nice. Too gentle to take care of himself among those rough men, I am sure." I think it quite possible that in the fullness of time Miss Amelia managed to take upon herself the care of our old friend Mr. Jack Morgan, commonly known as the Boss.

A tree is still pointed out at the bend as Ferguson's gum-tree. There is no need to enter into unsavoury details. Justice is short and sharp in primitive colonies, and the dwellers in Harvey's Sluice were a serious and practical race.

It is still the custom for a select party to meet on a Saturday evening in the snuggery of the Colonial Bar. On such occasions, if there be a stranger or guest to be entertained, the same solemn ceremony is always observed. Glasses are charged in silence; there is a tapping of the same upon the table, and then, with a deprecating cough, Jim Struggles comes forward and tells the tale of the April joke, and of what came of it. There is generally conceded to be something very artistic in the way in which he breaks off suddenly at the close of his narrative by waving his bumper in the air with "An' here's to Mr. and Mrs. Bones. God bless 'em!" a sentiment in which the stranger, if he be a prudent man, will most cordially acquiesce.

Selecting a Ghost

One of the few failings of the Sherlock Holmes saga—and Conan Doyle confessed it himself in his autobiography—is its lack of overt humor. There are a few chuckles to be found here and there in Holmes, but there is little evidence of the robust comic talent which bursts through from so much of Doyle's other writing. The adventures of his two other series heroes, Brigadier Gerard and Professor Challenger, are wildly comic in places. In 1893, he actually collaborated on a D'Oyley Carte musical comedy with James M. Barrie. Many of his novels and short stories are gently or bizarrely funny—he seemed equally at his ease with either form. If "Bones" represents an example of the former, then "Selecting a Ghost"—also known as "The Haunted Grange of Goresthorpe" and "The Secret of Goresthorpe Grange" but not to be confused with a different, unpublished story of similar title—is an epitome of the latter.

Perhaps the hallucinatory farce of "Selecting a Ghost" reflected Doyle's view of his own life at the time of its appearance in LONDON SOCIETY *for December 1883. For a year, he had been struggling to make a go of a medical practice in the Portsmouth suburb of Southsea, dreaming of success and desperately trying to keep up appearances. His sense of humor sustained him again and again. There was struggle in his writing career, too, for, after that first heady sale to* CHAMBERS'S, *he had been unable to make another and was reduced to contributing to the less distinguished—and less well-paying—publications such as* LONDON SOCIETY *and* THE BOY'S OWN PAPER. *Even in these early years, however, literature was more than just a sideline. He would never have been able to keep up his early practice had it not been for the sum of £7 15s. advanced to him by the editor of* LONDON SOCIETY. *No doubt "Selecting a Ghost" was intended in part to work off some of that debt, in part to laugh off some of his own privation.*

I AM SURE that Nature never intended me to be a self-made man. There are times when I can hardly bring myself to realize that twenty years of my life were spent behind the counter of a grocer's shop in the East End of London, and that it was through such an avenue that I reached a wealthy independence and the possession of Goresthorpe Grange. My habits are Conservative, and my tastes refined and aristocratic. I have a soul which spurns the vulgar herd. Our family, the D'Odds, date back to a prehistoric era, as is to be inferred from the fact that their advent into British history is not commented on by any trustworthy historian. Some instinct tells me that the blood of a Crusader runs in my veins. Even now, after the lapse of so many years, such exclamations as "By'r Lady!" rise naturally to my lips, and I feel that, should circumstances require it, I am capable of rising in my stirrups and dealing an infidel a blow — say with a mace — which would considerably astonish him.

Goresthorpe Grange is a feudal mansion — or so it was termed in the advertisement which originally brought it under my notice. Its right to this adjective had a most remarkable effect upon its price, and the advantages gained may possibly be more sentimental than real. Still, it is soothing to me to know that I have slits in my staircase through which I can discharge arrows; and there is a sense of power in the fact of possessing a complicated apparatus by means of which I am enabled to pour molten lead upon the head of the casual visitor. These things chime in with my peculiar humour, and I do not grudge to pay for them. I am proud of my battlements and of the circular uncovered sewer which girds me round. I am proud of my portcullis and donjon and keep. There is but one thing wanting to round off the mediaevalism of my abode, and to render it symmetrically and completely antique. Goresthorpe Grange is not provided with a ghost.

Any man with old-fashioned tastes and ideas as to how such establishments should be conducted would have been disappointed at the omission. In my case it was particularly unfortunate. From my childhood I had been an earnest student of the supernatural, and a firm believer in it. I have revelled in ghostly literature until there is hardly a tale bearing upon the subject which I have not perused. I learned the German language for the sole purpose of mastering a book upon demonology. When an infant I have secreted myself in dark rooms in the hope of seeing some of those bogies with which my nurse used to threaten me; and the same feeling is as strong in me now as then. It was a proud moment when I felt that a ghost was one of the luxuries which my money might command.

It is true that there was no mention of an apparition in the advertisement. On reviewing the mildewed walls, however, and the shadowy corridors, I had taken it for granted that there was such a thing on the premises. As the presence of a kennel presupposes that of a dog, so I imagined that it was impossible that such desirable quarters should be untenanted by one or more restless shades. Good heavens, what can the noble family from whom I purchased it have been doing during these hundreds of years! Was there no member of it spirited enough to make away with his sweetheart, or take some other steps calculated to establish a hereditary spectre? Even now I can hardly write with patience upon the subject.

For a long time I hoped against hope. Never did rat squeak behind the wainscot, or rain drip upon the attic-floor, without a wild thrill shooting through me as I thought that at last I had come upon traces of some unquiet soul. I felt no touch of fear upon these occasions. If it occurred in the night-time, I would send Mrs. D'Odd—who is a strong-minded woman—to investigate the matter while I covered up my head with the bedclothes and indulged in an ecstasy of expectation. Alas, the result was always the same! The suspicious sound would be traced to some cause so absurdly natural and commonplace that the most fervid imagination could not clothe it with any of the glamour of romance.

I might have reconciled myself to this state of things had it not been for Jorrocks of Havistock Farm. Jorrocks is a coarse, burly, matter-of-fact fellow whom I only happen to know through the accidental circumstance of his fields adjoining my demesne. Yet this man, though utterly devoid of all appreciation of archaeological unities, is in possession of a well authenticated and undeniable spectre. Its existence only dates back, I believe, to the reign of the Second George, when a young lady cut her throat upon hearing of the death of her lover at the battle of Dettingen. Still, even that gives the house an air of respectability, especially when coupled with bloodstains upon the floor. Jorrocks is densely unconscious of his good fortune; and his language when he reverts to the apparition is painful to listen to. He little dreams how I covet every one of those moans and nocturnal wails which he describes with unnecessary objurgation. Things are indeed coming to a pretty pass when democratic spectres are allowed to desert the landed proprietors and annul every social distinction by taking refuge in the houses of the great unrecognized.

I have a large amount of perseverance. Nothing else could have raised me into my rightful sphere, considering the uncongenial atmosphere in which I spent the earlier part of my life. I felt now that a ghost must be secured, but how to set about securing one was more than either Mrs. D'Odd or myself was able to determine. My reading taught me that such phenomena are usually the outcome of crime. What crime was to be done, then, and who was to do it? A wild idea entered my mind that Watkins, the house-steward, might be prevailed upon—for a consideration—to immolate himself or some one else in the interests of the establishment. I put the matter to him in a half jesting manner; but it did not seem to strike him in a favourable light. The other servants sympathized with him in his opinion—at least, I cannot account in any other way for their having left the house in a body the same afternoon.

"My dear," Mrs. D'Odd remarked to me one day after dinner, as I sat moodily sipping a cup of sack—I love the good old names—"my dear, that odious ghost of Jorrocks' has been gibbering again."

"Let it gibber," I answered recklessly.

Mrs. D'Odd struck a few chords on her virginal and looked thoughtfully into the fire.

"I'll tell you what it is, Argentine," she said at last, using the pet name which we usually substituted for Silas, "we must have a ghost sent down from London."

"How can you be so idiotic, Matilda?" I remarked severely. "Who could get us such a thing?"

"My cousin, Jack Brocket, could," she answered confidently.

Now, this cousin of Matilda's was rather a sore subject between us. He was a rakish clever young fellow, who had tried his hand at many things, but wanted perseverance to succeed at any. He was, at that time, in chambers in London, professing to be a general agent, and really living, to a great extent, upon his wits. Matilda managed so that most of our business should pass through his hands, which certainly saved me a great deal of trouble; but I found that Jack's commission was generally considerably larger than all the other items of the bill put together. It was this fact which made me feel inclined to rebel against any further negotiations with the young gentleman.

"O yes, he could," insisted Mrs. D., seeing the look of disapprobation upon my face. "You remember how well he managed that business about the crest?"

"It was only a resuscitation of the old family coat-of-arms, my dear," I protested.

Matilda smiled in an irritating manner. "There was a resuscitation of the family portraits, too, dear," she remarked. "You must allow that Jack selected them very judiciously."

I thought of the long line of faces which adorned the walls of my banqueting-hall, from the burly Norman robber, through every gradation of casque, plume, and ruff, to the sombre Chesterfieldian individual who appears to have staggered against a pillar in his agony at the return of a maiden MS. which he grips convulsively in his right hand. I was fain to confess that in that instance he had done his work well, and that it was only fair to give him an order—with the usual commission—for a family spectre, should such a thing be attainable.

It is one of my maxims to act promptly when once my mind is made up. Noon of the next day found me ascending the spiral stone staircase which leads to Mr. Brocket's chambers, and admiring the succession of arrows and fingers upon the whitewashed wall, all indicating the direction of that gentleman's sanctum. As it happened, artificial aids of the sort were entirely unnecessary, as an animated flap-dance overhead could proceed from no other quarter, though it was replaced by a deathly silence as I groped my way up the stair. The door was opened by a youth evidently astounded at the appearance of a client, and I was ushered into the presence of my young friend, who was writing furiously in a large ledger—upside down, as I afterwards discovered.

After the first greetings, I plunged into business at once.

"Look here, Jack," I said, "I want you to get me a spirit, if you can."

"Spirits, you mean!" shouted my wife's cousin, plunging his hand into the waste-paper basket and producing a bottle with the celerity of a conjuring trick. "Let's have a drink!"

I held up my hand as a mute appeal against such a proceeding so early in the day; but on lowering it again I found that I had almost involuntarily closed my fingers round the tumbler which my advisor had pressed upon me. I drank the contents hastily off, lest any one could come in upon us and set me down as a toper. After all, there was something very amusing about the young fellow's eccentricities.

"Not spirits," I explained smilingly; "an apparition — a ghost. If such a thing is to be had, I should be very willing to negotiate."

"A ghost for Goresthorpe Grange?" inquired Mr. Brocket, with as much coolness as if I had asked for a drawing-room suite.

"Quite so," I answered.

"Easiest thing in the world," said my companion, filling up my glass again in spite of my remonstrance. "Let us see!" Here he took down a large red note-book, with all the letters of the alphabet in a fringe down the edge. "A ghost you said, didn't you? That's G. G — gems — gimlets — gaspipes — gauntlets — guns — galleys. Ah, here we are. Ghosts. Volume nine, section six, page forty-one. Excuse me!" And Jack ran up a ladder and began rummaging among a pile of ledgers on a high shelf. I felt half inclined to empty my glass into the spittoon when his back was turned; but on second thoughts I disposed of it in a legitimate way.

"Here it is!" cried my London agent, jumping off the ladder with a crash, and depositing an enormous volume of manuscript upon the table. "I have all these things tabulated, so that I may lay my hands upon them in a moment. It's all right — it's quite weak" (here he filled our glasses again). "What were we looking up, again?"

"Ghosts," I suggested.

"Of course; page 41. Here we are. 'J. H. Fowler & Son, Dunkel Street, suppliers of mediums to the nobility and gentry;

charms sold—love-philtres—mummies—horoscopes cast.' Nothing in your line there, I suppose?"

I shook my head despondingly.

"Frederick Tabb," continued my wife's cousin, "sole channel of communication between the living and the dead. Proprietor of the spirits of Byron, Kirke White, Grimaldi, Tom Cribb, and Inigo Jones. That's about the figure!"

"Nothing romantic enough there," I objected. "Good heavens! Fancy a ghost with a black eye and a handkerchief tied round its waist, or turning somersaults, and saying, 'How are you tomorrow?'" The very idea made me so warm that I emptied my glass and filled it again.

"Here is another," said my companion. "'Christopher McCarthy; bi-weekly séances—attended by all the eminent spirits of ancient and modern times. Nativities—charms—abracadabras, messages from the dead.' He might be able to help us. However, I shall have a hunt round myself to-morrow, and see some of these fellows. I know their haunts, and it's odd if I can't pick up something cheap. So there's an end to business," he concluded, hurling the ledger into the corner, "and now we'll have something to drink."

We had several things to drink—so many that my inventive faculties were dulled next morning, and I had some little difficulty in explaining to Mrs. D'Odd why it was that I hung my boots and spectacles upon a peg along with my other garments before retiring to rest. The new hopes excited by the confident manner in which my agent had undertaken the commission caused me to rise superior to alcoholic reaction, and I paced about the rambling corridors and old-fashioned rooms, picturing to myself the appearance of my expected acquisition, and deciding what part of the building would harmonize best with its presence. After much consideration, I pitched upon the banqueting-hall as being, on the whole, most suitable for its reception. It was a long low room, hung round with valuable tapestry and interesting relics of the old family to whom it had belonged. Coats of mail and implements of war glimmered fitfully as the light of the fire played over them, and the wind crept under the door, moving the hangings to and fro with a ghastly rustling. At one end there was the raised daïs, on which in ancient times the host and his guests used to spread their table, while a descent of a couple of steps led to the lower part of the hall, where the vassals and retainers held wassail. The floor was uncovered by any sort of carpet, but a layer of rushes had been scattered over it by my direction. In the whole room there was nothing to remind one of the nineteenth century; except, indeed, my own solid silver plate, stamped with the resuscitated family arms, which was laid out upon an oak table in the centre. This, I determined, should be the haunted room, supposing my wife's cousin to succeed in his negotiation with the spirit-mongers. There was nothing for it now but to wait patiently until I heard some news of the result of his inquiries.

A letter came in the course of a few days, which, if it was short, was at least encouraging. It was scribbled in pencil on the back of a playbill, and sealed apparently with a tobacco-stopper. "Am on the track," it said. "Nothing of the sort to be had from any professional spiritualist, but picked up a fellow in a pub yesterday who says he can manage it for you. Will send him down unless you wire to the contrary. Abrahams is his name, and he has done one or two of these jobs before." The letter wound up with some incoherent allusions to a cheque, and was signed by my affectionate cousin, John Brocket.

I need hardly say that I did not wire, but awaited the arrival of Mr. Abrahams with all impatience. In spite of my belief in the supernatural, I could scarcely credit the fact that any mortal could have such a command over the spirit-world as to deal in them and barter them against mere earthly gold. Still, I had Jack's word for it that such a trade existed; and here was a gentleman with a Judaical name ready to demonstrate it by proof positive. How vulgar and commonplace Jorrocks' eighteenth-century ghost would appear should I succeed in securing a real mediaeval apparition! I almost thought that one had been sent down in advance, for, as I walked round the moat that night before retiring to rest, I came upon a dark figure engaged in surveying the machinery of my portcullis and drawbridge. His start of surprise, however, and the manner in which he hurried off into the darkness, speedily convinced me of his earthly origin, and I put him down as some admirer of one of my female retainers mourning over the muddy Hellespont which divided him from his love. Whoever he may have been, he disappeared and did not return, though I loitered about for some time in the hope of catching a glimpse of him and exercising my feudal rights upon his person.

Jack Brocket was as good as his word. The shades of another evening were beginning to darken round Goresthorpe Grange, when a peal at the outer bell, and the sound of a fly pulling up, announced the arrival of Mr. Abrahams. I hurried down to meet him, half expecting to see a choice assortment of ghosts crowding in at his rear. Instead, however, of being the sallow-faced melancholy-eyed man that I had pictured to myself, the ghost-dealer was a sturdy little podgy fellow, with a pair of wonderfully keen sparkling eyes and a mouth which was constantly stretched in a good-humoured, if somewhat artificial, grin. His sole stock-in-trade seemed to consist of a small leather bag jealously locked and strapped, which emitted a metallic chink upon being placed on the stone flags of the hall.

"And 'ow are you, sir?" he asked, wringing my hand with the utmost effusion. "And the missis, 'ow is she? And all the others —'ow's all their 'ealth?"

I intimated that we were all as well as could reasonably be expected; but Mr. Abrahams happened to catch a glimpse of Mrs. D'Odd in the distance, and at once plunged at her with another string of inquiries as to her health, delivered so volubly and with such an intense earnestness that I half expected to see him terminate his cross examination by feeling her pulse and demanding a sight of her tongue. All this time his little eyes rolled round and round, shifting perpetually from the floor to the ceiling, and from the ceiling to the walls, taking in apparently every article of furniture in a single comprehensive glance.

Having satisfied himself that neither of us was in a pathological condition, Mr. Abrahams suffered me to lead him up-stairs, where a repast had been laid out for him to which he did ample justice. The mysterious little bag he carried along with him, and deposited it under his chair during the meal. It was not until the table had been cleared and we were left together that he broached the matter on which he had come down.

"I hunderstand," he remarked, puffing at a trichinopoly, "that you want my 'elp in fitting up this 'ere 'ouse with a happarition."

I acknowledged the correctness of his surmise, while mentally

wondering at those restless eyes of his, which still danced about
the room as if he were making an inventory of the contents.

"And you won't find a better man for the job, though I says it
as shouldn't," continued my companion. "Wot did I say to the
young gent wot spoke to me in the bar of the Lame Dog? 'Can
you do it?' says he. 'Try me,' says I, 'me and my bag. Just try
me.' I couldn't say fairer than that."

My respect for Jack Brocket's business capabilities began to
go up very considerably. He certainly seemed to have managed
the matter wonderfully well. "You don't mean to say that you
carry ghosts about in bags!" I remarked, with diffidence.

Mr. Abrahams smiled a smile of superior knowledge. "You
wait," he said; "give me the right place and the right hour, with a
little of the essence of Lucoptolycus" — here he produced a small
bottle from his waistcoat pocket — "and you won't find no ghost
that I ain't up to. You'll see them yourself, and pick your own,
and I can't say fairer than that."

As all Mr. Abrahams' protestations of fairness were accompanied by a cunning leer and a wink from one or other of his
wicked little eyes, the impression of candour was somewhat
weakened.

"When are you going to do it?" I asked reverentially.

"Ten minutes to one in the morning," said Mr. Abrahams,
with decision. "Some says midnight, but I says ten to one, when
there ain't such a crowd, and you can pick your own ghost. And
now," he continued, rising to his feet, "suppose you trot me
round the premises, and let me see where you wants it; for
there's some places as attracts 'em, and some as they won't hear
of — not if there was no other place in the world."

Mr. Abrahams inspected our corridors and chambers with a
most critical and observant eye, fingering the old tapestry with
the air of a connoisseur, and remarking in an undertone that it
would "match uncommon nice." It was not until he reached the
banqueting-hall, however, which I had myself picked out, that
his admiration reached the pitch of enthusiasm. "'Ere's the
place!" he shouted, dancing, bag in hand, round the table on
which my plate was lying, and looking not unlike some quaint
little goblin himself. "'Ere's the place; we won't get nothin' to
beat this! A fine room — noble, solid, none of your electro-plate
trash! That's the way as things ought to be done, sir. Plenty of

room for 'em to glide here. Send up some brandy and the box of weeds; I'll sit here by the fire and do the preliminaries, which is more trouble than you'd think; for them ghosts carries on hawful at times, before they finds out who they've got to deal with. If you was in the room they'd tear you to pieces as like as not. You leave me alone to tackle them, and at half-past twelve come in, and I lay they'll be quiet enough by then."

Mr. Abrahams' request struck me as a reasonable one, so I left him with his feet upon the mantelpiece, and his chair in front of the fire, fortifying himself with stimulants against his refractory visitors. From the room beneath, in which I sat with Mrs. D'Odd, I could hear that after sitting for some time he rose up, and paced about the hall with quick impatient steps. We then heard him try the lock of the door, and afterwards drag some heavy article of furniture in the direction of the window, on which, apparently, he mounted, for I heard the creaking of the rusty hinges as the diamond-paned casement folded backwards, and I knew it to be situated several feet above the little man's reach. Mrs. D'Odd says that she could distinguish his voice speaking in low and rapid whispers after this, but that may have been her imagination. I confess that I began to feel more impressed than I had deemed it possible to be. There was something awesome in the thought of the solitary mortal standing by the open window and summoning in from the gloom outside the spirits of the nether world. It was with a trepidation which I could hardly disguise from Matilda that I observed that the clock was pointing to half-past twelve, and that the time had come for me to share the vigil of my visitor.

He was sitting in his old position when I entered, and there were no signs of the mysterious movements which I had overheard, though his chubby face was flushed as with recent exertion.

"Are you succeeding all right?" I asked as I came in, putting on as careless an air as possible, but glancing involuntarily round the room to see if we were alone.

"Only your help is needed to complete the matter," said Mr. Abrahams, in a solemn voice. "You shall sit by me and partake of the essence of Lucoptolycus, which removes the scales from our earthly eyes. Whatever you may chance to see, speak not and make no movement, lest you break the spell." His manner was subdued, and his usual cockney vulgarity had entirely disappeared. I took the chair which he indicated, and awaited the result.

My companion cleared the rushes from the floor in our neighbourhood, and, going down upon his hands and knees, described a half-circle with chalk, which enclosed the fireplace and ourselves. Round the edge of this half-circle he drew several hieroglyphics, not unlike the signs of the zodiac. He then stood up and uttered a long invocation, delivered so rapidly that it sounded like a single gigantic word in some uncouth guttural language. Having finished this prayer, if prayer it was, he pulled out the small bottle which he had produced before, and poured a couple of teaspoonfuls of clear transparent fluid into a phial, which he handed to me with an intimation that I should drink it.

The liquid had a faintly sweet odour, not unlike the aroma of certain sorts of apples. I hesitated a moment before applying it to my lips, but an impatient gesture from my companion overcame my scruples, and I tossed it off. The taste was not unpleasant; and, as it gave rise to no immediate effects, I leaned back in my chair and composed myself for what was to come. Mr. Abrahams seated himself beside me, and I felt that he was watching my face from time to time while repeating some more of the invocations in which he had indulged before.

A sense of delicious warmth and languor began gradually to steal over me, partly, perhaps, from the heat of the fire, and partly from some unexplained cause. An uncontrollable impulse to sleep weighed down my eyelids, while, at the same time, my brain worked actively, and a hundred beautiful and pleasing ideas flitted through it. So utterly lethargic did I feel that, though I was aware that my companion put his hand over the region of my heart, as if to feel how it were beating, I did not attempt to prevent him, nor did I even ask him for the reason of his action. Everything in the room appeared to be reeling slowly round in a drowsy dance, of which I was the centre. The great elk's head at the far end wagged solemnly backwards and forwards, while the massive salvers on the tables performed cotillons with the claret cooler and the epergne. My head fell upon my breast from sheer heaviness, and I should have become unconscious had I not been recalled to myself by the opening of the door at the other end of the hall.

This door led on to the raised daïs, which, as I have mentioned, the heads of the house used to reserve for their own use.
As it swung slowly back upon its hinges, I sat up in my chair,
clutching at the arms, and staring with a horrified glare at the
dark passage outside. Something was coming down it—something unformed and intangible, but still a *something*. Dim and
shadowy, I saw it flit across the threshold, while a blast of ice-
cold air swept down the room, which seemed to blow through
me, chilling my very heart. I was aware of the mysterious
presence, and then I heard it speak in a voice like the sighing of
an east wind among pine-trees on the banks of a desolate sea.

It said: "I am the invisible nonentity. I have affinities and am
subtle. I am electric, magnetic, and spiritualistic. I am the great
ethereal sigh-heaver. I kill dogs. Mortal, wilt thou choose me?"

I was about to speak, but the words seemed to be choked in
my throat; and, before I could get them out, the shadow flitted
across the hall and vanished in the darkness at the other side,
while a long-drawn melancholy sigh quivered through the
apartment.

I turned my eyes towards the door once more, and beheld, to
my astonishment, a very small old woman, who hobbled along
the corridor and into the hall. She passed backwards and
forwards several times, and then, crouching down at the very
edge of the circle upon the floor, she disclosed a face the horrible
malignity of which shall never be banished from my recollection.
Every foul passion appeared to have left its mark upon that
hideous countenance.

"Ha! ha!" she screamed, holding out her wizened hands like
the talons of an unclean bird. "You see what I am. I am the
fiendish old woman. I wear snuff-coloured silks. My curse
descends on people. Sir Walter was partial to me. Shall I be
thine, mortal?"

I endeavoured to shake my head in horror; on which she
aimed a blow at me with her crutch, and vanished with an
eldritch scream.

By this time my eyes turned naturally towards the open door,
and I was hardly surprised to see a man walk in of tall and noble
stature. His face was deadly pale, but was surmounted by a
fringe of dark hair which fell in ringlets down his back. A short
pointed beard covered his chin. He was dressed in loose-fitting

clothes, made apparently of yellow satin, and a large white ruff surrounded his neck. He paced across the room with slow and majestic strides. Then turning, he addressed me in a sweet, exquisitely-modulated voice.

"I am the cavalier," he remarked. "I pierce and am pierced. Here is my rapier. I clink steel. This is a blood-stain over my heart. I can emit hollow groans. I am patronized by many old Conservative families. I am the original manor-hour apparition. I work alone, or in company with shrieking damsels."

He bent his head courteously, as though awaiting my reply, but the same choking sensation prevented me from speaking; and, with a deep bow, he disappeared.

He had hardly gone before a feeling of intense horror stole over me and I was aware of the presence of a ghastly creature in the room of dim outlines and uncertain proportions. One moment it seemed to pervade the entire apartment, while at another it would become invisible, but always leaving behind it a distinct consciousness of its presence. Its voice, when it spoke, was quavering and gusty. It said, "I am the leaver of footsteps and the spiller of gouts of blood. I tramp upon corridors. Charles Dickens has alluded to me. I make strange and disagreeable noises. I snatch letters and place invisible hands on people's wrists. I am cheerful. I burst into peals of hideous laughter. Shall I do one now?" I raised my hand in a deprecating way, but too late to prevent one discordant outbreak which echoed through the room. Before I could lower it the apparition was gone.

I turned my head towards the door in time to see a man come hastily and stealthily into the chamber. He was a sunburned powerfully-built fellow, with earrings in his ears and a Barcelona handkerchief tied loosely round his neck. His head was bent upon his chest, and his whole aspect was that of one afflicted by intolerable remorse. He paced rapidly backwards and forwards like a caged tiger, and I observed that a drawn knife glittered in one of his hands, while he grasped what appeared to be a piece of parchment in the other. His voice, when he spoke, was deep and sonorous. He said, "I am a murderer. I am a ruffian. I crouch when I walk. I step noiselessly. I know something of the Spanish Main. I can do the lost treasure business. I have charts.

Am able-bodied and a good walker. Capable of haunting a large park." He looked towards me beseechingly, but before I could make a sign I was paralyzed by the horrible sight which appeared at the door.

It was a very tall man, if, indeed, it might be called a man, for the gaunt bones were protruding through the corroding flesh, and the features were of a leaden hue. A winding-sheet was wrapped round the figure, and formed a hood over the head, from under the shadow of which two fiendish eyes, deepset in their grisly sockets, blazed and sparkled like red-hot coals. The lower jaw had fallen upon the breast, disclosing a withered shrivelled tongue and two lines of black and jagged fangs. I shuddered and drew back as this fearful apparition advanced to the edge of the circle.

"I am the American blood-curdler," it said, in a voice which seemed to come in a hollow murmur from the earth beneath it. "None other is genuine. I am the embodiment of Edgar Allan Poe. I am circumstantial and horrible. I am a low-caste spirit-subduing spectre. Observe my blood and my bones. I am gristly and nauseous. No depending on artificial aid. Work with grave-clothes, a coffin-lid, and a galvanic battery. Turn hair white in a night." The creature stretched out its fleshless arms to me as if in entreaty, but I shook my head; and it vanished, leaving a low sickening repulsive odour behind it. I sank back in my chair, so overcome by terror and disgust that I would have very willingly resigned myself to dispensing with a ghost altogether, could I have been sure that this was the last of the hideous procession.

A faint sound of trailing garments warned me that it was not so. I looked up, and beheld a white figure emerging from the corridor into the light. As it stepped across the threshold I saw that it was that of a young and beautiful woman dressed in the fashion of a bygone day. Her hands were clasped in front of her, and her pale proud face bore traces of passion and of suffering. She crossed the hall with a gentle sound, like the rustling of autumn leaves, and then, turning her lovely and unutterably sad eyes upon me, she said:

"I am the plaintive and sentimental, the beautiful and ill-used. I have been forsaken and betrayed. I shriek in the night-time and glide down passages. My antecedents are highly respectable and generally aristocratic. My tastes are aesthetic. Old oak furniture like this would do, with a few more coats of mail and plenty of tapestry. Will you not take me?"

Her voice died away in a beautiful cadence as she concluded, and she held out her hands as if in supplication. I am always sensitive to female influences. Besides, what would Jorrocks' ghost be to this? Could anything be in better taste? Would I not be exposing myself to the chance of injuring my nervous system by interviews with such creatures as my last visitor, unless I decided at once? She gave me a seraphic smile, as if she knew what was passing in my mind. That smile settled the matter. "She will do!" I cried; "I choose this one"; and as, in my enthusiasm, I took a step towards her I passed over the magic circle which had girdled me round.

"Argentine, we have been robbed!"

I had an indistinct consciousness of these words being spoken, or rather screamed, in my ear a great number of times without my being able to grasp their meaning. A violent throbbing in my head seemed to adapt itself to their rhythm, and I closed my eyes to the lullaby of "Robbed, robbed, robbed." A vigorous shake caused me to open them again, however, and the sight of Mrs. D'Odd in the scantiest of costumes and most furious of tempers was sufficiently impressive to recall all my scattered thoughts, and make me realize that I was lying on my back on the floor, with my head among the ashes which had fallen from last night's fire, and a small glass phial in my hand.

I staggered to my feet, but felt so weak and giddy that I was compelled to fall back into a chair. As my brain became clearer, stimulated by the exclamations of Matilda, I began gradually to recollect the events of the night. There was the door through which my supernatural visitors had filed. There was the circle of chalk with the hieroglyphics round the edge. There was the cigar-box and brandy-bottle which had been honoured by the attentions of Mr. Abrahams. But the seer himself—where was he? and what was this open window with a rope running out of it? And where, O where, was the pride of Goresthorpe Grange, the glorious plate which was to have been the delectation of generations of D'Odds? And why was Mrs. D. standing in the gray light of dawn, wringing her hands and repeating her monotonous refrain? It was only very gradually that my misty brain took these things in, and grasped the connection between them.

Reader, I have never seen Mr. Abrahams since; I have never seen the plate stamped with the resuscitated family crest; hardest of all, I have never caught a glimpse of the melancholy spectre with the trailing garments, nor do I expect that I ever shall. In fact my night's experiences have cured me of my mania for the supernatural, and quite reconciled me to inhabiting the humdrum nineteenth century edifice on the outskirts of London which Mrs. D. has long had in her mind's eye.

As to the explanation of all that occurred — that is a matter which is open to several surmises. That Mr. Abrahams, the ghost-hunter, was identical with Jemmy Wilson, *alias* the Nottingham crackster, is considered more than probable at Scotland Yard, and certainly the description of that remarkable burglar tallied very well with the appearance of my visitor. The small bag which I have described was picked up in a neighbouring field next day, and found to contain a choice assortment of jemmies and centrebits. Footmarks deeply imprinted in the mud on either side of the moat showed that an accomplice from below had received the sack of precious metals which had been let down through the open window. No doubt the pair of scoundrels, while looking round for a job, had overheard Jack Brocket's indiscreet inquiries, and had promptly availed themselves of the tempting opening.

And now as to my less substantial visitors, and the curious grotesque vision which I had enjoyed — am I to lay it down to any real power over occult matters possessed by my Nottingham friend? For a long time I was doubtful upon the point, and eventually endeavoured to solve it by consulting a well-known analyst and medical man, sending him the few drops of the so-called essence of Lucoptolycus which remained in my phial. I append the letter which I received from him, only too happy to have the opportunity of winding up my little narrative by the weighty words of a man of learning.

"Arundel Street.

"Dear Sir, — Your very singular case has interested me extremely. The bottle which you sent contained a strong solution of chloral, and the quantity which you describe yourself as having swallowed must have amounted to at least eighty grains of the pure hydrate. This would of course have reduced you to a partial state of insensibility, gradually going on to complete coma. In this semi-conscious state of chloralism it is not unusual for circumstantial and *bizarre* visions to present themselves — more especially to individuals unaccustomed to the use of the drug. You tell me in your note that your mind was saturated with ghostly literature, and that you had long taken a morbid interest in classifying and recalling the various forms in which apparitions have been said to appear. You must also remember that you were expecting to see something of that very nature, and that your nervous system was worked up to an unnatural state of tension. Under the circumstances, I think that, far from the sequel being an astonishing one, it would have been very surprising indeed to any one versed in narcotics had you not experienced some such effects. — I remain, dear sir, sincerely yours,

"T. E. STUBE, M.D.

"Argentine D'Odd, Esq.
The Elms, Brixton."

The Recollections of
Captain Wilkie

It is hard to know when "The Recollections of Captain Wilkie" was written. It was first published in CHAMBERS'S JOURNAL *for January 19 and 26, 1895, but it was never permitted to be collected, for obvious reasons. By 1895, Sherlock Holmes had become a world-wide phenomenon, and Conan Doyle had every reason not to want the early "Captain Wilkie" to diffuse the image he had built up. A good guess would put the composition of this story around 1884 or 1885, when the fictional possibilities of Dr. Joseph Bell of Edinburgh were perhaps just beginning to stir in Doyle's mind but had not yet taken the form of Sherlock Holmes. It must have been written and sold before April 1886, when we know he began work on* A STUDY IN SCARLET, *the first Holmes tale.*

Here it is the doctor who has the deductive power; Doyle has not yet hit upon the idea of a professional detective or of separating his protagonist into two and presenting Watson as the physician who can transcribe—and by implication prescribe— Holmes's cold-blooded, scientific methods for the reading public. He has his concept, but its fabric is not yet complete. Fortunately for literature, though, CHAMBERS'S *held the story without publishing it, only to rediscover the manuscript a year after Holmes had met his supposed death at the hands of Professor Moriarty in the pages of the* STRAND. *"'Captain Wilkie' was written by Dr. Conan Doyle several years ago," the editors of* CHAMBERS'S *noted at the end of the piece when it finally appeared, "and is interesting, both as a vigorous story in itself and as being in the vein which he afterwards developed in the well-known Sherlock Holmes stories." Vigorous it is, indeed, and presented in an episodic and raconteurial fashion which is very unlike his usual storytelling style. One wonders, though— had "Captain Wilkie" been published when it was written, would*

*Conan Doyle, who did not like to repeat himself, have gone on
to create Sherlock Holmes? It gives one pause.*

"Wно can he be?" thought I, as I watched my companion
in the second-class carriage of the London and Dover
Railway.

I had been so full of the fact that my long-expected holiday
had come at last, and that for a few days at least the gaieties of
Paris were about to supersede the dull routine of the hospital
wards, that we were well out of London before I observed that I
was not alone in the compartment. In these days we have all
pretty well agreed that "Three is company and two is none" upon
the railway. At the time I write of, however, people were not so
morbidly sensitive about their travelling companions. It was
rather an agreeable surprise to me to find that there was some
chance of whiling away the hours of a tedious journey. I therefore pulled my cap down over my eyes, took a good look from
beneath it at my vis-à-vis, and repeated to myself, "Who can he
be?"

I used rather to pride myself on being able to spot a man's
trade or profession by a good look at his exterior. I had the
advantage of studying under a Professor at Edinburgh who was
a master of the art, and used to electrify both his patients and his
clinical classes by long shots, sometimes at the most unlikely of
pursuits, and never very far from the mark. "Well, my man," I
have heard him say, "I can see by your fingers that you play
some musical instrument for your livelihood, but it is a rather
curious one—something quite out of my line." The man afterwards informed us that he earned a few coppers by blowing *Rule
Britannia* on a coffee-pot, the spout of which was pierced to
form a rough flute. Though a novice in the art compared to the
shrewd Professor, I was still able to astonish my ward companions on occasion, and I never lost an opportunity of practising
myself. It was not mere curiosity, then, which led me to lean
back on the cushions and analyze the quiet middle-aged man in
front of me.

I used to do the thing systematically, and my train of reflec-
tions ran somewhat in this wise: "General appearance vulgar,

fairly opulent, and extremely self-possessed—looks like a man who could outchaff a bargee, and yet be at his ease in the best middle-class society. Eyes well set together, and nose rather prominent—would be a good long-range marksman. Cheeks flabby, but the softness of expression redeemed by a square-cut jaw and a well-set lower lip. On the whole, a powerful type. Now for the hands—rather disappointed there. Thought he was a self-made man by the look of him, but there is no callus in the palm, and no thickening at the joints. Has never been engaged in any real physical work, I should think. No tanning on the backs of the hands; on the contrary, they are very white, with blue projecting veins and long delicate fingers. Couldn't be an artist with that face, and yet he has the hands of a man engaged in delicate manipulations. No red acid spots upon his clothes, no ink-stains, no nitrate-of-silver marks upon the hands (this helps to negative my half-formed opinion that he was a photographer). Clothes not worn in any particular part. Coat made of tweed, and fairly old; but the left elbow, as far as I can see it, has as much of the fluff left on as the right, which is seldom the case with men who do much writing. Might be a commercial traveller, but the little pocket-book in the waistcoat is wanting, nor has he any of those handy valises suggestive of samples."

I give these brief headings of my ideas merely to demonstrate my method of arriving at a conclusion. As yet I had obtained nothing but negative results; but now, to use a chemical metaphor, I was in a position to pour off this solution of dissolved possibilities and examine the residue. I found myself reduced to a very limited number of occupations. He was neither a lawyer nor a clergyman, in spite of a soft felt hat, and a somewhat clerical cut about the necktie. I was wavering now between pawnbroker and horse-dealer; but there was too much character about his face for the former; and he lacked that extraordinary equine atmosphere which hangs about the latter even in his hours of relaxation; so I formed a provisional diagnosis of betting man of methodistical proclivities, the latter clause being inserted in deference to his hat and necktie.

Pray, do not think that I reasoned it out like this in my own mind. It is only now, sitting down with pen and paper, that I can see the successive steps. As it was, I had formed my conclusion within sixty seconds of the time when I drew my hat down over my eyes and uttered the mental ejaculation with which my narrative begins.

I did not feel quite satisfied even then with my deduction. However, as a leading question would—to pursue my chemical analogy—act as my litmus paper, I determined to try one. There was a *Times* lying by my companion, and I thought the opportunity too good to be neglected.

"Do you mind my looking at your paper?" I asked.

"Certainly, sir, certainly," said he most urbanely, handing it across.

I glanced down its columns until my eye rested upon the list of the latest betting.

"Hullo!" I said, "they are laying odds upon the favourite for the Cambridgeshire.—But perhaps," I added, looking up, "you are not interested in these matters?"

"Snares, sir!" said he violently, "wiles of the enemy! Mortals are but given a few years to live; how can they squander them so! —They have not even an eye to their poor worldly interests," he added in a quieter tone, "or they would never back a single horse at such short odds with a field of thirty."

There was something in this speech of his which tickled me immensely. I suppose it was the odd way in which he blended religious intolerance with worldly wisdom. I laid the *Times* aside with the conviction that I should be able to spend the next two hours to better purpose than in its perusal.

"You speak as if you understood the matter, at any rate," I remarked.

"Yes, sir," he answered; "few men in England understood these things better in the old days before I changed my profession. But that is all over now."

"Changed your profession?" said I interrogatively.

"Yes; I changed my name too."

"Indeed?" said I.

"Yes; you see, a man wants a real fresh start when his eyes become opened, so he has a new deal all round, so to speak. Then he gets a fair chance."

There was a short pause here, as I seemed to be on delicate ground in touching on my companion's antecedents, and he did not volunteer any information. I broke the silence by offering him a cheroot.

"No; thanks," said he; "I have given up tobacco. It was the hardest wrench of all, was that. It does me good to smell the whiff of your weed. — Tell me," he added suddenly, looking hard at me with his shrewd gray eyes, "why did you take stock of me so carefully before you spoke?"

"It is a habit of mine," said I. "I am a medical man, and observation is everything in my profession. I had no idea you were looking."

"I can see without looking," he answered. "I thought you were a detective, at first; but I couldn't recall your face at the time I knew the force."

"Were you a detective, then?" said I.

"No," he answered with a laugh; "I was the other thing — the detected, you know. Old scores are wiped out now, and the law cannot touch me, so I don't mind confessing to a gentleman like yourself what a scoundrel I have been in my time."

"We are none of us perfect," said I.

"No; but I was a real out-and-outer. A 'fake,' you know, to start with, and afterwards a 'cracksman.' It is easy to talk of these things now, for I've changed my spirit. It's as if I was talking of some other man, you see."

"Exactly so," said I. Being a medical man I had none of that shrinking from crime and criminals which many men possess. I could make all allowances for congenital influence and the force of circumstances. No company, therefore, could have been more acceptable to me than that of the old malefactor; and as I sat puffing at my cigar, I was delighted to observe that my air of interest was gradually loosening his tongue.

"Yes; I'm a changed man now," he continued, "and of course I am a happier man for that. And yet," he added wistfully, "there are times when I long for the old trade again, and fancy myself strolling out on a cloudy night with my jemmy in my pocket. I left a name behind me in my profession, sir. I was one of the old school, you know. It was very seldom that we bungled a job. We used to begin at the foot of the ladder, in my younger days, and then work our way up through the successive grades, so that we were what you might call good men all round."

"I see," said I.

"I was always reckoned a hard-working, conscientious man, and had talent too—the very cleverest of them allowed that. I began as a blacksmith, and then did a little engineering and carpentering, and then I took to sleight-of-hand tricks, and then to picking pockets. I remember, when I was home on a visit, how my poor old father used to wonder why I was always hovering around him. He little knew that I used to clear everything out of his pockets a dozen times a day, and then replace them, just to keep my hand in. He believes to this day that I am in an office in the City. There are few of them could touch me in that particular line of business, though."

"I suppose it is a matter of practice?" I remarked.

"To a great extent. Still, a man never quite loses it, if he has once been an adept.—Excuse me; you have dropped some cigar ash on your coat," and he waved his hand politely in front of my breast, as if to brush it off.—"There," he said, handing me my gold scarf pin, "you see I have not forgot my old cunning yet."

He had done it so quickly that I hardly saw the hand whisk over my bosom, nor did I feel his fingers touch me, and yet there was the pin glittering in his hand. "It is wonderful!" I said as I fixed it again in its place.

"Oh, that's nothing! But I have been in some really smart jobs. I was in the gang that picked the new patent safe. You remember the case. It was guaranteed to resist anything; and we managed to open the first that was ever issued, within a week of its appearance. It was done with graduated wedges, sir, the first so small that you could hardly see it against the light, and the last strong enough to prise it open. It was a cleverly managed affair."

"I remember it," said I. "But surely some one was convicted for that?"

"Yes, one was nabbed. But he didn't split, nor even let on how it was done. It would have been as much as his life was worth.— Perhaps I am boring you, talking about these old wicked days of mine?"

"On the contrary," I said, "you interest me extremely."

"I like to get a listener I can trust. It's a sort of blow-off, you know, and I feel lighter after it. When I am among my new and highly respectable acquaintances, I dare hardly think of what has gone before. — Now, I'll tell you about another job I was in. To this day, I cannot think about it without laughing."

I lit another cigar, and composed myself to listen.

"It was when I was a youngster," said he. "There was a big City man in those days who was known to have a very valuable gold watch. I followed him about for several days before I could get a chance; but when I did get one, you may be sure I did not throw it away. He found, to his disgust, when he got home that day, that there was nothing in his fob. I hurried off with my prize, and got it stowed away in safety, intending to have it melted down next day. Now, it happened that this watch possessed a special value in the owner's eyes because it was a sort of ancestral possession — presented to his father on coming of age, or something of that sort. I remember there was a long inscription on the back. He was determined not to lose it if he could help it, and accordingly he put an advertisement in an evening paper offering thirty pounds reward for its return, and promising that no questions should be asked. He gave the address of his house, 31 Caroline Square, at the end of the advertisement. The thing sounded good enough, so I set off for Caroline Square, leaving the watch in a parcel at a public-house which I passed on the way. When I got there, the gentleman was at dinner; but he came out quick enough when he heard that a young man wanted to see him. I suppose he guessed who the young man would prove to be. He was a genial-looking old fellow, and he led me away with him into his study.

" 'Well, my lad,' said he, 'what is it?'

" 'I've come about that watch of yours,' said I. 'I think I can lay my hands on it.'

" 'Oh, it was you that took it!' said he.

" 'No,' I answered; 'I know nothing whatever about how you lost it. I have been sent by another party to see you about it. Even if you have me arrested, you will not find out anything.'

" 'Well,' he said, 'I don't want to be hard on you. Hand it over, and here is my cheque for the amount.'

" 'Cheques won't do,' said I; 'I must have it in gold.'

" 'It will take me an hour or so to collect it in gold,' said he.

" 'That will just suit,' I answered, 'for I have not got the watch with me. I'll go back and fetch it, while you raise the money.'

"I started off, and got the watch where I had left it. When I came back, the old gentleman was sitting behind his study table, with the little heap of gold in front of him.

"'Here is your money,' he said, and pushed it over.

"'Here is your watch,' said I.

"He was evidently delighted to get it back; and after examining it carefully, and assuring himself that it was none the worse, he put it into the watch-pocket of his coat with a grunt of satisfaction.

"'Now, my lad,' he said, 'I know it was you that took the watch. Tell me how you did it, and I don't mind giving you an extra five-pound note.'

"'I wouldn't tell you in any case,' said I; 'but especially I wouldn't tell you when you have a witness hid behind that curtain.' You see, I had all my wits about me, and it didn't escape me that the curtain was drawn tighter than it had been before.

"'You are too sharp for us,' said he good-humouredly. 'Well, you have got your money, and that's an end of it. I'll take precious good care you don't get hold of my watch again in a hurry. — Good-night. — No; not that door,' he added as I marched towards a cupboard. 'This is the door,' and he stood up and opened it. I brushed past him, opened the hall door, and was round the corner of the square in no time. I don't know how long the old gentleman took to find it out, but in passing him at the door, I managed to pick his pocket for the second time, and next morning the family heirloom was in the melting-pot after all. — That wasn't bad, was it?"

The old war-horse was evidently getting his blood up now. There was a tone of triumph in the conclusion of his anecdote which showed that, sometimes at least, his pride in his smartness surpassed his repentance of his misdeeds. He seemed pleased at the astonishment and amusement I expressed at his adroitness.

"Yes," he continued with a laugh, "it was a capital joke. But sometimes the fun lies all the other way. Even the sharpest of us comes to grief at times. There was one rather curious incident which occurred in my career. You may possibly have seen the anecdote, for it got into print at the time."

"Pray, let me hear it," said I.

"Well, it is hard lines telling stories against one's self, but this was how it happened. I had made a rather good haul, and invested some of the swag in buying a very fine diamond ring. I thought it would be something to fall back upon when all the ready was gone and times were hard. I had just purchased it, and was going back to my lodgings in the omnibus, when, as luck would have it, a very stylishly dressed young lady came in and took her seat beside me. I didn't pay much attention to her at first; but after a time something hard in her dress knocked up against my hand, which my experienced touch soon made out to be a purse. It struck me that I could not pass the time more profitably or agreeably than by making this purse my own. I had to do it very carefully; but I managed at last to wriggle my hand into her rather tight pocket, and I thought the job was over. Just at this moment she rose abruptly to leave the 'bus, and I had hardly time to get my hand with the purse in it out of her pocket without detection. It was not until she had been gone some time that I found out that, in drawing out my hand in that hurried manner, the new and ill-fitting ring I wore had slipped over my finger and remained in the young lady's pocket. I sprang out, and ran in the direction in which she had gone, with the intention of picking her pocket once again. She had disappeared, however; and from that day to this I have never set eyes on her. To make the matter worse, there was only fourpence-halfpenny in coppers inside the purse. Sarve me right for trying to rob such a pretty girl; still, if I had that two hundred quid now, I should not be reduced to— Good heavens, forgive me! What am I saying?"

He seemed inclined to relapse into silence after this; but I was determined to draw him out a little more, if I could possibly manage it. "There is less personal risk in the branch you have been talking of," I remarked, "than there is in burglary."

"Ah!" he said, warming to his subject once again, "it is the higher game which is best worth aiming at. — Talk about sport, sir, talk about fishing or hunting! why, it is tame in comparison! Think of the great country-house with its men-servants and its dogs and its firearms, and you with only your jemmy and your centre-bit, and your mother-wit, which is best of all. It is the triumph of intellect over brute-force, sir, as represented by bolts and bars."

"People generally look upon it as quite the reverse," I remarked.

"I was never one of those blundering life-preserver fellows," said my companion. "I did try my hand at garrotting once; but it was against my principles, and I gave it up. I have tried everything. I have been a bedridden widow with three young children; but I do object to physical force."

"You have been what?" said I.

"A bedridden widow. Advertising, you know, and getting subscriptions. I have tried them all. — You seem interested in these experiences," he continued; "so I will tell you another anecdote. It was the narrowest escape for penal servitude that ever I had in my life. A pal and I had gone down on a country beat — it doesn't signify where it was — and taken up our head-quarters in a little provincial town. Somehow it got noised abroad that we were there, and householders were warned to be careful, as suspicious characters had been seen in the neighbour-hood. We should have changed our plans when we saw the game was up; but my chum was a plucky fellow, and wouldn't consent to back down. Poor little Jim! He was only thirty-four round the chest, and about twelve at the biceps; but there is not a measuring tape in England could have given the size of his heart. He said we were in for it, and we must stick to it; so I agreed to stay, and we chose Morley Hall, the country-house of a certain Colonel Morley, to begin with.

"Now, this Colonel Morley was about the last man in the world that we should have meddled with. He was a shrewd, cool-headed fellow, who had knocked about and seen the world, and it seems that he took a special pride in the detection of criminals. However, we knew nothing of all this at that time; so we set forth hopefully to have a try at the house.

"The reason that made us pick him out among the rest was that he had a good-for-nothing groom, who was a tool in our hands. This fellow had drawn up a rough plan of the premises for us. The place was pretty well locked up and guarded, and the only weak point we could see was a certain trap-door, the padlock of which was broken, and which opened from the roof into one of the lumber-rooms. If we could only find any method of reaching the roof, we might force a way securely from above. We both thought the plan rather a good one, and it had a spice of originality about it which pleased us. It is not the mere jewels or plate, you know, that a good cracksman thinks about. The neatness of the job, and his reputation for smartness, are almost as important in his eyes.

"We had been very quiet for a day or two, just to let suspicion die away. Then we set out one dark night, Jim and I, and got over the avenue railings and up to the house without meeting a soul. It was blowing hard, I remember, and the clouds hurrying across the sky. We had a good look at the front of the house, and then Jim went round to the garden side. He came running back in a minute or two in a great state of delight. 'Why, Bill,' he said, gripping me by the arm, 'there never was such a bit of luck! They've been repairing the roof or something, and they've left the ladder standing.' We went round together, and there, sure enough, was the ladder towering above our heads, and one or two labourers' hods lying about, which showed that some work had been going on during the day. We had a good look round, to see that everything was quiet, and then we climbed up, Jim first, and I after him. We got to the top, and were sitting on the slates, having a bit of a breather, before beginning business, when you can fancy our feelings to see the ladder that we came up by suddenly stand straight up in the air, and then slowly descend until it rested in the garden below! At first, we hoped it might have slipped, though that was bad enough; but we soon had that idea put out of our head.

" 'Hullo, up there!' cried a voice from below.

"We craned our heads over the edge, and there was a man dressed, as far as we could make out, in evening dress, and standing in the middle of the grass plot. We kept quiet.

" 'Hullo!' he shouted again. 'How do you feel yourselves? Pretty comfortable, eh? Ha! ha! You London rogues thought we were green in the country. What's your opinion now?'

We both lay still, though feeling pretty considerably small, as you may imagine.

" 'It's all right; I see you,' he continued. 'Why, I have been waiting behind that lilac bush every night for the last week, expecting to see you. I knew you couldn't resist going up that ladder, when you found the windows were too much for you. — Joe! Joe!'

" 'Yes, sir,' said a voice, and another man came from among the bushes.

" 'Just you keep your eye on the roof, will you, while I ride down to the station and fetch up a couple of constables? — *Au revoir,* gentlemen! You don't mind waiting, I suppose?' And Colonel Morley — for it was the owner of the house himself — strode off; and in a few minutes we heard the rattle of his horse's hoofs going down the avenue.

"Well, sir, we felt precious silly, as you may imagine. It wasn't so much having been nabbed that bothered us, as the feeling of being caught in such a simple trap. We looked at each other in blank disgust, and then, to save our lives, we couldn't help bursting into laughter at our own fix. However, it was no laughing matter; so we set to work going round the roof, and seeing if there was a likely water-pipe or anything that might give us a chance of escape. We had to give it up as a bad job; so we sat down again, and made up our minds to the worst. Suddenly an idea flashed into my head, and I groped my way over the roof until I felt wood under my feet. I bent down, and found that the Colonel had actually forgotten to secure the padlock! You will often notice, as you go through life, that it is the shrewdest and most cunning man who falls into the most absurd mistakes; and this was an example of it. You may guess that we did not lose much time, for we expected to hear the constables every moment. We dropped through into the lumber-room, slipped down-stairs, tore open the library shutters, and were out and away before the astonished groom could make out what had happened. There wasn't time enough to take any little souvenir with us, worse luck. I should have liked to have seen the Colonel's face when he came back with the constables and found that the birds were flown."

"Did you ever come across the Colonel again?" I asked.

"Yes; we skinned him of every bit of plate he had, down to the salt-spoons, a few years later. It was partly out of revenge, you see, that we did it. It was a very well-managed and daring thing, one of the best I ever saw, and all done in open daylight too."

"How in the world did you do it?" I asked.

"Well, there were three of us in it — Jim was one; and we set about it in this way. We wanted to begin by getting the Colonel out of the way, so I wrote him a note purporting to come from Squire Brotherwick, who lived about ten miles away, and was not always on the best of terms with the master of Morley Hall. I dressed myself up as a groom and delivered the note myself. It was to the effect that the Squire thought he was able to lay his hands on the scoundrels who had escaped from the Colonel a couple of years before, and that if the Colonel would ride over, they would have little difficulty in securing them. I was sure that this would have the desired effect; so, after handing it in, and remarking that I was the Squire's groom, I walked off again, as if on the way back to my master's.

"After getting out of sight of the house, I crouched down behind a hedge; and, as I expected, in less than a quarter of an hour the Colonel came swinging past me on his chestnut mare. Now, there is another accomplishment I possess which I have not mentioned to you yet, and that is, that I can copy any handwriting that I see. It is a very easy trick to pick up, if you only give your mind to it. I happened to have come across one of Colonel Morley's letters some days before, and I can write so that even now I defy an expert to detect a difference between the hands. This was a great assistance to me now, for I tore a leaf out of my pocket-book and wrote something to this effect:

"'As Squire Brotherwick has seen some suspicious characters about, and the house may be attempted again, I have sent down to the bank, and ordered them to send up their bank-cart to convey the whole of the plate to a place of safety. It will save us a good deal of anxiety to know that it is in absolute security. Have it packed up and ready, and give the bearer a glass of beer.'

"Having composed this precious epistle, I addressed it to the butler, and carried it back to the Hall, saying that their master had overtaken me on the way and asked me to deliver it. I was taken in and made much of down-stairs; while a great packing-case was dragged into the hall, and the plate stowed away among cotton-wool and stuffing. It was nearly ready, when I heard the sound of wheels upon the gravel, and sauntered round just in time to see a business-like closed car drive up to the door. One of my pals was sitting very demurely on the box; while Jim, with an official-looking hat, sprang out and bustled into the hall.

"'Now, then,' I heard him say, 'look sharp! What's for the bank? Come on!'

"'Wait a minute, sir,' said the butler.

" 'Can't wait. There's a panic all over the country, and they are clamouring for us everywhere. Must drive on to Lord Blackbury's place, unless you are ready.'

" 'Don't go, sir!' pleaded the butler. 'There's only this one rope to tie. — There; it is ready now. You'll look after it, won't you?'

" 'That we will. You'll never have any more trouble with it now,' said Jim, helping to push the great case into the car.

" 'I think I had better go with you and see it stowed away in the bank,' said the butler.

" 'All right!' said Jim, nothing abashed. 'You can't come in the car, though, for Lord Blackbury's box will take up all the spare room. — Let's see — it's twelve o'clock now. Well, you be waiting at the bank door at half-past one, and you will just catch us.'

" 'All right — half-past one,' said the butler.

" 'Good-day!' cried my chum; and away went the car, while I made a bit of a short cut and caught it round a turn of the road. We drove right off into the next county, got a down-train to London; and before midnight, the Colonel's silver was fused into a solid lump."

I could not help laughing at the versatility of the old scoundrel. "It was a daring game to play," I said.

"It is always the daring game which succeeds best," he answered.

At this point the train began to show symptoms of slowing down, and my companion put on his overcoat and gave other signs of being near the end of his journey. "You are going on to Dover?" he said.

"Yes."

"For the Continent?"

"Yes."

"How long do you intend to travel?"

"Only for a week or so."

"Well, I must leave you here. You will remember my name, won't you? John Wilkie, I am pleased to have met you. — Is my umbrella behind you?" he added, stretching across. — "No; I beg your pardon. Here it is in the corner"; and with an affable smile, the ex-cracksman stepped out, bowed, and disappeared among the crowd upon the platform.

I lit another cigar, laughed as I thought of my late companion, and lifted up the *Times,* which he had left behind him. The bell had rung, the wheels were already revolving, when, to my astonishment, a pallid face looked in at me through the window. It was so contorted and agitated, that I hardly recognized the features which I had been gazing upon during the last couple of hours. "Here, take it," he said—"take it. It's hardly worth my while to rob you of seven pounds four shillings; but I couldn't resist once more trying my hand"; and he flung something into the carriage and disappeared.

It was my old leather purse, with my return ticket, and the whole of my travelling expenses. How he had taken it he knows best himself; I suppose it was while he was bending over in search of an imaginary umbrella. His newly re-awakened conscience had then pricked him, so that he had been driven to instant restitution.

The Parson
of Jackman's Gulch

When "The Parson of Jackman's Gulch" was published in the Christmas issue of LONDON SOCIETY *for 1885, Dr. Conan Doyle was becoming a restless man. He had married in the previous August and was feeling the responsibility. His practice had grown until it could be described as "busy though ill-paying." And while he had finally won his way into the better magazines such as* CHAMBERS'S JOURNAL *and the* CORNHILL, *he had not found a style with which he was comfortable. He felt his work was uninspired and derivative. He chafed at lack of recognition. He penned two novels, neither of which sold. Meanwhile, "The Parson of Jackman's Gulch" was typical of the sort of thing he was writing. Significantly, it was his last contribution to* LONDON SOCIETY. *Four months later, he began work on* A STUDY IN SCARLET.

H E was known in the Gulch as the Reverend Elias B. Hopkins, but it was generally understood that the title was an honourary one, extorted by his many eminent qualities, and not borne out by any legal claim which he could adduce. "The Parson" was another of his *sobriquets,* which was sufficiently distinctive in a land where the flock was scattered and the shepherds few. To do him justice, he never pretended to have received any preliminary training for the ministry or any orthodox qualification to practise it. "We're all working in the claim of the Lord," he remarked one day, "and it don't matter a cent whether we're hired for the job or whether we waltzes in on our own account"—a piece of rough imagery which appealed directly to the instincts of Jackman's Gulch. It is quite certain that during the first few months his presence had a marked effect in diminishing the excessive use both of strong drinks and of stronger adjectives which had been characteristic of the little

mining settlement. Under his tuition, men began to understand
that the resources of their native language were less limited than
they had supposed, and that it was possible to convey their
impressions with accuracy without the aid of a gaudy halo of
profanity.

We were certainly in need of a regenerator at Jackman's Gulch
about the beginning of '53. Times were flush then over the whole
colony, but nowhere flusher than there. Our material prosperity
had had a bad effect upon our morals. The camp was a small
one, lying rather better than a hundred and twenty miles to the
south of Ballarat, at a spot where a mountain torrent finds its
way down a rugged ravine on its way tò join the Arrowsmith
River. History does not relate who the original Jackman may
have been, but at the time I speak of the camp it contained a
hundred or so adults, many of whom were men who had sought
an asylum there after making more civilized mining centres too
hot to hold them. They were a rough, murderous crew, hardly
leavened by the few respectable members of society who were
scattered among them.

Communication between Jackman's Gulch and the outside
world was difficult and uncertain. A portion of the bush between
it and Ballarat was infested by a redoubtable outlaw named
Conky Jim, who, with a small gang as desperate as himself,
made travelling a dangerous matter. It was customary, therefore,
at the Gulch, to shore up the dust and nuggets obtained from the
mines in a special store, each man's share being placed in a
separate bag on which his name was marked. A trusty man,
named Woburn, was deputed to watch over this primitive bank.
When the amount deposited became considerable, a wagon was
hired, and the whole treasure was conveyed to Ballarat, guarded
by the police and by a certain number of miners, who took it in
turn to perform the office. Once in Ballarat, it was forwarded on
to Melbourne by the regular gold wagons. By this plan the gold
was often kept for months in the Gulch before being dispatched;
but Conky Jim was effectually checkmated, as the escort party
were far too strong for him and his gang. He appeared, at the
time of which I write, to have forsaken his haunts in disgust, and
the road could be traversed by small parties with impunity.

Comparative order used to reign during the daytime at
Jackman's Gulch, for the majority of the inhabitants were out

with crowbar and pick among the quartz ledges, or washing clay and sand in their cradles by the banks of the little stream. As the sun sank down, however, the claims were gradually deserted, and their unkempt owners, clay-bespattered and shaggy, came lounging into camp, ripe for any form of mischief. Their first visit was to Woburn's gold store, where their clean-up of the day was duly deposited, the amount being entered in the store-keeper's book, and each miner retaining enough to cover his evening's expenses. After that all restraint was at an end, and each set to work to get rid of his surplus dust with the greatest rapidity possible. The focus of dissipation was the rough bar, formed by a couple of hogsheads spanned by planks, which was dignified by the name of the "Britannia Drinking Saloon." Here Nat Adams, the burly bar-keeper, dispensed bad whiskey at the rate of two shillings a noggin, or a guinea a bottle, while his brother Ben acted as croupier in a rude wooden shanty behind, which had been converted into a gambling hell and was crowded every night. There had been a third brother, but an unfortunate misunderstanding with a customer had shortened his existence. "He was too soft to live long," his brother Nathaniel feelingly observed on the occasion of his funeral. "Many's the time I've said to him, 'If you're arguin' a pint with a stranger, you should always draw first, then argue, and then shoot, if you judge that he's on the shoot.' Bill was too purlite. He must needs argue first and draw after, when he might just as well have kivered his man before talkin' it over with him." This amiable weakness of the deceased Bill was a blow to the firm of Adams, which became so short-handed that the concern could hardly be worked without the admission of a partner, which would mean a considerable decrease in the profits.

Nat Adams had had a roadside shanty in the Gulch before the discovery of gold, and might, therefore, claim to be the oldest inhabitant. These keepers of shanties were a peculiar race, and, at the cost of a digression, it may be interesting to explain how they managed to amass considerable sums of money in a land where travellers were few and far between. It was the custom of the "bushmen" — *i.e.,* bullock drivers, sheep tenders, and the other white hands who worked on the sheep-runs up country — to sign articles by which they agreed to serve their master for one, two, or three years at so much per year and certain daily rations. Liquor was never included in this agreement, and the men remained, perforce, total abstainers during the whole time. The money was paid in a lump sum at the end of the engagement. When that day came round, Jimmy, the stockman, would come slouching into his master's office, cabbage-tree hat in hand.

"Morning, master!" Jimmy would say. "My time's up. I guess I'll draw my cheque and ride down to town."

"You'll come back, Jimmy."

"Yes, I'll come back. Maybe I'll be away three weeks, maybe a month. I want some clothes, master, and my bloomin' boots are well nigh off my feet."

"How much, Jimmy?" asks his master, taking up his pen.

"There's sixty pound screw," Jimmy answers, thoughtfully; "and you mind, master, last March, when the brindled bull broke out o' the paddock. Two pound you promised me then. And a pound at the dipping. And a pound when Millar's sheep got mixed with ourn." And so he goes on, for bushmen can seldom write, but they have memories which nothing escapes.

His master writes the cheque and hands it across the table. "Don't get on the drink, Jimmy," he says.

"No fear of that, master," and the stockman slips the cheque into his leather pouch, and within an hour he is ambling off upon his long-limbed horse on his hundred-mile journey to town.

Now Jimmy has to pass some six or eight of the above-mentioned roadside shanties in his day's ride, and experience has taught him that if he once breaks his accustomed total abstinence, the unwonted stimulant has an overpowering effect upon his brain. Jimmy shakes his head warily as he determines that no earthly consideration will induce him to partake of any liquor until his business is over. His only chance is to avoid temptation; so, knowing that there is the first of these houses some half mile ahead, he plunges into a bypath through the bush which will lead him out at the other side.

Jimmy is riding resolutely along this narrow path, congratulating himself upon a danger escaped, when he becomes aware of a sunburned, black-bearded man who is leaning unconcernedly against a tree beside the track. This is none other than the shanty-keeper, who, having observed Jimmy's manoeuvre in the distance, has taken a short cut through the bush in order to intercept him.

"Morning, Jimmy!" he cries, as the horseman comes up to him.

"Morning, mate; morning!"

"Where are ye off to to-day, then?"

"Off to town," says Jimmy sturdily.

"No, now — are you, though? You'll have bully times down there for a bit. Come round and have a drink at my place — just by way of luck."

"No," says Jimmy, "I don't want a drink."

"Just a little damp."

"I tell ye I don't want one," says the stockman, angrily.

"Well, ye needn't be so darned short about it. It's nothin' to me whether you drinks or not. Good mornin'."

"Good mornin'," says Jimmy, and has ridden on about twenty yards when he hears the other calling on him to stop.

"See here, Jimmy!" he says, overtaking him again. "If you'll do me a kindness when you're up in town, I'd be obliged."

"What is it?"

"It's a letter, Jim, as I wants posted. It's an important one too, an' I wouldn't trust it with everyone; but I knows you, and if you'll take charge on it it'll be a powerful weight off my mind."

"Give it here," Jimmy says, laconically.

"I hain't got it here. It's round in my caboose. Come round for it with me. It ain't more'n quarter of a mile."

Jimmy consents reluctantly. When they reach the tumble-down hut the keeper asks him cheerily to dismount and to come in.

"Give me the letter," says Jimmy.

"It ain't altogether wrote yet, but you sit down here for a minute and it'll be right," and so the stockman is beguiled into the shanty.

At last the letter is ready and handed over. "Now, Jimmy," says the keeper, "one drink at my expense before you go."

"Not a taste," says Jimmy.

"Oh, that's it, is it?" the other says, in an aggrieved tone. "You're too damned proud to drink with a poor cove like me. Here — give us back that letter. I'm cursed if I'll accept a favour from a man who's too almighty big to have a drink with me."

"Well, well, mate, don't turn rusty," says Jim. "Give us one drink an' I'm off."

The keeper pours out about a half a pannikin of raw rum and hands it to the bushman. The moment he smells the old familiar smell his longing for it returns, and he swigs it off at a gulp. His eyes shine more brightly, and his face becomes flushed. The keeper watches him narrowly. "You can go now, Jim," he says.

"Steady, mate, steady," says the bushman. "I'm as good a man as you. If you stand a drink, I can stand one too, I suppose." So the pannikin is replenished, and Jimmy's eyes shine brighter still.

"Now, Jimmy, one last drink for the good of the house," says the keeper, "and then it's time you were off." The stockman has a third gulp from the pannikin, and with it all his scruples and good resolutions vanish forever.

"Look here," he says, somewhat huskily, taking his cheque out of his pouch. "You take this, mate. Whoever comes along this road, ask 'em what they'll have, and tell them it's my shout. Let me know when the money's done."

So Jimmy abandons the idea of ever getting to town, and for three weeks or a month he lies about the shanty in a state of extreme drunkenness, and reduces every wayfarer upon the road to the same condition. At last one fine morning the keeper comes to him. "The coin's done, Jimmy," he says; "it's about time you made some more." So Jimmy has a good wash to sober him, straps his blanket and his billy to his back, and rides off through the bush to the sheep-run, where he has another year of sobriety, terminating in another month of intoxication.

All this, though typical of the happy-go-lucky manners of the inhabitants, has no direct bearing upon Jackman's Gulch, so we must return to that Arcadian settlement. Additions to the population there were not numerous, and such as came about the time of which I speak were even rougher and fiercer than the original inhabitants. In particular, there came a brace of ruffians named Phillips and Maule, who rode into camp one day and started a claim upon the other side of the stream. They out-gulched the Gulch in the virulence and fluency of their blasphemy, in the truculence of their speech and manner, and in their reckless disregard of all social laws. They claimed to have come from Bendigo, and there were some among us who wished that the redoubted Conky Jim was on the track once more, as long as he would close it to such visitors as these. After their arrival the nightly proceedings at the "Britannia Bar" and at the gambling hell behind became more riotous than ever. Violent quarrels, frequently ending in bloodshed, were of constant occurrence. The more peaceable frequenters of the bar began to talk seriously of lynching the two strangers, who were the principal promoters of disorder. Things were in this unsatisfactory condition when our evangelist, Elias B. Hopkins, came limping into camp, travel-stained and footsore, with his spade strapped across his back and his Bible in the pocket of his moleskin jacket.

His presence was hardly noticed at first, so insignificant was the man. His manner was quiet and unobtrusive, his face pale, and his figure fragile. On better acquaintance, however, there was a squareness and firmness about his clean-shaven lower jaw, and an intelligence in his widely opened blue eyes, which marked him as a man of character. He erected a small hut for himself, and started a claim close to that occupied by the two strangers who had preceded him. This claim was chosen with a ludicrous disregard for all practical laws of mining, and at once stamped the new-comer as being a green hand at his work. It was piteous to observe him every morning, as we passed to our work, digging and delving with the greatest industry, but, as we knew well, without the smallest possibility of any result. He would pause for a moment as we went by, wipe his pale face with his bandanna handkerchief, and shout out to us a cordial morning greeting, and then fall to again with redoubled energy. By degrees we got into the way of making a half-pitying, half-contemptuous inquiry as to how he got on. "I hain't struck it yet, boys," he would answer, cheerily, leaning on his spade; "but the bedrock lies deep just hereabouts, and I reckon we'll get among the pay gravel to-day." Day after day he returned the same reply, with unvarying confidence and cheerfulness.

It was not long before he began to show us the stuff that was in him. One night the proceedings were unusually violent at the drinking saloon. A rich pocket had been struck during the day, and the striker was standing treat in a lavish and promiscuous fashion, which had reduced three parts of the settlement to a state of wild intoxication. A crowd of drunken idlers stood or lay about the bar, cursing, swearing, shouting, dancing, and here and there firing their pistols into the air out of pure wantonness. From the interior of the shanty behind there came a similar chorus. Maule, Phillips, and the roughs who followed them were in the ascendant, and all order and decency was swept away.

Suddenly, amid this tumult of oaths and drunken cries, men became conscious of a quiet monotone which underlay all other sounds and obtruded itself at every pause in the uproar. Gradually first one man and then another paused to listen, until there was a general cessation of the hubbub, and every eye was turned in the direction whence this quiet stream of words flowed. There, mounted upon a barrel, was Elias B. Hopkins, the newest of the inhabitants of Jackman's Gulch, with a good-humoured smile upon his resolute face. He held an open Bible in his hand, and was reading aloud a passage taken at random—an extract from the Apocalypse, if I remember right. The words were entirely irrelevant, and without the smallest bearing upon the scene before him; but he plodded on with great unction, waving his left hand slowly to the cadence of his words.

There was a general shout of laughter and applause at this apparition, and Jackman's Gulch gathered round the barrel approvingly, under the impression that this was some ornate joke, and that they were about to be treated to some mock sermon or parody of the chapter read. When, however, the reader, having finished the chapter, placidly commenced another, and having finished that rippled on into another one, the revellers came to the conclusion that the joke was somewhat too long-winded. The commencement of yet another chapter confirmed this opinion, and an angry chorus of shouts and cries, with suggestions as to gagging the reader, or knocking him off the barrel, rose from every side. In spite of roars and hoots, however, Elias B. Hopkins plodded away at the Apocalypse with the same serene countenance, looking as ineffably contented as though the babel around him were the most gratifying applause. Before long an occasional boot pattered against the barrel, or whistled past our parson's head; but here some of the more orderly of the inhabitants interfered in favour of peace and order, aided, curiously enough, by the afore-mentioned Maule and Phillips, who warmly espoused the cause of the little Scripture-reader. "The little cuss has got grit in him," the latter explained, rearing his bulky red-shirted form between the crowd and the object of its anger. "His ways ain't our ways, and we're all welcome to our opinions, and to sling them round from barrels or otherwise, if so minded. What I says, and Bill says, is, that when it comes to slingin' boots instead o' words it's too steep by half; an' if this man's wronged we'll chip in an' see him righted." This oratorical effort had the effect of checking the more active signs of disapproval, and the party of disorder attempted to settle down once more to their carouse, and to ignore the shower of Scripture which was poured upon them. The attempt was hopeless. The drunken portion fell asleep under the drowsy refrain, and the others, with many a sullen glance at the imperturbable reader, slouched off to their huts, leaving him still perched upon the barrel. Finding himself alone with the more orderly of the spectators, the little man rose, closed his book, after methodically marking with a lead pencil the exact spot at which he stopped, and descended from his perch. "To-morrow night, boys," he remarked in his quiet voice, "the reading will commence at the ninth verse of the fifteenth chapter of the Apocalypse," with which piece of information, disregarding our congratulations, he walked away with the air of a man who has performed an obvious duty.

We found that his parting words were no empty threat. Hardly had the crowd begun to assemble next night before he appeared once more upon the barrel and began to read with the same monotonous vigour tripping over words, muddling up sentences, but still boring along through chapter after chapter. Laughter, threats, chaff—every weapon short of actual violence —was used to deter him, but all with the same want of success. Soon it was found that there was a method in his proceedings. When silence reigned, or when the conversation was of an innocent nature, the reading ceased. A single word of blasphemy, however, set it going again, and it would ramble on for a quarter of an hour or so, when it stopped, only to be renewed upon similar provocation. The reading was pretty continuous during that second night, for the language of the opposition was still considerably free. At least it was an improvement upon the night before.

For more than a month Elias B. Hopkins carried on this campaign. There he would sit, night after night, with the open book upon his knee, and at the slightest provocation off he would go, like a musical box when the spring is touched. The monotonous drawl became unendurable, but it could only be avoided by conforming to the parson's code. A chronic swearer came to be looked upon with disfavour by the community, since the punishment of his transgression fell upon all. At the end of a fortnight the reader was silent more than half the time, and at the end of the month his position was a sinecure.

Never was a moral revolution brought about more rapidly and more completely. Our parson carried his principle into private life. I have seen him, on hearing an unguarded word from some worker in the gulches, rush across, Bible in hand, and perching himself upon the heap of red clay which surmounted the offender's claim, drawl through the genealogical tree at the commencement of the New Testament in a most earnest and impressive manner, as though it were especially appropriate to the occasion. In time an oath became a rare thing among us. Drunkenness was on the wane too. Casual travellers passing through the Gulch used to marvel at our state of grace, and rumours of it went as far as Ballarat, and excited much comment therein.

There were points about our evangelist which made him especially fitted for the work which he had undertaken. A man entirely without redeeming vices would have had no common basis on which to work, and no means of gaining the sympathy of his flock. As we came to know Elias B. Hopkins better, we discovered that in spite of his piety there was a leaven of old Adam in him, and that he had certainly known unregenerate days. He was no teetotaller. On the contrary, he could choose his liquor with discrimination, and lower it in an able manner. He played a masterly hand at poker, and there were few who could touch him at "cut-throat euchre." He and the two ex-ruffians, Phillips and Maule, used to play for hours in perfect harmony, except when the fall of the cards elicited an oath from one of his companions. At the first of these offences the parson would put on a pained smile and gaze reproachfully at the culprit. At the second he would reach for his Bible, and the game was over for the evening. He showed us he was a good revolver shot too, for when we were practicing at an empty brandy bottle outside Adams' bar he took up a friend's pistol and hit it plumb in the centre at twenty-four paces. There were few things he took up that he could not make a show at apparently, except gold-digging, and at that he was the veriest duffer alive. It was pitiful to see the little canvas bag, with his name printed across it, lying placid and empty upon the shelf at Woburn's store, while all the other bags were increasing daily, and some had assumed quite a portly rotundity of form, for the weeks were slipping by, and it was almost time for the gold-train to start off for Ballarat. We reckoned that the amount which we had stored at the time represented the greatest sum which had ever been taken by a single convoy out of Jackman's Gulch.

Although Elias B. Hopkins appeared to derive a certain quiet satisfaction from the wonderful change which he had effected in the camp, his joy was not yet rounded and complete. There was one thing for which he still yearned. He opened his heart to us about it one evening.

"We'd have a blessing on the camp, boys," he said, "if we only had a service o' some sort on the Lord's day. It's a temptin' o' Providence to go on in this way without takin' any notice of it except that maybe there's more whiskey drunk and more card-playin' than on any other day."

"We hain't got no parson," objected one of the crowd.

"Ye fool!" growled another, "hain't we got a man as is worth any three parsons, and can splash texts around like clay out o' a cradle? What more d'ye want?"

"We hain't got no church!" urged the same dissentient.

"Have it in the open air," one suggested.

"Or in Woburn's store," said another.

"Or in Adams' saloon."

The last proposal was received with a buzz of approval which showed that it was considered the most appropriate locality.

Adams' saloon was a substantial wooden building in the rear of the bar, which was used partly for storing liquor and partly for a gambling saloon. It was strongly built of rough-hewn logs, the proprietor rightly judging, in the unregenerate days of Jackman's Gulch, that hogsheads of brandy and rum were commodities which had best be secured under lock and key. A strong door opened into each end of the saloon, and the interior was spacious enough, when the table and lumber were cleared away, to accommodate the whole population. The spirit barrels were heaped together at one end by their owner, so as to make a very fair imitation of a pulpit.

At first the Gulch took but a mild interest in the proceedings, but when it became known that Elias B. Hopkins intended, after reading the service, to address the audience, the settlement began to warm up to the occasion. A real sermon was a novelty to all of them, and one coming from their own parson was additionally so. Rumour announced that it would be interspersed with local hits, and that the moral would be pointed by pungent personalities. Men began to fear that they would be unable to gain seats, and many applications were made to the brothers Adams. It was only when conclusively shown that the saloon could contain them all with a margin that the camp settled down into calm expectancy.

It was as well that the building was of such a size, for the assembly upon the Sunday morning was the largest which had ever occurred in the annals of Jackman's Gulch. At first it was thought that the whole population was present, but a little reflection showed that this was not so. Maule and Phillips had gone on a prospecting journey among the hills, and had not returned as yet; and Woburn, the gold-keeper, was unable to leave his store. Having a very large quantity of the precious metal under his charge, he stuck to his post, feeling that the responsibility was too great to trifle with. With these three exceptions the whole of the Gulch, with clean red shirts, and such other additions to their toilet as the occasion demanded, sauntered in a straggling line along the clayey pathway which led up to the saloon.

The interior of the building had been provided with rough benches; and the parson, with his quiet, good-humoured smile, was standing at the door to welcome them. "Good morning, boys," he cried cheerily, as each group came lounging up. "Pass in! pass in! You'll find this is as good a morning's work as any you've done. Leave your pistols in this barrel outside the door as you pass; you can pick them out as you come out again; but it isn't the thing to carry weapons into the house of peace." His request was good-humouredly complied with, and before the last of the congregation filed in there was a strange assortment of knives and fire-arms in this depository. When all had assembled the doors were shut and the service began—the first and the last which was ever performed at Jackman's Gulch.

The weather was sultry and the room close, yet the miners listened with exemplary patience. There was a sense of novelty

in the situation which had its attractions. To some it was entirely
new, others were wafted back by it to another land and other
days. Beyond a disposition which was exhibited by the uninitiated
to applaud at the end of certain prayers, by way of showing that
they sympathized with the sentiments expressed, no audience
could have behaved better. There was a murmur of interest,
however, when Elias B. Hopkins, looking down on the congregation from his rostrum of casks, began his address.

He had attired himself with care in honour of the occasion.
He wore a velveteen tunic, girt round the waist with a sash of
China silk, a pair of moleskin trousers, and held his cabbage-
tree hat in his left hand. He began speaking in a low tone, and it
was noticed at the time that he frequently glanced through the
small aperture which served for a window, which was placed
above the heads of those who sat beneath him.

"I've put you straight now," he said, in the course of his
address; "I've got you in the right rut, if you will but stick in it."
Here he looked very hard out of the window for some seconds.
"You've learned soberness and industry, and with those things
you can always make up any loss you may sustain. I guess there
isn't one of ye that won't remember my visit to this camp." He
paused for a moment, and three revolver shots rang out upon
the quiet summer air. "Keep your seats, damn ye!" roared our
preacher, as his audience rose in excitement. "If a man of ye
moves, down he goes! The door's locked on the outside, so ye
can't get out anyhow. Your seats, ye canting, chuckle-headed
fools! Down with ye, ye dogs, or I'll fire among ye!"

Astonishment and fear brought us back into our seats, and we
sat staring blankly at our pastor and each other. Elias B.
Hopkins, whose whole face and even figure appeared to have
undergone an extraordinary alteration, looked fiercely down on
us from his commanding position with a contemptuous smile on
his stern face.

"I have your lives in my hands," he remarked; and we noticed
as he spoke that he held a heavy revolver in his hand, and that
the butt of another one protruded from his sash. "I am armed
and you are not. If one of you moves or speaks, he is a dead
man. If not, I shall not harm you. You must wait here for an
hour. Why, you *fools*" (this with a hiss of contempt which rang
in our ears for many a long day), "do you know who it is that has

stuck you up? Do you know who it is that has been playing it upon you for months as a parson and a saint? Conky Jim, the bushranger, ye apes! And Phillips and Maule were my two right-hand men. They're off into the hills with your gold— Ha! would ye?" This to some restive member of the audience, who quieted down instantly before the fierce eye and the ready weapon of the bushranger. "In an hour they will be clear of any pursuit, and I advise you to make the best of it and not to follow, or you may lose more than your money. My horse is tethered outside this door behind me. When the time is up I shall pass through it, lock it on the outside, and be off. Then you may break your way out as best you can. I have no more to say to you, except that ye are the most cursed set of asses that ever trod in boot-leather."

We had time to indorse mentally this outspoken opinion during the long sixty minutes which followed; we were powerless before the resolute desperado. It is true that if we made a simultaneous rush we might bear him down at the cost of eight or ten of our number. But how could such a rush be organized without speaking, and who would attempt it without a previous agreement that he would be supported? There was nothing for it but submission. It seemed three hours at the least before the ranger snapped up his watch, stepped down from the barrel, walked backward, still covering us with his weapon, to the door behind him, and then passed rapidly through it. We heard the creaking of the rusty lock, and the clatter of his horse's hoofs as he galloped away.

It has been remarked that an oath had for the last few weeks been a rare thing in the camp. We made up for our temporary abstention during the next half-hour. Never was heard such symmetrical and heartfelt blasphemy. When at last we succeeded in getting the door off its hinges all sight of both rangers and treasure had disappeared, nor have we ever caught sight of either the one or the other since. Poor Woburn, true to his trust, lay shot through the head across the threshold of his empty store. The villains, Maule and Phillips, had descended upon the camp the instant that we had been enticed into the trap, murdered the keeper, loaded up a small cart with the booty, and got safe away to some wild fastness among the mountains, where they were joined by their wily leader.

Jackman's Gulch recovered from this blow, and is now a flourishing township. Social reformers are not in request there, however, and morality is at a discount. It is said that an inquest has been held lately upon an unoffending stranger who chanced to remark that in so large a place it would be advisable to have some form of Sunday service. The memory of their one and only pastor is still green among the inhabitants, and will be for many a long year to come.

Uncle Jeremy's Household

For five years, from December 1883 to December 1887, Conan Doyle contributed a story to the annual Christmas number of THE BOY'S OWN PAPER. *They varied in quality and content, as did much of what appeared in the* BOY'S OWN, *a weekly tabloid of immense popularity which ran historical articles, instructions for games and at-home experiments, and other features, but which especially favored the adventure serial, usually running two or three concurrently. It was neither a prestigious nor a lucrative publication, but Doyle always had a soft spot for children, and he remained loyal to the* BOY'S OWN *longer than to any other magazine until he took up with the* STRAND *in the 1890s. In addition to the annual Christmas stories, he wrote one serial for the* BOY'S OWN, *"Uncle Jeremy's Household," which was published in seven weekly parts during January and February 1887.* A STUDY IN SCARLET *had been written and sold by this time, although it had not yet been brought out. Even if he were still unknown to the public, Sherlock Holmes had been created. Stories of crime and mystery would come more often from Doyle's pen now, and the colonial adventure yarns were put behind him for good.*

*"Uncle Jeremy's Household" is the most interesting — and least known — of all Doyle's pre-*STRAND *mysteries. Indeed, it can be said to be his first true mystery tale, since* A STUDY IN SCARLET *did not appear in* BEETON'S CHRISTMAS ANNUAL *for 1887 until the year was nearly up. For motives unknown, though, he never allowed "Uncle Jeremy's Household" to be reprinted. Perhaps it bore too obvious a debt to Wilkie Collins's* THE MOONSTONE *or was too similar in some respects to his own 1889 novel* THE MYSTERY OF CLOOMBER. *Certainly the objection cannot be one of merit, for the plot is tightly knit and the characters credibly motivated, given the composition of Uncle Jeremy's singular household. Once again, there is the Watson-like narrator who is*

91

*more observer than participant, but in this story the central
character is a strong-willed woman, the very first of many female
protagonists who dominate some of Doyle's best works but who
remain unknown to those readers who know the author only
through Sherlock Holmes or Professor Challenger.*

*In its setting and subject matter, then, in its heroine, in its
length, in the depth of its characters' wickedness, "Uncle
Jeremy's Household" is a pivotal work in the Conan Doyle
corpus. It is difficult to believe it was written for a children's
publication. Its obscurity is truly undeserved.*

M Y LIFE has been a somewhat chequered one, and it has
fallen to my lot during the course of it to have had
several unusual experiences. There is one episode, however,
which is so surpassingly strange that whenever I look back to it,
it reduces the others to insignificance. It looms up out of the
mists of the past, gloomy and fantastic, overshadowing the
eventless years which preceded and which followed it.

It is not a story which I have often told. A few, but only a few,
who know me well have heard the facts from my lips. I have
been asked from time to time by these to narrate them to some
assemblage of friends, but I have invariably refused, for I have
no desire to gain a reputation as an amateur Munchausen. I have
yielded to their wishes, however, so far as to draw up this written
statement of the facts in connection with my visit to Dunkelthwaite.

Here is John Thurston's first letter to me. It is dated April,
1862. I take it from my desk and copy it as it stands:

"My dear Lawrence, — If you knew my utter loneliness and
complete *ennui* I am sure you would have pity upon me and
come up to share my solitude. You have often made vague
promises of visiting Dunkelthwaite and having a look at the
Yorkshire Fells. What time could suit you better than the
present? Of course I understand that you are hard at work, but
as you are not actually taking out classes you can read just as
well here as in Baker Street. Pack up your books, like a good
fellow, and come along! We have a snug little room, with

writing-desk and armchair, which will just do for your study. Let me know when we may expect you.

"When I say that I am lonely I do not mean that there is any lack of people in the house. On the contrary, we form rather a large household. First and foremost, of course, comes my poor Uncle Jeremy, garrulous and imbecile, shuffling about in his list slippers, and composing, as is his wont, innumerable bad verses. I think I told you when last we met of that trait in his character. It has attained such a pitch that he has an amanuensis, whose sole duty it is to copy down and preserve these effusions. This fellow, whose name is Copperthorne, has become as necessary to the old man as his foolscap or as the *Universal Rhyming Dictionary*. I can't say I care for him myself, but then I have always shared Caesar's prejudice against lean men — though, by the way, little Julius was rather inclined that way himself if we may believe the medals. Then we have the two children of my Uncle Samuel, who were adopted by Jeremy — there were three of them, but one has gone the way of all flesh — and their governess, a stylish-looking brunette with Indian blood in her veins. Besides all these, there are three maid-servants and the old groom, so you see we have quite a little world of our own in this out-of-the-way corner. For all that, my dear Hugh, I long for a familiar face and for a congenial companion. I am deep in chemistry myself, so I won't interrupt your studies. Write by return to your isolated friend,

"JOHN H. THURSTON."

At the time that I received this letter I was in lodgings in London, and was working hard for the final examination which should make me a qualified medical man. Thurston and I had been close friends at Cambridge before I took to the study of medicine, and I had a great desire to see him again. On the other hand, I was rather afraid that, in spite of his assurances, my studies might suffer by the change. I pictured to myself the childish old man, the lean secretary, the stylish governess, the two children, probably spoiled and noisy, and I came to the conclusion that when we were all cooped together in one country house there would be very little room for quiet reading. At the end of two days' cogitation I had almost made up my mind to refuse the invitation when I received another letter from York-shire even more pressing than the first.

"We expect to hear from you by every post," my friend said, "and there is never a knock that I do not think it is a telegram announcing your train. Your room is all ready, and I think you will find it comfortable. Uncle Jeremy bids me say how very happy he will be to see you. He would have written, but he is absorbed in a great epic poem of five thousand lines or so, and he spends his day trotting about the rooms, while Copperthorne stalks behind him like the monster in Frankenstein, with note-book and pencil, jotting down the words of wisdom as they drop from his lips. By the way, I think I mentioned the brunettish governess to you. I might throw her out as a bait to you if you retain your taste for ethnological studies. She is the child of an Indian chieftain, whose wife was an Englishwoman. He was killed in the mutiny, fighting against us, and, his estates being seized by Government, his daughter, then fifteen, was left almost destitute. Some charitable German merchant in Calcutta adopted her, it seems, and brought her over to Europe with him together with his own daughter. The latter died, and then Miss Warrender — as we call her, after her mother — answered uncle's advertisement; and here she is. Now, my dear boy, stand not upon the order of your coming, but come at once."

There were other things in this second letter which prevent me from quoting it in full.

There was no resisting the importunity of my old friend, so, with many inward grumbles, I hastily packed up my books, and, having telegraphed overnight, started for Yorkshire the first thing in the morning. I well remember that it was a miserable day, and that the journey seemed to be an interminable one as I sat huddled up in a corner of the draughty carriage, revolving in my mind many problems of surgery and of medicine. I had been warned that the little wayside station of Ingleton, some fifteen miles from Carnforth, was the nearest to my destination, and there I alighted just as John Thurston came dashing down the country road in a high dog-cart. He waved his whip enthusiasti-cally at the sight of me, and pulling up his horse with a jerk, sprang out and on to the platform.

"My dear Hugh," he cried, "I'm so delighted to see you! It's so kind of you to come!" He wrung my hand until my arm ached.

"I'm afraid you'll find me very bad company now that I am here," I answered; "I am up to my eyes in work."

"Of course, of course," he said, in his good-humoured way. "I reckoned on this. We'll have time for a crack at the rabbits for all that. It's a longish drive, and you must be bitterly cold, so let's start for home at once."

We rattled off along the dusty road.

"I think you'll like your room," my friend remarked. "You'll soon find yourself at home. You know it is not often that I visit Dunkelthwaite myself, and I am only just beginning to settle down and get my laboratory into working order. I have been here a fortnight. It's an open secret that I occupy a prominent position in old Uncle Jeremy's will, so my father thought it only right that I should come up and do the polite. Under the circumstances I can hardly do less than put myself out a little now and again."

"Certainly not," I said.

"And besides, he's a very good old fellow. You'll be amused at our *ménage*. A princess for governess — it sounds well, doesn't it? I think our imperturbable secretary is somewhat gone in that direction. Turn up your coat-collar, for the wind is very sharp."

The road ran over a succession of low bleak hills, which were devoid of all vegetation save a few scattered gorse-bushes and a thin covering of stiff wiry grass, which gave nourishment to a scattered flock of lean, hungry-looking sheep. Alternately we dipped down into a hollow or rose to the summit of an eminence from which we could see the road winding as a thin white track over successive hills beyond. Every here and there the monotony of the landscape was broken by jagged scarps, where the grey granite peeped grimly out, as though nature had been sorely wounded until her gaunt bones protruded through their covering. In the distance lay a range of mountains, with one great peak shooting up from amongst them coquettishly draped in a wreath of clouds which reflected the ruddy light of the setting sun.

"That's Ingleborough," my companion said, indicating the mountain with his whip, "and these are the Yorkshire Fells. You won't find a wilder, bleaker place in all England. They breed a good race of men. The raw militia who beat the Scotch chivalry at the Battle of the Standard came from this part of the country. Just jump down, old fellow, and open the gate."

We had pulled up at a place where a long moss-grown wall ran parallel to the road. It was broken by a dilapidated iron gate, flanked by two pillars, on the summit of which were stone devices which appeared to represent some heraldic animal, though wind and rain had reduced them to shapeless blocks. A ruined cottage, which may have served at some time as a lodge, stood on one side. I pushed the gate open and we drove up a long, winding avenue, grass-grown and uneven, but lined by magnificent oaks, which shot their branches so thickly over us that the evening twilight deepened suddenly into darkness.

"I'm afraid our avenue won't impress you much," Thurston said, with a laugh. "It's one of the old man's whims to let nature have her way in everything. Here we are at last at Dunkelthwaite."

As he spoke we swung round a curve in the avenue marked by a patriarchal oak which towered high above the others, and came upon a great square whitewashed house with a lawn in front of it. The lower part of the building was all in shadow, but up at the top a row of bloodshot windows glimmered out at the setting sun. At the sound of the wheels an old man in livery ran out and seized the horse's head when we pulled up.

"You can put her up, Elijah," my friend said, as we jumped down. "Hugh, let me introduce you to my Uncle Jeremy."

"How d'ye do? How d'ye do?" cried a wheezy cracked voice, and looking up I saw a little red-faced man who was standing waiting for us in the porch. He wore a cotton cloth tied round his head after the fashion of Pope and other eighteenth-century celebrities, and was further distinguished by a pair of enormous slippers. These contrasted so strangely with his thin spindle shanks that he appeared to be wearing snow-shoes, a resemblance which was heightened by the fact that when he walked he was compelled to slide his feet along the ground in order to retain his grip of these unwieldly appendages.

"You must be tired, sir. Yes, and cold, sir," he said, in a strange jerky way, as he shook me by the hand. "We must be hospitable to you, we must indeed. Hospitality is one of the old-world virtues which we still retain. Let me see, what are those lines? 'Ready and strong the Yorkshire arm, but oh, the Yorkshire heart is warm.' Neat and terse, sir. That comes from one of my poems. What poem is it, Copperthorne?"

" 'The Harrying of Borrodaile,' " said a voice behind him, and a tall long-visaged man stepped forward into the circle of light which was thrown by the lamp above the porch. John introduced us, and I remember that his hand as I shook it was cold and unpleasantly clammy.

This ceremony over, my friend led the way to my room, passing through many passages and corridors connected by old-fashioned and irregular staircases. I noticed as I passed the thickness of the walls and the strange slants and angles of the ceilings, suggestive of mysterious spaces above. The chamber set apart for me proved, as John had said, to be a cheery little sanctum with a crackling fire and a well-stocked bookcase. I began to think as I pulled on my slippers that I might have done worse after all than accept this Yorkshire invitation.

II

When we descended to the dining-room the rest of the household had already assembled for dinner. Old Jeremy, still wearing his quaint headgear, sat at the head of the table. Next to him, on his right, sat a very dark young lady with black hair and eyes, who was introduced to me as Miss Warrender. Beside her were two pretty children, a boy and a girl, who were evidently her charges. I sat opposite her, with Copperthorne on my left, while John faced his uncle. I can almost fancy now that I can see the yellow glare of the great oil lamp throwing Rembrandt-like lights and shades upon the ring of faces, some of which were soon to have so strange an interest for me.

It was a pleasant meal, apart from the excellence of the viands and the fact that the long journey had sharpened my appetite. Uncle Jeremy overflowed with anecdote and quotation, delighted to have found a new listener. Neither Miss Warrender nor Copperthorne spoke much, but all that the latter said bespoke the thoughtful and educated man. As to John, he had so much to say of college reminiscences and subsequent events that I fear his dinner was a scanty one.

When the dessert was put on the table Miss Warrender took the children away, and Uncle Jeremy withdrew into the library, where we could hear the dull murmur of his voice as he dictated to his amanuensis. My old friend and I sat for some time before the fire discussing the many things which had happened to both of us since our last meeting.

"And what do you think of our household?" he asked at last, with a smile.

I answered that I was very much interested with what I had seen of it. "Your uncle," I said, "is quite a character. I like him very much."

"Yes; he has a warm heart behind all his peculiarities. Your coming seems to have cheered him up, for he's never been quite himself since little Ethel's death. She was the youngest of Uncle Sam's children, and came here with the others, but she had a fit or something in the shrubbery a couple of months ago. They found her lying dead there in the evening. It was a great blow to the old man."

"It must have been to Miss Warrender too?" I remarked.

"Yes; she was very much cut up. She had only been here a week or two at the time. She had driven over to Kirkby Lonsdale that day to buy something."

"I was very much interested," I said, "in all that you told me about her. You were not chaffing, I suppose?"

"No, no; it's all true as gospel. Her father was Achmet Genghis Khan, a semi-independent chieftain somewhere in the Central Provinces. He was a bit of a heathen fanatic in spite of his Christian wife, and he became chummy with the Nana, and mixed himself up in the Cawnpore business, so Government came down heavily on him."

"She must have been quite a woman before she left her tribe," I said. "What view of religion does she take? Does she side with her father or mother?"

"We never press that question," my friend answered. "Between ourselves, I don't think she's very orthodox. Her mother must have been a good woman, and besides teaching her English, she is a good French scholar, and plays remarkably well. Why, there she goes!"

As he spoke the sound of a piano was heard from the next room, and we both paused to listen. At first the player struck a few isolated notes, as though uncertain how to proceed. Then came a series of clanging chords and jarring discords, until out of the chaos there suddenly swelled a strange barbaric march, with blare of trumpet and crash of cymbal. Louder and louder it pealed forth in a gust of wild melody, and then died away once more into the jerky chords which had preceded it. Then we heard the sound of the shutting of the piano, and the music was at an end.

"She does that every night," my friend remarked; "I suppose it is some Indian reminiscence. Picturesque, don't you think so? Now don't stay here longer than you wish. Your room is ready whenever you would like to study."

I took my companion at his word and left him with his uncle and Copperthorne, who had returned into the room, while I went upstairs and read Medical Jurisprudence for a couple of hours. I imagined that I should see no more of the inhabitants of Dunkelthwaite that night, but I was mistaken, for about ten o'clock Uncle Jeremy thrust his little red face into the room.

"All comfortable?" he asked.

"Excellent, thanks," I answered.

"That's right. Keep at it. Sure to succeed," he said, in his spasmodic way. "Good-night!"

"Good-night!" I answered.

"Good-night!" said another voice from the passage; and looking out I saw the tall figure of the secretary gliding along at the old man's heels like a long dark shadow.

I went back to my desk and worked for another hour, after which I retired to bed, where I pondered for some time before I dropped to sleep over the curious household of which I had become a member.

III

I was up betimes in the morning and out on the lawn, where I found Miss Warrender, who was picking primroses and making them into a little bunch for the breakfast-table. I approached her before she saw me, and I could not help admiring the beautiful litheness of her figure as she stooped over the flowers. There was a feline grace about her every movement such as I never remember to have seen in any woman. I recalled Thurston's words as to the impression which she had made upon the secretary, and ceased to wonder at it. As she heard my step she stood up and turned her dark handsome face towards me.

"Good morning, Miss Warrender," I said. "You are an early riser, like myself."

"Yes," she answered. "I have always been accustomed to rise at daybreak."

"What a strange, wild view!" I remarked, looking out over the wide stretch of fells. "I am a stranger to this part of the country, like yourself. How do you like it?"

"I don't like it," she said, frankly. "I detest it. It is cold and bleak and wretched. Look at these"—holding up her bunch of primroses—"they call these things flowers. They have not even a smell."

"You have been used to a more genial climate and a tropical vegetation?"

"Oh, then, Mr. Thurston has been telling you about me," she said, with a smile. "Yes, I have been used to something better than this."

We were standing together when a shadow fell between us, and looking round I found that Copperthorne was standing close behind us. He held out his thin white hand to me with a constrained smile.

"You seem to be able to find your way about already," he remarked, glancing backwards and forwards from my face to that of Miss Warrender. "Let me hold your flowers for you, miss."

"No, thank you," the other said, coldly. "I have picked enough and am going inside."

She swept past him and across the lawn to the house. Copperthorne looked after her with a frowning brow.

"You are a student of medicine, Mr. Lawrence?" he said, turning towards me and stamping one of his feet up and down in a jerky, nervous fashion, as he spoke.

"Yes, I am."

"Oh, we have heard of you students of medicine," he cried in a raised voice, with a little crackling laugh. "You are dreadful fellows, are you not? We have heard of you. There is no standing against you."

"A medical student, sir," I answered, "is usually a gentleman."

"Quite so," he said, in a changed voice. "Of course I was only joking." Nevertheless I could not help noticing that at breakfast he kept his eyes persistently fixed upon me while Miss Warrender was speaking, and if I chanced to make a remark he would flash a glance round at her as though to read in our faces what our thoughts were of each other. It was clear that he took a more than common interest in the beautiful governess, and it seemed to me to be equally evident that his feelings were by no means reciprocated.

We had an illustration that morning of the simple nature of these primitive Yorkshire folk. It appears that the housemaid and the cook, who sleep together, were alarmed during the night by something which their superstitious minds contorted into an apparition. I was sitting after breakfast with Uncle Jeremy, who, with the help of continual promptings from his secretary, was reciting some Border poetry, when there was a tap at the door and the housemaid appeared. Close at her heels came the cook, buxom but timorous, the two mutually encouraging and abetting each other. They told their story in a strophe and antistrophe, like a Greek chorus, Jane talking until her breath failed, when the narrative was taken up by the cook, who, in turn, was supplanted by the other. Much of what they said was almost unintelligible to me owing to their extraordinary dialect, but I could make out the main thread of their story. It appears that in the early morning the cook had been awakened by something touching her face, and starting up had seen a shadowy figure standing by her bed, which figure had at once glided noiselessly from the room. The housemaid was awakened by the cook's cry, and averred stoutly that she had seen the apparition. No amount of cross-examination or reasoning could shake them, and they wound up by both giving notice, which was a practical way of showing that they were honestly scared. They seemed considerably indignant at our want of belief, and ended by bouncing out of the room, leaving Uncle Jeremy angry, Copperthorne contemptuous, and myself very much amused.

I spent nearly the whole of the second day of my visit in my room, and got over a considerable amount of work. In the evening John and I went down to the rabbit-warren with our

guns. I told John as we came back of the absurd scene with the
servants in the morning, but it did not seem to strike him in the
same ridiculous light that it had me.

"The fact is," he said, "in very old houses like ours, where you
have the timber rotten and warped, you get curious effects
sometimes which predispose the mind to superstition. I have
heard one or two things at night during this visit which might
have frightened a nervous man, and still more an uneducated
servant. Of course all this about apparitions is mere nonsense,
but when once the imagination is excited there's no checking it."

"What have you heard, then?" I asked with interest.

"Oh, nothing of any importance," he answered. "Here are the
youngsters and Miss Warrender. We mustn't talk about these
things before her, or else we shall have her giving warning too,
and that would be a loss to the establishment."

She was sitting on a little stile which stood on the outskirts of
the wood which surrounds Dunkelthwaite, and the two children
were leaning up against her, one on either side, with their hands
clasped round her arms, and their chubby faces turned up to
hers. It was a pretty picture and we both paused to look at it. She
had heard our approach, however, and springing lightly down
she came towards us, with the two little ones toddling behind
her.

"You must aid me with the weight of your authority," she said
to John. "These little rebels are fond of the night air and won't
be persuaded to come indoors."

"Don't want to come," said the boy, with decision. "Want to
hear the rest of the story."

"Yes — the 'tory," lisped the younger one.

"You shall hear the rest of the story to-morrow if you are
good. Here is Mr. Lawrence, who is a doctor — he will tell you
how bad it is for little boys and girls to be out when the dew
falls."

"So you have been hearing a story?" John said as we moved
on together.

"Yes — such a good story!" the little chap said with enthusiasm.
"Uncle Jeremy tells us stories, but they are in po'try and they are
not nearly so nice as Miss Warrender's stories. This one was
about elephants — "

"And tigers — and gold — " said the other.

"Yes, and wars and fighting, and the king of the Cheroots——"

"Rajpoots, my dear," said the governess.

"And the scattered tribes that know each other by signs, and the man that was killed in the wood. She knows splendid stories. Why don't you make her tell you some, Cousin John?"

"Really, Miss Warrender, you have excited our curiosity," my companion said. "You must tell us of these wonders."

"They would seem stupid enough to you," she answered, with a laugh. "They are merely a few reminiscences of my early life."

As we strolled along the pathway which led through the wood we met Copperthorne coming from the opposite direction.

"I was looking for you all," he said, with an ungainly attempt at geniality. "I wanted to tell you that it was dinner-time."

"Our watches told us that," said John, rather ungraciously as I thought.

"And you have been all rabbiting together?" the secretary continued, as he stalked along beside us.

"Not at all," I answered. "We met Miss Warrender and the children on our way back."

"Oh, Miss Warrender came to meet you as you came back!" said he. This quick contortion of my words, together with the sneering way in which he spoke, vexed me so much that I should have made a sharp rejoinder had it not been for the lady's presence.

I happened to turn my eyes towards the governess at the moment, and I saw her glance at the speaker with an angry sparkle in her eyes which showed that she shared my indignation. I was surprised, however, that same night when about ten o'clock I chanced to look out of the window of my study, to see the two of them walking up and down in the moonlight engaged in deep conversation. I don't know how it was, but the sight disturbed me so much that after several fruitless attempts to continue my studies I threw my books aside and gave up work for the night. About eleven I glanced out again, but they were gone, and shortly afterwards I heard the shuffling step of Uncle Jeremy, and the firm heavy footfall of the secretary, as they ascended the staircase which led to their bedrooms upon the upper floor.

IV

John Thurston was never a very observant man, and I believe that before I had been three days under his uncle's roof I knew more of what was going on there than he did. My friend was ardently devoted to chemistry, and spent his days happily among his test-tubes and solutions, perfectly contented so long as he had a congenial companion at hand to whom he could communicate his results. For myself, I have always had a weakness for the study and analysis of human character, and I found much that was interesting in the microcosm in which I lived. Indeed, I became so absorbed in my observations that I fear my studies suffered to a considerable extent.

In the first place, I discovered beyond all doubt that the real master of Dunkelthwaite was not Uncle Jeremy, but Uncle Jeremy's amanuensis. My medical instinct told me that the absorbing love of poetry, which had been nothing more than a harmless eccentricity in the old man's younger days, had now become a complete monomania, which filled his mind to the exclusion of every other subject. Copperthorne, by humouring his employer upon this one point until he had made himself indispensable to him, had succeeded in gaining complete power over him in everything else. He managed his money matters and the affairs of the house unquestioned and uncontrolled. He had sense enough, however, to exert his authority so lightly that it galled no one's neck, and therefore excited no opposition. My friend, busy with his distillations and analyses, was never allowed to realize that he was really a nonentity in the establishment.

I have already expressed my conviction that though Copperthorne had some tender feeling for the governess, she by no means favoured his addresses. After a few days I came to think, however, that there existed besides this unrequited affection some other link which bound the pair together. I have seen him more than once assume an air towards her which can only be described as one of authority. Two or three times also I had observed them pacing the lawn and conversing earnestly in the early hours of the night. I could not guess what mutual understanding existed between them, and the mystery piqued my curiosity.

It is proverbially easy to fall in love in a country house, but my nature has never been a sentimental one, and my judgment was not warped by any such feeling towards Miss Warrender. On the contrary, I set myself to study her as an entomologist might a specimen, critically, but without bias. With this object I used to arrange my studies in such a way as to be free at the times when she took the children out for exercise, so that we had many walks together, and I gained a deeper insight into her character than I should otherwise have done.

She was fairly well read, and had a superficial acquaintance with several languages, as well as a great natural taste for music. Underneath this veneer of culture, however, there was a great dash of the savage in her nature. In the course of her conversation she would every now and again drop some remark which would almost startle me by its primitive reasoning, and by its disregard for the conventionalities of civilization. I could hardly wonder at this, however, when I reflected that she had been a woman before she left the wild tribe which her father ruled.

I remember one instance which struck me as particularly characteristic, in which her wild original habits suddenly asserted themselves. We were walking along the country road, talking of Germany, in which she had spent some months, when she suddenly stopped short and laid her finger upon her lips. "Lend me your stick!" she said, in a whisper. I handed it to her, and at once, to my astonishment, she darted lightly and noiselessly through a gap in the hedge, and, bending her body, crept swiftly along under the shelter of a little knoll. I was still looking after her in amazement, when a rabbit rose suddenly in front of her and scuttled away. She hurled the stick after it and struck it, but the creature made good its escape, though trailing one leg behind it.

She came back to me exultant and panting. "I saw it move among the grass," she said. "I hit it."

"Yes, you hit it. You broke its leg," I said, somewhat coldly.

"You hurt it," the little boy cried, ruefully.

"Poor little beast!" she exclaimed, with a sudden change in her whole manner. "I am sorry I harmed it." She seemed completely cast down by the incident, and spoke little during the remainder of our walk. For my own part I could not blame her much. It was evidently an outbreak of the old predatory instinct of the

savage, though with a somewhat incongruous effect in the case
of a fashionably dressed young lady on an English high road.

John Thurston made me peep into her private sitting-room
one day when she was out. She had a thousand little Indian
knickknacks there which showed that she had come well-laden
from her native land. Her Oriental love for bright colours had
exhibited itself in an amusing fashion. She had gone down to the
market town and bought numerous sheets of pink and blue
paper, and these she had pinned in patches over the sombre
covering which had lined the walls before. She had some tinsel
too, which she had put in the most conspicuous places. The
whole effect was ludicrously tawdry and glaring, and yet there
seemed to me to be a touch of pathos in this attempt to reproduce
the brilliance of the tropics in the cold English dwelling-house.

During the first few days of my visit the curious relationship
which existed between Miss Warrender and the secretary had
simply excited my curiosity, but as the weeks passed and I
became more interested in the beautiful Anglo-Indian a deeper
and more personal feeling took possession of me. I puzzled my
brains as to what tie could exist between them. Why was it that
while she showed every symptom of being averse to his company
during the day she should walk about with him alone after
nightfall? Could it be that the distaste which she showed for him
before others was a blind to conceal her real feelings? Such a
supposition seemed to involve a depth of dissimulation in her
nature which appeared to be incompatible with her frank eyes
and clear-cut proud features. And yet, what other hypothesis
could account for the power which he most certainly exercised
over her?

This power showed itself in many ways, but was exerted so
quietly and silently that none but a close observer could have
known that it existed. I have seen him glance at her with a look
so commanding, and, as it seemed to me, so menacing, that next
moment I could hardly believe that his white impassive face
could be capable of so intense an expression. When he looked at
her in this manner she would wince and quiver as though she had
been in physical pain. "Decidedly," I thought, "it is fear and not
love which produces such effects."

I was so interested in the question that I spoke to my friend
John about it. He was in his little laboratory at the time, and was

deeply immersed in a series of manipulations and distillations, which ended in the production of an evil-smelling gas, which set us both coughing and choking. I took advantage of our enforced retreat into the fresh air to question him upon one or two points on which I wanted information.

"How long did you say that Miss Warrender had been with your uncle?" I asked.

John looked at me slyly, and shook his acid-stained finger.

"You seem to be wonderfully interested about the daughter of the late lamented Achmet Genghis," he said.

"Who could help it?" I answered, frankly. "I think she is one of the most romantic characters I ever met."

"Take care of the studies, my boy," John said, paternally. "This sort of thing doesn't do before examinations."

"Don't be ridiculous!" I remonstrated. "Any one would think that I was in love with Miss Warrender to hear the way in which you talk. I look on her as an interesting psychological problem, nothing more."

"Quite so—an interesting psychological problem, nothing more."

John seemed to have some of the vapours of the gas still hanging about his system, for his manner was decidedly irritating.

"To revert to my original question," I said. "How long has she been here?"

"About ten weeks."

"And Copperthorne?"

"Over two years."

"Do you imagine that they could have known each other before?"

"Impossible!" said John, with decision. "She came from Germany. I saw the letter from the old merchant, in which he traced her previous life. Copperthorne has always been in Yorkshire except for two years at Cambridge. He had to leave the university under a cloud."

"What sort of a cloud?"

"Don't know," John answered. "They kept it very quiet. I fancy Uncle Jeremy knows. He's very fond of taking rapscallions up and giving them what he calls another start. Some of them will give him a start some of these fine days."

"And so Copperthorne and Miss Warrender were absolute strangers until the last few weeks?"

"Quite so; and now I think we can go back and analyze the sediment."

"Never mind the sediment," I cried, detaining him. "There's more I want to talk to you about. If these two have only known each other for this short time, how has he managed to gain his power over her?"

John stared at me open-eyed.

"His power?" he said.

"Yes, the power which he exercises over her."

"My dear Hugh," my friend said, gravely, "I'm not in the habit of thus quoting Scripture, but there is one text which occurs irresistibly to my mind, and that is, that 'Much learning hath made thee mad.' You've been reading too hard."

"Do you mean to say," I cried, "that you have never observed that there is some secret understanding between your uncle's governess and his amanuensis?"

"Try bromide of potassium," said John. "It's very soothing in twenty-grain doses."

"Try a pair of spectacles," I retorted, "you most certainly need them"; with which parting shot I turned on my heel and went off in high dudgeon. I had not gone twenty yards down the gravel walk of the garden before I saw the very couple of whom we had just been speaking. They were some little way off, she leaning against the sundial, he standing in front of her and speaking earnestly, with occasional jerky gesticulations. With his tall, gaunt figure towering above her, and the spasmodic motions of his long arms, he might have been some great bat fluttering over a victim. I remember that that was the simile which rose in my mind at the time, heightened perhaps by the suggestion of shrinking and of fear which seemed to me to lie in every curve of her beautiful figure.

The little picture was such an illustration of the text upon which I had been preaching, that I had half a mind to go back to the laboratory and bring the incredulous John out to witness it. Before I had time to come to a conclusion, however, Copperthorne caught a glimpse of me, and turning away, he strolled slowly in the opposite direction into the shrubbery, his companion walking by his side and cutting at the flowers as she passed with her sunshade.

I went up to my room after this small episode with the intention of pushing on with my studies, but do what I would my mind wandered away from my books in order to speculate upon this mystery.

I had learned from John that Copperthorne's antecedents were not of the best, and yet he had obviously gained enormous power over his almost imbecile employer. I could understand this fact by observing the infinite pains with which he devoted himself to the old man's hobby, and the consummate tact with which he humoured and encouraged his strange poetic whims. But how could I account for the to me equally obvious power which he wielded over the governess? She had no whims to be humoured. Mutual love might account for the tie between them, but my instinct as a man of the world and as an observer of human nature told me most conclusively that no such love existed. If not love, it must be fear—a supposition which was favoured by all that I had seen.

What, then, had occurred during these two months to cause this high-spirited, dark-eyed princess to fear the white-faced Englishman with the soft voice and the gentle manner? That was the problem which I set myself to solve with an energy and earnestness which eclipsed my ardour for study, and rendered me superior to the terrors of my approaching examination.

I ventured to approach the subject that same afternoon to Miss Warrender, whom I found alone in the library, the two little children having gone to spend the day in the nursery of a neighbouring squire.

"You must be rather lonely when there are no visitors," I remarked. "It does not seem to be a very lively part of the country."

"Children are always good companions," she answered. "Nevertheless I shall miss both Mr. Thornton and yourself very much when you go."

"I shall be sorry when the time comes," I said. "I never expected to enjoy this visit as I have done; still, you won't be quite companionless when we are gone, you'll always have Mr. Copperthorne."

"Yes; we shall always have Mr. Copperthorne." She spoke with a weary intonation.

"He's a pleasant companion," I remarked; "quiet, well informed, and amiable. I don't wonder that old Mr. Thurston is so fond of him."

As I spoke in this way I watched my companion intently. There was a slight flush on her dark cheeks, and she'd drummed her fingers impatiently against the arms of the chair.

"His manner may be a little cold sometimes——" I was continuing, but she interrupted me, turning on me furiously, with an angry glare in her black eyes.

"What do you want to talk to me about him for?" she asked.

"I beg pardon," I answered, submissively, "I did not know it was a forbidden subject."

"I don't wish ever to hear his name," she cried, passionately. "I hate it and I hate him. Oh, if I had only some one who loved me — that is, as men love away over the seas in my own land — I know what I should say to him."

"What would you say?" I asked, astonished at this extraordinary outburst.

She leaned forward until I seemed to feel the quick pants of her warm breath upon my face.

"Kill Copperthorne," she said. "That is what I should say to him. Kill Copperthorne. Then you can come and talk of love to me."

Nothing can describe the intensity of fierceness with which she hissed these words out from between her white teeth.

She looked so venomous as she spoke that I involuntarily shrank away from her. Could this pythoness be the demure young lady who sat every day so primly and quietly at the table of Uncle Jeremy? I had hoped to gain some insight into her character by my leading question, but I had never expected to conjure up such a spirit as this. She must have seen the horror and surprise which was depicted on my face, for her manner changed and she laughed nervously.

"You must really think me mad," she said. "You see, it is the Indian training breaking out again. We do nothing by halves over there — either loving or hating."

"And why is it that you hate Mr. Copperthorne?" I asked.

"Ah, well," she answered, in a subdued voice, "perhaps hate is rather too strong a term after all. Dislike would be better. There are some people you cannot help having an antipathy to, even though you are unable to give any exact reason."

It was evident that she regretted her recent outburst and was endeavouring to explain it away.

As I saw that she wished to change the conversation, I aided her to do so, and made some remark about a book of Indian prints which she had taken down before I came in, and which still lay upon her lap. Uncle Jeremy's collection was an extensive one, and was particularly rich in works of this class.

"They are not very accurate," she said, turning over the many-coloured leaves. "This is good, though," she continued, picking out a picture of a chieftain clad in chain mail with a picturesque turban upon his head. "This is very good indeed. My father was dressed like that when he rode down on his white charger and led all the warriors of the Dooab to do battle with the Feringhees. My father was chosen out from amongst them all, for they knew that Achmet Genghis Khan was a great priest as well as a great soldier. The people would be led by none but a tried Borka. He is dead now, and of all those who followed his banner there are none who are not scattered or slain, whilst I, his daughter, am a servant in a far land."

"No doubt you will go back to India some day," I said, in a somewhat feeble attempt at consolation.

She turned the pages over listlessly for a few moments without answering. Then she gave a sudden little cry of pleasure as she paused at one of the prints.

"Look at this," she cried, eagerly. "It is one of our wanderers. He is a Bhuttotee. It is very like."

The picture which excited her so was one which represented a particularly uninviting-looking native with a small instrument which looked like a minature pickaxe in one hand, and a striped handkerchief or roll of linen in the other.

"That handkerchief is his roomal," she said. "Of course he wouldn't go about with it openly like that, nor would he bear the sacred axe, but in every other respect he is as he should be. Many a time have I been with such upon the moonless nights when the Lughaees were on ahead and the heedless stranger heard the Pilhaoo away to the left and knew not what it might mean. Ah! that was a life that was worth the living!"

"And what may a roomal be—and the Lughaee and all the rest of it?" I asked.

"Oh, they are Indian terms," she answered, with a laugh. "You would not understand them."

"But," I said, "this picture is marked as Dacoit, and I always thought that a Dacoit was a robber."

"That is because the English know no better," she observed. "Of course, Dacoits are robbers, but they call many people robbers who are not really so. Now this man is a holy man and in all probability a Gooroo."

She might have given me more information upon Indian manners and customs, for it was a subject upon which she loved to talk; but suddenly as I watched her I saw a change come over her face, and she gazed with a rigid stare at the window behind me. I looked round, and there peering stealthily round the corner at us was the face of the amanuensis. I confess that I was startled myself at the sight, for, with its corpse-like pallor, the head might have been one which had been severed from his shoulders. He threw open the sash when he saw that he was observed.

"I'm sorry to interrupt you," he said, looking in, "but don't you think, Miss Warrender, that it is a pity to be boxed up on such a fine day in a close room? Won't you come out and take a stroll?"

Though his words were courteous they were uttered in a harsh and almost menacing voice, so as to sound more like a command than a request. The governess rose, and without protest or remark glided away to put on her bonnet. It was another example of Copperthorne's authority over her. As he looked in at me through the open window a mocking smile played about his thin lips, as though he would have liked to have taunted me with this display of his power. With the sun shining in behind him he might have been a demon in a halo. He stood in this manner for a few moments gazing in at me with concentrated malice upon his face. Then I heard his heavy footfall scrunching along the gravel path as he walked round in the direction of the door.

V

For some days after the interview in which Miss Warrender confessed her hatred of the secretary, things ran smoothly at Dunkelthwaite. I had several long conversations with her as we rambled about the woods and fields with the two little children, but I was never able to bring her round to the subject of her outburst in the library, nor did she tell me anything which threw any light at all upon the problem which interested me so deeply. Whenever I made any remark which might lead in that direction she either answered me in a guarded manner or else discovered suddenly that it was high time that the children were back in their nursery, so that I came to despair of ever learning anything from her lips.

During this time I studied spasmodically and irregularly. Occasionally old Uncle Jeremy would shuffle into my room with a roll of manuscript in his hand, and would read me extracts from his great epic poem. Whenever I felt in need of company I used to go a-visiting to John's laboratory, and he in his turn would come to my chamber if he were lonely. Sometimes I used to vary the monotony of my studies by taking my books out into an arbour in the shrubbery and working there during the day. As to Copperthorne, I avoided him as much as possible, and he, for his part, appeared to be by no means anxious to cultivate my acquaintance.

One day about the second week in June, John came to me with a telegram in his hand and a look of considerable disgust upon his face. "Here's a pretty go!" he cried. "The governor wants me to go up at once and meet him in London. It's some legal business, I suppose. He was always threatening to set his affairs in order, and now he has got an energetic fit and intends to do it."

"I suppose you won't be gone long?" I said.

"A week or two perhaps. It's rather a nuisance, just when I was in a fair way towards separating that alkaloid."

"You'll find it there when you come back," I said, laughing. "There's no one here who is likely to separate it in your absence."

"What bothers me most is leaving you here," he continued. "It seems such an inhospitable thing to ask a fellow down to a lonely place like this and then to run away and leave him."

"Don't you mind about me," I answered, "I have too much to do to be lonely. Besides, I have found attractions in this place which I never expected. I don't think any six weeks of my life have ever passed more quickly than the last."

"Oh, they passed quickly, did they?" said John, and sniggered to himself. I am convinced that he was still under the delusion that I was hopelessly in love with the governess.

He went off that day by the early train, promising to write and tell us his address in town, for he did not know yet at which hotel his father would put up. I little knew what a difference this trifle would make, nor what was to occur before I set eyes upon my friend once more. At the time I was by no means grieved at his departure. It brought the four of us who were left into closer apposition, and seemed to favour the solving of that problem in which I found myself from day to day becoming more interested.

About a quarter of a mile from the house of Dunkelthwaite there is a straggling little village of the same name, consisting of some twenty or thirty slate-roofed cottages, with an ivy-clad church hard by and the inevitable beerhouse. On the afternoon of the very day on which John left us, Miss Warrender and the two children walked down to the post-office there, and I volunteered to accompany them.

Copperthwaite would have liked well to have either prevented the excursion or to have gone with us, but fortunately Uncle Jeremy was in the throes of composition, and the services of his secretary were indispensable to him. It was a pleasant walk, I remember, for the road was well shaded by trees, and the birds were singing merrily overhead. We strolled along together, talking of many things, while the little boy and girl ran on, laughing and romping.

Before you get to the post-office you have to pass the beer-house already mentioned. As we walked down the village street we became conscious that a small knot of people had assembled in front of this building. There were a dozen or so ragged boys and draggle-tailed girls, with a few bonnetless women, and a couple of loungers from the bar—probably as large an assemblage as ever met together in the annals of that quiet neighbourhood. We could not see what it was that was exciting their curiosity, but the children scampered on and quickly returned brimful of information.

"Oh, Miss Warrender," Johnnie cried, as he dashed up, panting and eager, "there's a black man there like the ones you tell us stories about!"

"A gipsy, I suppose," I said.

"No, no," said Johnnie, with decision; "he is blacker than that, isn't he, May?"

"Blacker than that," the little girl echoed.

"I suppose we had better go and see what this wonderful apparition is," I said.

As I spoke I glanced at my companion. To my surprise, she was very pale, and her great black eyes appeared to be luminous with suppressed excitement.

"Aren't you well?" I asked.

"Oh, yes. Come on!" she cried, eagerly, quickening her step; "come on!"

It was certainly a curious sight which met our eyes when we joined the little circle of rustics. It reminded me of the description of the opium-eating Malay whom De Quincey saw in the farmhouse in Scotland. In the centre of the circle of homely Yorkshire folk there stood an Oriental wanderer, tall, lithe, and graceful, his linen clothes stained with dust and his brown feet projecting through his rude shoes. It was evident that he had travelled far and long. He had a heavy stick in his hand, on which he leaned, while his dark eyes looked thoughtfully away into space, careless apparently of the throng around him. His picturesque attire, with his coloured turban and swarthy face, had a strange and incongruous effect amongst all the prosaic surroundings.

"Poor fellow!" Miss Warrender said to me, speaking in an excited, gasping voice. "He is tired and hungry, no doubt, and cannot explain his wants. I will speak to him"; and, going up to the Indian, she said a few words in his native dialect.

Never shall I forget the effect which those few syllables produced. Without a word the wanderer fell straight down upon his face on the dusty road and absolutely grovelled at the feet of my companion. I had read of Eastern forms of abasement when in the presence of a superior, but I could not have imagined that any human being could have expressed such abject humility as was indicated in this man's attitude.

Miss Warrender spoke again in a sharp and commanding

voice, on which he sprang to his feet and stood with his hands clasped and his eyes cast down, like a slave in the presence of his mistress. The little crowd, who seemed to think that the sudden prostration had been the prelude to some conjuring feat or acrobatic entertainment, looked on amused and interested.

"Should you mind walking on with the children and posting the letters?" the governess said; "I should like to have a word with this man."

I complied with her request, and when I returned in a few minutes the two were still conversing. The Indian appeared to be giving a narrative of his adventures or detailing the causes of his journey, for he spoke rapidly and excitedly, with quivering fingers and gleaming eyes. Miss Warrender listened intently, giving an occasional start or exclamation, which showed how deeply the man's statement interested her.

"I must apologize for detaining you so long in the sun," she said, turning to me at last. "We must go home, or we shall be late for dinner."

With a few parting sentences, which sounded like commands, she left her dusky acquaintance still standing in the village street, and we strolled homewards with the children.

"Well?" I asked, with natural curiosity, when we were out of earshot of the visitors. "Who is he, and what is he?"

"He comes from the Central Provinces, near the land of the Mahrattas. He is one of us. It has been quite a shock to me to meet a fellow-countryman so unexpectedly; I feel quite upset."

"It must have been pleasant for you," I remarked.

"Yes, very pleasant," she said, heartily.

"And why did he fall down like that?"

"Because he knew me to be the daughter of Achmet Genghis Khan," she said, proudly.

"And what chance has brought him here?"

"Oh, it's a long story," she said, carelessly. "He has led a wandering life. How dark it is in this avenue, and how the great branches shoot across! If you were to crouch on one of those you could drop down on the back of any one who passed, and they would never know that you were there until they felt your fingers on their throat."

"What a horrible idea!" I exclaimed.

"Gloomy places always give me gloomy thoughts," she said,

lightly. "By the way, I want you to do me a favour, Mr. Lawrence."

"What is that?" I asked.

"Don't say anything at the house about this poor compatriot of mine. They might think him a rogue and a vagabond, you know, and order him to be driven from the village."

"I'm sure Mr. Thurston would do nothing so unkind."

"No; but Mr. Copperthorne might."

"Just as you like," I said; "but the children are sure to tell."

"No, I think not," she answered.

I don't know how she managed to curb their little prattling tongues, but they certainly preserved silence upon the point, and there was no talk that evening of the strange visitor who had wandered into our little hamlet.

I had a shrewd suspicion that this stranger from the tropics was no chance wanderer, but had come to Dunkelthwaite upon some set errand. Next day I had the best possible evidence that he was still in the vicinity, for I met Miss Warrender coming down the garden walk with a basketful of scraps of bread and of meat in her hand. She was in the habit of taking these leavings to sundry old women in the neighbourhood, so I offered to accompany her.

"Is it old Dame Venables or old Dame Taylforth to-day?" I asked.

"Neither one nor the other," she said, with a smile. "I'll tell you the truth, Mr. Lawrence, because you have always been a good friend to me, and I feel I can trust you. These scraps are for my poor countryman. I'll hang the basket here on this branch, and he will get it."

"Oh, he's still about, then," I observed.

"Yes, he's still in the neighbourhood."

"You think he will find it?"

"Oh, trust him for that," she said. "You don't blame me for helping him, do you? You would do the same if you lived among Indians and suddenly came upon an Englishman. Come to the hothouse and look at the flowers."

We walked round to the conservatory together. When we came back the basket was still hanging to the branch, but the contents were gone. She took it down with a laugh and carried it in with her.

It seemed to me that since this interview with her countryman the day before her spirits had become higher and her step freer and more elastic. It may have been imagination, but it appeared to me also that she was not as constrained as usual in the presence of Copperthorne, and that she met his glances more fearlessly, and was less under the influence of his will.

And now I am coming to that part of this statement of mine which describes how I first gained an insight into the relation which existed between those two strange mortals, and learned the terrible truth about Miss Warrender, or of the Princess Achmet Genghis, as I should prefer to call her, for assuredly she was the descendant of the fierce fanatical warrior rather than of her gentle mother.

To me the revelation came as a shock, the effect of which I can never forget. It is possible that in the way in which I have told the story, emphasizing those facts which had a bearing upon her, and omitting those which had not, my readers have already detected the strain which ran in her blood. As for myself, I solemnly aver that up to the last moment I had not the smallest suspicion of the truth. Little did I know what manner of woman this was, whose hand I pressed in friendship, and whose voice was music to my ears. Yet it is my belief, looking back, that she was really well disposed to me, and would not willingly have harmed me.

It was in this manner that the revelation came about. I think I have mentioned that there was a certain arbour in the shrubbery in which I was accustomed to study during the daytime. One night, about ten o'clock, I found on going to my room that I had left a book on gynaecology in this summer-house, and as I intended to do a couple of hours' work before turning in, I started off with the intention of getting it. Uncle Jeremy and the servants had already gone to bed, so I slipped downstairs very quietly and turned the key gently in the front door. Once in the open air, I hurried rapidly across the lawn, and so into the shrubbery, with the intention of regaining my property and returning as rapidly as possible.

I had hardly passed the little wooden gate and entered the plantation before I heard the sound of talking, and knew that I had chanced to stumble upon one of those nocturnal conclaves which I had observed from my window. The voices were those of the secretary and of the governess, and it was clear to me, from the direction in which they sounded, that they were sitting in the arbour and conversing together without any suspicion of the presence of a third person. I have ever held that eavesdropping, under any circumstances, is a dishonourable practice, and curious as I was to know what passed between these two, I was about to cough or give some other signal of my presence, when suddenly I heard some words of Copperthorne's which brought me to a halt with every faculty overwhelmed with horrified amazement.

"They'll think he died of apoplexy," were the words which sounded clearly and distinctly through the peaceful air in the incisive tones of the amanuensis.

I stood breathless, listening with all my ears. Every thought of announcing my presence had left me. What was the crime which these ill-assorted conspirators were hatching upon this lovely summer's night?

I heard the deep sweet tones of her voice, but she spoke so rapidly, and in such a subdued manner, that I could not catch the words. I could tell by the intonation that she was under the influence of deep emotion. I drew nearer on tiptoe, with my ears straining to catch every sound. The moon was not up yet, and under the shadows of the trees it was very dark. There was little chance of my being observed.

"Eaten his bread, indeed!" the secretary said, derisively. "You are not usually so squeamish. You did not think of that in the case of little Ethel."

"I was mad! I was mad!" she ejaculated in a broken voice. "I had prayed much to Buddha and to the great Bhowanee, and it seemed to me that in this land of unbelievers it would be a great and glorious thing for me, a lonely woman, to act up to the teachings of my great father. There are few women who are admitted into the secrets of our faith, and it was but by an accident that the honour came upon me. Yet, having once had the path pointed out to me, I have walked straight and fearlessly, and the great Gooroo Ramdeen Singh has said that even in my fourteenth year I was worthy to sit upon the cloth of the Tupounee with the other Bhuttotees. Yet I swear by the sacred pickaxe that I have grieved much over this, for what had the poor child done that she should be sacrificed!"

"I fancy that my having caught you has had more to do with your repentance than the moral aspect of the case," Copperthorne said, with a sneer. "I may have had my misgivings before, but it was only when I saw you rising up with the handkerchief in your hand that I knew for certain that we were honoured by the presence of a Princess of the Thugs. An English scaffold would be rather a prosaic end for such a romantic being."

"And you have used your knowledge ever since to crush all the life out of me," she said, bitterly. "You have made my existence a burden to me."

"A burden to you!" he said, in an altered voice. "You know what my feelings are towards you. If I have occasionally governed you by the fear of exposure it was only because I found you were insensible to the milder influence of love."

"Love!" she cried, bitterly. "How could I love a man who held a shameful death for ever before my eyes. But let us come to the point. You promise me my unconditional liberty if I do this one thing for you?"

"Yes," Copperthorne answered; "you may go where you will when this is done. I shall forget what I saw here in the shrubbery."

"You swear it?"

"Yes, I swear it."

"I would do anything for my freedom," she said.

"We can never have such a chance again," Copperthorne cried. "Young Thurston is gone, and this friend of his sleeps heavily, and is too stupid to suspect. The will is made out in my favour, and if the old man dies every stick and stone of the great estate will be mine."

"Why don't you do it yourself, then?" she asked.

"It's not in my line," he said. "Besides, I have not got the knack. That roomal, or whatever you call it, leaves no mark. That's the advantage of it."

"It is an accursed thing to slay one's benefactor."

"But it is a great thing to serve Bhowanee, the goddess of murder. I know enough of your religion to know that. Would not your father do it if he were here?"

"My father was the greatest of all the Borkas of Jublepore," she said, proudly. "He has slain more than there are days in the year."

"I wouldn't have met him for a thousand pounds," Copper-

thorne remarked, with a laugh. "But what would Achmet
Genghis Khan say now if he saw his daughter hesitate with such
a chance before her of serving the gods? You have done excel-
lently so far. He may well have smiled when the infant soul of
young Ethel was wafted up to this god or ghoul of yours.
Perhaps this is not the first sacrifice you have made. How about
the daughter of this charitable German merchant? Ah, I see in
your face that I am right again! After such deeds you do wrong
to hesitate now when there is no danger and all shall be made
easy to you. Besides that, the deed will free you from your
existence here, which cannot be particularly pleasant with a
rope, so to speak, round your neck the whole time. If it is to be
done it must be done at once. He might rewrite his will at any
moment, for he is fond of the lad, and is as changeable as a
weathercock."

There was a long pause, and a silence so profound that I
seemed to hear my own heart throbbing in the darkness.

"When shall it be done?" she asked at last.

"Why not to-morrow night?"

"How am I to get to him?"

"I shall leave his door open," Copperthorne said. "He sleeps
heavily, and I shall leave a night-light burning, so that you may
see your way."

"And afterwards?"

"Afterwards you will return to your room. In the morning it
will be discovered that our poor employer has passed away in his
sleep. It will also be found that he has left all his worldly goods
as a slight return for the devoted labours of his faithful secretary.
Then the services of Miss Warrender the governess being no
longer required, she may go back to her beloved country or to
anywhere else that she fancies. She can run away with Mr. Hugh
Lawrence, student of medicine, if she pleases."

"You insult me," she said, angrily; and then, after a pause,
"You must meet me to-morrow night before I do this."

"Why so?" he asked.

"Because there may be some last instructions which I may
require."

"Let it be here, then, at twelve," he said.

"No, not here. It is too near the house. Let us meet under the
great oak at the head of the avenue."

"Where you will," he answered, sulkily; "but mind, I'm not going to be with you when you do it."

"I shall not ask you," she said, scornfully. "I think we have said all that need be said to-night."

I heard the sound of one or other of them rising to their feet, and though they continued to talk I did not stop to hear more, but crept quietly out from my place of concealment and scudded across the dark lawn and in through the door, which I closed behind me. It was only when I had regained my room and had sunk back into my armchair that I was able to collect my shattered senses and to think over the terrible conversation to which I had listened. Long into the hours of the night I sat motionless, meditating over every word that I had heard and endeavouring to form in my mind some plan of action for the future.

VI

The Thugs! I had heard of the wild fanatics of that name who are found in the central part of India, and whose distorted religion represents murder as being the highest and purest of all the gifts which a mortal can offer to the Creator. I remember an account of them which I had read in the works of Colonel Meadows Taylor, of their secrecy, their organization, their relentlessness, and the terrible power which their homicidal craze has over every other mental or moral faculty. I even recalled now that the roomal—a word which I had heard her mention more than once—was the sacred handkerchief with which they were wont to work their diabolical purpose. She was already a woman when she had left them, and being, according to her own account, the daughter of their principal leader, it was no wonder that the varnish of civilization had not eradicated all her early impressions or prevented the breaking out of occasional fits of fanaticism. In one of these apparently she had put an end to poor Ethel, having carefully prepared an alibi to conceal her crime, and it was Copperthorne's accidental discovery of this murder which gave him his power over his strange associate. Of all deaths that by hanging is considered among these tribes to be the most impious and degrading, and her knowledge that she had subjected herself to this death by the law of the land was evidently the reason why she had found herself compelled to subject her will and tame her imperious nature when in the presence of the amanuensis.

As to Copperthorne himself, as I thought over what he had done, and what he proposed to do, a great horror and loathing filled my whole soul. Was this his return for the kindness lavished upon him by the poor old man? He had already cozened him into signing away his estates, and now, for fear some prickings of conscience should cause him to change his mind, he had determined to put it out of his power ever to write a codicil. All this was bad enough, but the acme of all seemed to be that, too cowardly to effect his purpose with his own hand, he had made use of this unfortunate woman's horrible conceptions of religion in order to remove Uncle Jeremy in such a way that no suspicion could possibly fall upon the real culprit. I determined in my mind that, come what might, the amanuensis should not escape from the punishment due to his crimes.

But what was I to do? Had I known my friend's address I should have telegraphed for him in the morning, and he could have been back in Dunkelthwaite before nightfall. Unfortunately John was the worst of correspondents, and though he had been gone for some days we had had no word yet of his whereabouts. There were three maid-servants in the house, but no man, with the exception of old Elijah; nor did I know of any upon whom I could rely in the neighbourhood. This, however, was a small matter, for I knew that in personal strength I was more than a match for the secretary, and I had confidence enough in myself to feel that my resistance alone would prevent any possibility of the plot being carried out.

The question was, what were the best steps for me to take under the circumstances? My first impulse was to wait until morning, and then to quietly go or send to the nearest police-station and summon a couple of constables. I could then hand Copperthorne and his female accomplice over to justice and narrate the conversation which I had overheard. On second thoughts this plan struck me as being a very impracticable one. What grain of evidence had I against them except my story? which, to people who did not know me, would certainly appear a very wild and improbable one. I could well imagine too the plausible voice and imperturbable manner with which Copperthorne would oppose the accusation, and how he would dilate upon the ill-will which I bore both him and his companion on account of their mutual affection. How easy it would be for him to make a third person believe that I was trumping up a story in the hope of injuring a rival, and how difficult for me to make any one credit that this clerical-looking gentleman and this stylishly-dressed young lady were two beasts of prey who were hunting in couples! I felt that it would be a great mistake for me to show my hand before I was sure of the game.

The alternative was to say nothing and to let things take their course, being always ready to step in when the evidence against the conspirators appeared to be conclusive. This was the course which recommended itself to my young adventurous disposition, and it also appeared to be the one most likely to lead to conclusive results. When at last at early dawn I stretched myself upon my bed I had fully made up my mind to retain my knowledge in my own breast, and to trust to myself entirely for the defeat of the murderous plot which I had overheard.

Old Uncle Jeremy was in high spirits next morning after breakfast, and insisted upon reading aloud a scene from Shelley's "Cenci," a work for which he had a profound admiration. Copperthorne sat silent and inscrutable by his side, save when he threw in a suggestion or uttered an exclamation of admiration. Miss Warrender appeared to be lost in thought, and it seemed to me more than once that I saw tears in her dark eyes. It was strange for me to watch the three of them and to think of the real relation in which they stood to each other. My heart warmed towards my little red-faced host with the quaint head-gear and the old-fashioned ways. I vowed to myself that no harm should befall him while I had power to prevent it.

The day wore along slowly and drearily. It was impossible for me to settle down to work, so I wandered restlessly about the corridors of the old-fashioned house and over the garden. Copperthorne was with Uncle Jeremy upstairs, and I saw little of him. Twice when I was striding up and down outside I perceived the governess coming with the children in my direction, but on each occasion I avoided her by hurrying away. I felt that I could not speak to her without showing the intense horror with which she inspired me, and so betraying my knowledge of what had transpired the night before. She noticed that I shunned her, for at luncheon, when my eyes caught hers for a moment, she flashed across a surprised and injured glance, to which, however, I made no response.

The afternoon post brought a letter from John telling us that he was stopping at the Langham. I knew that it was now impossible for him to be of any use to me in the way of sharing the responsibility of whatever might occur, but I nevertheless thought it my duty to telegraph to him and let him know that his presence was desirable. This involved a long walk to the station, but that was useful as helping me to while away the time, and I felt a weight off my mind when I heard the clicking of the needles which told me that my message was flying upon its way.

When I reached the avenue gate on my return from Ingleton I found our old serving-man Elijah standing there, apparently in a violent passion.

"They says as one rat brings others," he said to me, touching his hat, "and it seems as it be the same with they darkies."

He had always disliked the governess on account of what he called her "uppish ways."

"What's the matter, then?" I asked.

"It's one o' they furriners a-hidin' and a-prowlin'," said the old man. "I seed him here among the bushes, and I sent him off wi' a bit o' my mind. Lookin' after the hens as like as not, or maybe wantin' to burn the house and murder us all in our beds. I'll go down to the village, Muster Lawrence, and see what he's after," and he hurried away in a paroxysm of senile anger.

This little incident made a considerable impression on me, and I thought seriously over it as I walked up the long avenue. It was clear that the wandering Hindoo was still hanging about the premises. He was a factor whom I had forgotten to take into account. If his compatriot enlisted him as an accomplice in her dark plans, it was possible that the three of them might be too many for me. Still it appeared to me to be improbable that she should do so, since she had taken such pains to conceal his presence from Copperthorne.

I was half tempted to take Elijah into my confidence, but on second thoughts I came to the conclusion that a man of his age would be worse than useless as an ally.

About seven o'clock I was going up to my room when I met the secretary, who asked me whether I could tell him where Miss Warrender was. I answered that I had not seen her.

"It's a singular thing," he said, "that no one has seen her since dinner-time. The children don't know where she is. I particularly want to speak to her."

He hurried on with an agitated and disturbed expression upon his features.

As to me, Miss Warrender's absence did not seem a matter of surprise. No doubt she was out in the shrubbery somewhere, nerving herself for the terrible piece of work which she had undertaken to do. I closed my door behind me and sat down, with a book in my hand, but with my mind too much excited to comprehend the contents. My plan of campaign had been already formed. I determined to be within sight of their trysting-place, to follow them, and to interfere at the moment when my interference would have most effect. I had chosen a thick, knobby stick, dear to my student heart, and with this I knew that I was master of the situation, for I had ascertained that Copperthorne had no firearms.

I do not remember any period of my life when the hours passed so slowly as did those which I spent in my room that night. Far away I heard the mellow tones of the Dunkelthwaite clock as it struck the hours of eight and then of nine, and then, after an interminable pause, of ten. After that it seemed as though time had stopped altogether as I paced my little room, fearing and yet longing for the hour as men will when some great ordeal has to be faced. All things have an end, however, and at last there came pealing through the still night air the first clear stroke which announced the eleventh hour. Then I rose, and, putting on my soft slippers, I seized my stick and slipped quietly out of my room and down the creaking old-fashioned staircase. I could hear the stertorous snoring of Uncle Jeremy upon the floor above. I managed to feel my way to the door through the darkness, and having opened it passed out into the beautiful starlit night.

I had to be very careful of my movements, because the moon shone so brightly that it was almost as light as day. I hugged the shadow of the house until I reached the garden hedge, and then, crawling down in its shelter, I found myself safe in the shrubbery in which I had been the night before. Through this I made my way, treading very cautiously and gingerly, so that not a stick snapped beneath my feet. In this way I advanced until I found myself among the brushwood at the edge of the plantation and within full view of the great oak tree which stood at the upper end of the avenue.

There was some one standing under the shadow of the oak. At first I could hardly make out who it was, but presently the figure began to move, and, coming out into a silvery patch where the moon shone down between two branches, looked impatiently to left and to right. Then I saw that it was Copperthorne, who was waiting alone. The governess apparently had not yet kept her appointment.

As I wished to hear as well as to see, I wormed my way along under the dark shadows of the trunks in the direction of the oak. When I stopped I was not more than fifteen paces from the spot where the tall gaunt figure of the amanuensis looked grim and ghastly in the shifting light. He paced about uneasily, now disappearing in the shadow, now reappearing in the silvery patches where the moon broke through the covering above him. It was evident from his movements that he was puzzled and disconcerted at the non-appearance of his accomplice. Finally he stationed himself under a great branch which concealed his figure, while from beneath it he commanded a view of the gravel drive which led down from the house, and along which, no doubt, he expected Miss Warrender to come.

I was still lying in my hiding-place, congratulating myself inwardly at having gained a point from which I could hear all without risk of discovery, when my eye lit suddenly upon something which made my heart rise to my mouth and almost caused me to utter an ejaculation which would have betrayed my presence.

I have said that Copperthorne was standing immediately under one of the great branches of the oak tree. Beneath this all was plunged in the deepest shadow, but the upper part of the branch itself was silvered over by the light of the moon. As I gazed I became conscious that down this luminous branch something was crawling—a flickering, inchoate something, almost indistinguishable from the branch itself, and yet slowly and steadily writhing its way down it. My eyes, as I looked, became more accustomed to the light, and then this indefinite something took form and substance. It was a human being—a

man—the Indian whom I had seen in the village. With his arms
and legs twined round the great limb, he was shuffling his way
down as silently and almost as rapidly as one of his native snakes.

Before I had time to conjecture the meaning of his presence he
was directly over the spot where the secretary stood, his bronzed
body showing out hard and clear against the disc of moon
behind him. I saw him take something from round his waist,
hesitate for a moment, as though judging his distance, and then
spring downwards, crashing through the intervening foliage.
There was a heavy thud, as of two bodies falling together, and
then there rose on the night air a noise as of some one gargling
his throat, followed by a succession of croaking sounds, the
remembrance of which will haunt me to my dying day.

Whilst this tragedy had been enacted before my eyes its entire
unexpectedness and its horror had bereft me of the power of
acting in any way. Only those who have been in a similar position
can imagine the utter paralysis of mind and body which comes
upon a man in such straits, and prevents him from doing the
thousand and one things which may be suggested afterwards as
having been appropriate to the occasion. When those notes of
death, however, reached my ears I shook off my lethargy and ran
forward with a loud cry from my place of concealment. At the
sound the young Thug sprang from his victim with a snarl like a
wild beast driven from a carcase, and made off down the avenue
at such a pace that I felt it to be impossible for me to overtake
him. I ran to the secretary and raised his head. His face was
purple and horribly distorted. I loosened his shirt-collar and did
all I could to restore him, but it was useless. The roomal had
done its work, and he was dead.

I have little more to add to this strange tale of mine. If I have
been somewhat long-winded in the telling of it, I feel that I owe
no apology for that, for I have simply set the successive events
down in a plain unvarnished fashion, and the narrative would be
incomplete without any one of them. It transpired afterwards
that Miss Warrender had caught the 7.20 London train, and was
safe in the metropolis before any search could be made for her.
As to the messenger of death whom she had left behind to keep
her appointment with Copperthorne under the old oak tree, he
was never either heard of or seen again. There was a hue and cry

over the whole country side, but nothing came of it. No doubt the fugitive passed the days in sheltered places, and travelled rapidly at night, living on such scraps as can sustain an Oriental, until he was out of danger.

John Thurston returned next day, and I poured all the facts into his astonished ears. He agreed with me that it was best perhaps not to speak of what I knew concerning Copperthorne's plans and the reasons which kept him out so late upon that summer's night. Thus even the county police have never known the full story of that strange tragedy, and they certainly never shall, unless, indeed, the eyes of some of them should chance to fall upon this narrative. Poor Uncle Jeremy mourned the loss of his secretary for months, and many were the verses which he poured forth in the form of epitaphs and of "In Memoriam" poems. He has been gathered to his fathers himself since then, and the greater part of his estate has, I am glad to say, descended to the rightful heir, his nephew.

There is only one point on which I should like to make a remark. How was it that the wandering Thug came to Dunkelthwaite? This question has never been cleared up; but I have not the slightest doubt in my own mind, nor I think can any one have who considers the facts of the case, that there was no chance about his appearance. The sect in India were a large and powerful body, and when they came to look around for a fresh leader, they naturally bethought them of the beautiful daughter of their late chief. It would be no difficult matter to trace her to Calcutta, to Germany, and finally to Dunkelthwaite. He had come, no doubt, with the message that she was not forgotten in India, and that a warm welcome awaited her if she chose to join her scattered tribesmen. This may seem far-fetched, but it is the opinion which I have always entertained upon the matter.

I began this statement by a quotation from a letter, and I shall end it by one. This was from an old friend, Dr. B. C. Haller, a man of encyclopaedic knowledge, and particularly well versed in Indian manners and customs. It is through his kindness that I am able to reproduce the various native words which I heard from time to time from the lips of Miss Warrender, but which I should not have been able to recall to my memory had he not suggested them to me. This is a letter in which he comments

upon the matter, which I had mentioned to him in conversation
some time previously:

"My dear Lawrence, — I promised to write to you *re* Thuggee,
but my time has been so occupied that it is only now that I can
redeem my pledge. I was much interested in your unique experience, and should much like to have further talk with you upon
the subject. I may inform you that it is most unusual for a
woman to be initiated into the mysteries of Thuggee, and it arose
in this case probably from her having accidentally or by design
tasted the sacred goor, which was the sacrifice offered by the
gang after each murder. Any one doing this must become an
acting Thug, whatever the rank, sex, or condition. Being of
noble blood she would then rapidly pass through the different
grades of Tilhaee, or scout, Lughaee, or grave-digger, Shum-
sheea, or holder of the victim's hands, and finally of Bhuttotee,
or strangler. In all this she would be instructed by her Gooroo,
or spiritual adviser, whom she mentions in your account as
having been her own father, who was a Borka, or an expert
Thug. Having once attained this position, I do not wonder that
her fanatical instincts broke out at times. The Pilhaoo which she
mentions in one place was the omen on the left hand, which, if it
is followed by the Thibaoo, or omen on the right, was considered
to be an indication that all would go well. By the way, you
mention that the old coachman saw the Hindoo lurking about
among the bushes in the morning. Do you know what he was
doing? I am very much mistaken if he was not digging Copperthorne's grave, for it is quite opposed to Thug customs to kill a
man without having some receptacle prepared for his body. As
far as I know only one English officer in India has ever fallen a
victim to the fraternity, and that was Lieutenant Monsell, in
1812. Since then Colonel Sleeman has stamped it out to a great
extent, though it is unquestionable that it flourishes far more
than the authorities suppose. Truly 'the dark places of the earth
are full of cruelty,' and nothing but the Gospel will ever effectually dispel that darkness. You are very welcome to publish
these few remarks if they seem to you to throw any light upon
your narrative.

                              "Yours very sincerely,
                                   "B. C. HALLER."

The Bravoes
of Market-Drayton

Short, cynical, and savage—that is "The Bravoes of Market-Drayton." It defies description, and it is like nothing Doyle ever wrote, before or since. The origins of its style and subject are as great a mystery as its author's reasons for never collecting this fine story after its publication in CHAMBERS'S JOURNAL *in 1889. It appears here in book form for the first time.*

To the north of the Wrekin, amid the rolling pastoral country which forms the borders of the counties of Shropshire and Staffordshire, there lies as fair a stretch of rustic England as could be found in the length and breadth of the land. Away to the south-east lie the great Staffordshire potteries; and farther south still, a long dusky pall marks the region of coal and of iron. On the banks of the Torn, however, there are sprinkled pretty country villages, and sleepy market towns which have altered little during the last hundred years, save that the mosses have grown longer, and the red bricks have faded into a more mellow tint. The traveller who in the days of our grandfathers was whirled through this beautiful region upon the box-seat of the Liverpool and Shrewsbury coach, was deeply impressed by the Arcadian simplicity of the peasants, and congratulated himself that innocence, long pushed out of the great cities, could still find a refuge amid these peaceful scenes. Most likely he would have smiled incredulously had he been informed that neither in the dens of Whitechapel nor in the slums of Birmingham was morality so lax or human life so cheap as in the fair region which he was admiring.

How such a state of things came about it is difficult now to determine. It may be that the very quiet and beauty of the place caused those precautions and safeguards to be relaxed which may nip crime in the bud. Sir Robert Peel's new police had not yet been established. Even in London the inefficient "Charley" still reigned supreme, and was only replaced by the more efficient Bow Street "runner" after the crime had been committed. It may be imagined, therefore, that among the cider orchards and sheep-walks of Shropshire the arm of Justice, however powerful to revenge, could do little to protect. No doubt, small offenses undetected had led to larger ones, and those to larger still, until, in the year 1828, a large portion of the peasant population were banded together to defeat the law and to screen each other from the consequence of their misdeeds. This secret society might have succeeded in its object, had it not been for the unparalleled and most unnatural villainy of one of its members, whose absolutely callous and selfish conduct throws into the shade even the cold-blooded cruelty of his companions.

In the year 1827 a fine-looking young peasant named Thomas Ellson, in the prime of his manhood, was arrested at Market-Drayton upon two charges — the one of stealing potatoes, and the other of sheep-lifting, which in those days was still a hanging matter. The case for the prosecution broke down at the last moment on account of the inexplicable absence of an important witness named James Harrison. The crier of the court having three times summoned the absentee without any response, the charge was dismissed, and Thomas Ellson discharged with a caution. A louder crier still would have been needed to arouse James Harrison, for he was lying at that moment foully murdered in a hastily scooped grave within a mile of the court-house.

It appears that the gang which infested the country had, amidst their countless vices, one questionable virtue in their grim fidelity to each other. No red Macgregor attempting to free a clansman from the grasp of the Sassenach could have shown a more staunch and unscrupulous allegiance. The feeling was increased by the fact that the members of the league were generally connected with one another either by birth or marriage. When it became evident that Ellson's deliverance could only be wrought by the silencing of James Harrison, there appears to have been no hesitation as to the course to be followed.

The prime movers in the business were Ann Harris, who was the mother of Ellson by a former husband; and John Cox, his father-in-law. The latter was a fierce and turbulent old man, with two grown-up sons as savage as himself; while Mrs. Harris is described as being a ruddy-faced pleasant country woman, remarkable only for the brightness of her eyes. This pair of worthies having put their heads together, decided that James Harrison should be poisoned and that arsenic should be the drug. They applied, therefore, at several chemists', but without success. It is a remarkable commentary upon the general morality of Market-Drayton at this period that on applying at the local shop and being asked why she wanted the arsenic, Mrs. Harris ingenuously answered that it was simply "to poison that scoundrel, James Harrison." The drug was refused; but the speech appears to have been passed by as a very ordinary one, for no steps were taken to inform the authorities or to warn the threatened man.

Being unable to effect their purpose in this manner, the mother and the father-in-law determined to resort to violence. Being old and feeble themselves, they resolved to hire assassins for the job, which appears to have been neither a difficult nor an expensive matter in those regions. For five pounds, three stout young men were procured who were prepared to deal in human lives as readily as any Italian bravo who ever handled a stiletto. Two of these were the sons of old Cox, John and Robert. The third was a young fellow named Pugh, who lodged in the same house as the proposed victim. The spectacle of three smock-frocked English yokels selling themselves at thirty-three shillings and fourpence a head to murder a man against whom they had no personal grudge is one which is happily unique in the annals of crime.

The men earned their blood-money. On the next evening, Pugh proposed to the unsuspecting Harrison that they should slip out together and steal bacon, an invitation which appears to have had a fatal seduction to the Draytonian of the period. Harrison accompanied him upon the expedition, and presently, in a lonely corner, they came upon the two Coxes. One of them was digging in the ditch. Harrison expressed some curiosity as to what work he could have on hand at that time of night. He little dreamed that it was his own grave upon which he was looking. Presently, Pugh seized him by the throat, John Cox tripped up his heels, and together they strangled him. They bundled the body into the hole, covered it carefully up, and calmly returned to their beds. Next morning, as already recorded, the court crier cried in vain, and Thomas Ellson became a free man once more.

Upon his liberation, his associates naturally enough explained to him with some exultation the means which they had adopted to silence the witness for the prosecution. The young Coxes, Pugh, and his mother all told him the same story. The unfortunate Mrs. Harris had already found occasion to regret the steps which she had taken, for Pugh, who appears to have been a most hardened young scoundrel, had already begun to extort money out of her on the strength of his knowledge. Robert Cox, too, had remarked to her with an oath: "If thee doesn't give me more money, I will fetch him and rear him up against thy door." The rustic villains seem to have seen their way to unlimited beer by working upon the feelings of the old country woman.

One would think that the lowest depths of human infamy had been already plumbed in this matter; but it remained for Thomas Ellson, the rescued man, to cap all the iniquities of his companions. About a year after his release, he was apprehended upon a charge of fowl-stealing, and in order to escape the trifling punishment allotted to that offense, he instantly told the whole story of the doing away with James Harrison. Had his confession come from horror at their crime, it might have been laudable; but the whole circumstances of the case showed that it was merely a cold-blooded bid for the remission of a small sentence at the cost of the lives of his own mother and his associates. Deep as their guilt was, it had at least been incurred in order to save this heartless villain from the fate which he had well deserved.

The trial which ensued excited the utmost interest in all parts of England. Ann Harris, John Cox, John Cox the younger, Robert Cox, and James Pugh were all arraigned for the murder of James Harrison. The wretched remnant of mortality had been dug up from the ditch, and could only be recognized by the clothes and by the colour of the hair. The whole case against the accused rested upon the very flimsiest evidence, save for Thomas Ellson's statement, which was delivered with a clearness and precision which no cross-examination could shake. He recounted the various conversations in which the different prisoners, including his mother, had admitted their guilt, as calmly and as imperturbably as though there were nothing at stake upon it. From the time when Pugh " 'ticed un out o' feyther's house to steal some bacon," to the final tragedy, when he "gripped un by the throat," every detail came out in its due order. He met his mother's gaze steadily as he swore that she had confided to him that she had contributed fifty shillings towards the removing of the witness. No more repulsive spectacle has ever been witnessed in an English court of justice than this cold-blooded villain calmly swearing away the life of the woman who bore him, whose crime had arisen from her extravagant affection for him, and all to save himself from a temporary inconvenience.

Mr. Phillips, the counsel for the defense, did all that he could to shake Ellson's evidence; but though he aroused the loathing of the whole court by the skillful way in which he brought out the scoundrel's motives and character, he was unable to shake him as to his facts. A verdict of guilty was returned against the whole band, and sentence of death duly passed upon them.

On the 4th of July 1828 the awful punishment was actually carried out upon Pugh and the younger Cox, the two who had laid hands upon the deceased. Pugh declared that death was a relief to him, as Harrison was always, night and day, by his side. Cox, on the other hand, died sullenly, without any sign of repentance for the terrible crime for which his life was forfeited. Thomas Ellson was compelled to be present at the execution, as a warning to him to discontinue his evil practices.

Mrs. Harris and the elder Cox were carried across the seas, and passed the short remainder of their lives in the dreary convict barracks which stood upon the site of what is now the beautiful town of Sydney. The air of the Shropshire downs was the sweeter for the dispersal of the precious band; and it is on record that this salutary example brought it home to the rustics that the law was still a power in the land, and that, looking upon it as a mere commercial transaction, the trade of the bravo was not one which could flourish upon English soil.

Our Midnight Visitor

When "Our Midnight Visitor" appeared in the literary magazine TEMPLE BAR *in February 1891, Arthur Conan Doyle was on the brink of greatness. After the lukewarm receptions given his first three books,* A STUDY IN SCARLET, THE MYSTERY OF CLOOMBER, *and* THE SIGN OF THE FOUR, *he had finally found critical and popular success with his historical romance* MICAH CLARKE. *His new novel* THE WHITE COMPANY *had just begun its serialization in the* CORNHILL. *He had given up his Southsea practice after eight years and, at the very moment that "Our Midnight Visitor" was brought out, was in Vienna, studying the diseases of the eye, preparatory to setting up in an ophthalmological practice in London. Not a single patient ever crossed the threshold of his new consulting room — not one! — and he whiled away the spring of 1891 writing stories for the newly-begun* STRAND *magazine featuring his detective character, Sherlock Holmes.*

With his changed surroundings came a different literary expression. "Our Midnight Visitor" displays Doyle's new maturity. All his former vigor is there, yet now it is tempered with greater assurance and a more sustained and polished narrative. But a loss of innocence is evident too. Gone is the naïveté and unalloyed idealism of his previous writing. There appears a new willingness to examine the nature of cruelty, greed, and compulsion. It cannot be that he had been unaware of the baser side of man and life. It must be that until now he had been reluctant to address them fully, no doubt in deference to the image of respectability he had so carefully cultivated in Southsea. Now that he had no need of it, he gave it up, and his work improved overnight.

O N the western side of the island of Arran, seldom visited, and almost unknown to tourists, is the little island named Uffa. Between the two lies a strait or roost, two miles and a half broad, with a dangerous current which sets in from the north. Even on the calmest day there are ripples, and swirls, and dimples on the surface of the roost, which suggest hidden influences, but when the wind blows from the west, and the great Atlantic waves choke up the inlet and meet their brethren which have raced round the other side of the island, there is such seething and turmoil that old sailors say they have never seen the like. God help the boat that is caught there on such a day!

My father owned one-third part of the island of Uffa, and I was born and bred there. Our farm or croft was a small one enough, for if a good thrower were to pick up a stone on the shore at Carracuil (which was our place) he could manage, in three shies, to clear all our arable land, and it was hardly longer than it was broad. Behind this narrow track, on which we grew corn and potatoes, was the homesteading of Carracuil — a rather bleak-looking grey stone house with a red-tiled byre buttressed against one side of it, and behind this again the barren undulating moorland stretched away up to Beg-na-sacher and Beg-na-phail, two rugged knowes which marked the centre of the island. We had grazing ground for a couple of cows, and eight or ten sheep, and we had our boat anchored down in Carravoe. When the fishing failed, there was more time to devote to the crops, and if the season was bad, as likely as not the herring would be thick on the coast. Taking one thing with another a crofter in Uffa had as much chance of laying by a penny or two as most men on the mainland.

Besides our own family, the McDonalds of Carracuil, there were two others on the island. These were the Gibbs of Arden and the Fullartons of Corriemains. There was no priority claimed among us, for none had any legend of the coming of the others. We had all three held our farms by direct descent for many generations, paying rent to the Duke of Hamilton and all prospering in a moderate way. My father had been enabled to send me to begin the study of medicine at the University of Glasgow, and I had attended lectures there for two winter sessions, but whether from caprice or from some lessening in his funds, he had recalled me, and in the year 1865 I found myself cribbed up in this little island with just education enough to wish for more, and with no associate at home but the grim, stern old man, for my mother had been dead some years, and I had neither brother nor sister.

There were two youths about my own age in the island, Geordie and Jock Gibbs, but they were rough, loutish fellows, good-hearted enough, but with no ideas above fishing and farming. More to my taste was the society of Minnie Fullarton, the pretty daughter of old Fullarton of Corriemains. We had been children together, and it was natural that when she blossomed into a buxom, fresh-faced girl, and I into a square-shouldered, long-legged youth, there should be something warmer than friendship between us. Her elder brother was a corn chandler in Ardrossan, and was said to be doing well, so that the match was an eligible one, but for some reason my father objected very strongly to our intimacy and even forbade me entirely to meet her. I laughed at his commands, for I was a hot-headed, irreverent youngster, and continued to see Minnie, but when it came to his ears, it caused many violent scenes between us, which nearly went the length of blows. We had a quarrel of this sort just before the equinoctial gales in the spring of the year in which my story begins, and I left the old man with his face flushed, and his great bony hands shaking with passion, while I went jauntily off to our usual trysting-place. I have often regretted since that I was not more submissive, but how was I to guess the dark things which were to come upon us?

I can remember that day well. Many bitter thoughts rose in my heart as I strode along the narrow pathway, cutting savagely at the thistles on either side with my stick. One side of our little estate was bordered by the Combera cliffs, which rose straight out of the water to the height of a couple of hundred feet. The top of these cliffs was covered with green sward and commanded a noble view on every side. I stretched myself on the turf there and watched the breakers dancing over the Winner sands and listened to the gurgling of the water down beneath me in the caves of the Combera. We faced the western side of the island, and from where I lay I could see the whole stretch of the Irish Sea, right across to where a long hazy line upon the horizon marked the northern coast of the sister isle. The wind was blowing freshly from the north-west and the great Atlantic rollers were racing merrily in, one behind the other, dark brown below, light green above, and breaking with a sullen roar at the base of the cliffs. Now and again a sluggish one would be overtaken by its successor, and the two would come crashing in together and send the spray right over me as I lay. The whole air was prickly with the smack of the sea. Away to the north there was a piling up of clouds, and the peak of Goatfell in Arran looked lurid and distinct. There were no craft in the offing except one little eager, panting steamer making for the shelter of the Clyde, and a trim brigantine tacking along the coast. I was speculating as to her destination when I heard a light springy footstep, and Minnie Fullarton was standing beside me, her face rosy with exercise and her brown hair floating behind her.

"Wha's been vexing you, Archie?" she asked with the quick intuition of womanhood. "The auld man has been speaking aboot me again; has he no'?"

It was strange how pretty and mellow the accents were in her mouth which came so raspingly from my father. We sat down on a little green hillock together, her hand in mine, while I told her of our quarrel in the morning.

"You see they're bent on parting us," I said; "but indeed they'll find they have the wrong man to deal with if they try to frighten me away from you."

"I'm no' worth it, Archie," she answered, sighing. "I'm over hamely and simple for one like you that speaks well and is a scholar forbye."

"You're too good and true for any one, Minnie," I answered, though in my heart I thought there was some truth in what she said.

"I'll no' trouble any one lang," she continued, looking earnestly into my face. "I got my call last nicht; I saw a ghaist, Archie."

"Saw a ghost!" I ejaculated.

"Yes, and I doubt it was a call for me. When my cousin Steevie deed he saw one the same way."

"Tell me about it, dear," I said, impressed by her solemnity.

"There's no' much to tell: it was last nicht aboot twelve, or maybe one o'clock. I was lying awake thinking o' this and that wi' my een fixed on the window. Suddenly I saw a face looking in at me through the glass—an awfu'-like face, Archie. It was na the face of any one on the island. I canna tell what it was like—it was just awfu'. It was there maybe a minute looking tae way and tither into the room. I could see the glint o' his very een—for it was a man's face—and his nose was white where it was pressed against the glass. My very blood ran cauld and I couldna scream for fright. Then it went awa' as quickly and as sudden as it came."

"Who could it have been?" I exclaimed.

"A wraith or a bogle," said Minnie positively.

"Are you sure it wasn't Tommy Gibbs?" I suggested.

"Na, na, it wasna Tammy. It was a dark, hard, dour sort of face."

"Well," I said, laughing, "I hope the fellow will give me a look up, whoever he is. I'll soon learn who he is and where he comes from. But we won't talk of it, or you'll be frightening yourself to-night again. It'll be a dreary night as it is."

"A bad nicht for the puir sailors," she answered sadly, glancing at the dark wrack hurrying up from the northward, and at the white line of breakers on the Winner sands. "I wonder what yon brig is after! Unless it gets roond to Lamlash or Brodick Bay, it'll find itself on a nasty coast."

She was watching the trim brigantine which had already attracted my attention. She was still standing off the coast, and evidently expected rough weather, for her foresail had been taken in and her topsail reefed down.

"It's too cold for you up here!" I exclaimed at last, as the clouds covered the sun, and the keen north wind came in more frequent gusts. We walked back together, until we were close to Carracuil, when she left me, taking the footpath to Corriemains, which was about a mile from our bothy. I hoped that my father had not observed us together, but he met me at the door, fuming with passion. His face was quite livid with rage, and he held his shotgun in his hands. I forget if I mentioned that in spite of his age he was one of the most powerful men I ever met in my life.

"So you've come!" he roared, shaking the gun at me. "You great gowk——" I did not wait for the string of adjectives which I knew was coming.

"You keep a civil tongue in your head," I said.

"You dare!" he shouted, raising his arm as if to strike me. "You wunna come in here. You can gang back where you came frae!"

"You can go to the devil!" I answered, losing my temper completely, on which he jabbed at me with the butt-end of the gun, but I warded it off with my stick. For a moment the devil was busy in me, and my throat was full of oaths, but I choked them down, and, turning on my heel, walked back to Corrie-mains, where I spent the day with the Fullartons. It seemed to me that my father, who had long been a miser, was rapidly becoming a madman — and a dangerous one to boot.

II

My mind was so busy with my grievance that I was poor company, I fear, and drank perhaps more whisky than was good for me. I remember that I stumbled over a stool once and that Minnie looked surprised and tearful, while old Fullarton sniggered to himself and coughed to hide it. I did not set out for home till half-past nine, which was a very late hour for the island. I knew my father would be asleep, and that if I climbed through my bedroom window I should have one night in peace.

It was blowing great guns by this time, and I had to put my shoulder against the gale as I came along the winding path which led down to Carracuil. I must still have been under the influence of liquor, for I remember that I sang uproariously and joined my feeble pipe to the howling of the wind. I had just got to the enclosure of our croft when a little incident occurred which helped to sober me.

White is a colour so rare in nature that in an island like ours, where even paper was a precious commodity, it would arrest the attention at once. Something white fluttered across my path and stuck flapping upon a furze bush. I lifted it up and discovered, to my very great surprise, that it was a linen pocket-handkerchief — and scented. Now I was very sure that beyond my own there was no such thing as a white pocket-handkerchief in the island. A small community like ours knew each other's wardrobes to a nicety. But as to scent in Uffa — it was preposterous! Who did the handkerchief belong to then? Was Minnie right, and was there really a stranger in the island? I walked on very thoughtfully, holding my discovery in my hand and thinking of what Minnie had seen the night before.

When I got into my bedroom and lit my rushlight I examined it again. It was clean and new, with the initials A. W. worked in red silk in the corner. There was no other indication as to who it might belong to, though from its size it was evidently a man's. The incident struck me as so extraordinary that I sat for some time on the side of my bed turning it over in my befuddled mind, but without getting any nearer a conclusion. I might even have taken my father into confidence, but his hoarse snoring in the adjoining room showed that he was fast asleep. It is as well that it was so, for I was in no humour to be bullied, and we might have had words. The old man had little longer to live, and it is some solace to me now that that little was unmarred by any further strife between us.

I did not take my clothes off, for my brain was getting swimmy after its temporary clearness, so I dropped my head upon the pillow and sank into profound slumber. I must have slept about four hours when I woke with a violent start. To this day I have never known what it was that roused me. Everything was perfectly still, and yet I found all my faculties in a state of extreme tension. Was there someone in the room? It was very dark, but I peered about, leaning on my elbow. There was nothing to be seen, but still that eerie feeling haunted me. At that moment the flying scud passed away from the face of the moon and a flood of cold light was poured into my chamber. I turned my eyes up instinctively, and – good God! – there at the window was the face, an evil, malicious face, hard-cut, and distinct against the silvery radiance, glaring in at me as Minnie had seen it the night before. For one moment I tingled and palpitated like a frightened child, the next both glass and sash were gone and I was rolling over and over on the gravel path with my arms round a tall strong man – the two of us worrying each other like a pair of dogs. Almost by intuition I knew as we went down together that he had slipped his hand into his side pocket, and I clung to that wrist like grim death. He tried hard to free it but I was too strong for him, and we staggered on to our feet again in the same position, panting and snarling.

"Let go my hand, damn you!" he said.

"Let go that pistol then," I gasped.

We looked hard at each other in the moonlight, and then he laughed and opened his fingers. A heavy glittering object, which I could see was a revolver, dropped with a clink on to the gravel. I put my foot on it and let go my grip of him.

"Well, matey, how now?" he said with another laugh. "Is that an end of a round, or the end of the battle? You islanders seem a hospitable lot. You're so ready to welcome a stranger, that you can't wait to find the door, but must come flying through the window like infernal fireworks."

"What do you want to come prowling round people's houses at night for, with weapons in your pocket?" I asked sternly.

"I should think I needed a weapon," he answered, "when there are young devils like you knocking around. Hullo! here's another of the family."

I turned my head, and there was my father, almost at my elbow. He had come round from the front door. His grey woollen nightdress and grizzled hair were streaming in the wind, and he was evidently much excited. He had in his hand the double-barrelled gun with which he had threatened me in the morning. He put this up to his shoulder, and would most certainly have blown out either my brains or those of the stranger, had I not turned away the barrel with my hand.

"Wait a bit, father," I said, "let us hear what he has to say for himself. And you," I continued, turning to the stranger, "can come inside with us and justify yourself if you can. But remember we are in a majority, so keep your tongue between your teeth."

"Not so fast, my young bantam," he grumbled; "you've got my six-shooter, but I have a Derringer in my pocket. I learned in Colorado to carry them both. However, come along into this shanty of yours, and let us get the damned palaver over. I'm wet through, and most infernally hungry."

My father was still mumbling to himself, and fidgeting with his gun, but he did not oppose my taking the stranger into the house. I struck a match, and lit the oil lamp in the kitchen, on which our prisoner stooped down to it and began smoking a cigarette. As the light fell full on his face, both my father and I took a good look at him. He was a man of about forty, remarkably handsome, of rather a Spanish type, with blue-black hair and beard, and sun-burned features. His eyes were very bright, and their gaze so intense that you would think they projected somewhat, unless you saw him in profile. There was a dash of recklessness and devilry about them, which, with his wiry, powerful frame and jaunty manner, gave the impression of a man whose past had been an adventurous one. He was elegantly dressed in a velveteen jacket, and greyish trousers of a foreign cut. Without in the least resenting our prolonged scrutiny, he seated himself upon the dresser, swinging his legs, and blowing little blue wreaths from his cigarette. His appearance seemed to reassure my father, or perhaps it was the sight of the rings which flashed on the stranger's left hand every time he raised it to his lips.

"Ye munna mind Archie, sir," he said in a cringing voice. "He was aye a fashious bairn, ower quick wi' his hands, and wi' mair muscle than brains. I was fashed mysel' wi' the sudden stour, but as tae shootin' at ye, sir, that was a' an auld man's havers. Nae doobt ye're a veesitor, or maybe it's a shipwreck—it's no a shipwreck, is 't?" The idea awoke the covetous devil in my father's soul, and it looked out through his glistening eyes, and set his long stringy hands a-shaking.

"I came here in a boat," said the stranger shortly. "This was the first house I came to after I left the shore, and I'm not likely to forget the reception that you have given me. That young hopeful of yours has nearly broken my back."

"A good job too!" I interrupted hotly, "why couldn't you come up to the door like a man, instead of skulking at the window?"

"Hush, Archie, hush!" said my father imploringly; while our visitor grinned across at me as amicably as if my speech had been most conciliatory.

"I don't blame you," he said—he spoke with a strange mixture of accents, sometimes with a foreign lisp, sometimes with a slight Yankee intonation, and at other times very purely indeed. "I have done the same, mate. Maybe you noticed a brigantine standing on and off the shore yesterday?"

I nodded my head.

"That was mine," he said. "I'm owner, skipper, and everything else. Why shouldn't a man spend his money in his own way? I like cruising about, and I like new experiences. I suppose there's no harm in that. I was in the Mediterranean last month, but I'm sick of blue skies and fine weather. Chios is a damnable paradise of a place. I've come up here for a little fresh air and freedom. I cruised all down the western isles, and when we came abreast of this place of yours it rather took my fancy, so I hauled the foreyard aback and came ashore last night to prospect. It wasn't this house I struck, but another farther to the west'ard; however, I saw enough to be sure it was a place after my own heart — a real quiet corner. So I went back and set everything straight aboard yesterday, and now here I am. You can put me up for a few weeks, I suppose. I'm not hard to please, and I can pay my way; suppose we say ten dollars a week for board and lodging, and a fortnight to be paid in advance."

He put his hand in his pocket and produced four shining napoleons, which he pushed along the dresser to my father, who grabbed them up eagerly.

"I'm sorry I gave you such a rough reception," I said, rather awkwardly. "I was hardly awake at the time."

"Say no more, mate, say no more!" he shouted heartily, holding out his hand and clasping mine. "Hard knocks are nothing to me. I suppose we may consider the bargain settled then?"

"Ye can bide as lang as ye wull, sir," answered my father, still fingering the four coins. "Archie and me 'll do a' we can to mak' your veesit a pleasant ane. It's no' such a dreary place as ye might think. When the Lamlash boats come in we get the papers and a' the news."

It struck me that the stranger looked anything but overjoyed by this piece of information. "You don't mean to say that you get the papers here," he said.

" 'Oo aye, the *Scotsman* an' the *Glasgey Herald*. But maybe you would like Archie and me to row ower to your ship in the morn, an' fetch your luggage."

"The brig is fifty miles away by this time," said our visitor. "She is running before the wind for Marseilles. I told the mate to bring her round again in a month or so. As to luggage, I always travel light in that matter. If a man's purse is only full he can do with very little else. All I have is in a bundle under your window. By the way, my name is Digby — Charles Digby."

"I thought your initials were A. W.," I remarked.

He sprang off the dresser as if he had been stung, and his face turned quite grey for a moment. "What the devil do you mean by that?" he said.

"I thought this might be yours," I answered, handing him the handkerchief I had found.

"Oh, is that all!" he said with rather a forced laugh. "I didn't quite see what you were driving at. That's all right. It belongs to Whittingdale, my second officer. I'll keep it until I see him again. And now suppose you give me something to eat, for I'm about famished."

We brought him out such rough fare as was to be found in our larder, and he ate ravenously, and tossed off a stiff glass of whisky and water. Afterwards my father showed him into the solitary spare bedroom, with which he professed himself well pleased, and we all settled down for the night. As I went back to my couch I noticed that the gale had freshened up, and I saw long streamers of seaweed flying past my broken window in the moonlight. A great bat fluttered into the room, which is reckoned a sure sign of misfortune in the islands — but I was never superstitious, and let the poor thing find its way out again unmolested.

III

In the morning it was still blowing a whole gale, though the sky was blue for the most part. Our guest was up betimes and we walked down to the beach together. It was a sight to see the great rollers sweeping in, overtopping one another like a herd of oxen, and then bursting with a roar, sending the Carracuil pebbles flying before them like grapeshot, and filling the whole air with drifting spume.

We were standing together watching the scene, when looking round I saw my father hurrying towards us. He had been up and out since early dawn. When he saw us looking, he began waving his hands and shouting, but the wind carried his voice away. We ran towards him however, seeing that he was heavy with news.

"The brig's wrecked, and they're a' drowned!" he cried as we met him.

"What!" roared our visitor.

If ever I heard exceeding great joy compressed into a monosyllable it vibrated in that one.

"They're a' drowned and naething saved!" repeated my father. "Come yoursel' and see."

We followed him across the Combera to the level sands on the other side. They were strewn with wreckage, broken pieces of bulwark and handrail, panelling of a cabin, and an occasional cask. A single large spar was tossing in the waves close to the shore, occasionally shooting up towards the sky like some giant's javelin, then sinking and disappearing in the trough of the great scooping seas. Digby hurried up to the nearest piece of timber, and stooping over it examined it intently.

"By God!" he said at last, taking in a long breath between his teeth, "you are right. It's the *Proserpine,* and all hands are lost. What a terrible thing!"

His face was very solemn as he spoke, but his eyes danced and glittered. I was beginning to conceive a great repugnance and distrust towards this man.

"Is there no chance of any one having got ashore?" he said.

"Na, na, nor cargo neither," my father answered with real grief in his voice. "Ye dinna ken this coast. There's an awful undertow outside the Winners, and it's a' swept round to Holy Isle. De'il take it, if there was to be a shipwreck what for should they no' run their ship agroond to the east'ard o' the point and let an honest mun have the pickings instead o' they rascally loons in Arran? An empty barrel might float in here, but there's no chance o' a sea-chest, let alane a body."

"Poor fellows!" said Digby. "But there — we must meet it some day, and why not here and now? I've lost my ship, but thank Heaven I can buy another. It is sad about them, though — very sad. I warned Lamarck that he was waiting too long with a low barometer and an ugly shore under his lee. He has himself to thank. He was my first officer, a prying, covetous, meddlesome hound."

"Don't call him names," I said. "He's dead."

"Well said, my young prig!" he answered. "Perhaps you wouldn't be so mealy-mouthed yourself if you lost five thousand pounds before breakfast. But there — there's no use crying over spilt milk. *Vogue la galère!* as the French say. Things are never so bad but that they might be worse."

My father and Digby stayed at the scene of the wreck, but I walked over to Corriemains to reassure Minnie's mind as to the

apparition at the window. Her opinion, when I had told her all,
coincided with mine, that perhaps the crew of the brig knew
more about the stranger than he cared for. We agreed that I
should keep a close eye upon him without letting him know that
he was watched.

"But oh, Archie," she said, "ye munna cross him or anger him
while he carries them awfu' weapons. Ye maun be douce and
saft, and no' gainsay him."

I laughed, and promised her to be very prudent, which
reassured her a little. Old Fullarton walked back with me in the
hope of picking up a piece of timber, and both he and my father
patrolled the shore for many days, without, however, finding
any prize of importance, for the under current off the Winners
was very strong, and everything had probably drifted right
round to Lamlash Bay in Arran.

It was wonderful how quickly the stranger accommodated
himself to our insular ways, and how useful he made himself
about the homesteading. Within a fortnight he knew the island
almost as well as I did myself. Had it not been for that one
unpleasant recollection of the shipwreck which rankled in my
remembrance, I could have found it in my heart to become fond
of him. His nature was a tropical one—fiercely depressed at
times, but sunny as a rule, bursting continually into jest and
song from pure instinct, in a manner which is unknown among
us Northerners. In his graver moments he was a most interesting
companion, talking shrewdly and eloquently of men and
manners, and his own innumerable and strange adventures. I
have seldom heard a more brilliant conversationalist. Of an
evening he would keep my father and myself spell-bound by the
kitchen fire for hours and hours, while he chatted away in a
desultory fashion and smoked his cigarettes. It seemed to me
that the packet he had brought with him on the first night must
have consisted entirely of tobacco. I noticed that in these
conversations, which were mostly addressed to my father, he
used, unconsciously perhaps, to play upon the weak side of the
old man's nature. Tales of cunning, of smartness, of various
ways in which mankind had been cheated and money gained,
came most readily to his lips, and were relished by an eager
listener. I could not help one night remarking upon it, when my
father had gone out of the room, laughing hoarsely, and vibrat-

ing with amusement over some story of how the Biscayan peasants will strap lanterns to a bullock's horns, and taking the beast some distance inland on a stormy night, will make it prance and rear so that the ships at sea may imagine it to be the lights of a vessel, and steer fearlessly in that direction, only to find themselves on a rockbound coast.

"You shouldn't tell such tales to an old man," I said.

"My dear fellow," he answered very kindly, "you have seen nothing of the world yet. You have formed fine ideas no doubt, and notions of delicacy and such things, and you are very dogmatic about them, as clever men of your age always are. I had notions of right and wrong once, but it has been all knocked out of me. It's just a sort of varnish which the rough friction of the world soon rubs off. I started with a whole soul, but there are more gashes and seams and scars in it now than there are in my body, and that's pretty fair as you'll allow"—with which he pulled open his tunic and showed me his chest.

"Good heavens!" I said. "How on earth did you get those?"

"This was a bullet," he said, pointing to a deep bluish pucker underneath his collar bone. "I got it behind the barricades in Berlin in '48. Langenback said it just missed the subclavian artery. And this," he went on, indicating a pair of curious elliptical scars upon his throat, "was a bite from a Sioux chief, when I was under Custer on the plains—I've got an arrow wound on my leg from the same party. This is from a mutinous Lascar aboard ship, and the others are mere scratches—Californian vaccination marks. You can excuse my being a little ready with my own irons, though, when I've been dropped so often."

"What's this?" I asked, pointing to a little chamois-leather bag which was hung by a strong cord round his neck. "It looks like a charm."

He buttoned up his tunic again hastily, looking extremely disconcerted. "It is nothing," he said brusquely. "I am a Roman Catholic, and it is what we call a scapular." I could hardly get another word out of him that night, and even next day he was reserved and appeared to avoid me. This little incident made me very thoughtful, the more so as I noticed shortly afterwards when standing over him, that the string was no longer round his neck. Apparently he had taken it off after my remark about it. What could there be in that leather bag which needed such secrecy and precaution! Had I but known it, I would sooner have put my left hand in the fire than have pursued that inquiry.

One of the peculiarities of our visitor was that in all his plans for the future, with which he often regaled us, he seemed entirely untrammelled by any monetary considerations. He would talk in the lightest and most off-hand way of schemes which would involve the outlay of much wealth. My father's eyes would glisten as he heard him talk carelessly of sums which to our frugal minds appeared enormous. It seemed strange to both of us that a man who by his own confession had been a vagabond and adventurer all his life, should be in possession of such a fortune. My father was inclined to put it down to some stroke of luck on the American goldfields. I had my own ideas even then — chaotic and half-formed as yet, but tending in the right direction.

It was not long before these suspicions began to assume a more definite shape, which came about in this way. Minnie and I made the summit of the Combera cliff a favourite trysting-place, as I think I mentioned before, and it was rare for a day to pass without our spending two or three hours there. One morning, not long after my chat with our guest, we were seated together in a little nook there, which we had chosen as sheltering us from the wind as well as from my father's observation, when Minnie caught sight of Digby walking along the Carracuil beach. He sauntered up to the base of the cliff, which was boulder-studded and slimy from the receding tide, but instead of turning back he kept on climbing over the great green slippery stones, and threading his way among the pools until he was standing immediately beneath us so that we looked straight down at him. To him the spot must have seemed the very acme of seclusion, with the great sea in front, the rocks on each side, and the precipice behind. Even had he looked up, he could hardly have made out the two human faces, which peered down at him from the distant ledge. He gave a hurried glance round, and then slipping his hand into his pocket, he pulled out the leather bag which I had noticed, and took out of it a small object which he held in the palm of his hand and looked at long, and, as it were, lovingly. We both had an excellent view of it from where we lay. He then replaced it in the bag, and shoving it down to the very bottom of his pocket picked his way back more cheerily than he had come.

Minnie and I looked at each other. She was smiling; I was serious.

"Did you see it?" I asked.

"Yon? Aye, I saw it."

"What did you think it was, then?"

"A wee bit of glass," she answered, looking at me with wondering eyes.

"No," I cried excitedly, "glass could never catch the sun's rays so. It was a diamond, and if I mistake not, one of extraordinary value. It was as large as all I have seen put together, and must be worth a fortune."

A diamond was a mere name to poor, simple Minnie, who had never seen one before, nor had any conception of their value, and she prattled away to me about this and that, but I hardly heard her. In vain she exhausted all her little wiles in attempting to recall my attention. My mind was full of what I had seen. Look where I would, the glistening of the breakers, or the sparkling of the mica-laden rocks, recalled the brilliant facets of the gem which I had seen. I was moody and distraught, and eventually let Minnie walk back to Corriemains by herself, while I made my way to the homesteading. My father and Digby were just sitting down to the midday meal, and the latter hailed me cheerily.

"Come along, mate," he cried, pushing over a stool, "we were just wondering what had become of you. Ah! you rogue, I'll bet my bottom dollar it was that pretty wench I saw the other day who kept you."

"Mind your own affairs," I answered angrily.

"Don't be thin-skinned," he said; "young people should control their tempers, and you've got a mighty bad one, my lad. Have you heard that I am going to leave you?"

"I'm sorry to hear it," I said frankly; "when do you intend to go?"

"Next week," he answered, "but don't be afraid; you'll see me again. I've had too good a time here to forget you easily. I'm going to buy a good steam yacht — 250 tons or thereabouts — and I'll bring her round in a few months and give you a cruise."

"What would be a fair price for a craft of that sort?" I asked.

"Forty thousand dollars," said our visitor, carelessly.

"You must be very rich," I remarked, "to throw away so much money on pleasure."

"Rich!" echoed my companion, his Southern blood mantling up for a moment. "Rich, why man, there is hardly a limit—but there, I was romancing a bit. I'm fairly well off, or shall be shortly."

"How did you make your money?" I asked. The question came so glibly to my lips that I had no time to check it, though I felt the moment afterwards that I had made a mistake. Our guest drew himself into himself at once, and took no notice of my query, while my father said:

"Hush, Archie laddie, ye munna speer they questions o' the gentleman!" I could see, however, from the old man's eager grey eyes, looking out from under the great thatch of his brows, that he was meditating over the same problem himself.

During the next couple of days I hesitated very often as to whether I should tell my father of what I had seen and the opinions I had formed about our visitor; but he forestalled me by making a discovery himself which supplemented mine and explained all that had been dark. It was one day when the stranger was out for a ramble, that, entering the kitchen, I found my father sitting by the fire deeply engaged in perusing a newspaper, spelling out the words laboriously, and following the lines with his great forefinger. As I came in he crumpled up the paper as if his instinct were to conceal it, but then spreading it out again on his knee he beckoned me over to him.

"Wha d'ye think this chiel Digby is?" he asked. I could see by his manner that he was much excited.

"No good," I answered.

"Come here, laddie, come here!" he croaked. "You're a braw scholar. Read this tae me alood—read it and tell me if you dinna think I've fitted the cap on the right heid. It's a *Glasgey Herald* only four days auld—a Loch Ranza feeshin' boat brought it in the morn. Begin frae here—'Oor Paris Letter.' Here it is, 'Fuller details'; read it a' to me."

I began at the spot indicated, which was a paragraph of the ordinary French correspondence of the Glasgow paper. It ran in this way. "Fuller details have now come before the public of the diamond robbery by which the Duchess de Rochevieille lost her celebrated gem. The diamond is a pure brilliant weighing eighty-three and a half carats, and is supposed to be the third largest in France, and the seventeenth in Europe. It came into the possession of the family through the great grand-uncle of the Duchess, who fought under Bussy in India, and brought it back to Europe with him. It represented a fortune then, but its value now is simply enormous. It was taken, as will be remembered, from the jewel case of the Duchess two months ago during the night, and though the police have made every effort, no real clue has been obtained as to the thief. They are very reticent upon the subject, but it seems that they have reason to suspect one Achille Wolff, an Americanized native of Lorraine, who had called at the Château a short time before. He is an eccentric man, of Bohemian habits, and it is just possible that his sudden disappearance at the time of the robbery may have been a coincidence. In appearance he is described as romantic-looking, with an artistic face, dark eyes and hair, and a brusque manner. A large reward is offered for his capture."

When I finished reading this, my father and I sat looking at each other in silence for a minute or so. Then my father jerked his finger over his shoulder. "Yon's him," he said.

"Yes, it must be he," I answered, thinking of the initials on the handkerchief.

Again we were silent for a time. My father took one of the faggots out of the grate and twisted it about in his hands. "It maun be a muckle stane," he said. "He canna hae it aboot him. Likely he's left it in France."

"No, he has it with him," I said, like a cursed fool as I was.

"Hoo d'ye ken that?" asked the old man, looking up quickly with eager eyes.

"Because I have seen it."

The faggot which he held broke in two in his grip, but he said nothing more. Shortly afterwards our guest came in, and we had dinner, but neither of us alluded to the arrival of the paper.

IV

I have often been amused, when reading stories told in the first person, to see how the narrator makes himself out as a matter of course to be a perfect and spotless man. All around may have their passions, and weaknesses, and vices, but he remains a cold and blameless nonentity, running like a colourless thread through the tangled skein of the story. I shall not fall into this error. I see myself as I was in those days, shallow-hearted, hot-headed, and with little principle of any kind. Such I was, and such I depict myself.

From the time that I finally identified our visitor Digby with Achille Wolff the diamond robber, my resolution was taken. Some might have been squeamish in the matter, and thought that because he had shaken their hand and broken their bread he had earned some sort of grace from them. I was not troubled with sentimentality of this sort. He was criminal escaping from justice. Some providence had thrown him into our hands, and an enormous reward awaited his betrayers. I never hesitated for a moment as to what was to be done.

The more I thought of it the more I admired the cleverness with which he had managed the whole business. It was clear that he had had a vessel ready, manned either by confederates or by unsuspecting fishermen. Hence he would be independent of all those parts where the police would be on the look-out for him. Again if he had made for England or for America, he could hardly have escaped ultimate capture, but by choosing one of the most desolate and lonely spots in Europe he had thrown them off his track for a time, while destruction of the brig seemed to destroy the last clue as to his whereabouts. At present he was entirely at our mercy, since he could not move from the island without our help. There was no necessity for us to hurry therefore, and we could mature our plans at our leisure.

Both my father and I showed no change in our manner towards our guest, and he himself was as cheery and light-hearted as ever. It was pleasant to hear him singing as we mended the nets or caulked the boat. His voice was a very high tenor and one of the most melodious I ever listened to. I am convinced that he could have made a name upon the operatic stage, but like most versatile scoundrels, he placed small account upon the genuine talents which he possessed, and cultivated the worse portion of his nature. My father used sometimes to eye him sideways in a strange manner, and I thought I knew what he was thinking about — but there I made a mistake.

One day, about a week after our conversation, I was fixing up one of the rails of our fence which had been snapped in the gale, when my father came along the seashore, plodding heavily among the pebbles, and sat down on a stone at my elbow. I went on knocking in the nails, but looked at him from the corner of my eye, as he pulled away at his short black pipe. I could see that he had something weighty on his mind, for he knitted his brows, and his lips projected.

"D'ye mind what was in yon paper?" he said at last, knocking his ashes out against the stone.

"Yes," I answered shortly.

"Well, what's your opeenion?" he asked.

"Why, that we should have the reward, of course!" I replied.

"The reward!" he said, with a fierce snarl. "You would tak' the reward. You'd let the stane that's worth thoosands an' thoosands gang awa' back tae some furrin Papist, an' a' for the sake o' a few pund that they'd fling till ye, as they fling a bane to a dog when the meat's a' gone. It's a clean flingin' awa' o' the gifts o' Providence."

"Well, father," I said, laying down the hammer, "you must be satisfied with what you can get. You can only have what is offered."

"But if we got the stane itsel'," whispered my father, with a leer on his face.

"He'd never give it up," I said.

"But if he deed while he's here—if he was suddenly—"

"Drop it, father, drop it!" I cried, for the old man looked like a fiend out of the pit. I saw now what he was aiming at.

"If he deed," he shouted, "wha saw him come, and wha wad speer where he'd ganged till? If an accident happened, if he came by a dud on the heid, or woke some nicht to find a knife at his thrapple, wha wad be the wiser?"

"You mustn't speak so, father," I said, though I was thinking many things at the same time.

"It may as well be oot as in," he answered, and went away rather sulkily, turning round after a few yards and holding his finger towards me to impress the necessity of caution.

My father did not speak of this matter to me again, but what he said rankled in my mind. I could hardly realize that he meant his words, for he had always, as far as I knew, been an upright, righteous man, hard in his ways, and grasping in his nature, but guiltless of any great sin. Perhaps it was that he was removed from temptation, for isothermal lines of crime might be drawn on the map through places where it is hard to walk straight, and there are others where it is as hard to fall. It was easy to be a saint in the island of Uffa.

One day we were finishing breakfast when our guest asked if the boat was mended (one of the thole-pins had been broken). I answered that it was.

"I want you two," he said, "to take me round to Lamlash to-day. You shall have a couple of sovereigns for the job. I don't know that I may not come back with you—but I may stay."

My eyes met those of my father for a flash. "There's no' vera much wind," he said.

"What there is, is in the right direction," returned Digby, as I must call him.

"The new foresail has no' been bent," persisted my father.

"There's no use throwing difficulties in the way," said our visitor angrily. "If you won't come, I'll get Tommy Gibbs and his father, but go I shall. Is it a bargain or not?"

"I'll gang," my father replied sullenly, and went down to get the boat ready. I followed, and helped him to bend on the new foresail. I felt nervous and excited.

"What do you intend to do?" I asked.

"I dinna ken," he said irritably. "Gin the worst come to the worst we can gie him up at Lamlash—but oh, it wad be a peety, an awfu' peety. You're young an' strong, laddie; can we no' master him between us?"

"No," I said, "I'm ready to give him up, but I'm damned if I lay a hand on him."

"You're a cooardly, white-livered loon!" he cried, but I was not to be moved by taunts, and left him mumbling to himself and picking at the sail with nervous fingers.

It was about two o'clock before the boat was ready, but as there was a slight breeze from the north we reckoned on reaching Lamlash before nightfall. There was just a pleasant ripple upon the dark blue water, and as we stood on the beach before shoving off, we could see the Carlin's leap and Goatfell bathed in a purple mist, while beyond them along the horizon loomed the long line of the Argyleshire hills. Away to the south the great bald summit of Ailsa crag glittered in the sun, and a single white fleck showed where a fishing boat was beating up from the Scotch coast. Digby and I stepped into the boat, but my father ran back to where I had been mending the rails, and came back with the hatchet in his hand, which he stowed away under the thwarts.

"What d'ye want with the axe?" our visitor asked.

"It's a handy thing to hae aboot a boat," my father answered with averted eyes, and shoved us off. We set the foresail jib, and mainsail, and shot away across the Roost, with the blue water splashing merrily under our bows. Looking back, I saw the coastline of our little island extend rapidly on either side. There was Carravoe which we had left, and our own beach of Carracuil and the steep brown face of the Combera, and away behind the rugged crests of Beg-na-phail and Beg-na-sacher. I could see the red tiles of the byre of our homesteading, and across the moor a thin blue reek in the air which marked the position of Corrie-mains. My heart warmed towards the place which had been my home since childhood.

We were about half-way across the Roost when it fell a dead calm, and the sails flapped against the mast. We were perfectly motionless except for the drift of the current, which runs from north to south. I had been steering and my father managing the sails, while the stranger smoked his eternal cigarettes and admired the scenery; but at his suggestion we now got the sculls out to row. I shall never know how it began, but as I was stooping down to pick up an oar I heard our visitor give a great scream that he was murdered, and looking up I saw him with his face all in a sputter of blood leaning against the mast, while my father made at him with the hatchet. Before I could move hand or foot Digby rushed at the old man and caught him round the waist. "You grey-headed devil," he cried in a husky voice. "I feel that you have done for me. But you'll never get what you want. No—never! never! never!" Nothing can ever erase from my memory the intense and concentrated malice of those words. My father gave a raucous cry, they swayed and balanced for a moment and then over they went into the sea. I rushed to the side, boat-hook in hand, but they never came up. As the long rings caused by the splash widened out however and left an unruffled space in the centre, I saw them once again. The water was very clear, and far far down I could see the shimmer of two white faces coming and going, faces which seemed to look up at me with an expression of unutterable horror. Slowly they went down, revolving in each other's embrace until they were nothing but a dark loom, and then faded from my view for ever. There they shall lie, the Frenchman and the Scot, till the great trumpet shall sound and the sea give up its dead. Storms may rage above them and great ships labour and creak, but their slumber shall be dreamless and unruffled in the silent green depths of the Roost of Uffa. I trust when the great day shall come that they will bring up the cursed stone with them, that they may show the sore temptation which the devil had placed in their way, as some slight extenuation of their errors while in this mortal flesh.

It was a weary and waesome journey back to Carravoe. I remember tug-tugging at the oars as though to snap them in trying to relieve the tension in my mind. Towards evening a breeze sprang up and helped me on my way, and before nightfall I was back in the lonely homesteading once more, and all that had passed that spring afternoon lay behind me like some horrible nightmare.

I did not remain in Uffa. The croft and the boat were sold by public roup in the market-place of Ardrossan, and the sum realized was sufficient to enable me to continue my medical studies at the University. I fled from the island as from a cursed place, nor did I ever set foot on it again. Gibbs and his son, and even Minnie Fullarton too, passed out of my life completely and for ever. She missed me for a time, no doubt, but I have heard that young McBane, who took the farm, went a-wooing to Corriemains after the white fishing, and as he was a comely fellow enough he may have consoled her for my loss. As for myself, I have settled quietly down into a large middle-class practice in Paisley. It has been in the brief intervals of profes-sional work that I have jotted down these reminiscences of the events which led up to my father's death. Achille Wolff and the Rochevieille diamond are things of the past now, but there may be some who will care to hear of how they visited the island of Uffa.

De Profundis

And now he was wealthy and world famous. The Sherlock Holmes stories in the STRAND *were the making of both the author and the magazine. It was a lasting partnership, continuing right up to Doyle's death in 1930. Almost exclusively until 1908, and in large part thereafter, he contributed series episodes and serialized novels to the* STRAND. *His non-series fiction appeared principally in* HARPER'S *and* McCLURE'S *in the United States and at home in a newly-established little magazine by and about the world of British letters called* THE IDLER. *Since moving to London, he had been thrown much into the company of* THE IDLER'S *circle, which included many of the emerging young English writers of the 1890s, even playing on the magazine's unofficial cricket team. The very first story he had contributed, in March 1892, was "De Profundis," a hypnotic blend of subtle styling and Conan Doyle's own variety of rational deduction.*

As long as the oceans are the ligaments which bind together the great broad-cast British Empire, so long there will be a dash of romance in our slow old Frisian minds. For the soul is swayed by the waters, as the waters are by the moon, and when the great highways of an Empire are along such roads as those, so full of strange sights and sounds, with danger ever running like a hedge on either side of the course, it is a dull mind indeed which does not bear away with it some trace of such a passage. And now, Britain lies far beyond herself, for in truth the three mile limit of every seaboard is her frontier, which has been won by hammer and loom and pick, rather than by arts of war. For it is written in history that neither a king in his might, nor an army with banners, can bar the path to the man who having twopence in his strong box, and knowing well where he can turn it to threepence, sets his mind to that one end. And as the Empire has broadened, the mind of Britain has broadened too, spreading out into free speech, free press, free trade, until all men can see that the ways of the island are continental, even as those of the continent are insular.

But for this a price must be paid, and the price is a grievous one. As the beast of old must have one young human life as a tribute every year, so to our Empire we throw from day to day the pick and flower of our youth. The engine is world-wide and strong, but the only fuel that will drive it is the lives of British men. Thus it is that in the grey old cathedrals, as we look round upon the brasses on the walls, we see strange names, such names as they who reared those walls had never heard, for it is in Peshawur, and Umballah, and Korti and Fort Pearson that the youngsters die, leaving only a precedent and a brass behind them. But if every man had his obelisk, even where he lay, then no frontier line need be drawn, for a cordon of British graves would ever show how high the Anglo-Saxon tide had lapped.

And this too, as well as the waters which separate us from France, and join us to the world, has done something to tinge us with romance. For when so many have their loved ones over the seas, walking amid hillmen's bullets, or swamp malaria, where death is sudden and distance great, then mind communes with mind, and strange stories arise of dream, presentiment or vision, where the mother sees her dying son, and is past the first bitterness of her grief ere the message comes which should have broke the news. The learned have of late looked into the matter, and have even labelled it with a name, but what can we know more of it save that a poor stricken soul, when hard-pressed and driven, can shoot across the earth some ten-thousand-mile-long picture of its trouble to the mind which is most akin to it. Far be it from me to say that there lies no such power within us, for of all things which the brain will grasp the last will be itself, but yet it is well to be very cautious over such matters, for once at least I have known that which was within the laws of nature to seem to be far upon the further side of them.

John Vansittart was the younger partner of the firm of Hudson and Vansittart, coffee exporters of the Island of Ceylon, three-quarters Dutchman by descent, but wholly English in his sympathies. For years I had been his agent in London, and when in '72 he came over to England for a three months' holiday, he turned to me for the introductions which would enable him to see something of town and country life. Armed with seven letters he left my offices, and for many weeks scrappy notes from different parts of the country let me know that he had found favour in the eyes of my friends. Then came word of his engagement to Emily Lawson, of a cadet branch of the Hereford Lawsons, and at the very tail of the first flying rumour the news of his absolute marriage, for the wooing of a wanderer must be short, and the days were already crowding on towards the date when he must be upon his homeward journey. They were to return together to Columbo in one of the firm's own thousand ton barque-rigged sailing ships, and this was to be their princely honeymoon, at once a necessity and a delight.

Those were the royal days of coffee planting in Ceylon, before a single season and a rotting fungus drove a whole community through years of despair to one of the greatest commercial victories which pluck and ingenuity ever won. Not often is it that men have the heart when their one great industry is withered to rear up in a few years another as rich to take its place, and the teafields of Ceylon are as true a monument to courage as is the lion at Waterloo. But in '72 there was no cloud yet above the skyline, and the hopes of the planters were as high and as bright as the hill-sides on which they reared their crops. Vansittart came down to London with his young and beautiful wife. I was introduced, dined with them, and it was finally arranged that I, since business called me also to Ceylon, should be a fellow-passenger with them on the *Eastern Star,* which was timed to sail upon the following Monday.

It was on the Sunday evening that I saw him again. He was shown up into my rooms about nine o'clock at night, with the air of a man who is bothered and out of sorts. His hand, as I shook it, was hot and dry.

"I wish, Atkinson," said he, "that you could give me a little lime juice and water. I have a beastly thirst upon me, and the more I take the more I seem to want."

I rang and ordered in a caraffe and glasses. "You are flushed," said I. "You don't look the thing."

"No, I'm clean off colour. Got a touch of rheumatism in my back, and don't seem to taste my food. It is this vile London that is choking me. I'm not used to breathing air which has been used

up by four million lungs all sucking away on every side of you."
He flapped his crooked hands before his face, like a man who
really struggles for his breath.

"A touch of the sea will soon set you right."

"Yes, I'm of one mind with you there. That's the thing for me.
I want no other doctor. If I don't get to sea to-morrow I'll have
an illness. There are no two ways about it." He drank off a
tumbler of lime juice, and clapped his two hands with his
knuckles doubled up into the small of his back.

"That seems to ease me," said he, looking at me with a filmy
eye. "Now I want your help, Atkinson, for I am rather awkwardly placed."

"As how?"

"This way. My wife's mother got ill and wired for her. I
couldn't go — you know best yourself how tied I have been — so
she had to go alone. Now I've had another wire to say that she
can't come to-morrow, but that she will pick up the ship at
Falmouth on Wednesday. We put in there, you know, and in,
and in, though I count it hard, Atkinson, that a man should be
asked to believe in a mystery, and cursed if he can't do it.
Cursed, mind you, no less." He leaned forward and began to
draw a catchy breath like a man who is poised on the very edge
of a sob.

Then it first came into my mind that I had heard much of the
hard drinking life of the island, and that from brandy came
these wild words and fevered hands. The flushed cheek and the
glazing eye were those of one whose drink is strong upon him.
Sad it was to see so noble a young man in the grip of that most
bestial of all the devils.

"You should lie down," I said, with some severity.

He screwed up his eyes, like a man who is striving to wake
himself, and looked up with an air of surprise.

"So I shall presently," said he, quite rationally. "I felt quite
swimmy just now, but I am my own man again now. Let me see,
what was I talking about? Oh ah, of course, about the wife. She
joins the ship at Falmouth. Now I want to go round by water. I
believe my health depends upon it. I just want a little clean first-
hand air to set me on my feet again. Now I want you, like a good
fellow, to go to Falmouth by rail, so that in case we should be
late you may be there to look after the wife. Put up at the Royal

Hotel, and I will wire her that you are there. Her sister will bring her down, so that it will be all plain sailing."

"I'll do it with pleasure," said I. "In fact, I should rather go by rail, for we shall have enough and to spare of the sea before we reach Columbo. I believe too that you badly need a change. Now I should go and turn in, if I were you."

"Yes, I will. I sleep aboard to-night. You know," he continued, as the film settled down again over his eyes, "I've not slept well the last few nights. I've been troubled with theolololog — that is to say, theolological — hang it," with a desperate effort, "with the doubts of theolologicians. Wondering why the Almighty made us, you know, and why He made our heads swimmy, and fixed little pains into the small of our backs. Maybe I'll do better to-night." He rose, and steadied himself with an effort against the corner of the chair back.

"Look here, Vansittart," said I gravely, stepping up to him, and laying my hand upon his sleeve, "I can give you a shakedown here. You are not fit to go out. You are all over the place. You've been mixing your drinks."

"Drinks!" he stared at me stupidly.

"You used to carry your liquor better than this."

"I give you my word, Atkinson, that I have not had a drain for two days. It's not drink. I don't know what it is. I suppose you think this is drink." He took up my hand in his burning grasp, and passed it over his own forehead.

"Great Lord!" said I.

His skin felt like a thin sheet of velvet beneath which lies a close packed layer of small shot. It was smooth to the touch at any one place, but, to a finger passed along it, rough as a nutmeg grater.

"It's all right," said he, smiling at my startled face. "I've had the prickly heat nearly as bad."

"But this is never prickly heat."

"No, it's London. It's breathing bad air. But to-morrow it'll be all right. There's a surgeon aboard, so I shall be in safe hands. I must be off now."

"Not you," said I, pushing him back into a chair. "This is past a joke. You don't move from here until a doctor sees you. Just stay where you are." I caught up my hat, and rushing round to the house of a neighbouring physician, I brought him back with me. The room was empty and Vansittart gone. I rang the bell. The servant said that the gentleman had ordered a cab the instant that I had left, and had gone off in it. He had told the cabman to drive to the docks.

"Did the gentleman seem ill?" I asked.

"Ill!" The man smiled. "No, sir, he was singin' his 'ardest all the time."

The information was not as reassuring as my servant seemed to think, but I reflected that he was going straight back to the *Eastern Star,* and that there was a doctor aboard of her, so that there was nothing which I could do in the matter. None the less, when I thought of his thirst, his burning hands, his heavy eye, his tripping speech, and lastly, of that leprous forehead, I carried with me to bed an unpleasant memory of my visitor and his visit.

At eleven o'clock next day I was at the docks, but the *Eastern Star* had already moved down the river, and was nearly at Gravesend. To Gravesend I went by train, but only to see her topmasts far off, with a plume of smoke from a tug in front of her. I would hear no more of my friend until I rejoined him at Falmouth. When I got back to my offices a telegram was awaiting for me from Mrs. Vansittart, asking me to meet her, and next evening found us both at the Royal Hotel, Falmouth, where we were to wait for the *Eastern Star.* Ten days passed, and there came no news of her.

They were ten days which I am not likely to forget. On the very day that the *Eastern Star* had cleared from the Thames, a furious easterly gale had sprung up, and blew on from day to day for the greater part of a week without the sign of a lull. Such a screaming, raving, longdrawn storm has never been known on the southerly coast. From our hotel windows the sea view was all banked in with haze, with a little rain-swept half circle under our very eyes, churned and lashed into one tossing stretch of foam. So heavy was the wind upon the waves that little sea could rise, for the crest of each billow was torn shrieking from it, and lashed broadcast over the bay. Clouds, wind, sea, all were rushing to the west, and there, looking down at this mad jumble of elements, I waited on day after day, my sole companion a white, silent woman, with terror in her eyes, her forehead pressed ever against the bar of the window, her gaze from early morning to the fall of night fixed upon that wall of grey haze through which the loom of a vessel might come. She said nothing, but that face of hers was one long wail of fear.

On the fifth day I took counsel with an old seaman. I should have preferred to have done so alone, but she saw me speak with him, and was at our side in an instant, with parted lips and a prayer in her eyes.

"Seven days out from London," said he, "and five in the gale. Well, the Channel's swept as clear as clear by this wind. There's three things for it. She may have popped into port on the French side. That's like enough."

"No, no, he knew we were here. He would have telegraphed."

"Ah, yes, so he would. Well then, he might have run for it, and if he did that he won't be very far from Madeira by now. That'll be it, marm, you may depend."

"Or else? You said there was a third chance."

"Did I, marm. No, only two, I think. I don't think I said anything of a third. Your ship's out there, depend upon it, away out in the Atlantic, and you'll hear of it time enough, for the weather is breaking; now don't you fret, marm, and wait quiet, and you'll find a real blue Cornish sky to-morrow."

The old seaman was right in his surmise, for the next day broke calm and bright, with only a low dwindling cloud in the west to mark the last trailing wreaths of the storm wrack. But still there came no word from the sea, and no sign of the ship. Three more weary days had passed, the weariest that I have ever spent, when there came a seafaring man to the hotel with a letter. I gave a shout of joy. It was from the Captain of the *Eastern Star*. As I read the first lines of it I whisked my hand over it, but she laid her own upon it and drew it away. "I have seen it," said she, in a cold, quiet voice; "I may as well see the rest, too."

"Dear Sir," said the letter, "Mr. Vansittart is down with the small-pox, and we are blown so far on our course that we don't know what to do, he being off his head and unfit to tell us. By dead reckoning we are but three hundred miles from Funchal, so I take it that it is best that we should push on there, get Mr. V. into hospital, and wait in the Bay until you come. There's a sailing ship due from Falmouth to Funchal in a few days' time, as I understand. This goes by the brig *Marian,* of Falmouth, and five pounds is due to the master.

> "Yours respectfully,
>   "JNO. HINES."

She was a wonderful woman that, only a chit of a girl fresh from school, but as quiet and strong as a man. She said nothing — only pressed her lips together tight, and put on her bonnet.

"You are going out?" I asked.

"Yes."

"Can I be of use?"

"No, I am going to the doctor's."

"To the doctor's?"

"Yes. To learn how to nurse a small-pox case."

She was busy at that all evening, and next morning we were off with a fine ten-knot breeze in the barque *Rose of Sharon* for Madeira. For five days we made good time, and were no great way from the island, but on the sixth there fell a calm, and we lay without motion on a sea of oil, heaving slowly, but making not a foot of weigh.

At ten o'clock that night Emily Vansittart and I stood leaning on the starboard railing of the poop, with a full moon shining at our backs, and casting a black shadow of the barque, and of our own two heads upon the shining water. From the shadow on, a broadening path of moonshine stretched away to the lonely skyline, flickering and shimmering in the gentle heave of the swell. We were talking with bent heads, chatting of the calm, of the chances of wind, of the look of the sky, when there came a sudden plop, like a rising salmon, and there in the clear light John Vansittart sprang out of the water and looked up at us.

I never saw anything clearer in my life than I saw that man. The moon shone full upon him, and he was but three oars' lengths away. His face was more puffed than when I had seen him last, mottled here and there with dark scabs, his mouth and eyes open as one who is struck with some overpowering surprise. He had some white stuff streaming from his shoulders, and one hand was raised to his ear, the other crooked across his breast. I saw him leap from the water into the air, and in the dead calm the waves of his coming lapped up against the sides of the vessel. Then his figure sank back into the water again, and I heard a rending, crackling sound like a bundle of brushwood snapping in the fire upon a frosty night. There were no signs of him when I looked again, but a swift swirl and eddy on the still sea still marked the spot where he had been. How long I stood there, tingling to my finger-tips, holding up an unconscious woman with one hand, clutching at the rail of the vessel with the other, was more than I could afterwards tell. I had been noted as a man of slow and unresponsive emotions, but this time at least I was shaken to the core. Once and twice I struck my foot upon the deck to be certain that I was indeed the master of my own senses, and that this was not some mad prank of an unruly brain. As I stood, still marvelling, the woman shivered, opened her eyes, gasped, and then standing erect with her hands upon the rail, looked out over the moonlit sea with a face which had aged ten years in a summer night.

"You saw his vision?" she murmured.

"I saw something."

"It was he. It was John. He is dead."

I muttered some lame words of doubt.

"Doubtless he died at this hour," she whispered. "In hospital at Madeira. I have read of such things. His thoughts were with me. His vision came to me. Oh, my John, my dear, dear, lost John!"

She broke out suddenly into a storm of weeping, and I led her down into her cabin, where I left her with her sorrow. That night a brisk breeze blew up from the east, and in the evening of the next day we passed the two islets of Los Desertos, and dropped anchor at sundown in the Bay of Funchal. The *Eastern Star* lay no great distance from us, with the quarantine flag flying from her main, and her Jack half way up her peak.

"You see," said Mrs. Vansittart quickly. She was dry-eyed now, for she had known how it would be.

That night we received permission from the authorities to move on board the *Eastern Star*. The Captain, Hines, was waiting upon deck with confusion and grief contending upon his bluff face as he sought for words with which to break this heavy tidings, but she took the story from his lips.

"I know that my husband is dead," she said. "He died yesterday night, about ten o'clock, in hospital at Madeira, did he not?"

The seaman stared aghast. "No, marm, he died eight days ago at sea, and we had to bury him out there, for we lay in a belt of calm, and could not say when we might make the land."

Well, those are the main facts about the death of John Vansittart, and his appearance to his wife somewhere about lat. 35° N. and long. 15° W. A clearer case of a wraith has seldom been made out, and since then it has been told as such, and put into print as such, and endorsed by a learned society as such, and so floated off with many others to support the recent theory of telepathy. For myself I hold telepathy to be proved, but I would snatch this one case from amid the evidence, and say that I do not think that it was the wraith of John Vansittart, but John Vansittart himself whom we saw that night leaping into the moonlight out of the depths of the Atlantic. It has ever been my belief that some strange chance, one of these chances which seem so improbable and yet so constantly occur, had becalmed us over the very spot where the man had been buried a week before. For the rest the surgeon tells me that the leaden weight was not too firmly fixed, and that seven days bring about changes which are wont to fetch a body to the surface. Coming from the depth which the weight would have sunk it to, he explains that it might well attain such a velocity as to carry it clear of the water. Such is my own explanation of the matter, and if you ask me what then became of the body, I must recall to you that snapping, crackling sound, with the swirl in the water. The shark is a surface feeder and is plentiful in those parts.

Lot No. 249

The best horror stories are those written as mysteries. Where there is no mystery, there is no horror. "Familiarity with a subject robs it of those vague and undefined terrors which are the most appalling to the imaginative mind," Doyle himself remarked later in the story of "The Brown Hand" (1898). But in few of Doyle's horror tales does the hero resolve the puzzle through his own efforts, and the classic "Lot No. 249" is the welcome exception. While the seemingly occult events of "De Profundis" prove to have a factual explanation, the nightmare in this story is genuinely unnatural. The clues by which young Abercrombie Smith pieces the answer together are by now obvious to any casual watcher of The Late Show, but several experts have proclaimed "Lot No. 249," originally published in HARPER'S *in 1892, to be the very first story of its kind ever written. Knowing the outcome will only permit the reader to appreciate all the more Doyle's uncanny ability to develop to its fullest any concept to which he turned his pen and his unfailing talent for conveying mood through narrative, for "Lot No. 249" is as superbly suspenseful as anything he ever wrote.*

OF the dealings of Edward Bellingham with William Monk-house Lee, and of the cause of the great terror of Abercrombie Smith, it may be that no absolute and final judgment will ever be delivered. It is true that we have the full and clear narrative of Smith himself, and such corroboration as he could look for from Thomas Styles the servant, from the Reverend Plumptree Peterson, Fellow of Old's, and from such other people as chanced to gain some passing glance at this or that incident in a singular chain of events. Yet, in the main, the story must rest upon Smith alone, and the most will think that it is more likely that one brain, however outwardly sane, has some subtle warp in its texture, some strange flaw in its workings, than that the path of Nature has been overstepped in open day in so famed a centre of learning and light as the University of Oxford. Yet when we think how narrow and how devious this path of Nature is, how dimly we can trace it, for all our lamps of science, and how from the darkness that girds it round great and terrible possibilities loom ever shadowly upward, it is a bold and confident man who will put a limit to the strange bypaths into which the human spirit may wander.

In a certain wing of what we will call Old College in Oxford there is a corner turret of an exceeding great age. The heavy arch that spans the open door has bent downward in the centre under the weight of its years, and the grey, lichen-blotched blocks of stone are bound and knitted together with withes and strands of ivy, as though the old mother had set herself to brace them up against wind and weather. From the door a stone stair curves upward spirally, passing two landings, and terminating in a third one, its steps all shapeless and hollowed by the tread of so many generations of the seekers after knowledge. Life has flowed like water down this winding stair, and, waterlike, has left these smooth-worn grooves behind it. From the long-gowned, pedantic scholars of Plantagenet days down to the young bloods of a later age, how full and strong had been that tide of young, English life. And what was left now of all those hopes, those strivings, those fiery energies, save here and there in some old-world churchyard a few scratches upon a stone, and perchance a handful of dust in a moldering coffin? Yet here were the silent stair and the grey, old wall, with bend and saltire and many another heraldic device still to be read upon its surface, like grotesque shadows thrown back from the days that had passed.

In the month of May, in the year 1884, three young men occupied the sets of rooms which opened on to the separate landings of the old stair. Each set consisted simply of a sitting-room and of a bedroom, while the two corresponding rooms upon the ground floor were used, the one as a coal cellar, and the other as the living room of the servant, or scout, Thomas Styles, whose duty it was to wait upon the three men above him. To right and to left was a line of lecture rooms and of offices, so that the dwellers in the old turret enjoyed a certain seclusion, which made the chambers popular among the more studious under-graduates. Such were the three who occupied them now—Abercrombie Smith above, Edward Bellingham beneath him, and William Monkhouse Lee upon the lowest storey.

It was ten o'clock on a bright, spring night, and Abercrombie Smith lay back in his armchair, his feet upon the fender, and his brier-root pipe between his lips. In a similar chair, and equally at his ease, there lounged on the other side of the fireplace his old school friend Jephro Hastie. Both men were in flannels, for they had spent their evening upon the river, but apart from their dress no one could look at their hard-cut, alert faces without seeing that they were open-air men—men whose minds and tastes turned naturally to all that was manly and robust. Hastie, indeed, was stroke of his college boat, and Smith was an even better oar, but a coming examination had already cast its shadow over him and held him to his work, save for the few hours a week which health demanded. A litter of medical books upon the table, with scattered bones, models, and anatomical plates, pointed to the extent as well as the nature of his studies, while a couple of singlesticks and a set of boxing gloves above the mantelpiece hinted at the means by which, with Hastie's help, he might take his exercise in its most compressed and least distant form. They knew each other very well—so well that they could sit now in that soothing silence which is the very highest development of companionship.

"Have some whisky," said Abercrombie Smith at last between two cloudbursts. "Scotch in the jug and Irish in the bottle."

"No, thanks. I'm in for the sculls. I don't liquor when I'm training. How about you?"

"I'm reading hard. I think it best to leave it alone."

Hastie nodded, and they relapsed into a contented silence.

"By the way, Smith," asked Hastie, presently, "have you made the acquaintance of either of the fellows on your stair yet?"

"Just a nod when we pass. Nothing more."

"Hum! I should be inclined to let it stand at that. I know something of them both. Not much, but as much as I want. I don't think I should take them to my bosom if I were you. Not that there's much amiss with Monkhouse Lee."

"Meaning the thin one?"

"Precisely. He is a gentlemanly little fellow. I don't think there is any vice in him. But then you can't know him without knowing Bellingham."

"Meaning the fat one?"

"Yes, the fat one. And he's a man whom I, for one, would rather not know."

Abercrombie Smith raised his eyebrows and glanced across at his companion.

"What's up, then?" he asked. "Drink? Cards? Cad? You used not to be censorious."

"Ah! you evidently don't know the man, or you wouldn't ask. There's something damnable about him—something reptilian. My gorge always rises at him. I should put him down as a man with secret vices—an evil liver. He's no fool, though. They say that he is one of the best men in his line that they have ever had in the college."

"Medicine or classics?"

"Eastern languages. He's a demon at them. Chillingworth met him somewhere above the second cataract last summer vacation, and he told me that he just prattled to the Arabs as if he had been born and nursed and weaned among them. He talked Coptic to the Copts, and Hebrew to the Jews, and Arabic to the Bedouins, and they were all ready to kiss the hem of his frock coat. There are some old hermit Johnnies up in those parts who sit on rocks and scowl and spit at the casual stranger. Well, when they saw this chap Bellingham, before he had said five words they just lay down on their bellies and wriggled. Chillingworth said that he never saw anything like it. Bellingham seemed to take it as his right, too, and strutted about among them and talked down to them like a Dutch uncle. Pretty good for an undergrad of Old's, wasn't it?"

"Why do you say you can't know Lee without knowing Bellingham?"

"Because Bellingham is engaged to his sister Eveline. Such a bright little girl, Smith! I know the whole family well. It's disgusting to see that brute with her. A toad and a dove, that's what they always remind me of."

Abercrombie Smith grinned and knocked his ashes out against the side of the grate.

"You show every card in your hand, old chap," said he. "What a prejudiced, green-eyed, evil-thinking old man it is! You have really nothing against the fellow except that."

"Well, I've known her ever since she was as long as that cherrywood pipe, and I don't like to see her taking risks. And it is a risk. He looks beastly. And he has a beastly temper, a venomous temper. You remember his row with Long Norton?"

"No; you always forget that I am a freshman."

"Ah, it was last winter. Of course. Well, you know the tow-path along by the river. There were several fellows going along it, Bellingham in front, when they came on an old market woman coming the other way. It had been raining — you know what those fields are like when it has rained — and the path ran between the river and a great puddle that was nearly as broad. Well, what does this swine do but keep the path, and push the old girl into the mud, where she and her marketings came to terrible grief. It was a blackguard thing to do, and Long Norton, who is as gentle a fellow as ever stepped, told him what he thought of it. One word led to another, and it ended in Norton laying his stick across the fellow's shoulders. There was the deuce of a fuss about it, and it's a treat to see the way in which Bellingham looks at Norton when they meet now. By Jove, Smith, it's nearly eleven o'clock!"

"No hurry. Light your pipe again."

"Not I. I'm supposed to be in training. Here I've been sitting gossiping when I ought to have been safely tucked up. I'll borrow your skull, if you can share it. Williams has had mine for a month. I'll take the little bones of your ear, too, if you are sure you won't need them. Thanks very much. Never mind a bag, I can carry them very well under my arm. Good night, my son, and take my tip as to your neighbour."

When Hastie, bearing his anatomical plunder, had clattered off down the winding stair, Abercrombie Smith hurled his pipe into the wastepaper basket, and drawing his chair nearer to the lamp, plunged into a formidable, green-covered volume, adorned with great, coloured maps of that strange, internal kingdom of which we are the hapless and helpless monarchs. Though a freshman at Oxford, the student was not so in medicine, for he had worked for four years at Glasgow and at Berlin, and this coming examination would place him finally as a member of his profession. With his firm mouth, broad forehead, and clear-cut, somewhat hard-featured face, he was a man who, if he had no brilliant talent, was yet so dogged, so patient, and so strong that he might in the end overtop a more showy genius. A man who can hold his own among Scotchmen and North Germans is not a man to be easily set back. Smith had left a name at Glasgow and at Berlin, and he was bent upon doing as much at Oxford, if hard work and devotion could accomplish it.

He had sat reading for about an hour, and the hands of the noisy carriage clock upon the side table were rapidly closing together upon the twelve, when a sudden sound fell upon his student's ear — a sharp, rather shrill sound, like the hissing intake of a man's breath who gasps under some strong emotion. Smith laid down his book and slanted his ear to listen. There was no one on either side or above him, so that the interruption came certainly from the neighbour beneath — the same neighbour of whom Hastie had given so unsavoury an account. Smith knew him only as a flabby, pale-faced man of silent and studious habits, a man whose lamp threw a golden bar from the old turret even after he had extinguished his own. This community in lateness had formed a certain silent bond between them. It was soothing to Smith when the hours stole on towards dawn to feel that there was another so close who set as small a value upon his sleep as he did. Even now, as his thoughts turned towards him, Smith's feelings were kindly. Hastie was a good fellow, but he was rough, strong-fibred, with no imagination or sympathy. He could not tolerate departures from what he looked upon as the model type of manliness. If a man could not be measured by a public-school standard, then he was beyond the pale with Hastie. Like so many who are themselves robust, he was apt to confuse the consitution with the character, to ascribe to want of principle what was really a want of circulation. Smith, with his stronger mind, knew his friend's habit, and made allowances for it now as his thoughts turned towards the man beneath him.

There was no return of the singular sound, and Smith was about to turn to his work once more, when suddenly there broke out in the silence of the night a hoarse cry, a positive scream — the call of a man who is moved and shaken beyond all control. Smith sprang out of his chair and dropped his book. He was a man of fairly firm fibre, but there was something in this sudden, uncontrollable shriek of horror that chilled his blood and pringled in his skin. Coming in such a place and at such an hour, it brought a thousand fantastic possibilities into his head. Should he rush down, or was it better to wait? He had all the national hatred of making a scene, and he knew so little of his neighbour that he would not lightly intrude upon his affairs. For a moment he stood in doubt and even as he balanced the matter there was a quick rattle of footsteps upon the stairs, and young Monkhouse Lee, half-dressed and as white as ashes, burst into his room.

"Come down!" he gasped. "Bellingham's ill."

Abercrombie Smith followed him closely downstairs into the sitting-room which was beneath his own, and intent as he was upon the matter in hand, he could not but take an amazed glance round him as he crossed the threshold. It was such a chamber as he had never seen before — a museum rather than a study. Walls and ceiling were thickly covered with a thousand strange relics from Egypt and the East. Tall, angular figures bearing burdens or weapons stalked in an uncouth frieze round the apartment. Above were bull-headed, stork-headed, cat-headed, owl-headed statues, with viper-crowned, almond-eyed monarchs, and strange, beetlelike deities cut out of the blue Egyptian lapis lazuli. Horus and Isis and Osiris peeped down from every niche and shelf, while across the ceiling a true son of Old Nile, a great, hanging-jawed crocodile, was slung in a double noose.

In the centre of this singular chamber was a large, square table, littered with papers, bottles, and the dried leaves of some graceful, palmlike plant. These varied objects had all been heaped together in order to make room for a mummy case, which had been conveyed from the wall, as was evident from the gap there, and laid across the front of the table. The mummy itself, a horrid, black, withered thing, like a charred head on a gnarled bush, was lying half out of the case, with its clawlike hand and bony forearm resting upon the table. Propped up against the sarcophagus was an old, yellow scroll of papyrus, and in front of it, in a wooden armchair, sat the owner of the room, his head thrown back, his widely opened eyes directed in a horrified stare to the crocodile above him, and his blue, thick lips puffing loudly with every expiration.

"My God! He's dying!" cried Monkhouse Lee, distractedly.

He was a slim, handsome young fellow, olive-skinned and

dark-eyed, of a Spanish rather than of an English type, with a Celtic intensity of manner which contrasted with the Saxon phlegm of Abercrombie Smith.

"Only a faint, I think," said the medical student. "Just give me a hand with him. You take his feet. Now on to the sofa. Can you kick all those little wooden devils off? What a litter it is! Now he will be all right if we undo his collar and give him some water. What has he been up to at all?"

"I don't know. I heard him cry out. I ran up. I know him pretty well, you know. It is very good of you to come down."

"His heart is going like a pair of castanets," said Smith, laying his hand on the breast of the unconscious man. "He seems to me to be frightened all to pieces. Chuck the water over him! What a face he has got on him!"

It was indeed a strange and most repellent face, for colour and outline were equally unnatural. It was white, not with the ordinary pallor of fear, but with an absolutely bloodless white, like the underside of a sole. He was very fat, but gave the impression of having at some time been considerably fatter, for his skin hung loosely in creases and folds, and was shot with a meshwork of wrinkles. Short, stubby brown hair bristled up from his scalp, with a pair of thick, wrinkled ears protruding at the sides. His light grey eyes were still open, the pupils dilated and the balls projecting in a fixed and horrid stare. It seemed to Smith as he looked down upon him that he had never seen Nature's danger signals flying so plainly upon a man's countenance, and his thoughts turned more seriously to the warning which Hastie had given him an hour before.

"What the deuce can have frightened him so?" he asked.

"It's the mummy."

"The mummy? How, then?"

"I don't know. It's beastly and morbid. I wish he would drop it. It's the second fright he has given me. It was the same last winter. I found him just like this, with that horrid thing in front of him."

"What does he want with the mummy, then?"

"Oh, he's a crank, you know. It's his hobby. He knows more about these things than any man in England. But I wish he wouldn't! Ah, he's beginning to come to."

A faint tinge of colour had begun to steal back into Bellingham's ghastly cheeks, and his eyelids shivered like a sail after a calm. He clasped and unclasped his hands, drew a long, thin breath between his teeth, and suddenly jerking up his head, threw a glance of recognition round him. As his eyes fell upon the mummy, he sprang off the sofa, seized the roll of papyrus, thrust it into a drawer, turned the key, and then staggered back on to the sofa.

"What's up?" he asked. "What do you chaps want?"

"You've been shrieking out and making no end of a fuss," said Monkhouse Lee. "If our neighbour here from above hadn't come down, I'm sure I don't know what I should have done with you."

"Ah, it's Abercrombie Smith," said Bellingham, glancing up at him. "How very good of you to come in! What a fool I am! Oh, my God, what a fool I am!"

He sank his head on to his hands, and burst into peal after peal of hysterical laughter.

"Look here! Drop it!" cried Smith, shaking him roughly by the shoulder.

"Your nerves are all in a jangle. You must drop these little midnight games with mummies, or you'll be going off your chump. You're all on wires now."

"I wonder," said Bellingham, "whether you would be as cool as I am if you had seen ——"

"What then?"

"Oh, nothing. I meant that I wonder if you could sit up at night with a mummy without trying your nerves. I have no doubt that you are quite right. I dare say that I have been taking it out of myself too much lately. But I am all right now. Please don't go, though. Just wait for a few minutes until I am quite myself."

"The room is very close," remarked Lee, throwing open the window and letting in the cool night air.

"It's balsamic resin," said Bellingham. He lifted up one of the dried palmate leaves from the table and frizzled it over the chimney of the lamp. It broke away into heavy smoke wreaths, and a pungent, biting odour filled the chamber. "It's the sacred plant — the plant of the priests," he remarked. "Do you know anything of Eastern languages, Smith?"

"Nothing at all. Not a word."

The answer seemed to lift a weight from the Egyptologist's mind.

"By the way," he continued, "how long was it from the time that you ran down until I came to my senses?"

"Not long. Some four or five minutes."

"I thought it could not be very long," said he, drawing a long breath. "But what a strange thing unconsciousness is! There is no measurement to it. I could not tell from my own sensations if it were seconds or weeks. Now that gentleman on the table was packed up in the days of the eleventh dynasty, some forty centuries ago, and yet if he could find his tongue, he would tell us that this lapse of time has been but a closing of the eyes and a reopening of them. He is a singularly fine mummy, Smith."

Smith stepped over to the table and looked down with a professional eye at the black and twisted form in front of him. The features, though horribly discoloured, were perfect, and two little nutlike eyes still lurked in the depths of the black, hollow sockets. The blotched skin was drawn tightly from bone to bone, and a tangled wrap of black, coarse hair fell over the ears. Two thin teeth, like those of a rat, overlay the shrivelled lower lip. In its crouching position, with bent joints and craned head, there was a suggestion of energy about the horrid thing which made Smith's gorge rise. The gaunt ribs, with their parchmentlike covering, were exposed, and the sunken, leaden-hued abdomen, with the long slit where the embalmer had left his mark; but the lower limbs were wrapped round with coarse, yellow bandages. A number of little clovelike pieces of myrrh and of cassia were sprinkled over the body, and lay scattered on the inside of the case.

"I don't know his name," said Bellingham, passing his hand over the shrivelled head. "You see the outer sarcophagus with the inscriptions is missing. Lot 249 is all the title he has now. You see it printed on his case. That was his number in the auction at which I picked him up."

"He has been a very pretty sort of fellow in his day," remarked Abercrombie Smith.

"He has been a giant. His mummy is six feet seven in length, and that would be a giant over there, for they were never a very robust race. Feel these great, knotted bones, too. He would be a nasty fellow to tackle."

"Perhaps these very hands helped to build the stones into the pyramids," suggested Monkhouse Lee, looking down with disgust in his eyes at the crooked, unclean talons.

"No fear. This fellow has been pickled in natron, and looked after in the most approved style. They did not serve hodsmen in that fashion. Salt or bitumen was enough for them. It has been calculated that this sort of thing cost about seven hundred and thirty pounds in our money. Our friend was a noble at the least. What do you make of that small inscription near his feet, Smith?"

"I told you that I know no Eastern tongue."

"Ah, so you did. It is the name of the embalmer, I take it. A very conscientious worker he must have been. I wonder how many modern works will survive four thousand years?"

He kept on speaking lightly and rapidly, but it was evident to Abercrombie Smith that he was still palpitating with fear. His hands shook, his lower lip trembled, and look where he would, his eye always came sliding round to his gruesome companion. Through all his fear, however, there was a suspicion of triumph in his tone and manner. His eyes shone, and his footstep, as he paced the room, was brisk and jaunty. He gave the impression of a man who has gone through an ordeal, the marks of which he still bears upon him, but which has helped him to his end.

"You're not going yet?" he cried, as Smith rose from the sofa.

At the prospect of solitude, his fears seemed to crowd back upon him, and he stretched out a hand to detain him.

"Yes, I must go. I have my work to do. You are all right now. I think that with your nervous system you should take up some less morbid study."

"Oh, I am not nervous as a rule; and I have unwrapped mummies before."

"You fainted last time," observed Monkhouse Lee.

"Ah, yes, so I did. Well, I must have a nerve tonic or a course of electricity. You are not going, Lee?"

"I'll do whatever you wish, Ned."

"Then I'll come down with you and have a shakedown on your sofa. Good-night, Smith. I am so sorry to have disturbed you with my foolishness."

They shook hands, and as the medical student stumbled up the spiral and irregular stair he heard a key turn in a door, and the steps of his two new acquaintances as they descended to the lower floor.

In this strange way began the acquaintance between Edward Bellingham and Abercrombie Smith, an acquaintance which the latter, at least, had no desire to push further. Bellingham, however, appeared to have taken a fancy to his rough-spoken neighbour, and made his advances in such a way that he could hardly be repulsed without absolute brutality. Twice he called to thank Smith for his assistance, and many times afterwards he looked in with books, papers, and such other civilities as two bachelor neighbours can offer each other. He was, as Smith soon found, a man of wide reading, with catholic tastes and an extra-ordinary memory. His manner, too, was so pleasing and suave that one came, after a time, to overlook his repellent appearance. For a jaded and wearied man he was no unpleasant companion, and Smith found himself, after a time, looking forward to his visits, and even returning them.

Clever as he undoubtedly was, however, the medical student seemed to detect a dash of insanity in the man. He broke out at times into a high, inflated style of talk which was in contrast with the simplicity of his life.

"It is a wonderful thing," he cried, "to feel that one can command powers of good and evil—a ministering angel or a demon of vengeance." And again, of Monkhouse Lee, he said—"Lee is a good fellow, an honest fellow, but he is without strength or ambition. He would not make a fit partner for a man with a great enterprise. He would not make a fit partner for me."

At such hints and innuendoes stolid Smith, puffing solemnly at his pipe, would simply raise his eyebrows and shake his head, with little interjections of medical wisdom as to earlier hours and fresher air.

One habit Bellingham had developed of late which Smith knew to be a frequent herald of a weakening mind. He appeared to be forever talking to himself. At late hours of the night, when there could be no visitor with him, Smith could still hear his voice beneath him in a low, muffled monologue, sunk almost to a whisper, and yet very audible in the silence. This solitary babbling annoyed and distracted the student, so that he spoke more than once to his neighbour about it. Bellingham, however, flushed up at the charge, and denied curtly that he had uttered a sound; indeed, he showed more annoyance over the matter than the occasion seemed to demand.

Had Abercrombie Smith had any doubt as to his own ears he had not to go far to find corroboration. Tom Styles, the little wrinkled man-servant who had attended to the wants of the lodgers in the turret for a longer time than any man's memory could carry him, was sorely put to it over the same matter.

"If you please, sir," said he, as he tidied down the top chamber one morning, "do you think Mr. Bellingham is all right, sir?"

"All right, Styles?"

"Yes, sir. Right in his head, sir."

"Why should he not be, then?"

"Well, I don't know, sir. His habits has changed of late. He's not the same man he used to be, though I make free to say that he was never quite one of my gentlemen, like Mr. Hastie or yourself, sir. He's took to talkin' to himself something awful. I wonder it don't disturb you. I don't know what to make of him, sir."

"I don't know what business it is of yours, Styles."

"Well, I takes an interest, Mr. Smith. It may be forward of me, but I can't help it. I feel sometimes as if I was mother and father to my young gentlemen. It all falls on me when things go wrong and the relations come. But Mr. Bellingham, sir. I want to know what it is that walks about his room sometimes when he's out and when the door's locked on the outside."

"Eh? You're talking nonsense, Styles."

"Maybe so, sir; but I heard it more'n once with my own ears."

"Rubbish, Styles."

"Very good, sir. You'll ring the bell if you want me."

Abercrombie Smith gave little heed to the gossip of the old man-servant, but a small incident occurred a few days later which left an unpleasant effect upon his mind, and brought the words of Styles forcibly to his memory.

Bellingham had come up to see him late one night, and was entertaining him with an interesting account of the rock tombs of Beni Hassan in Upper Egypt, when Smith, whose hearing was remarkably acute, distinctly heard the sound of a door opening on the landing below.

"There's some fellow gone in or out of your room," he remarked.

Bellingham sprang up and stood helpless for a moment, with
the expression of a man who is half incredulous and half afraid.

"I surely locked it. I am almost positive that I locked it," he
stammered. "No one could have opened it."

"Why, I hear someone coming up the steps now," said Smith.

Bellingham rushed out through the door, slammed it loudly
behind him, and hurried down the stairs. About halfway down
Smith heard him stop, and thought he caught the sound of
whispering. A moment later the door beneath him shut, a key
creaked in a lock, and Bellingham, with beads of moisture upon
his pale face, ascended the stairs once more, and re-entered the
room.

"It's all right," he said, throwing himself down in a chair. "It
was that fool of a dog. He had pushed the door open. I don't
know how I came to forget to lock it."

"I didn't know you kept a dog," said Smith, looking very
thoughtfully at the disturbed face of his companion.

"Yes, I haven't had him long. I must get rid of him. He's a
great nuisance."

"He must be, if you find it so hard to shut him up. I should
have thought that shutting the door would have been enough,
without locking it."

"I want to prevent old Styles from letting him out. He's of
some value, you know, and it would be awkward to lose him."

"I am a bit of a dog fancier myself," said Smith, still gazing
hard at his companion from the corner of his eyes. "Perhaps
you'll let me have a look at it."

"Certainly. But I am afraid it cannot be to-night; I have an
appointment. Is that clock right? Then I am a quarter of an hour
late already. You'll excuse me, I am sure."

He picked up his cap and hurried from the room. In spite of
his appointment, Smith heard him re-enter his own chamber and
lock his door upon the inside.

This interview left a disagreeable impression upon the medical
student's mind. Bellingham had lied to him, and lied so clumsily
that it looked as if he had desperate reasons for concealing the
truth. Smith knew that his neighbour had no dog. He knew,
also, that the step which he had heard upon the stairs was not the
step of an animal. But if it were not, then what could it be?
There was old Styles's statement about the something that used

to pace the room at times when the owner was absent. Could it be a woman? Smith rather inclined to the view. If so, it would mean disgrace and expulsion to Bellingham if it were discovered by the authorities, so that his anxiety and falsehoods might be accounted for. And yet it was inconceivable that an undergraduate could keep a woman in his rooms without being instantly detected. Be the explanation what it might, there was something ugly about it, and Smith determined, as he turned to his books, to discourage all further attempts at intimacy on the part of his soft-spoken and ill-favoured neighbour.

But his work was destined to interruption that night. He had hardly caught up the broken threads when a firm, heavy footfall came three steps at a time from below, and Hastie, in blazer and flannels, burst into the room.

"Still at it!" said he, plumping down into his wonted armchair. "What a chap you are to stew! I believe an earthquake might come and knock Oxford into a cocked hat, and you would sit perfectly placid with your books among the ruins. However, I won't bore you long. Three whiffs of baccy, and I am off."

"What's the news, then?" asked Smith, cramming a plug of bird's-eye into his brier with his forefinger.

"Nothing very much. Wilson made seventy for the freshmen against the eleven. They say that they will play him instead of Buddicomb, for Buddicomb is clean off colour. He used to be able to bowl a little, but it's nothing but half volleys and long hops now."

"Medium right," suggested Smith, with the intense gravity that comes upon a 'varsity man when he speaks of athletics.

"Inclining to fast, with a work from leg. Comes with the arm about three inches or so. He used to be nasty on a wet wicket. Oh, by the way, have you heard about Long Norton?"

"What's that?"

"He's been attacked."

"Attacked?"

"Yes, just as he was turning out of the High Street, and within a hundred yards of the gate of Old's."

"But who — "

"Ah, that's the rub! If you said 'what,' you would be more grammatical. Norton swears that it was not human, and, indeed, from the scratches on his throat, I should be inclined to agree with him."

"What, then? Have we come down to spooks?"

Abercrombie Smith puffed his scientific contempt.

"Well, no; I don't think that is quite the idea, either. I am inclined to think that if any showman has lost a great ape lately, and the brute is in these parts, a jury would find a true bill against it. Norton passes that way every night, you know, about the same hour. There's a tree that hangs low over the path—the big elm from Rainy's garden. Norton thinks the thing dropped on him out of the tree. Anyhow, he was nearly strangled by two arms, which, he says, were as strong and as thin as steel bands. He saw nothing; only those beastly arms that tightened and tightened on him. He yelled his head off, and a couple of chaps came running, and the thing went over the wall like a cat. He never got a fair sight of it the whole time. It gave Norton a shake up, I can tell you. I tell him it has been as good as a change at the seaside for him."

"A garroter, most likely," said Smith.

"Very possibly. Norton says not; but we don't mind what he says. The garroter has long nails, and was pretty smart at swinging himself over walls. By the way, your beautiful neighbour would be pleased if he heard about it. He had a grudge against Norton, and he's not a man, from what I know of him, to forget his little debts. But hallo, old chap, what have you got in your noddle?"

"Nothing," Smith answered curtly.

He had started in his chair, and the look had flashed over his face which comes upon a man who is struck suddenly by some unpleasant idea.

"You looked as if something I had said had taken you on the raw. By the way, you have made the acquaintance of Master B. since I looked in last, have you not? Young Monkhouse Lee told me something to that effect."

"Yes; I know him slightly. He has been up here once or twice."

"Well, you're big enough and ugly enough to take care of yourself. He's not what I should call exactly a healthy sort of Johnny, though, no doubt, he's very clever, and all that. But you'll soon find out for yourself. Lee is all right; he's a very decent little fellow. Well, so long, old chap! I row Mullins for the Vice-Chancellor's pot on Wednesday week, so mind you come down, in case I don't see you before."

Bovine Smith laid down his pipe and turned stolidly to his books once more. But with all the will in the world, he found it very hard to keep his mind upon his work. It would slip away to brood upon the man beneath him, and upon the little mystery which hung round his chambers. Then his thoughts turned to this singular attack of which Hastie had spoken, and to the grudge which Bellingham was said to owe the object of it. The two ideas would persist in rising together in his mind, as though there were some close and intimate connection between them. And yet the suspicion was so dim and vague that it could not be put down in words.

"Confound the chap!" cried Smith, as he shied his book on pathology across the room. "He has spoiled my night's reading, and that's reason enough, if there were no other, why I should steer clear of him in the future."

For ten days the medical student confined himself so closely to his studies that he neither saw nor heard anything of either of the men beneath him. At the hours when Bellingham had been accustomed to visit him, he took care to sport his oak, and though he more than once heard a knocking at his outer door, he resolutely refused to answer it. One afternoon, however, he was descending the stairs when, just as he was passing it, Bellingham's door flew open, and young Monkhouse Lee came out with his eyes sparkling and a dark flush of anger upon his olive cheeks. Close at his heels followed Bellingham, his fat, unhealthy face all quivering with malignant passion.

"You fool!" he hissed. "You'll be sorry."

"Very likely," cried the other. "Mind what I say. It's off! I won't hear of it!"

"You've promised, anyhow."

"Oh, I'll keep that! I won't speak. But I'd rather little Eva was in her grave. Once for all, it's off. She'll do what I say. We don't want to see you again."

So much Smith could not avoid hearing, but he hurried on, for he had no wish to be involved in their dispute. There had been a serious breach between them, that was clear enough, and Lee was going to cause the engagement with his sister to be broken off. Smith thought of Hastie's comparison of the toad and the dove, and was glad to think that the matter was at an end. Bellingham's face when he was in a passion was not pleasant to look upon. He was not a man to whom an innocent girl could be trusted for life. As he walked, Smith wondered languidly what could have caused the quarrel, and what the promise might be which Bellingham had been so anxious that Monkhouse Lee should keep.

It was the day of the sculling match between Hastie and Mullins, and a stream of men were making their way down to the banks of the Isis. A May sun was shining brightly, and the yellow path was barred with the black shadows of the tall elm trees. On either side the grey colleges lay back from the road, the hoary old mothers of minds looking out from their high, mullioned windows at the tide of young life which swept so merrily past them. Black-clad tutors, prim officials, pale reading men, brown-faced straw-hatted young athletes in white sweaters or many-coloured blazers, all were hurrying towards the blue, winding river which curves through the Oxford meadows.

Abercrombie Smith, with the intuition of an old oarsman, chose his position at the point where he knew that the struggle, if there were a struggle, would come. Far off he heard the hum that announced the start, the gathering roar of the approach, the thunder of running feet, and the shouts of the men in the boats beneath him. A spray of half-clad, deep-breathing runners shot past him, and craning over their shoulders, he saw Hastie pulling a steady thirty-six, while his opponent, with a jerky forty, was a good boat's length behind him. Smith gave a cheer for his friend, and pulling out his watch, was starting off again for his chambers, when he felt a touch upon his shoulder, and found that young Monkhouse Lee was beside him.

"I saw you there," he said, in a timid, deprecating way. "I wanted to speak to you, if you could spare me a half hour. This cottage is mine. I share it with Harrington of King's. Come in and have a cup of tea."

"I must be back presently," said Smith. "I am hard on the grind at present. But I'll come in for a few minutes with pleasure. I wouldn't have come out only Hastie is a friend of mine."

"So he is of mine. Hasn't he a beautiful style? Mullins wasn't in it. But come into the cottage. It's a little den of a place, but it is pleasant to work in during the summer months."

It was a small, square, white building, with green doors and shutters, and a rustic trelliswork porch, standing back some fifty

yards from the river's bank. Inside, the main room was roughly
fitted up as a study—deal table, unpainted shelves with books,
and a few cheap oleographs upon the wall. A kettle sang upon a
spirit-stove, and there were tea things upon a tray on the table.

"Try that chair and have a cigarette," said Lee. "Let me pour
you out a cup of tea. It's so good of you to come in, for I know
that your time is a good deal taken up. I wanted to say to you
that, if I were you, I should change my rooms at once."

"Eh?"

Smith sat staring with a lighted match in one hand and his
unlit cigarette in the other.

"Yes; it must seem very extraordinary, and the worst of it is
that I cannot give my reasons, for I am under a solemn promise
—a very solemn promise. But I may go so far as to say that I
don't think Bellingham is a very safe man to live near. I intend to
camp out here as much as I can for a time."

"Not safe! What do you mean?"

"Ah, that's what I mustn't say. But do take my advice and
move your rooms. We had a grand row today. You must have
heard us, for you came down the stairs."

"I saw that you had fallen out."

"He's a horrible chap, Smith. That is the only word for him. I
have had doubts about him ever since that night when he fainted
—you remember, when you came down. I taxed him today, and
he told me things that made my hair rise, and wanted me to
stand in with him. I'm not straight-laced, but I am a clergyman's
son, you know, and I think there are some things which are quite
beyond the pale. I only thank God that I found him out before it
was too late, for he was to have married into my family."

"That is all very fine, Lee," said Abercrombie Smith curtly.
"But either you are saying a great deal too much or a great deal
too little."

"I give you a warning."

"If there is real reason for warning, no promise can bind you.
If I see a rascal about to blow a place up with dynamite no
pledge will stand in my way of preventing him."

"Ah, but I cannot prevent him, and I can do nothing but warn
you."

"Without saying what you warn me against."

"Against Bellingham."

"But that is childish. Why should I fear him, or any man?"

"I can't tell you. I can only entreat you to change your rooms. You are in danger where you are. I don't even say that Bellingham would wish to injure you. But it might happen, for he is a dangerous neighbour just now."

"Perhaps I know more than you think," said Smith, looking keenly at the young man's boyish, earnest face. "Suppose I tell you that someone else shares Bellingham's rooms."

Monkhouse Lee sprang from his chair in uncontrollable excitement.

"You know, then?" he gasped.

"A woman."

Lee dropped back again with a groan.

"My lips are sealed," he said. "I must not speak."

"Well, anyhow," said Smith, rising, "it is not likely that I should allow myself to be frightened out of rooms which suit me very nicely. It would be a little too feeble for me to move out all my goods and chattels because you say that Bellingham might in some unexplained way do me an injury. I think that I'll just take my chance, and stay where I am, and as I see that it's nearly five o'clock, I must ask you to excuse me."

He bade the young student adieu in a few curt words, and made his way homeward through the sweet spring evening, feeling half ruffled, half amused, as any other strong, unimaginative man might who has been menaced by a vague and shadowy danger.

There was one little indulgence which Abercrombie Smith always allowed himself, however closely his work might press upon him. Twice a week, on the Tuesday and the Friday, it was his invariable custom to walk over to Farlingford, the residence of Dr. Plumptree Peterson, situated about a mile and a half out of Oxford. Peterson had been a close friend of Smith's elder brother, Francis, and as he was a bachelor, fairly well-to-do, with a good cellar and a better library, his house was a pleasant goal for a man who was in need of a brisk walk. Twice a week, then, the medical student would swing out there along the dark country roads and spend a pleasant hour in Peterson's comfortable study, discussing, over a glass of old port, the gossip of the 'varsity or the latest developments of medicine or of surgery.

On the day that followed his interview with Monkhouse Lee,

Smith shut up his books at a quarter past eight, the hour when
he usually started for his friend's house. As he was leaving the
room, however, his eyes chanced to fall upon one of the books
which Bellingham had lent him, and his conscience pricked him
for not having returned it. However repellent the man might be,
he should not be treated with discourtesy. Taking the book, he
walked down-stairs and knocked at his neighbour's door. There
was no answer; but on turning the handle he found that it was
unlocked. Pleased at the thought of avoiding an interview, he
stepped inside, and placed the book with his card upon the table.

The lamp was turned half down, but Smith could see the
details of the room plainly enough. It was all much as he had
seen it before — the frieze, the animal-headed gods, the hanging
crocodile, and the table littered over with papers and dried
leaves. The mummy case stood upright against the wall, but the
mummy itself was missing. There was no sign of any second
occupant of the room, and he felt as he withdrew that he had
probably done Bellingham an injustice. Had he a guilty secret to
preserve, he would hardly leave his door open so that all the
world might enter.

The spiral stair was as black as pitch, and Smith was slowly
making his way down its irregular steps, when he was suddenly
conscious that something had passed him in the darkness. There
was a faint sound, a whiff of air, a light brushing past his elbow,
but so slight that he could scarcely be certain of it. He stopped
and listened, but the wind was rustling among the ivy outside,
and he could hear nothing else.

"Is that you, Styles?" he shouted.

There was no answer, and all was still behind him. It must
have been a sudden gust of air, for there were crannies and
cracks in the old turret. And yet he could almost have sworn that
he heard a footfall by his very side. He had emerged into the
quadrangle, still turning the matter over in his head, when a man
came running swiftly across the smooth-cropped lawn.

"Is that you, Smith?"

"Hullo, Hastie!"

"For God's sake come at once! Young Lee is drowned! Here's
Harrington of King's with the news. The doctor is out. You'll
do, but come along at once. There may be life in him."

"Have you brandy?"

"No."

"I'll bring some. There's a flask on my table."

Smith bounded up the stairs, taking three at a time, seized the flask, and was rushing down with it, when, as he passed Bellingham's room his eyes fell upon something which left him gasping and staring upon the landing.

The door, which he had closed behind him, was now open, and right in front of him, with the lamplight shining upon it, was the mummy case. Three minutes ago it had been empty. He could swear to that. Now it framed the lank body of its horrible occupant, who stood, grim and stark, with his black, shrivelled face towards the door. The form was lifeless and inert, but it seemed to Smith as he gazed that there still lingered a lurid spark of vitality, some faint sign of consciousness in the little eyes which lurked in the depths of the hollow sockets. So astounded and shaken was he that he had forgotten his errand, and was still staring at the lean, sunken figure when the voice of his friend below recalled him to himself.

"Come on, Smith!" he shouted. "It's life and death, you know. Hurry up! Now, then," he added, as the medical student reappeared, "let us do a sprint. It is well under a mile, and we should do it in five minutes. A human life is better worth running for than a pot."

Neck and neck they dashed through the darkness, and did not pull up until, panting and spent, they had reached the little cottage by the river. Young Lee, limp and dripping like a broken water plant, was stretched upon the sofa, the green scum of the river upon his black hair, and a fringe of white foam upon his leaden-hued lips. Beside him knelt his fellow student, Harrington, endeavouring to chafe some warmth back into his rigid limbs.

"I think there's life in him," said Smith, with his hands to the lad's side. "Put your watch glass to his lips. Yes, there's dimming on it. You take one arm, Hastie. Now work it as I do, and we'll soon pull him round."

For ten minutes they worked in silence, inflating and depressing the chest of the unconscious man. At the end of that time a shiver ran through his body, his lips trembled, and he opened his eyes. The three students burst out into an irrepressible cheer.

"Wake up, old chap. You've frightened us quite enough."

"Have some brandy. Take a sip from the flask."

"He's all right now," said his companion Harrington. "Heavens, what a fright I got! I was reading here, and he had gone out for a stroll as far as the river, when I heard a scream and a splash. Out I ran, and by the time I could find him and fish him out, all life seemed to have gone. Then Simpson couldn't get a doctor, for he has a game leg, and I had to run, and I don't know what I'd have done without you fellows. That's right, old chap. Sit up."

Monkhouse Lee had raised himself on his hands, and looked wildly about him.

"What's up?" he asked. "I've been in the water. Ah, yes; I remember."

A look of fear came into his eyes, and he sank his face into his hands.

"How did you fall in?"

"I didn't fall in."

"How then?"

"I was thrown in. I was standing by the bank, and something from behind picked me up like a feather and hurled me in. I heard nothing, and I saw nothing. But I know what it was, for all that."

"And so do I," whispered Smith.

Lee looked up with a quick glance of surprise.

"You've learned, then?" he said. "You remember the advice I gave you?"

"Yes, and I begin to think that I shall take it."

"I don't know what the deuce you fellows are talking about," said Hastie, "but I think, if I were you, Harrington, I should get Lee to bed at once. It will be time enough to discuss the why and the wherefore when he is a little stronger. I think, Smith, you and I can leave him alone now. I am walking back to college; if you are coming in that direction, we can have a chat."

But it was little chat that they had upon their homeward path. Smith's mind was too full of the incidents of the evening, the absence of the mummy from his neighbour's rooms, the step that passed him on the stair, the reappearance—the extraordinary, inexplicable reappearance—of the grisly thing, and then this attack upon Lee, corresponding so closely to the previous outrage upon another man against whom Bellingham bore a grudge. All this settled in his thoughts, together with the many little incidents which had previously turned him against his neighbour, and the singular circumstances under which he was first called in to him. What had been a dim suspicion, a vague, fantastic conjecture, had suddenly taken form, and stood out in his mind as a grim fact, a thing not to be denied. And yet, how monstrous it was! how unheard of! how entirely beyond all bounds of human experience. An impartial judge, or even the friend who walked by his side, would simply tell him that his eyes deceived him, that the mummy had been there all the time, that young Lee had tumbled into the river as any other man tumbles into a river, and the blue pill was the best thing for a disordered liver. He felt that he would have said as much if the positions had been reversed. And yet he could swear that Bellingham was a murderer at heart, and that he wielded a weapon such as no man had ever used in all the grim history of crime.

Hastie had branched off to his rooms with a few crisp and emphatic comments upon his friend's unsociability, and Abercrombie Smith crossed the quadrangle to his corner turret with a strong feeling of repulsion for his chambers and their associations. He would take Lee's advice, and move his quarters as soon as possible, for how could a man study when his ear was ever straining for every murmur or footstep in the room below? He observed, as he crossed over the lawn, that the light was still shining in Bellingham's window, and as he passed up the staircase the door opened, and the man himself looked out at him. With his fat, evil face he was like some bloated spider fresh from the weaving of his poisonous web.

"Good evening," said he. "Won't you come in?"

"No," cried Smith fiercely.

"No? You are as busy as ever? I wanted to ask you about Lee. I was sorry to hear that there was a rumour that something was amiss with him."

His features were grave, but there was the gleam of a hidden laugh in his eyes as he spoke. Smith saw it, and he could have knocked him down for it.

"You'll be sorrier still to hear that Monkhouse Lee is doing very well, and is out of all danger," he answered. "Your hellish tricks have not come off this time. Oh, you needn't try to brazen it out. I know all about it."

Bellingham took a step back from the angry student, and half closed the door as if to protect himself.

"You are mad," he said. "What do you mean? Do you assert that I had anything to do with Lee's accident?"

"Yes," thundered Smith. "You and that bag of bones behind you; you worked it between you. I tell you what it is, Master B., they have given up burning folk like you, but we still keep a hangman, and, by George! if any man in this college meets his death while you are here, I'll have you up, and if you don't swing for it, it won't be my fault. You'll find that your filthy Egyptian tricks won't answer in England."

"You're a raving lunatic," said Bellingham.

"All right. You just remember what I say, for you'll find that I'll be better than my word."

The door slammed, and Smith went fuming up to his chamber, where he locked the door upon the inside, and spent half the night in smoking his old brier, and brooding over the strange events of the evening.

Next morning Abercrombie Smith heard nothing of his neighbour, but Harrington called upon him in the afternoon to say that Lee was almost himself again. All day Smith stuck fast to his work, but in the evening he determined to pay the visit to his friend Dr. Peterson upon which he had started the night before. A good walk and a friendly chat would be welcome to his jangled nerves.

Bellingham's door was shut as he passed, but glancing back when he was some distance from the turret, he saw his neighbour's head at the window outlined against the lamplight, his face pressed apparently against the glass as he gazed out into the darkness. It was a blessing to be away from all contact with him, if but for a few hours, and Smith stepped out briskly, and breathed the soft spring air into his lungs. The half moon lay in the west between two Gothic pinnacles, and threw upon the silvered street a dark tracery from the stonework above. There was a brisk breeze, and light, fleecy clouds drifted swiftly across the sky. Old's was on the very border of the town, and in five minutes Smith found himself beyond the houses and between the hedges of a May-scented Oxfordshire lane.

It was a lonely and little-frequented road which led to his friend's house. Early as it was, Smith did not meet a single soul upon his way. He walked briskly along until he came to the avenue gate, which opened into the long, gravel drive leading up to Farlingford. In front of him he could see the cozy, red light of the windows glimmering through the foliage. He stood with his hand upon the iron latch of the swinging gate, and he glanced back at the road along which he had come. Something was coming swiftly down it.

It moved in the shadow of the hedge, silently and furtively, a dark, crouching figure, dimly visible against the black background. Even as he gazed back at it, it had lessened its distance by twenty paces, and was fast closing upon him. Out of the darkness he had a glimpse of a scraggy neck, and of two eyes that will ever haunt him in his dreams. He turned, and with a cry of terror he ran for his life up the avenue. There were the red lights, the signals of safety, almost within a stone's throw of him. He was a famous runner, but never had he run as he ran that night.

The heavy gate had swung into place behind him but he heard it dash open again before his pursuer. As he rushed madly and wildly through the night, he could hear a swift, dry patter behind him, and could see, as he threw back a glance, that this horror was bounding like a tiger at his heels, with blazing eyes and one stringy arm outthrown. Thank God, the door was ajar. He could see the thin bar of light which shot from the lamp in the hall. Nearer yet sounded the clatter from behind. He heard a hoarse gurgling at his very shoulder. With a shriek he flung himself against the door, slammed and bolted it behind him, and sank half fainting on the hall chair.

"My goodness, Smith, what's the matter?" asked Peterson, appearing at the door of his study.

"Give me some brandy."

Peterson disappeared, and came rushing out again with a glass and a decanter.

"You need it," he said, as his visitor drank off what he poured out for him. "Why, man, you are as white as a cheese."

Smith laid down his glass, rose up, and took a deep breath.

"I am my own man again now," said he. "I was never so unmanned before. But, with your leave, Peterson, I will sleep here to-night, for I don't think I could face that road again except by daylight. It's weak, I know, but I can't help it."

Peterson looked at his visitor with a very questioning eye.

"Of course you shall sleep here if you wish. I'll tell Mrs.
Burney to make up the spare bed. Where are you off to now?"

"Come up with me to the window that overlooks the door. I
want you to see what I have seen."

They went up to the window of the upper hall whence they
could look down upon the approach to the house. The drive and
the fields on either side lay quiet and still, bathed in the peaceful
moonlight.

"Well, really, Smith," remarked Peterson, "it is well that I
know you to be an abstemious man. What in the world can have
frightened you?"

"I'll tell you presently. But where can it have gone? Ah, now,
look, look! See the curve of the road just beyond your gate."

"Yes, I see; you needn't pinch my arm off. I saw someone
pass. I should say a man, rather thin, apparently, and tall, very
tall. But what of him? And what of yourself? You are still
shaking like an aspen leaf."

"I have been within handgrip of the devil, that's all. But come
down to your study, and I shall tell you the whole story."

He did so. Under the cheery lamplight with a glass of wine on
the table beside him, and the portly form and florid face of his
friend in front, he narrated, in their order, all the events, great
and small, which had formed so singular a chain, from the night
on which he had found Bellingham fainting in front of the
mummy case until this horrid experience of an hour ago.

"There now," he said as he concluded, "that's the whole, black
business. It is monstrous and incredible, but it is true."

Doctor Plumptree Peterson sat for some time in silence with a
very puzzled expression upon his face.

"I never heard of such a thing in my life, never!" he said at
last. "You have told me the facts. Now tell me your inferences."

"You can draw your own."

"But I should like to hear yours. You have thought over the
matter, and I have not."

"Well, it must be a little vague in detail, but the main points
seem to me to be clear enough. This fellow Bellingham, in his
Eastern studies, has got hold of some infernal secret by which a
mummy—or possibly only this particular mummy—can be
temporarily brought to life. He was trying this disgusting

business on the night when he fainted. No doubt the sight of the creature moving had shaken his nerve, even though he had expected it. You remember that almost the first words he said were to call out upon himself as a fool. Well, he got more hardened afterward, and carried the matter through without fainting. The vitality which he could put into it was evidently only a passing thing, for I have seen it continually in its case as dead as this table. He has some elaborate process, I fancy, by which he brings the thing to pass. Having done it, he naturally bethought him that he might use the creature as an agent. It has intelligence and it has strength. For some purpose he took Lee into his confidence; but Lee, like a decent Christian, would have nothing to do with such a business. Then they had a row, and Lee vowed that he would tell his sister of Bellingham's true character. Bellingham's game was to prevent him, and he nearly managed it, by setting this creature of his on his track. He had already tried its powers upon another man — Norton — towards whom he had a grudge. It is the merest chance that he has not two murders upon his soul. Then, when I taxed him with the matter, he had the strongest reasons for wishing to get me out of the way before I could convey my knowledge to anyone else. He got his chance when I went out, for he knew my habits and where I was bound for. I have had a narrow shave, Peterson, and it is mere luck you didn't find me on your doorstep in the morning. I'm not a nervous man as a rule, and I never thought to have the fear of death put upon me as it was to-night."

"My dear boy, you take the matter too seriously," said his companion. "Your nerves are out of order with your work, and you make too much of it. How could such a thing as this stride about the streets of Oxford, even at night, without being seen?"

"It has been seen. There is quite a scare in the town about an escaped ape, as they imagine the creature to be. It is the talk of the place."

"Well, it's a striking chain of events. And yet, my dear fellow, you must allow that each incident in itself is capable of a more natural explanation."

"What! even my adventure of to-night?"

"Certainly. You come out with your nerves all unstrung, and your head full of this theory of yours. Some gaunt, half-famished tramp steals after you, and seeing you run, is emboldened to pursue you. Your fears and imagination do the rest."

"It won't do, Peterson; it won't do."

"And again, in the instance of your finding the mummy case empty, and then a few moments later with an occupant, you know that it was lamplight, that the lamp was half-turned down, and that you had no special reason to look hard at the case. It is quite possible that you may have overlooked the creature in the first instance."

"No, no; it is out of the question."

"And then Lee may have fallen into the river, and Norton been garroted. It is certainly a formidable indictment that you have against Bellingham; but if you were to place it before a police magistrate, he would simply laugh in your face."

"I know he would. That is why I mean to take the matter into my own hands."

"Eh?"

"Yes; I feel that a public duty rests upon me, and, besides, I must do it for my own safety, unless I choose to allow myself to be hunted by this beast out of the college, and that would be a little too feeble. I have quite made up my mind what I shall do. And first of all, may I use your paper and pens for an hour?"

"Most certainly. You will find all that you want upon that side table."

Abercrombie Smith sat down before a sheet of foolscap, and for an hour, and then for a second hour, his pen travelled swiftly over it. Page after page was finished and tossed aside while his friend leaned back in his armchair, looking across at him with patient curiosity. At last, with an exclamation of satisfaction, Smith sprang to his feet, gathered his papers up into order, and laid the last one upon Peterson's desk.

"Kindly sign this as a witness," he said.

"A witness? Of what?"

"Of my signature, and of the date. The date is the most important. Why, Peterson, my life might hang upon it."

"My dear Smith, you are talking wildly. Let me beg you to go to bed."

"On the contrary, I never spoke so deliberately in my life. And I will promise to go to bed the moment you have signed it."

"But what is it?"

"It is a statement of all that I have been telling you to-night. I wish you to witness it."

"Certainly," said Peterson, signing his name under that of his companion. "There you are! But what is the idea?"

"You will kindly retain it, and produce it in case I am arrested."

"Arrested? For what?"

"For murder. It is quite on the cards. I wish to be ready for every event. There is only one course open to me, and I am determined to take it."

"For heaven's sake, don't do anything rash!"

"Believe me, it would be far more rash to adopt any other course. I hope that we won't need to bother you, but it will ease my mind to know that you have this statement of my motives. And now I am ready to take your advice and to go to roost, for I want to be at my best in the morning."

Abercrombie Smith was not an entirely pleasant man to have as an enemy. Slow and easy tempered, he was formidable when driven to action. He brought to every purpose in life the same deliberate resoluteness that had distinguished him as a scientific student. He had laid his studies aside for a day, but he intended that the day should not be wasted. Not a word did he say to his host as to his plans, but by nine o'clock he was well on his way to Oxford.

In the High Street he stopped at Clifford's, the gunmaker's, and bought a heavy revolver, with a box of centre-fire cartridges. Six of them he slipped into the chambers, and half cocking the weapon, placed it in the pocket of his coat. He then made his way to Hastie's rooms, where the big oarsman was lounging over his breakfast, with the *Sporting Times* propped up against the coffee pot.

"Hullo! What's up?" he asked. "Have some coffee?"

"No, thank you. I want you to come with me, Hastie, and do what I ask you."

"Certainly, my boy."

"And bring a heavy stick with you."

"Hullo!" Hastie stared. "Here's a hunting crop that would fell an ox."

"One other thing. You have a box of amputating knives. Give me the longest of them."

"There you are. You seem to be fairly on the war trail. Anything else?"

"No; that will do." Smith placed the knife inside his coat, and led the way to the quadrangle. "We are neither of us chickens, Hastie," said he. "I think I can do this job alone, but I take you as a precaution. I am going to have a little talk with Bellingham. If I have only him to deal with, I won't, of course, need you. If I shout, however, up you come, and lam out with your whip as hard as you can lick. Do you understand?"

"All right. I'll come if I hear you bellow."

"Stay here, then. I may be a little time, but don't budge until I come down."

"I'm a fixture."

Smith ascended the stairs, opened Bellingham's door and stepped in. Bellingham was seated behind his table, writing. Beside him, among his litter of strange possessions, towered the mummy case, with its sale number 249 still stuck upon its front, and its hideous occupant stiff and stark within it. Smith looked very deliberately round him, closed the door, and then, stepping across to the fireplace, struck a match and set the fire alight. Bellingham sat staring, with amazement and rage upon his bloated face.

"Well, really now, you make yourself at home," he gasped.

Smith sat himself deliberately down, placing his watch upon the table, drew out his pistol, cocked it, and laid it in his lap. Then he took the long amputation knife from his bosom, and threw it down in front of Bellingham.

"Now, then," said he, "just get to work and cut up that mummy."

"Oh, is that it?" said Bellingham with a sneer.

"Yes, that is it. They tell me that the law can't touch you. But I have a law that will set matters straight. If in five minutes you have not set to work, I swear by the God who made me that I will put a bullet through your brain!"

"You would murder me?"

Bellingham had half risen, and his face was the colour of putty.

"Yes."

"And for what?"

"To stop your mischief. One minute has gone."

"But what have I done?"

"I know and you know."

"This is mere bullying."

"Two minutes are gone."

"But you must give reasons. You are a madman—a dangerous madman. Why should I destroy my own property? It is a valuable mummy."

"You must cut it up, and you must burn it."

"I will do no such thing."

"Four minutes are gone."

Smith took up the pistol and he looked toward Bellingham with an inexorable face. As the second-hand stole round, he raised his hand, and the finger twitched on the trigger.

"There! there! I'll do it!" screamed Bellingham.

In frantic haste he caught up the knife and hacked at the figure of the mummy, ever glancing round to see the eye and the weapon of his terrible visitor bent upon him. The creature crackled and snapped under every stab of the keen blade. A thick, yellow dust rose up from it. Spices and dried essences rained down upon the floor. Suddenly, with a rending crack, its backbone snapped asunder, and it fell, a brown heap of sprawling limbs, upon the floor.

"Now into the fire!" said Smith.

The flames leaped and roared as the dried and tinderlike débris was piled upon it. The little room was like the stokehole of a steamer and the sweat ran down the faces of the two men; but still the one stooped and worked, while the other sat watching him with a set face. A thick, fat smoke oozed out from the fire, and a heavy smell of burned resin and singed hair filled the air. In a quarter of an hour a few charred and brittle sticks were all that was left of Lot No. 249.

"Perhaps that will satisfy you," snarled Bellingham, with hate and fear in his little grey eyes as he glanced back at his tormentor.

"No; I must make a clean sweep of all your materials. We must have no more devil's tricks. In with all these leaves! They may have something to do with it."

"And what now?" asked Bellingham, when the leaves also had been added to the blaze.

"Now the roll of papyrus which you had on the table that night. It is in that drawer, I think."

"No, no," shouted Bellingham. "Don't burn that! Why, man, you don't know what you do. It is unique; it contains wisdom which is nowhere else to be found."

"Out with it!"

"But look here, Smith, you can't really mean it. I'll share the knowledge with you. I'll teach you all that is in it. Or, stay, let me only copy it before you burn it!"

Smith stepped forward and turned the key in the drawer. Taking out the yellow, curled roll of paper, he threw it into the fire, and pressed it down with his heel. Bellingham screamed, and grabbed at it; but Smith pushed him back and stood over it until it was reduced to a formless, grey ash.

"Now, Master B.," said he, "I think I have pretty well drawn your teeth. You'll hear from me again, if you return to your old tricks. And now good morning, for I must go back to my studies."

And such is the narrative of Abercrombie Smith as to the singular events that occurred in Old College, Oxford, in the spring of '84. As Bellingham left the university immediately afterwards, and was last heard of in the Soudan, there is no one who can contradict his statement. But the wisdom of men is small, and the ways of Nature are strange, and who shall put a bound to the dark things that may be found by those who seek for them?

The Los Amigos Fiasco

Doyle was a prolific contributor to the pages of THE IDLER *during 1892–95, and his subjects ranged from a nonfiction article on the Arctic to stories of medical life to an autobiographical novel. In "The Los Amigos Fiasco," he even indulged in a little nineteenth-century science fiction, and had the good sense to infuse it with the kind of outrageous humor at which he excelled.*

I USED to be the leading practitioner of Los Amigos. Of course, everyone has heard of the great electrical generating gear there. The town is wide spread, and there are dozens of little townlets and villages all round, which receive their supply from the same centre, so that the works are on a very large scale. The Los Amigos folk say that they are the largest upon earth, but then we claim that for everything in Los Amigos except the gaol and the death-rate. Those are said to be the smallest.

Now, with so fine an electrical supply, it seemed to be a sinful waste of hemp that Los Amigos criminals should perish in the old-fashioned manner. And then came the news of the electro-cutions in the East, and how the results had not after all been so instantaneous as had been hoped. The Western engineers raised their eyebrows when they read of the puny shocks by which these men had perished, and they vowed in Los Amigos that when an irreclaimable came their way he should be dealt handsomely by, and have the run of all the big dynamos. There should be no reserve, said the engineers, but he should have all that they had got. And what the result of that would be none could predict, save that it must be absolutely blasting and deadly. Never before had a man been so charged with electricity as they would charge him. He was to be smitten by the essence of ten thunderbolts. Some prophesied combustion, and some disintegration and disappearance. They were waiting eagerly to settle the question

by actual demonstration, and it was just at that moment that
Duncan Warner came that way.

Warner had been wanted by the law, and by nobody else, for
many years. Desperado, murderer, train robber, and road agent,
he was a man beyond the pale of human pity. He had deserved a
dozen deaths, and the Los Amigos folk grudged him so gaudy a
one as that. He seemed to feel himself to be unworthy of it, for
he made two frenzied attempts at escape. He was a powerful,
muscular man, with a lion head, tangled black locks, and a
sweeping beard which covered his broad chest. When he was
tried, there was no finer head in all the crowded court. It's no
new thing to find the best face looking from the dock. But his
good looks could not balance his bad deeds. His advocate did all
he knew, but the cards lay against him, and Duncan Warner was
handed over to the mercy of the big Los Amigos dynamos.

I was there at the committee meeting when the matter was
discussed. The town council had chosen four experts to look
after the arrangements. Three of them were admirable. There
was Joseph M'Connor, the very man who had designed the
dynamos, and there was Joshua Westmacott, the chairman of
the Los Amigos Electrical Supply Company, Limited. Then
there was myself as the chief medical man, and lastly an old
German of the name of Peter Stulpnagel. The Germans were a
strong body at Los Amigos, and they all voted for their man.
That was how he got on the committee. It was said that he had
been a wonderful electrician at home, and he was eternally
working with wires and insulators and Leyden jars; but, as he
never seemed to get any further, or to have any results worth
publishing, he came at last to be regarded as a harmless crank,
who had made science his hobby. We three practical men smiled
when we heard that he had been elected as our colleague, and at
the meeting we fixed it all up very nicely among ourselves without
much thought of the old fellow who sat with his ears scooped
forward in his hands, for he was a trifle hard of hearing, taking
no more part in the proceedings than the gentlemen of the press
who scribbled their notes on the back benches.

We did not take long to settle it all. In New York a strength of
some two thousand volts had been used, and death had not been
instantaneous. Evidently their shock had been too weak. Los
Amigos should not fall into that error. The charge should be six

times greater, and therefore, of course, it would be six times more effective. Nothing could possibly be more logical. The whole concentrated force of the great dynamos should be employed on Duncan Warner.

So we three settled it, and had already risen to break up the meeting, when our silent companion opened his mouth for the first time.

"Gentlemen," said he, "you appear to me to show an extraordinary ignorance upon the subject of electricity. You have not mastered the first principles of its actions upon a human being."

The committee was about to break into an angry reply to this brusque comment, but the chairman of the Electrical Company tapped his forehead to claim its indulgence for the crankiness of the speaker.

"Pray tell us, sir," said he, with an ironical smile, "what is there in our conclusions with which you find fault?"

"With your assumption that a large dose of electricity will merely increase the effect of a small dose. Do you not think it possible that it might have an entirely different result? Do you know anything, by actual experiment, of the effect of such powerful shocks?"

"We know it by analogy," said the chairman, pompously. "All drugs increase their effect when they increase their dose; for example — for example — "

"Whisky," said Joseph M'Connor.

"Quite so. Whisky. You see it there."

Peter Stulpnagel smiled and shook his head.

"Your argument is not very good," said he. "When I used to take whisky, I used to find that one glass would excite me, but that six would send me to sleep, which is just the opposite. Now, suppose that electricity were to act in just the opposite way also, what then?"

We three practical men burst out laughing. We had known that our colleague was queer, but we never had thought that he would be as queer as this.

"What then?" repeated Peter Stulpnagel.

"We'll take our chances," said the chairman.

"Pray consider," said Peter, "that workmen who have touched the wires, and who have received shocks of only a few hundred volts, have died instantly. The fact is well known. And yet when a much greater force was used upon a criminal at New York, the man struggled for some little time. Do you not clearly see that the smaller dose is the more deadly?"

"I think, gentlemen, that this discussion has been carried on quite long enough," said the chairman, rising again. "The point, I take it, has already been decided by the majority of the committee, and Duncan Warner shall be electrocuted on Tuesday by the full strength of the Los Amigos dynamos. Is it not so?"

"I agree," said Joseph M'Connor.

"I agree," said I.

"And I protest," said Peter Stulpnagel.

"Then the motion is carried, and your protest will be duly entered in the minutes," said the chairman, and so the sitting was dissolved.

The attendance at the electrocution was a very small one. We four members of the committee were, of course, present with the executioner, who was to act under their orders. The others were the United States Marshal, the governor of the gaol, the chaplain, and three members of the press. The room was a small brick chamber, forming an out-house to the Central Electrical station. It had been used as a laundry, and had an oven and copper at one side, but no other furniture save a single chair for the condemned man. A metal plate for his feet was placed in front of it, to which ran a thick, insulated wire. Above, another wire depended from the ceiling, which could be connected with a small metallic rod projecting from a cap which was to be placed upon his head. When this connection was established Duncan Warner's hour was come.

There was a solemn hush as we waited for the coming of the prisoner. The practical engineers looked a little pale, and fidgeted nervously with the wires. Even the hardened Marshal was ill at ease, for a mere hanging was one thing, and this blasting of flesh and blood a very different one. As to the pressmen, their faces were whiter than the sheets which lay before them. The only man who appeared to feel none of the influence of these preparations was the little German crank, who strolled from one to the other with a smile on his lips and mischief in his eyes. More than once he even went so far as to burst into a shout of laughter, until the chaplain sternly rebuked him for his ill-timed levity.

"How can you so far forget yourself, Mr. Stulpnagel," said he, "as to jest in the presence of death?"

But the German was quite unabashed.

"If I were in the presence of death I should not jest," said he, "but since I am not I may do what I choose."

This flippant reply was about to draw another and a sterner reproof from the chaplain, when the door was swung open and two warders entered leading Duncan Warner between them. He glanced round him with a set face, stepped resolutely forward, and seated himself upon the chair.

"Touch her off!" said he.

It was barbarous to keep him in suspense. The chaplain murmured a few words in his ear, the attendant placed the cap upon his head, and then, while we all held our breath, the wire and the metal were brought in contact.

"Great Scott!" shouted Duncan Warner.

He had bounded in his chair as the frightful shock crashed through his system. But he was not dead. On the contrary, his eyes gleamed far more brightly than they had done before. There was only one change, but it was a singular one. The black had passed from his hair and beard as the shadow passes from a landscape. They were both as white as snow. And yet there was no other sign of decay. His skin was smooth and plump and lustrous as a child's.

The Marshal looked at the committee with a reproachful eye.

"There seems to be some hitch here, gentlemen," said he.

We three practical men looked at each other.

Peter Stulpnagel smiled pensively.

"I think that another one should do it," said I.

Again the connection was made, and again Duncan Warner sprang in his chair and shouted, but, indeed, were it not that he still remained in the chair none of us would have recognized him. His hair and his beard had shredded off in an instant, and the room looked like a barber's shop on a Saturday night. There he sat, his eyes still shining, his skin radiant with the glow of perfect health, but with a scalp as bald as a Dutch cheese, and a chin without so much as a trace of down. He began to revolve one of his arms, slowly and doubtfully at first, but with more confidence as he went on.

"That jint," said he, "has puzzled half the doctors on the Pacific Slope. It's as good as new, and as limber as a hickory twig."

"You are feeling pretty well?" asked the old German.

"Never better in my life," said Duncan Warner cheerily.

The situation was a painful one. The Marshal glared at the committee. Peter Stulpnagel grinned and rubbed his hands. The engineers scratched their heads. The bald-headed prisoner revolved his arm and looked pleased.

"I think that one more shock — " began the chairman.

"No, sir," said the Marshal; "we've had foolery enough for one morning. We are here for an execution, and an execution we'll have."

"What do you propose?"

"There's a hook handy upon the ceiling. Fetch in a rope, and we'll soon set this matter straight."

There was another awkward delay while the warders departed for the cord. Peter Stulpnagel bent over Duncan Warner, and whispered something in his ear. The desperado started in surprise.

"You don't say?" he asked.

The German nodded.

"What! No ways?"

Peter shook his head, and the two began to laugh as though they shared some huge joke between them.

The rope was brought, and the Marshal himself slipped the noose over the criminal's neck. Then the two warders, the assistant and he swung their victim into the air. For half an hour he hung — a dreadful sight — from the ceiling. Then in solemn silence they lowered him down, and one of the warders went out to order the shell to be brought round. But as he touched ground again what was our amazement when Duncan Warner put his hands up to his neck, loosened the noose, and took a long, deep breath.

"Paul Jefferson's sale is goin' well," he remarked, "I could see the crowd from up yonder," and he nodded at the hook in the ceiling.

"Up with him again!" shouted the Marshal, "we'll get the life out of him somehow."

In an instant the victim was up at the hook once more.

They kept him there for an hour, but when he came down he was perfectly garrulous.

"Old man Plunket goes too much to the Arcady Saloon," said he. "Three times he's been there in an hour; and him with a family. Old man Plunket would do well to swear off."

It was monstrous and incredible, but there it was. There was no getting round it. The man was there talking when he ought to have been dead. We all sat staring in amazement, but United States Marshal Carpenter was not a man to be euchred so easily. He motioned the others to one side, so that the prisoner was left standing alone.

"Duncan Warner," said he, slowly, "you are here to play your part, and I am here to play mine. Your game is to live if you can, and my game is to carry out the sentence of the law. You've beat us on electricity. I'll give you one there. And you've beat us on hanging, for you seem to thrive on it. But it's my turn to beat you now, for my duty has to be done."

He pulled a six-shooter from his coat as he spoke, and fired all the shots through the body of the prisoner. The room was so filled with smoke that we could see nothing, but when it cleared the prisoner was still standing there, looking down in disgust at the front of his coat.

"Coats must be cheap where you come from," said he. "Thirty dollars it cost me, and look at it now. The six holes in front are bad enough, but four of the balls have passed out, and a pretty state the back must be in."

The Marshal's revolver fell from his hand, and he dropped his arms to his sides, a beaten man.

"Maybe some of you gentlemen can tell me what this means," said he, looking helplessly at the committee.

Peter Stulpnagel took a step forward.

"I'll tell you all about it," said he.

"You seem to be the only person who knows anything."

"I *am* the only person who knows anything. I should have warned these gentlemen; but, as they would not listen to me, I have allowed them to learn by experience. What you have done with your electricity is that you have increased this man's vitality until he can defy death for centuries."

"Centuries!"

"Yes, it will take the wear of hundreds of years to exhaust the enormous nervous energy with which you have drenched him. Electricity is life, and you have charged him with it to the utmost. Perhaps in fifty years you might execute him, but I am not sanguine about it."

"Great Scott! What shall I do with him?" cried the unhappy Marshal.

Peter Stulpnagel shrugged his shoulders.

"It seems to me that it does not much matter what you do with him now," said he.

"Maybe we could drain the electricity out of him again. Suppose we hang him up by the heels?"

"No, no, it's out of the question."

"Well, well, he shall do no more mischief in Los Amigos, anyhow," said the Marshal, with decision. "He shall go into the new gaol. The prison will wear him out."

"On the contrary," said Peter Stulpnagel, "I think that it is much more probable that he will wear out the prison."

It was rather a fiasco and for years we didn't talk more about it than we could help, but it's no secret now and I thought you might like to jot down the facts in your case-book.

The Case of Lady Sannox

In his time, Conan Doyle was as well known for his doctor stories as for Sherlock Holmes or historical romances. Indeed, he was as much a pioneer of medical fiction as he was of the crime story, and it comes as no surprise that once or twice he combined the two forms, as he did in this now-classic tale written for THE IDLER *in 1893.*

THE RELATIONS between Douglas Stone and the notorious Lady Sannox were very well known both among the fashionable circles of which she was a brilliant member, and the scientific bodies which numbered him among their most illustrious *confréres*. There was naturally, therefore, a very widespread interest when it was announced one morning that the lady had absolutely and for ever taken the veil, and that the world would see her no more. When, at the very tail of this rumour, there came the assurance that the celebrated operating surgeon, the man of steel nerves, had been found in the morning by his valet, seated on one side of his bed, smiling pleasantly upon the universe, with both legs jammed into one side of his breeches and his great brain about as valuable as a cap full of porridge, the matter was strong enough to give quite a little thrill of interest to folk who had never hoped that their jaded nerves were capable of such a sensation.

Douglas Stone in his prime was one of the most remarkable men in England. Indeed, he could hardly be said to have ever reached his prime, for he was but nine-and-thirty at the time of this little incident. Those who knew him best were aware that, famous as he was as a surgeon, he might have succeeded with even greater rapidity in any of a dozen lines of life. He could have cut his way to fame as a soldier, struggled to it as an explorer, bullied for it in the courts, or built it out of stone and iron as an engineer. He was born to be great, for he could plan what another man dare not do, and he could do what another man dare not plan. In surgery none could follow him. His nerve, his judgment, his intuition, were things apart. Again and again his knife cut away death, but grazed the very springs of life in doing it, until his assistants were as white as the patient. His energy, his audacity, his full-blooded self-confidence — does not the memory of them still linger to the south of Marylebone Road and the north of Oxford Street?

His vices were as magnificent as his virtues, and infinitely more picturesque. Large as was his income, and it was the third largest of all professional men in London, it was far beneath the luxury of his living. Deep in his complex nature lay a rich vein of sensualism, at the sport of which he placed all the prizes of his life. The eye, the ear, the touch, the palate — all were his masters. The bouquet of old vintages, the scent of rare exotics, the curves and tints of the daintiest potteries of Europe — it was to these that the quick-running stream of gold was transformed. And then there came his sudden mad passion for Lady Sannox, when a single interview with two challenging glances and a whispered word set him ablaze. She was the loveliest woman in London, and the only one to him. He was one of the handsomest men in London, but not the only one to her. She had a liking for new experiences, and was gracious to most men who wooed her. It may have been cause or it may have been effect that Lord Sannox looked fifty, though he was six-and-thirty.

He was a quiet, silent, neutral-tinted man, this lord, with thin lips and heavy eyelids, much given to gardening, and full of home-like habits. He had at one time been fond of acting, had even rented a theatre in London, and on its boards had first seen Miss Marion Dawson, to whom he had offered his hand, his title, and the third of a county. Since his marriage this early hobby had become distasteful to him. Even in private theatricals it was no longer possible to persuade him to exercise the talent which he had often shown that he possessed. He was happier with a spud and a watering-can among his orchids and chrysanthemums.

It was quite an interesting problem whether he was absolutely devoid of sense, or miserably wanting in spirit. Did he know his lady's ways and condone them, or was he a mere blind, doting fool? It was a point to be discussed over the teacups in snug little drawing-rooms, or with the aid of a cigar in the bow windows of clubs. Bitter and plain were the comments among men upon his conduct. There was but one who had a good word to say for him, and he was the most silent member in the smoking-room. He had seen him break in a horse at the university, and it seemed to have left an impression upon his mind.

But when Douglas Stone became the favourite, all doubts as to Lord Sannox's knowledge or ignorance were set for ever at rest. There was no subterfuge about Stone. In his high-handed, impetuous fashion, he set all caution and discretion at defiance. The scandal became notorious. A learned body intimated that his name had been struck from the list of its vice-presidents. Two friends implored him to consider his professional credit. He cursed them all three, and spent forty guineas on a bangle to take with him to the lady. He was at her house every evening, and she drove in his carriage in the afternoons. There was not an attempt on either side to conceal their relations; but there came at last a little incident to interrupt them.

It was a dismal winter's night, very cold and gusty, with the wind whooping in the chimneys and blustering against the window-panes. A thin spatter of rain tinkled on the glass with each fresh sough of the gale, drowning for the instant the dull gurgle and drip from the eaves. Douglas Stone had finished his dinner, and sat by his fire in the study, a glass of rich port upon the malachite table at his elbow. As he raised it to his lips, he held it up against the lamplight, and watched with the eye of a connoisseur the tiny scales of beeswing which floated in its rich ruby depths. The fire, as it spurted up, threw fitful lights upon his bold, clear-cut face, with its widely-opened grey eyes, its thick and yet firm lips, and the deep, square jaw, which had something Roman in its strength and its animalism. He smiled from time to time as he nestled back in his luxurious chair. Indeed, he had a right to feel well pleased, for, against the advice of six colleagues, he had performed an operation that day of which only two cases were on record, and the result had been brilliant beyond all expectation. No other man in London would have had the daring to plan, or the skill to execute, such a heroic measure.

But he had promised Lady Sannox to see her that evening and

it was already half-past eight. His hand was outstretched to the bell to order the carriage when he heard the dull thud of the knocker. An instant later there was the shuffling of feet in the hall, and the sharp closing of a door.

"A patient to see you, sir, in the consulting-room," said the butler.

"About himself?"

"No, sir; I think he wants you to go out."

"It is too late," cried Douglas Stone peevishly. "I won't go."

"This is his card, sir."

The butler presented it upon the gold salver which had been given to his master by the wife of a Prime Minister.

"'Hamil Ali, Smyrna.' Hum! The fellow is a Turk, I suppose."

"Yes, sir. He seems as if he came from abroad, sir. And he's in a terrible way."

"Tut, tut! I have an engagement. I must go somewhere else. But I'll see him. Show him in here, Pim."

A few moments later the butler swung open the door and ushered in a small and decrepit man, who walked with a bent back and with the forward push of the face and blink of the eyes which goes with extreme short sight. His face was swarthy, and his hair and beard of the deepest black. In one hand he held a turban of white muslin striped with red, in the other a small chamois leather bag.

"Good evening," said Douglas Stone, when the butler had closed the door. "You speak English, I presume?"

"Yes, sir. I am from Asia Minor, but I speak English when I speak slow."

"You wanted me to go out, I understand?"

"Yes, sir. I wanted very much that you should see my wife."

"I could come in the morning, but I have an engagement which prevents me from seeing your wife to-night."

The Turk's answer was a singular one. He pulled the string which closed the mouth of the chamois leather bag, and poured a flood of gold on to the table.

"There are one hundred pounds there," said he, "and I promise you that it will not take you an hour. I have a cab ready at the door."

Douglas Stone glanced at his watch. An hour would not make it too late to visit Lady Sannox. He had been there later. And the fee was an extraordinarily high one. He had been pressed by his creditors lately, and he could not afford to let such a chance pass. He would go.

"What is the case?" he asked.

"Oh, it is so sad a one! So sad a one! You have not, perhaps, heard of the daggers of the Almohades?"

"Never."

"Ah, they are Eastern daggers of a great age and of a singular shape, with the hilt like what you call a stirrup. I am a curiosity dealer, you understand, and that is why I have come to England from Smyrna, but next week I go back once more. Many things I brought with me, and I have a few things left, but among them, to my sorrow, is one of these daggers."

"You will remember that I have an appointment, sir," said the surgeon, with some irritation. "Pray confine yourself to the necessary details."

"You will see that it is necessary. To-day my wife fell down in a faint in the room in which I keep my wares, and she cut her lower lip upon this cursed dagger of Almohades."

"I see," said Douglas Stone, rising. "And you wish me to dress the wound?"

"No, no, it is worse than that."

"What then?"

"These daggers are poisoned."

"Poisoned!"

"Yes, and there is no man, East or West, who can tell now what is the poison or what the cure. But all that is known I know, for my father was in this trade before me, and we have had much to do with these poisoned weapons."

"What are the symptoms?"

"Deep sleep, and death in thirty hours."

"And you say there is no cure. Why then should you pay me this considerable fee?"

"No drug can cure, but the knife may."

"And how?"

"The poison is slow of absorption. It remains for hours in the wound."

"Washing, then, might cleanse it?"

"No more than in a snake-bite. It is too subtle and too deadly."

"Excision of the wound, then?"

"That is it. If it be on the finger, take the finger off. So said my father always. But think of where this wound is, and that it is my wife. It is dreadful!"

But familiarity with such grim matters may take the finer edge from a man's sympathy. To Douglas Stone this was already an interesting case, and he brushed aside as irrelevant the feeble objections of the husband.

"It appears to be that or nothing," said he brusquely. "It is better to lose a lip than a life."

"Ah, yes, I know that you are right. Well, well, it is kismet, and must be faced. I have the cab, and you will come with me and do this thing."

Douglas Stone took his case of bistouries from a drawer, and placed it with a roll of bandage and a compress of lint in his pocket. He must waste no more time if he were to see Lady Sannox.

"I am ready," said he, pulling on his overcoat. "Will you take a glass of wine before you go out into this cold air?"

His visitor shrank away, with a protesting hand upraised.

"You forget that I am a Mussulman, and a true follower of the Prophet," said he. "But tell me what is the bottle of green glass which you have placed in your pocket?"

"It is chloroform."

"Ah, that also is forbidden to us. It is a spirit, and we make no use of such things."

"What! You would allow your wife to go through an operation without an anaesthetic?"

"Ah! she will feel nothing, poor soul. The deep sleep has already come on, which is the first working of the poison. And then I have given her of our Smyrna opium. Come, sir, for already an hour has passed."

As they stepped out into the darkness, a sheet of rain was driven in upon their faces, and the hall lamp, which dangled from the arm of a marble caryatid, went out with a fluff. Pim, the butler, pushed the heavy door to, straining hard with his shoulder against the wind, while the two men groped their way towards the yellow glare which showed where the cab was waiting. An instant later they were rattling upon their journey.

"Is it far?" asked Douglas Stone.

"Oh, no. We have a very little quiet place off the Euston Road."

The surgeon pressed the spring of his repeater and listened to the little tings which told him the hour. It was a quarter past nine. He calculated the distances, and the short time which it would take him to perform so trivial an operation. He ought to reach Lady Sannox by ten o'clock. Through the fogged windows he saw the blurred gas-lamps dancing past, with occasionally the broader glare of a shop front. The rain was pelting and rattling upon the leathern top of the carriage, and the wheels swashed as they rolled through puddle and mud. Opposite to him the white headgear of his companion gleamed faintly through the obscurity. The surgeon felt in his pockets and arranged his needles, his ligatures and his safety-pins, that no time might be wasted when they arrived. He chafed with impatience and drummed his foot upon the floor.

But the cab slowed down at last and pulled up. In an instant Douglas Stone was out, and the Smyrna merchant's toe was at his very heel.

"You can wait," said he to the driver.

It was a mean-looking house in a narrow and sordid street. The surgeon, who knew his London well, cast a swift glance into the shadows, but there was nothing distinctive—no shop, no movement, nothing but a double line of dull, flat-faced houses, a double stretch of wet flagstones which gleamed in the lamplight, and a double rush of water in the gutters which swirled and gurgled towards the sewer gratings. The door which faced them was blotched and discoloured, and a faint light in the fan pane above it served to show the dust and the grime which covered it. Above, in one of the bedroom windows, there was a dull yellow glimmer. The merchant knocked loudly, and, as he turned his dark face towards the light, Douglas Stone could see that it was contracted with anxiety. A bolt was drawn, and an elderly woman with a taper stood in the doorway, shielding the thin flame with her gnarled hand.

"Is all well?" gasped the merchant.

"She is as you left her, sir."

"She has not spoken?"

"No; she is in a deep sleep."

The merchant closed the door, and Douglas Stone walked down the narrow passage, glancing about him in some surprise as he did so. There was no oilcloth, no mat, no hat-rack. Deep grey dust and heavy festoons of cobwebs met his eyes everywhere. Following the old woman up the winding stair, his firm footfall echoed harshly through the silent house. There was no carpet.

The bedroom was on the second landing. Douglas Stone followed the old nurse into it, with the merchant at his heels. Here, at least, there was furniture and to spare. The floor was littered and the corners piled with Turkish cabinets, inlaid tables, coats of chain mail, strange pipes, and grotesque weapons. A single small lamp stood upon a bracket on the wall. Douglas Stone took it down, and picking his way among the lumber, walked over to a couch in the corner, on which lay a woman dressed in the Turkish fashion, with yashmak and veil. The lower part of the face was exposed, and the surgeon saw a jagged cut which zigzagged along the border of the under lip.

"You will forgive the yashmak," said the Turk. "You know our views about woman in the East."

But the surgeon was not thinking about the yashmak. This was no longer a woman to him. It was a case. He stooped and examined the wound carefully.

"There are no signs of irritation," said he. "We might delay the operation until local symptoms develop."

The husband wrung his hands in incontrollable agitation.

"Oh! sir, sir!" he cried. "Do not trifle. You do not know. It is deadly. I know, and I give you my assurance that an operation is absolutely necessary. Only the knife can save her."

"And yet I am inclined to wait," said Douglas Stone.

"That is enough!" the Turk cried, angrily. "Every minute is of importance, and I cannot stand here and see my wife allowed to sink. It only remains for me to give you my thanks for having come, and to call in some other surgeon before it is too late."

Douglas Stone hesitated. To refund that hundred pounds was no pleasant matter. But of course if he left the case he must return the money. And if the Turk were right and the woman died, his position before a coroner might be an embarrassing one.

"You have had personal experience of this poison?" he asked.

"I have."

"And you assure me that an operation is needful."

"I swear it by all that I hold sacred."

"The disfigurement will be frightful."

"I can understand that the mouth will not be a pretty one to kiss."

Douglas Stone turned fiercely upon the man. The speech was a brutal one. But the Turk has his own fashion of talk and of thought, and there was no time for wrangling. Douglas Stone drew a bistoury from his case, opened it and felt the straight edge with his forefinger. Then he held the lamp closer to the bed. Two dark eyes were gazing up at him through the slit in the yashmak. They were all iris, and the pupil was hardly to be seen.

"You have given her a very heavy dose of opium."

"Yes, she has had a good dose."

He glanced again at the dark eyes which looked straight at his own. They were dull and lustreless, but, even as he gazed, a little shifting sparkle came into them, and the lips quivered.

"She is not absolutely unconscious," said he.

"Would it not be well to use the knife while it would be painless?"

The same thought had crossed the surgeon's mind. He grasped the wounded lip with his forceps, and with two swift cuts he took out a broad V-shaped piece. The woman sprang up on the couch with a dreadful gurgling scream. Her covering was torn from her face. It was a face that he knew. In spite of that protruding upper lip and that slobber of blood, it was a face that he knew. She kept on putting her hand up to the gap and screaming. Douglas Stone sat down at the foot of the couch with his knife and his forceps. The room was whirling round, and he had felt something go like a ripping seam behind his ear. A bystander would have said that his face was the more ghastly of the two. As in a dream, or as if he had been looking at something at the play, he was conscious that the Turk's hair and beard lay upon the table, and that Lord Sannox was leaning against the wall with his hand to his side, laughing silently. The screams had died away now, and the dreadful head had dropped back again upon the pillow, but Douglas Stone still sat motionless, and Lord Sannox still chuckled quietly to himself.

"It was really very necessary for Marion, this operation," said he, "not physically, but morally, you know, morally."

Douglas Stone stooped forwards and began to play with the fringe of the coverlet. His knife tinkled down upon the ground, but he still held the forceps and something more.

"I had long intended to make a little example," said Lord Sannox, suavely. "Your note of Wednesday miscarried, and I have it here in my pocket-book. I took some pains in carrying out my idea. The wound, by the way, was from nothing more dangerous than my signet ring."

He glanced keenly at his silent companion, and cocked the small revolver which he held in his coat pocket. But Douglas Stone was still picking at the coverlet.

"You see you have kept your appointment after all," said Lord Sannox.

And at that Douglas Stone began to laugh. He laughed long and loudly. But Lord Sannox did not laugh now. Something like fear sharpened and hardened his features. He walked from the room, and he walked on tiptoe. The old woman was waiting outside.

"Attend to your mistress when she awakes," said Lord Sannox.

Then he went down to the street. The cab was at the door, and the driver raised his hand to his hat.

"John," said Lord Sannox, "you will take the doctor home first. He will want leading down-stairs, I think. Tell his butler that he has been taken ill at a case."

"Very good, sir."

"Then you can take Lady Sannox home."

"And how about yourself, sir?"

"Oh, my address for the next few months will be Hotel di Roma, Venice. Just see that the letters are sent on. And tell Stevens to exhibit all the purple chrysanthemums next Monday and to wire me the result."

The Parasite

And then, tragedy. Louise Doyle, his wife of eight years, was diagnosed a consumptive. In 1893, such diagnosis was a sentence of death. The question was only how long she might be expected to survive.

Doyle's father had died of an epileptic seizure less than a month before. Now Louise had tuberculosis, and he realized that he, a physician, had been aware of her symptoms for a year without recognizing them for what they were. Loss and guilt plunged him into a welter of depression — but not of despair. In November 1893, he took two important steps. He took Louise away to Davos, in Switzerland, a place having a climate which had proven especially conducive to the remission of tuberculosis. And he joined the Society for Psychical Research.

At Davos, to occupy his mind, he threw himself into his writing. He missed the outcries of rage and dismay when "The Final Problem" appeared in the STRAND *in December and the British public learned of the death of Sherlock Holmes at the hand of Professor Moriarty. In January, he finished* THE STARK MUNRO LETTERS, *the autobiographical novel which he had been planning for more than two years. That done, he immediately began work on* THE PARASITE.

Nothing in Conan Doyle's work reflects as clearly the influence of immediate events and his own emotional state. He had for years been interested in spiritualism, having attended his first séance in 1879, not long before renouncing his Catholic faith. That he wrote THE PARASITE *just weeks after reading an address on the subject of mesmerism by Arthur Balfour, future Prime Minister of Britain and then President of the Society for Psychical Research, is, to use one of Doyle's own phrases, beyond coincidence. That the emphasis of the work is on the darkly sexual is equally telling, for marital relations for consumptives were considered out of the question and Doyle must have been adjusting himself, at the virile age of 34, to a celibate marriage, rejecting temptations of several sorts just as the first-person hero of* THE PARASITE *does. That the tale revealed something more of its author than he had originally intended is evident from the fact that it was suppressed almost immediately after publication.*

It was serialized in four parts in HARPER'S WEEKLY *in the U.S. in November and December 1894 and brought out as a small book by Constable in England, by Harper in America. It was almost universally hailed by the critics as one of the best things Doyle had ever written — and then it was dashed into obscurity by the author himself, who publicly disavowed the ideas presented there and refused to allow further editions.* THE PARASITE *remained unpublished after 1897, its brilliance unknown to the public and ignored even by Doyle scholars.*

But the book proved to be the purging of its author's black mood. Still at Davos, he created Brigadier Gerard, the rollicking Hussar officer in the service of Napoleon. In the spring — it is true, however farfetched it may sound — he introduced into Switzerland the sport of cross-country skiing, which he had learned during a trip to Norway two years before. In the summer, he went on a triumphal lecture tour of the United States. And Louise Doyle, through the devoted ministerings of her husband, lived on for another twelve years.

MARCH 24TH. — The spring is fairly with us now. Outside my laboratory window the great chestnut tree is all covered with the big glutinous gummy buds, some of which have already begun to break into little green shuttle-cocks. As you walk down the lanes you are conscious of the rich silent forces of nature working all around you. The wet earth smells fruitful and luscious. Green shoots are peeping out everywhere. The twigs are stiff with their sap; and the moist heavy English air is laden with a faintly resinous perfume. Buds in the hedges, lambs beneath them — everywhere the work of reproduction going forward!

I can see it without and I can feel it within. We also have our spring when the little arterioles dilate, the lymph flows in a brisker stream, the glands work harder, winnowing and straining. Every year Nature readjusts the whole machine. I can feel the ferment in my blood at this very moment, and as the cool sunshine pours through my window I could dance about in it like a gnat. So I should, only that Charles Sadler would rush upstairs to know what was the matter. Besides, I must remember that I am Professor Gilroy. An old professor may afford to be natural, but when fortune has given one of the first chairs in the university to a man of four-and-thirty he must try and act the part consistently.

What a fellow Wilson is! If I could only throw the same enthusiasm into physiology that he does into psychology I should become a Claude Bernard at the least. His whole life and soul and energy works to one end. He drops to sleep collating his results of the past day, and he wakes to plan his researches for the coming one. And yet, outside the narrow circle who follow his proceedings he gets so little credit for it. Physiology is a recognized science. If I add even a brick to the edifice every one sees and applauds it. But Wilson is trying to dig the foundations for a science of the future. His work is underground and does not show. Yet he goes on uncomplainingly, corresponding with a hundred semi-maniacs in the hope of finding one reliable witness, sifting a hundred lies on the chance of gaining one little speck of truth, collating old books, devouring new ones, experimenting, lecturing, trying to light up in others the fiery interest which is consuming him. I am filled with wonder and admiration when I think of him; and yet, when he asks me to associate myself with his researches I am compelled to tell him that in their present state they offer little attraction to a man who is devoted to exact science. If he could show me something positive and objective, I might then be tempted to approach the question from its physiological side. So long as half his subjects are tainted with charlatanry and the other half with hysteria, we physiologists must content ourselves with the body and leave the mind to our descendants.

No doubt I am a materialist. Agatha says that I am a rank one. I tell her that is an excellent reason for shortening our engagement, since I am in such urgent need of her spirituality. And yet I may claim to be a curious example of the effect of education upon temperament, for by nature I am, unless I deceive myself, a highly psychic man. I was a nervous, sensitive boy, a dreamer, a somnambulist, full of impressions and intuitions. My black hair, my dark eyes, my thin olive face, my tapering fingers are all characteristic of my real temperament, and cause experts like Wilson to claim me as their own. But my brain is soaked with exact knowledge. I have trained myself to deal only with fact and with proof. Surmise and fancy have no place in my scheme of thought. Show me what I can see with my microscope, cut with my scalpel, weigh in my balance, and I will devote a lifetime to its investigation. But when you ask me to study feelings, impressions, suggestions, you ask me to do what is distasteful and even demoralizing. A departure from pure reason affects me like an evil smell or a musical discord.

Which is a very sufficient reason why I am a little loth to go to Professor Wilson's to-night. Still, I feel that I could hardly get out of the invitation without positive rudeness — and now that Mrs. Marden and Agatha are going, of course I would not if I could. But I had rather meet them anywhere else. I know that Wilson would draw me into this nebulous semi-science of his if he could. In his enthusiasm he is perfectly impervious to hints or remonstrances. Nothing short of a positive quarrel will make him realize my aversion to the whole business. I have no doubt that he has some new mesmerist, or clairvoyant, or medium, or trickster of some sort whom he is going to exhibit to us, for even his entertainments bear upon his hobby. Well, it will be a treat for Agatha at any rate. She is interested in it, as woman usually is in whatever is vague and mystical and indefinite.

10.50 P.M. — This diary-keeping of mine is, I fancy, the outcome of that scientific habit of mind about which I wrote this morning. I like to register impressions while they are fresh. Once a day at least I endeavour to define my own mental position. It is a useful piece of self-analysis, and has, I fancy, a steadying effect upon the character. Frankly, I must confess that my own needs what stiffening I can give it. I fear that after all much of my neurotic temperament survives, and that I am far from that cool, calm precision which characterizes Murdoch or Pratt-Haldane. Otherwise, why should the tomfoolery which I have witnessed this evening have set my nerves thrilling so that even now I am all unstrung? My only comfort is that neither Wilson, nor Miss Penelosa, nor even Agatha could have possibly known my weakness.

And what in the world was there to excite me? Nothing, or so little that it will seem ludicrous when I set it down.

The Mardens got to Wilson's before me. In fact I was one of the last to arrive, and found the room crowded. I had hardly time to say a word to Mrs. Marden and to Agatha, who was looking charming in white and pink with glittering wheat-ears in her hair, when Wilson came twitching at my sleeve.

"You want something positive, Gilroy," said he, drawing me apart into a corner. "My dear fellow, I have a phenomenon—a phenomenon."

I should have been more impressed had I not heard the same before. His sanguine spirit turns every firefly into a star.

"No possible question about the *bona fides* this time," said he, in answer perhaps to some little gleam of amusement in my eyes. "My wife has known her for many years. They both come from Trinidad, you know. Miss Penelosa has only been in England a month or two, and knows no one outside the university circle; but I assure you that the things she has told us suffice in themselves to establish clairvoyance upon an absolutely scientific basis. There is nothing like her, amateur or professional. Come and be introduced!"

I like none of these mystery-mongers, but the amateur least of all. With the paid performer you may pounce upon him and expose him the instant that you have seen through his trick. He is there to deceive you, and you are there to find him out. But what are you to do with the friend of your host's wife? Are you to turn on a light suddenly and expose her slapping a surreptitious banjo? Or are you to hurl cochineal over her evening frock when she steals round with her phosphorous bottle and her supernatural platitude? There would be a scene, and you would be looked upon as a brute. So you have your choice of being that or a dupe. I was in no very good humour as I followed Wilson to the lady.

Any one less like my idea of a West Indian could not be imagined. She was a small, frail creature, well over forty, I should say, with a pale, peaky face, and hair of a very light shade of chestnut. Her presence was insignificant and her manner retiring. In any group of women she would have been the last whom one would have picked out. Her eyes were perhaps her most remarkable, and also, I am compelled to say, her least pleasant feature. They were grey in colour — grey with a shade of green — and their expression struck me as being decidedly furtive. I wonder if furtive is the word, or should I have said fierce? On second thoughts, feline would have expressed it better. A crutch leaning against the wall told me, what was painfully evident when she rose, that one of her legs was crippled.

So I was introduced to Miss Penelosa, and it did not escape me that as my name was mentioned she glanced across at Agatha. Wilson had evidently been talking. And presently no doubt, thought I, she will inform me by occult means that I am engaged to a young lady with wheat-ears in her hair. I wondered how much more Wilson had been telling her about me.

"Professor Gilroy is a terrible sceptic," said he; "I hope, Miss Penelosa, that you will be able to convert him."

She looked keenly up at me.

"Professor Gilroy is quite right to be sceptical if he has not seen anything convincing," said she. "I should have thought," she added, "that you would yourself have been an excellent subject."

"For what, may I ask?" said I.

"Well, for mesmerism, for example."

"My experience has been, that mesmerists go for their subjects to those who are mentally unsound. All their results are vitiated, as it seems to me, by the fact that they are dealing with abnormal organisms."

"Which of these ladies would you say possessed a normal organism?" she asked. "I should like you to select the one who seems to you to have the best-balanced mind. Should we say the girl in pink and white — Miss Agatha Marden, I think the name is?"

"Yes, I should attach weight to any results from her."

"I have never tried how far she is impressionable. Of course some people respond much more rapidly than others. May I ask how far your scepticism extends? I suppose that you admit the mesmeric sleep and the power of suggestion."

"I admit nothing, Miss Penelosa."

"Dear me, I thought science had got further than that. Of course I know nothing about the scientific side of it. I only know what I can do. You see the girl in red, for example, over near the Japanese jar. I shall will that she come across to us."

She bent forward as she spoke and dropped her fan upon the floor. The girl whisked round and came straight towards us, with an inquiring look upon her face as if some one had called her.

"What do you think of that, Gilroy?" cried Wilson in a kind of ecstasy.

I did not dare to tell him what I thought of it. To me it was the most barefaced, shameless piece of imposture that I had ever witnessed. The collusion and the signal had really been too obvious.

"Professor Gilroy is not satisfied," said she, glancing up at me with her strange little eyes. "My poor fan is to get the credit of that experiment. Well, we must try something else. Miss Marden, would you have any objection to my putting you off?"

"Oh, I should love it!" cried Agatha.

By this time all the company had gathered round us in a circle, the shirt-fronted men and the white-throated women, some awed, some critical, as though it were something between a religious ceremony and a conjurer's entertainment. A red velvet armchair had been pushed into the centre, and Agatha lay back in it, a little flushed and trembling slightly from excitement. I could see it from the vibration of the wheat-ears. Miss Penelosa rose from her seat and stood over her, leaning upon her crutch.

And there was a change in the woman. She no longer seemed small or insignificant. Twenty years were gone from her age. Her eyes were shining, a tinge of colour had come into her sallow cheeks, her whole figure had expanded. So I have seen a dull-eyed, listless lad change in an instant into briskness and life when given a task of which he felt himself master. She looked down at Agatha with an expression which I resented from the bottom of my soul—the expression with which a Roman empress might have looked at her kneeling slave. Then, with a quick commanding gesture, she tossed up her arms and swept them slowly down in front of her.

I was watching Agatha narrowly. During three passes she seemed to be simply amused. At the fourth I observed a slight glazing of her eyes, accompanied by some dilation of her pupils. At the sixth there was a momentary rigor. At the seventh her lids began to drop. At the tenth her eyes were closed, and her breathing was slower and fuller than usual. I tried as I watched to preserve my scientific calm, but a foolish, causeless agitation convulsed me. I trust that I hid it, but I felt as a child feels in the dark. I could not have believed that I was still open to such weakness.

"She is in the trance," said Miss Penelosa.

"She is sleeping," I cried.

"Wake her, then!"

I pulled her by the arm and shouted in her ear. She might have been dead for all the impression that I could make. Her body was there on the velvet chair. Her organs were acting, her heart, her lungs. But her soul! It had slipped from beyond our ken. Whither had it gone? What power had dispossessed it? I was puzzled and disconcerted.

"So much for the mesmeric sleep," said Miss Penelosa. "As regards suggestion, whatever I may suggest Miss Marden will infallibly do, whether it be now or after she has awakened from her trance. Do you demand proof of it?"

"Certainly," said I.

"You shall have it."

I saw a smile pass over her face as though an amusing thought had struck her. She stopped and whispered earnestly into her subject's ear. Agatha, who had been so deaf to me, nodded her head as she listened.

"Awake!" cried Miss Penelosa, with a sharp tap of her crutch upon the floor. The eyes opened, the glazing cleared slowly away, and the soul looked out once more after its strange eclipse.

We went away early. Agatha was none the worse for her strange excursion, but I was nervous and unstrung, unable to listen to or answer the stream of comments which Wilson was pouring out for my benefit. As I bade her good-night, Miss Penelosa slipped a piece of paper into my hand.

"Pray forgive me," said she, "if I take means to overcome your scepticism. Open this note at ten o'clock to-morrow morning. It is a little private test."

I can't imagine what she means, but there is the note, and it shall be opened as she directs. My head is aching, and I have written enough for to-night. To-morrow I dare say that what seems so inexplicable will take quite another complexion. I shall not surrender my convictions without a struggle.

March 25th. — I am amazed — confounded. It is clear that I must reconsider my opinion upon this matter. But first, let me place on record what has occurred.

I had finished breakfast and was looking over some diagrams with which my lecture is to be illustrated when my housekeeper entered to tell me that Agatha was in my study, and wished to see me immediately. I glanced at the clock, and saw with surprise that it was only half-past nine.

When I entered the room she was standing on the hearthrug facing me. Something in her pose chilled me, and checked the words which were rising to my lips. Her veil was half down, but I could see that she was pale, and that her expression was constrained.

"Austin," she said, "I have come to tell you that our engagement is at an end."

I staggered. I believe that I literally did stagger. I know that I found myself leaning against the bookcase for support.

"But — but — " I stammered, "this is very sudden, Agatha."

"Yes, Austin, I have come here to tell you that our engagement is at an end."

"But surely," I cried, "you will give me some reason. This is unlike you, Agatha. Tell me how I have been unfortunate enough to offend you."

"It is all over, Austin."

"But why? You must be under some delusion, Agatha. Perhaps you have been told some falsehood about me. Or you may have misunderstood something that I have said to you. Only let me know what it is, and a word may set it all right."

"We must consider it all at an end."

"But you left me last night without a hint at any disagreement. What could have occurred in the interval to change you so? It must have been something that happened last night. You have been thinking it over, and you have disapproved of my conduct. Was it the mesmerism? Did you blame me for letting that woman exercise her power over you? You know that at the least sign I should have interfered."

"It is useless, Austin. All is over." Her voice was cold and measured; her manner strangely formal and hard. It seemed to me that she was absolutely resolved not to drawn into any argument or explanation. As for me, I was shaking with agitation, and I turned my face aside, so ashamed was I that she should see my want of control.

"You must know what this means to me," I cried. "It is the blasting of all my hopes and the ruin of my life. You surely will not inflict such a punishment upon me unheard. You will let me know what is the matter. Consider how impossible it would be for me, under any circumstances, to treat you so. For God's sake, Agatha, let me know what I have done."

She walked past me without a word and opened the door.

"It is quite useless, Austin," said she. "You must consider our engagement at an end." An instant later she was gone, and before I could recover myself sufficiently to follow her I heard the hall door close behind her.

I rushed into my room to change my coat, with the idea of hurrying round to Mrs. Marden's to learn from her what the cause of my misfortune might be. So shaken was I that I could hardly lace my boots. Never shall I forget those horrible ten minutes.

I had just pulled on my overcoat when the clock upon the mantelpiece struck ten.

Ten! I associated the idea with Miss Penelosa's note. It was lying before me on the table, and I tore it open. It was scribbled in pencil in a peculiarly angular handwriting.

"My dear Professor Gilroy," it said, "pray excuse the personal nature of the test which I am giving you. Professor Wilson happened to mention the relations between you and my subject of this evening, and it struck me that nothing could be more convincing to you than if I were to suggest to Miss Marden that she should call upon you at half-past nine to-morrow morning and suspend your engagement for half an hour or so. Science is so exacting that it is difficult to give a satisfying test, but I am convinced that this, at least, will be an action which she would be most unlikely to do of her own free-will. Forget anything that she may have said, as she has really nothing whatever to do with it, and will certainly not recollect anything about it. I write this note to shorten your anxiety, and to beg you to forgive me for the momentary unhappiness which my suggestion must have caused you.

"Yours faithfully,
"HELEN PENELOSA."

Really when I had read the note I was too relieved to be angry. It was a liberty. Certainly it was a very great liberty indeed on the part of a lady whom I had only met once. But after all I had challenged her by my scepticism. It may have been, as she said, a little difficult to devise a test which would satisfy me.

And she had done that. There could be no question at all upon the point. For me hypnotic suggestion was finally established. It took its place from now onwards as one of the facts of life. That Agatha, who of all women of my acquaintance has the best-balanced mind, had been reduced to a condition of automatism appeared to be certain. A person at a distance had worked her as an engineer on the shore might guide a Brennan torpedo. A second soul had slipped in, as it were, had pushed her own aside, and had seized her nervous mechanism, saying, "I will work this for half an hour." And Agatha must have been unconscious as she came and as she returned. Could she make her way in safety through the streets in such a state! I put on my hat and hurried round to see if all was well with her.

Yes. She was at home. I was shown into the drawing-room, and found her sitting with a book upon her lap.

"You are an early visitor, Austin," said she, smiling.

"And you have been an even earlier one," I answered.

She looked puzzled. "What do you mean?" she asked.

"You have not been out to-day?"

"No, certainly not."

"Agatha," said I seriously. "Would you mind telling me exactly what you have done this morning?"

She laughed at my earnestness.

"You've got on your professorial look, Austin. See what comes of being engaged to a man of science. However, I will tell you, though I can't imagine what you want to know for. I got up at eight. I breakfasted at half-past. I came into this room at ten minutes past nine and began to read *The Memoirs of Madame de Rémusat*. In a few minutes I did the French lady the bad compliment of dropping to sleep over her pages, and I did you, sir, the very flattering one of dreaming about you. It is only a few minutes since I woke up."

"And found yourself where you had been before?"

"Why, where else should I find himself?"

"Would you mind telling me, Agatha, what it was that you dreamed about me? It really is not mere curiosity on my part."

"I merely had a vague impression that you came into it. I cannot recall anything definite."

"If you have not been out to-day, Agatha, how is it that your shoes are dusty."

A pained look came over her face.

"Really, Austin, I do not know what is the matter with you this morning. One would almost think that you doubted my word. If my boots are dusty, it must be, of course, that I have put on a pair which the maid had not cleaned."

It was perfectly evident that she knew nothing whatever about the matter, and I reflected that after all perhaps it was better that I should not enlighten her. It might frighten her, and could serve no good purpose that I could see. I said no more about it, therefore, and left shortly afterwards to give my lecture.

But I am immensely impressed. My horizon of scientific possibilities has suddenly been enormously extended. I no longer wonder at Wilson's demoniac energy and enthusiasm. Who would not work hard who had a vast virgin field ready to his hand? Why, I have known the novel shape of a nucleolus, or a trifling peculiarity of striped muscular fibre seen under a 300 diametre lens to fill me with exultation. How petty do such researches seem when compared with this one which strikes at the very roots of life, and the nature of the soul! I had always looked upon spirit as a product of matter. The brain, I thought, secreted the mind, as the liver does the bile. But how can this be when I see mind working from a distance, and playing upon matter as a musician might upon a violin? The body does not give rise to the soul then, but is rather the rough instrument by which the spirit manifests itself. The windmill does not give rise to the wind, but only indicates it. It was opposed to my whole habit of thought, and yet it was undeniably possible and worthy of investigation.

And why should I not investigate it? I see that under yesterday's date I said, "If I could see something positive and objective

I might be tempted to approach it from the physiological aspect."
Well, I have got my test. I shall be as good as my word. The
investigation would, I am sure, be of immense interest. Some of
my colleagues might look askance at it, for science is full of
unreasoning prejudices, but if Wilson has the courage of his
convictions, I can afford to have it also. I shall go to him to-
morrow morning — to him and to Miss Penelosa. If she can show
us so much it is probable that she can show us more.

March 26th. — Wilson was, as I had anticipated, very exultant
over my conversion, and Miss Penelosa was also demurely
pleased at the result of her experiment. Strange what a silent
colourless creature she is, save only when she exercises her
power! Even talking about it gives her colour and life. She seems
to take a singular interest in me. I cannot help observing how her
eyes follow me about the room.

We had the most interesting conversation about her own
powers. It is just as well to put her views on record, though they
cannot of course claim any scientific weight.

"You are on the very fringe of the subject," said she, when I
had expressed wonder at the remarkable instance of suggestion
which she had shown me. "I had no direct influence upon Miss
Marden when she came round to you. I was not even thinking of
her that morning. What I did was to set her mind as I might set
the alarum of a clock so that at the hour named it would go off
of its own accord. If six months instead of twelve hours had
been suggested, it would have been the same."

"And if the suggestion had been to assassinate me?"

"She would most inevitably have done so."

"But this is a terrible power!" I cried.

"It is, as you say, a terrible power," she answered gravely.
"And the more you know of it the more terrible will it seem to
you."

"May I ask," said I, "what you meant when you said that this
matter of suggestion is only at the fringe of it? What do you
consider the essential?"

"I had rather not tell you."

I was surprised at the decision of her answer.

"You understand," said I, "that it is not out of curiosity I ask, but in the hope that I may find some scientific explanation for the facts with which you furnish me."

"Frankly, Professor Gilroy," said she, "I am not at all interested in science, nor do I care whether it can or can not classify these powers."

"But I was hoping — "

"Ah, that is quite another thing. If you make it a personal matter," said she, with the pleasantest of smiles, "I shall be only too happy to tell you anything you wish to know. Let me see! What was it you asked me? Oh, about the further powers. Professor Wilson won't believe in them, but they are quite true all the same. For example, it is possible for an operator to gain complete command over his subject — presuming that the latter is a good one. Without any previous suggestion he may make him do whatever he likes."

"Without the subject's knowledge?"

"That depends. If the force were strongly exerted he would know no more about it than Miss Marden did when she came round and frightened you so. Or, if the influence were less powerful, he might be conscious of what he was doing but be quite unable to prevent himself from doing it."

"Would he have lost his own will-power, then?"

"It would be overridden by another, stronger, one."

"Have you ever exercised this power yourself?"

"Several times."

"Is your own will so strong, then?"

"Well, it does not entirely depend upon that. Many have strong wills which are not detachable from themselves. The thing is to have the gift of projecting it into another person and superseding their own. I find that the power varies with my own strength and health."

"Practically, you send your soul into another person's body."

"Well, you might put it that way."

"And what does your own body do?"

"It merely feels lethargic."

"Well, but is there no danger to your own health?" I asked.

"There might be a little. You have to be careful never to let your own consciousness absolutely go, otherwise you might experience some difficulty in finding your way back again. You must always preserve the connection, as it were. I am afraid I express myself very badly, Professor Gilroy, but of course I don't know how to put these things in a scientific way. I am just giving you my own experiences and my own explanations."

Well, I read this over now at my leisure, and I marvel at myself! Is this Austin Gilroy, the man who has won his way to the front by his hard reasoning power and by his devotion to fact? Here I am gravely retailing the gossip of a woman, who tells me how her soul may be projected from her body, and how, while she lies in a lethargy, she can control the actions of people at a distance! Do I accept it? Certainly not. She must prove and re-prove before I yield a point. But if I am still a sceptic I have at least ceased to be a scoffer. We are to have a sitting this evening and she is to try if she can produce any mesmeric effect upon me. If she can it will make an excellent starting-point for our investigation. No one can accuse me, at any rate, of complicity. If she cannot, we must try and find some subject who will be like Caesar's wife. Wilson is perfectly impervious.

10 P.M. — I believe that I am on the threshold of an epoch-making investigation. To have the power of examining these phenomena from inside — to have an organism which will respond, and, at the same time, a brain which will appreciate and criticize — that is surely a unique advantage. I am quite sure that Wilson would give five years of his life to be as susceptible as I have proven myself to be.

There was no one present except Wilson and his wife. I was seated with my head leaning back, and Miss Penelosa, standing in front and a little way to the left, used the same long sweeping strokes as with Agatha. At each of them a warm current of air seemed to strike me and to suffuse a thrill and glow all through me from head to foot. My eyes were fixed upon Miss Penelosa's face, but as I gazed the features seemed to blur and to fade away. I was conscious only of her own eyes looking down at me, grey, deep, inscrutable. Larger they grew and larger, until they changed suddenly into two mountain lakes towards which I seemed to be falling with horrible rapidity. I shuddered, and as I did so some deeper stratum of thought told me that the shudder represented the rigor which I had observed in Agatha. An instant later I struck the surface of the lakes, now joined into one, and down I went beneath the water with a fulness in my head and a buzzing in my ears. Down I went, down, down, and then with a swoop up again until I could see the light streaming brightly through the green water. I was almost at the surface when the word "Awake!" rang through my head, and with a start I found myself back in the armchair, with Miss Penelosa leaning on her crutch, and Wilson, his note-book in his hand, peeping over her shoulder. No heaviness or weariness was left behind. On the contrary, though it is only an hour or so since the experiment, I feel so wakeful that I am more inclined for my study than my bedroom. I see quite a vista of interesting experiments extending before us, and am all impatience to begin upon them.

March 27th. — A blank day, as Miss Penelosa goes with Wilson and his wife to the Suttons. Have begun Binet and Ferré's *Animal Magnetism*. What strange deep waters these are! Results, results, results — and the cause an absolute mystery. It is stimulating to the imagination, but I must be on my guard against that. Let us have no inferences nor deductions, and nothing but solid facts. I know that the mesmeric trance is true, I know that mesmeric suggestion is true, I know that I am myself sensitive to this force. That is my present position. I have a large new note-book, which shall be devoted entirely to scientific detail.

Long talk with Agatha and Mrs. Marden in the evening about our marriage. We think that the summer vac. (the beginning of it) would be the best time for the wedding. Why should we delay? I grudge even those few months. Still, as Mrs. Marden says, there are a good many things to be arranged.

March 28th. — Mesmerized again by Miss Penelosa. Experience much the same as before, save that insensibility came on more quickly. See Note-book A for temperature of room, barometric pressure, pulse and respiration, as taken by Professor Wilson.

March 29th. — Mesmerized again. Details in Note-book A.

March 30th. — Sunday, and a blank day. I grudge any interruption of our experiments. At present they merely embrace the physical signs which go with slight, with complete, and with extreme insensibility. Afterwards we hope to pass on to the phenomena of suggestion and of lucidity. Professors have demonstrated these things upon women at Nancy, and at the Saltpetrière. It will be more convincing when a woman demonstrates it upon a professor, with a second professor as a witness. And that I should be the subject, I the sceptic, the materialist! At least I have shown that my devotion to science is greater than to my own personal consistency. The eating of our own words is the greatest sacrifice which truth ever requires of us.

My neighbour, Charles Sadler, the handsome young demonstrator of Anatomy, came in this evening to return a volume of Virchow's Archives which I had lent him. I call him young, but, as a matter of fact, he is a year older than I am.

"I understand, Gilroy," said he, "that you are being experimented upon by Miss Penelosa.

"Well," he went on, when I had acknowledged it, "if I were you I should not let it go any further. You will think me very impertinent, no doubt, but none the less I feel it to be my duty to advise you to have no more to do with her."

Of course I asked him why.

"I am so placed that I cannot enter into particulars as freely as I could wish," said he. "Miss Penelosa is the friend of my friend, and my position is a delicate one. I can only say this, that I have myself been the subject of some of the woman's experiments, and that they have left a most unpleasant impression upon my mind."

He could hardly expect me to be satisfied with that, and I tried hard to get something more definite out of him, but without success. Is it conceivable that he could be jealous at my having superseded him! Or is he one of those men of science who feel personally injured when facts run counter to their preconceived opinions? He cannot seriously suppose that because he has some vague grievance I am therefore to abandon a series of experiments which promise to be so fruitful of results. He appeared to be annoyed at the light way in which I treated his shadowy warnings, and we parted with some little coldness on both sides.

March 31st. — Mesmerized by Miss P.

April 1st. — Mesmerized by Miss P. (Note-book A.)

April 2nd. — Mesmerized by Miss P. (Sphygmographical chart taken by Professor Wilson.)

April 3rd. — It is possible that this course of mesmerism may be a little trying to the general constitution. Agatha says that I am thinner, and darker under the eyes. I am conscious of a nervous irritability which I had not observed in myself before. The least noise, for example, makes me start, and the stupidity of a student causes me exasperation instead of amusement. Agatha wishes me to stop; but I tell her that every course of study is trying, and that one can never attain a result without paying some price for it. When she sees the sensation which my forthcoming paper on "The Relation between Mind and Matter" may make, she will understand that it is worth a little nervous wear-and-tear. I should not be surprised if I got my F.R.S. over it.

Mesmerized again in the evening. The effect is produced more rapidly now, and the subjective visions are less marked. I keep full notes of each sitting. Wilson is leaving for town for a week or ten days, but we shall not interrupt the experiments, which depend for their value as much upon my sensations as on his observations.

April 4th. — I must be carefully on my guard. A complication has crept into our experiments which I had not reckoned upon. In my eagerness for scientific facts I have been foolishly blind to the human relations between Miss Penelosa and myself. I can write here what I would not breathe to a living soul. The unhappy woman appears to have formed an attachment for me.

I should not say such a thing even in the privacy of my own intimate journal if it had not come to such a pass that it is impossible to ignore it. For some time — that is, for the last week — there have been signs, which I have brushed aside and refused to think of. Her brightness when I come, her dejection when I go, her eagerness that I should come often, the expression of her eyes, the tone of her voice. I tried to think that they meant nothing and were perhaps only her ardent West Indian manner. But last night as I woke from the mesmeric sleep I put out my hand, unconsciously, involuntarily, and clasped hers. When I came fully to myself we were sitting with them locked, she looking up at me with an expectant smile. And the horrible thing was that I felt impelled to say what she expected me to say. What a false wretch I should have been! How I should have loathed myself to-day had I yielded to the temptation of that moment! But, thank God, I was strong enough to spring up and to hurry from the room. I was rude, I fear, but I could not—no, I could not trust myself another moment. I, a gentleman, a man of honour, engaged to one of the sweetest girls in England—and yet in a moment of reasonless passion I nearly professed love for this woman whom I hardly know! She is far older than myself, and a cripple. It is monstrous—odious—and yet the impulse was so strong that had I stayed another minute in her presence I should have committed myself. What was it? I have to teach others the workings of our organism, and what do I know of it myself! Was it the sudden uncropping of some lower stratum in my nature—a brutal primitive instinct suddenly asserting itself? I could almost believe the tales of obsession by evil spirits, so overmastering was the feeling.

Well, the incident places me in a most unfortunate position. On the one hand, I am very loth to abandon a series of experiments which have already gone so far, and which promise such brilliant results. On the other, if this unhappy woman has conceived a passion for me—but surely even now I must have made some hideous mistake. She, with her age and her deformity. It is impossible. And then she knew about Agatha. She understood how I was placed. She only smiled out of amusement, perhaps, when in my dazed state I seized her hand. It was my half-mesmerized brain which gave it a meaning, and sprang with such bestial swiftness to meet it. I wish I could persuade myself that it was indeed so. On the whole, perhaps, my wisest plan would be to postpone our other experiments until Wilson's return. I have written a note to Miss Penelosa, therefore, making no allusion to last night, but saying that a press of work would cause me to interrupt our sittings for a few days. She has answered, formally enough, to say that if I should change my mind I should find her at home at the usual hour.

10 P.M.—Well, well, what a thing of straw I am! I am coming to know myself better of late, and the more I know the lower I fall in my own estimation. Surely I was not always so weak as

this. At four o'clock I should have smiled had any one told me that I should go to Miss Penelosa's to-night; and yet at eight I was at Wilson's door as usual. I don't know how it occurred. The influence of habit, I suppose. Perhaps there is a mesmeric craze as there is an opium craze, and I am a victim to it. I only know that as I worked in my study I became more and more uneasy. I fidgeted. I worried. I could not concentrate my mind upon the papers in front of me. And then, at last, almost before I knew what I was doing, I seized my hat and hurried round to keep my usual appointment.

We had an interesting evening. Mrs. Wilson was present during most of the time, which prevented the embarrassment which one at least of us must have felt. Miss Penelosa's manner was quite the same as usual, and she expressed no surprise at my having come in spite of my note. There was nothing in her bearing to show that yesterday's incident had made any impression upon her, and so I am inclined to hope that I overrated it.

April 6th (evening). — No, no, I did not overrate it. I can no longer attempt to conceal from myself that this woman has conceived a passion for me. It is monstrous, but it is true. Again, to-night, I awoke from the mesmeric trance to find my hand in hers, and to suffer that odious feeling which urges me to throw away my honour, my career — everything — for the sake of this creature who, as I can plainly see when I am away from her influence, possesses no single charm upon earth. But when I am near her I do not feel this. She rouses something in me — something evil — something I had rather not think of. She paralyzes my better nature, too, at the moment when she stimulates my worse. Decidedly it is not good for me to be near her.

Last night was worse than before. Instead of flying I actually sat for some time with my hand in hers, talking over the most intimate subjects with her. We spoke of Agatha among other things. What could I have been dreaming of! Miss Penelosa said that she was conventional, and I agreed with her. She spoke once or twice in a disparaging way of her, and I did not protest. What a creature I have been!

Weak as I have proved myself to be, I am still strong enough to bring this sort of thing to an end. It shall not happen again. I have sense enough to fly when I cannot fight. From this Sunday

night onwards I shall never sit with Miss Penelosa again. Never!
Let the experiments go, let the research come to an end, anything
is better than facing this monstrous temptation which drags me
so low. I have said nothing to Miss Penelosa, but I shall simply
stay away. She can tell the reason without any words of mine.

April 7th. — Have stayed away as I said. It is a pity to ruin
such an interesting investigation, but it would be a greater pity
still to ruin my life, and I know that I cannot trust myself with
that woman.

11 P.M. — God help me! What is the matter with me! Am I
going mad? Let me try and be calm and reason with myself. First
of all I shall set down exactly what occurred.

It was nearly eight when I wrote the lines with which this day
begins. Feeling strangely restless and uneasy, I left my rooms
and walked round to spend the evening with Agatha and her
mother. They both remarked that I was pale and haggard.
About nine Professor Pratt-Haldane came in, and we played a
game of whist. I tried hard to concentrate my attention upon the
cards, but the feeling of restlessness grew and grew until I found
it impossible to struggle against it. I simply could not sit still at
the table. At last, in the very middle of a hand, I threw my cards
down, and, with some sort of an incoherent apology about
having an appointment, I rushed from the room. As if in a
dream, I have a vague recollection of tearing through the hall,
snatching my hat from the stand, and slamming the door behind
me. As in a dream, too, I have the impression of the double line
of gas-lamps, and my bespattered boots tell me that I must have
run down the middle of the road. It was all misty and strange
and unnatural. I came to Wilson's house, I saw Mrs. Wilson and
I saw Miss Penelosa. I hardly recall what we talked about, but I
do remember that Miss Penelosa shook the head of her crutch at
me in a playful way, and accused me of being late and of losing
interest in our experiments. There was no mesmerism, but I
stayed some time and have only just returned.

My brain is quite clear again, now, and I can think over what
has occurred. It is absurd to suppose that it is merely weakness
and force of habit. I tried to explain it in that way the other
night, but it will no longer suffice. It is something much deeper
and more terrible than that. Why, when I was at the Mardens'

whist-table I was dragged away, as if the noose of a rope had been cast round me. I can no longer disguise it from myself. The woman has her grip upon me. I am in her clutch. But I must keep my head and reason it out, and see what is best to be done.

But what a blind fool I have been! In my enthusiasm over my research I have walked straight into the pit, although it lay gaping before me. Did she not herself warn me? Did she not tell me, as I can read in my own journal, that when she has acquired power over a subject she can make him do her will? And she has acquired that power over me. I am, for the moment, at the beck and call of this creature with the crutch. I must come when she wills it. I must do as she wills. Worst of all, I must feel as she wills. I loathe her and fear her, yet while I am under the spell she can doubtless make me love her.

There is some consolation in the thought, then, that these odious impulses for which I have blamed myself do not really come from me at all. They are all transferred from her, little as I could have guessed it at the time. I feel cleaner and lighter for the thought.

April 8th. — Yes, now in broad daylight, writing coolly and with time for reflection, I am compelled to confirm everything which I find in my journal last night. I am in a horrible position, but, above all, I must not lose my head. I must pit my intellect against her powers. After all, I am no silly puppet to dance at the end of a string. I have energy, brains, courage. For all her devil's tricks I may beat her yet. May! I must, or what is to become of me?

Let me try to reason it out. This woman, by her own explanation, can dominate my nervous organism. She can project herself into my body and take command of it. She has a parasitic soul — yes, she is a parasite, a monstrous parasite. She creeps into my frame as the hermit crab does into the whelk's shell. I am powerless! What can I do? I am dealing with forces of which I know nothing. And I can tell no one of my trouble. They would set me down as a madman. Certainly, if it got noised abroad, the university would say that they had no need of a devil-ridden professor. And Agatha! No, no, I must face it alone.

I read over my notes of what the woman said when she spoke about her powers. There is one point which fills me with dismay.

She implies that when the influence is slight the subject knows what he is doing but cannot control himself, whereas, when it is strongly exerted, he is absolutely unconscious. Now, I have always known what I did, though less so last night than on the previous occasion. That seems to mean that she has never yet exerted her full powers upon me. Was ever a man so placed before!

Yes, perhaps there was, and very near me too. Charles Sadler must know something of this! His vague words of warning take a meaning now. Oh, if I had only listened to him then, before I helped by those repeated sittings to forge the links of the chain which binds me. But I will see him to-day. I will apologize to him for having treated his warning so lightly. I will see if he can advise me.

4 P.M. — No, he cannot. I have talked with him, and he showed such surprise at the first words in which I tried to express my unspeakable secret that I went no further. As far as I can gather (by hints and inferences rather than by any statement), his own experience was limited to some words or looks such as I have myself endured. His abandonment of Miss Penelosa is in itself a sign that he was never really in her toils. Oh, if he only knew his escape! He has to thank his phlegmatic Saxon temperament for it. I am black and Celtic, and this hag's clutch is deep in my nerves. Shall I ever get it out? Shall I ever be the same man that I was just one short fortnight ago?

Let me consider what I had better do. I cannot leave the university in the middle of the term. If I were free my course would be obvious. I should start at once and travel in Persia. But would she allow me to start? And could her influence not reach me in Persia, and bring me back to within touch of her crutch? I can only find out the limits of this hellish power by my own bitter experience. I will fight and fight and fight — and what can I do more?

I know very well that about eight o'clock to-night that craving for her society — that irresistible restlessness — will come upon me. How shall I overcome it? What shall I do? I must make it impossible for me to leave the room. I shall lock the door and throw the key out of the window. But then, what am I to do in the morning? Never mind about the morning. I must at all costs break this chain which holds me.

April 9th. — Victory! I have done splendidly! At seven o'clock last night I took a hasty dinner and then locked myself up in my bedroom and dropped the key into the garden. I chose a cheery novel, and lay in bed for three hours trying to read it, but really in a horrible state of trepidation, expecting every instant that I should become conscious of the impulse. Nothing of the sort occurred, however, and I awoke this morning with the feeling that a black nightmare had been lifted off me. Perhaps the creature realized what I had done, and understood that it was useless to try to influence me. At any rate, I have beaten her once, and if I can do it once I can do it again.

It was most awkward about the key in the morning. Luckily there was an under-gardener below, and I asked him to throw it up. No doubt he thought I had just dropped it. I will have doors and windows screwed up and six stout men to hold me down in my bed before I will surrender myself to be hag-ridden in this way.

I had a note from Mrs. Marden this afternoon asking me to go round and see her. I intended to do so in any case, but had not expected to find bad news waiting for me. It seems that the Armstrongs, from whom Agatha has expectations, are due home from Adelaide in the *Aurora,* and that they have written to Mrs. Marden and her to meet them in town. They will probably be away for a month or six weeks, and as the *Aurora* is due on Wednesday they must go at once — to-morrow if they are ready in time. My consolation is that when we meet again there will be no more parting between Agatha and me.

"I want you to do one thing, Agatha," said I, when we were alone together. "If you should happen to meet Miss Penelosa, either in town or here, you must promise me never again to allow her to mesmerize you."

Agatha opened her eyes.

"Why, it was only the other day that you were saying how interesting it all was, and how determined you were to finish your experiments."

"I know, but I have changed my mind since then."

"And you won't have it any more?"

"No."

"I am so glad, Austin. You can't think how pale and worn you have been lately. It was really our principal objection to going to London now, that we did not wish to leave you when you were so pulled down. And your manner has been so strange occasionally — especially that night when you left poor Professor Pratt-Haldane to play dummy. I am convinced that these experiments are very bad for your nerves."

"I think so too, dear."

"And for Miss Penelosa's nerves as well. You have heard that she is ill?"

"No."

"Mrs. Wilson told us so last night. She described it as a nervous fever. Professor Wilson is coming back this week, and of course Mrs. Wilson is very anxious that Miss Penelosa should be well again then, for he has quite a programme of experiments which he is anxious to carry out."

I was glad to have Agatha's promise, for it was enough that this woman should have one of us in her clutch. On the other hand, I was disturbed to hear about Miss Penelosa's illness. It rather discounts the victory which I appeared to win last night. I remember that she said that loss of health interfered with her power. That may be why I was able to hold my own so easily. Well, well, I must take the same precautions to-night and see what comes of it. I am childishly frightened when I think of her.

April 10th. — All went very well last night. I was amused at the gardener's face when I had again to hail him this morning and to ask him to throw up my key. I shall get a name among the servants if this sort of thing goes on. But the great point is that I stayed in my room without the slightest inclination to leave it. I do believe that I am shaking myself clear of this incredible bond — or is it only that the woman's power is in abeyance until she recovers her strength? I can but pray for the best.

The Mardens left this morning, and the brightness seems to have gone out of the spring sunshine. And yet it is very beautiful also as it gleams on the green chestnuts opposite my windows, and gives a touch of gaiety to the heavy lichen-mottled walls of the old colleges. How sweet and gentle and soothing is Nature! Who would think that there lurked in her also such vile forces, such odious possibilities! For of course I understand that this dreadful thing which has sprung out at me is neither supernatural nor even preternatural. No, it is a natural force which this woman can use and society is ignorant of. The mere fact that it ebbs with her strength shows how entirely it is subject to physical laws. If I had time I might probe it to the bottom and lay my hands upon its antidote. But you cannot tame the tiger when you are beneath his claws. You can but try to writhe away from him. Ah, when I look in the glass and see my own dark eyes and clear-cut Spanish face I long for a vitriol splash or a bout of the small-pox. One or the other might have saved me from this calamity.

I am inclined to think that I may have trouble to-night. There are two things which make me fear so. One is, that I met Mrs. Wilson on the street and that she tells me that Miss Penelosa is better, though still weak. I find myself wishing in my heart that the illness had been her last. The other is, that Professor Wilson comes back in a day or two, and his presence would act as a constraint upon her. I should not fear our interviews, if a third person were present. For both these reasons I have a presentiment of trouble to-night, and I shall take the same precautions as before.

April 10th. — No, thank God, all went well last night. I really could not face the gardener again. I locked my door and thrust the key underneath it, so that I had to ask the maid to let me out in the morning. But the precaution was really not needed, for I never had any inclination to go out at all. Three evenings in succession at home! I am surely near the end of my troubles, for Wilson will be home again either to-day or to-morrow. Shall I tell him of what I have gone through or not? I am convinced that I should not have the slightest sympathy from him. He would look upon me as an interesting case, and read a paper about me at the next meeting of the Psychical Society, in which he would gravely discuss the possibility of my being a deliberate liar, and weigh it against the chances of my being in an early stage of lunacy. No, I shall get no comfort out of Wilson.

I am feeling wonderfully fit and well. I don't think I ever lectured with greater spirit. Oh, if I could only get this shadow off my life how happy I should be! Young, fairly wealthy, in the front rank of my profession, engaged to a beautiful and charming girl — have I not everything which a man could ask for? Only one thing to trouble me, but what a thing it is!

MIDNIGHT. — I shall go mad. Yes, that will be the end of it. I
shall go mad. I am not far from it now. My head throbs as I rest
it on my hot hand. I am quivering all over like a scared horse.
Oh, what a night I have had! And yet I have some cause to be
satisfied also.

At the risk of becoming the laughing-stock of my own servant
I again slipped my key under the door, imprisoning myself for
the night. Then, finding it too early to go to bed, I lay down with
my clothes on and began to read one of Dumas' novels. Suddenly
I was gripped — gripped and dragged from the couch. It is only
thus that I can describe the overpowering nature of the force
which pounced upon me. I clawed at the coverlet. I clung to the
woodwork. I believe that I screamed out in my frenzy. It was all
useless — hopeless. I must go. There was no way out of it. It was
only at the outset that I resisted. The force soon became too
overmastering for that. I thank goodness that there were no
watchers there to interfere with me. I could not have answered
for myself if there had been. And besides the determination to
get out, there came to me also the keenest and coolest judgment
in choosing my means. I lit a candle and endeavoured, kneeling
in front of the door, to pull the key through with the feather-end
of a quill pen. It was just too short and pushed it further away.
Then with quiet persistence I got a paper-knife out of one of the
drawers, and with that I managed to draw the key back. I
opened the door, stepped into my study, took a photograph of
myself from the bureau, wrote something across it, placed it in
the inside pocket of my coat, and then started off for Wilson's.

It was all wonderfully clear, and yet disassociated from the
rest of my life, as the incidents of even the most vivid dream
might be. A peculiar double consciousness possessed me. There
was the predominant alien will, which was bent upon drawing
me to the side of its owner, and there was the feebler protesting
personality, which I recognized as being myself, tugging feebly
at the overmastering impulse as a led terrier might at its chain. I
can remember recognizing these two conflicting forces, but I
recall nothing of my walk, nor of how I was admitted to the
house. Very vivid, however, is my recollection of how I met Miss
Penelosa. She was reclining on the sofa in the little boudoir in
which our experiments had usually been carried out. Her head
was rested on her hand, and a tiger-skin rug had been partly

drawn over her. She looked up expectantly as I entered, and, as the lamplight fell upon her face, I could see that she was very pale and thin, with dark hollows under her eyes. She smiled at me and pointed to a stool beside her. It was with her left hand that she pointed, and I, running eagerly forward, seized it — I loathe myself as I think of it — and pressed it passionately to my lips. Then, seating myself upon the stool, and still retaining her hand, I gave her the photograph which I had brought with me, and talked, and talked, and talked, of my love for her, of my grief over her illness, of my joy at her recovery, of the misery it was to me to be absent a single evening from her side. She lay quietly looking down at me with imperious eyes and her provocative smile. Once I remember that she passed her hand over my hair as one caresses a dog. And it gave me pleasure, the caress. I thrilled under it. I was her slave, body and soul, and for the moment I rejoiced in my slavery.

And then came the blessed change. Never tell me that there is not a Providence. I was on the brink of perdition. My feet were on the edge. Was it a coincidence that at that very instant help should come! No, no, no, there is a Providence, and His hand has drawn me back. There is something in the universe stronger than this devil woman with her tricks. Ah, what a balm to my heart it is to think so!

As I looked up at her I was conscious of a change in her. Her face, which had been pale before, was now ghastly. Her eyes were dull and the lids drooped heavily over them. Above all, the look of serene confidence had gone from her features. Her mouth had weakened. Her forehead had puckered. She was frightened and undecided. And, as I watched the change, my own spirit fluttered and struggled, trying hard to tear itself from the grip which held it — a grip which from moment to moment grew less secure.

"Austin," she whispered, "I have tried to do too much. I was not strong enough. I have not recovered yet from my illness. But I could not live longer without seeing you. You won't leave me, Austin. This is only a passing weakness. If you will only give me five minutes I shall be myself again. Give me the small decanter from the table in the window."

But I had regained my soul. With her waning strength the influence had cleared away from me and left me free. And I was aggressive—bitterly, fiercely aggressive. For once, at least, I could make this woman understand what my real feelings towards her were. My soul was filled with a hatred as bestial as the love against which it was a reaction. It was the savage, murderous passion of the revolted serf. I could have taken the crutch from her side and beaten her face in with it. She threw her hands up, as if to avoid a blow, and cowered away from me into the corner of the settee.

"The brandy!" she gasped. "The brandy!"

I took the decanter and poured it over the roots of a palm in the window. Then I snatched the photograph from her hand and tore it into a hundred pieces.

"You vile woman!" I said. "If I did my duty to society you would never leave the room alive."

"I love you, Austin. I love you," she wailed.

"Yes," I cried. "And Charles Sadler before. And how many others before that?"

"Charles Sadler!" she gasped. "He has spoken to you! So, Charles Sadler, Charles Sadler!" Her voice came through her white lips like a snake's hiss.

"Yes, I know you, and others shall know you too. You shameless creature! You knew how I stood. And yet you used your vile power to bring me to your side. You may perhaps do so again, but at least you will remember that you have heard me say that I love Miss Marden from the bottom of my soul, and that I loathe you, abhor you. The very sight of you and the sound of your voice fill me with horror and disgust. The thought of you is repulsive. That is how I feel towards you, and if it pleases you by your tricks to draw me again to your side, as you have done to-night, you will at least, I should think, have little satisfaction in trying to make a lover out of a man who has told you his real opinion of you. You may put what words you will into my mouth, but you cannot help remembering——"

I stopped, for the woman's head had fallen back and she had fainted. She could not bear to hear what I had to say to her. What a glow of satisfaction it gives me to think that come what may in the future she can never misunderstand my true feelings towards her. But what will occur in the future? What will she do next? I dare not think of it. Oh, if only I could hope that she will leave me alone! But when I think of what I said to her—never mind, I have been stronger than she for once.

April 11th.—I hardly slept last night, and found myself in the morning so unstrung and feverish that I was compelled to ask Pratt-Haldane to do my lecture for me. It is the first that I have ever missed. I rose at midday; but my head is aching, my hands quivering, and my nerves in a pitiable state.

Who should come round this evening but Wilson. He has just come back from London, where he has lectured, read papers, convened meetings, exposed a medium, conducted a series of experiments on thought transference, entertained Professor Richet of Paris, spent hours gazing into a crystal, and obtained some evidence as to the passage of matter through matter. All this he poured into my ears in a single gust.

"But you," he cried at last, "you are not looking well. And Miss Penelosa is quite prostrated to-day. How about the experiments?"

"I have abandoned them."

"Tut, tut! Why?"

"The subject seems to me to be a dangerous one."

Out came his big brown note-book.

"This is of great interest," said he. "What are your grounds for saying that it is a dangerous one? Please give your facts in chronological order with approximate dates, and names of reliable witnesses with their permanent addresses."

"First of all," I asked, "would you tell me whether you have collected any cases where the mesmerist has gained a command over the subject and has used it for evil purposes?"

"Dozens," he cried exultantly. "Crime by suggestion——"

"I don't mean suggestion. I mean where a sudden impulse comes from a person at a distance—an uncontrollable impulse."

"Obsession!" he shrieked, in an ecstasy of delight. "It is the rarest condition. We have eight cases, five well attested. You don't mean to say——" His exultation made him hardly articulate.

"No, I don't," said I. "Good evening! You will excuse me, but I am not very well to-night." And so at last I got rid of him, still brandishing his pencil and his note-book. My troubles may be bad to bear, but at least it is better to hug them to myself than to have myself exhibited by Wilson, like a freak at a fair. He has lost sight of human beings. Everything to him is a case and a phenomenon. I will die before I speak to him again upon the matter.

April 12th. — Yesterday was a blessed day of quiet, and I enjoyed an uneventful night. Wilson's presence is a great consolation. What can the woman do now? Surely when she has heard me say what I have said she will conceive the same disgust for me which I have for her. She could not — no, she could not — desire to have a lover who had insulted her so. No, I believe I am free from her love — but how about her hate? Might she not use these powers of hers for revenge? Tut, why should I frighten myself over shadows! She will forget about me and I shall forget about her, and all will be well.

April 13th. — My nerves have quite recovered their tone. I really believe that I have conquered the creature. But I must confess to living in some suspense. She is well again, for I hear that she was driving with Mrs. Wilson in the High Street in the afternoon.

April 14th. — I do wish I could get away from the place altogether. I shall fly to Agatha's side the very day that the term closes. I suppose it is pitiably weak of me, but this woman gets upon my nerves most terribly. I have seen her again, and I have spoken with her.

It was just after lunch, and I was smoking a cigarette in my study when I heard the step of my servant Murray in the passage. I was languidly conscious that a second step was audible behind, and had hardly troubled myself to speculate who it might be, when suddenly a slight noise brought me out of my chair with my skin creeping with apprehension. I had never particularly observed before what sort of sound the tapping of a crutch was, but my quivering nerves told me that I heard it now in the sharp wooden clack which alternated with the muffled thud of the footfall. Another instant and my servant had shown her in.

I did not attempt the usual conventions of society, nor did she. I simply stood with the smouldering cigarette in my hand and gazed at her. She in her turn looked silently at me, and at her look I remembered how in these very pages I had tried to define the expression of her eyes, whether they were furtive or fierce. To-day they were fierce — coldly and inexorably so.

"Well," said she at last, "are you still of the same mind as when I saw you last?"

"I have always been of the same mind."

"Let us understand each other, Professor Gilroy," said she slowly. "I am not a very safe person to trifle with, as you should realize by now. It was you who asked me to enter into a series of experiments with you, it was you who won my affections, it was you who professed your love for me, it was you who brought me your own photograph with words of affection upon it, and finally, it was you who on the very same evening thought fit to insult me most outrageously, addressing me as no man has ever dared to speak to me yet. Tell me that those words came from you in a moment of passion, and I am prepared to forget and to forgive them. You did not mean what you said, Austin? You do not really hate me?"

I might have pitied this deformed woman — such a longing for love broke suddenly through the menace of her eyes. But then I thought of what I had gone through, and my heart set like flint.

"If you ever heard me speak of love," said I, "you know very well that it was your voice which spoke and not mine. The only words of truth which I have ever been able to say to you are those which you heard when last we met."

"I know. Some one has set you against me. It was he." She tapped with her crutch upon the floor. "Well, you know very well that I could bring you this instant crouching like a spaniel to my feet. You will not find me again in my hours of weakness when you can insult me with impunity. Have a care what you are doing, Professor Gilroy. You stand in a terrible position. You have not yet realized the hold which I have upon you."

I shrugged my shoulders and turned away.

"Well," said she, after a pause, "if you despise my love I must see what can be done with fear. You smile, but the day will come when you will come screaming to me for pardon. Yes, you will grovel on the ground before me, proud as you are, and you will curse the day that ever you turned me from your best friend into your most bitter enemy. Have a care, Professor Gilroy." I saw a white hand shaking in the air, and a face which was scarcely human so convulsed was it with passion. An instant later she was gone, and I heard the quick hobble and tap receding down the passage.

But she has left a weight upon my heart. Vague presentiments of coming misfortune lie heavy upon me. I try in vain to persuade myself that these are only words of empty anger. I can remember those relentless eyes too clearly to think so. What shall I do – ah, what shall I do? I am no longer master of my own soul. At any moment this loathsome parasite may creep into me, and then — ? I must tell some one my hideous secret – I must tell it or go mad. If I had some one to sympathize and advise! Wilson is out of the question. Charles Sadler would understand me only so far as his own experience carries him. Pratt-Haldane! He is a well-balanced man, a man of great common sense and resource. I will go to him. I will tell him everything. God grant that he may be able to advise me!

6.45 P.M. – No, it is useless. There is no human help for me. I must fight this out single-handed. Two courses lie before me: I might become the woman's lover, or I must endure such persecutions as she can inflict upon me. Even if none come I shall live in a hell of apprehension. But she may torture me, she may drive me mad, she may kill me, I will never, never, never give in. What can she inflict which would be worse than the loss of Agatha, and the knowledge that I am a perjured liar and have forfeited the name of gentleman?

Pratt-Haldane was most amiable, and listened with all politeness to my story. But when I looked at his heavy set features, his slow eyes, and the ponderous study furniture which surrounded him, I could hardly tell him what I had come to say. It was all so substantial, so material. And besides, what would I myself have said a short month ago if one of my colleagues had come to me with a story of demoniac possession? Perhaps I should have been less patient than he was. As it was, he took notes of my statement, asked me how much tea I drank, how many hours I slept, whether I had been over-working much, had I had sudden pains in the head, evil dreams, singing in the ears, flashes before the eyes – all questions which pointed to his belief that brain congestion was at the bottom of my trouble. Finally, he dismissed me with a great many platitudes about open-air exercise and avoidance of nervous excitement. His prescription, which was for chloral and bromide, I rolled up and threw into the gutter.

No, I can look for no help from any human being. If I consult any more they may put their heads together and I may find myself in an asylum. I can but grip my courage with both hands and pray that an honest man may not be abandoned.

April 15th. — It is the sweetest spring within the memory of man. So green, so mild, so beautiful! Ah, what a contrast between Nature without and my own soul, so torn with doubt and terror! It has been an uneventful day, but I know that I am on the edge of an abyss. I know it, and yet I go on with the routine of my life. The one bright spot is that Agatha is happy and well, and out of all danger. If this creature had a hand on each of us, what might she not do?

April 16th. — The woman is ingenious in her torments. She knows how fond I am of my work, and how highly my lectures are thought of. So it is from that point that she now attacks me. It will end, I can see, in my losing my professorship, but I will fight to the finish. She shall not drive me out of it without a struggle.

I was not conscious of any change during my lecture this morning, save that for a minute or two I had a dizziness and swimminess which rapidly passed away. On the contrary, I congratulated myself upon having made my subject (the functions of the red corpuscles) both interesting and clear. I was surprised, therefore, when a student came into my laboratory immediately after the lecture and complained of being puzzled by the discrepancy between my statements and those in the textbooks. He showed me his note-book, in which I was reported as having in one portion of the lecture championed the most outrageous and unscientific heresies. Of course I denied it, and declared that he had misunderstood me; but on comparing his notes with those of his companions, it became clear that he was right, and that I really had made some most preposterous statements. Of course I shall explain it away as being the result of a moment of aberration, but I feel only too sure that it will be the first of a series. It is but a month now to the end of the session, and I pray that I may be able to hold out until then.

April 26th. — Ten days have elapsed since I have had the heart to make any entry in my journal. Why should I record my own humiliation and degradation! I had vowed never to open it again. And yet the force of habit is strong, and here I find myself taking up once more the record of my own dreadful experiences — in much the same spirit in which a suicide has been known to take notes of the effects of the poison which killed him.

Well, the crash which I had foreseen has come — and that no further back than yesterday. The university authorities have taken my lectureship from me. It has been done in the most delicate way, purporting to be a temporary measure to relieve me from the effects of overwork and to give me the opportunity of recovering my health. None the less it has been done, and I am no longer Professor Gilroy. The laboratory is still in my charge, but I have little doubt that that also will soon go.

The fact is that my lectures had become the laughing-stock of the university. My class was crowded with students who came to see and hear what the eccentric professor would do or say next. I cannot go into the detail of my humiliation. Oh, that devilish woman! There is no depth of buffoonery and imbecility to which she has not forced me. I would begin my lecture clearly and well — but always with the sense of a coming eclipse. Then as I felt the influence I would struggle against it, striving with clenched hands and beads of sweat upon my brow to get the better of it, while the students, hearing my incoherent words and watching my contortions, would roar with laughter at the antics of their professor. And then, when she had once fairly mastered me, out would come the most outrageous things: silly jokes, sentiments as though I were proposing a toast, snatches of ballads, personal abuse even against some member of my class. And then in a moment my brain would clear again and my lecture proceed decorously to the end. No wonder that my conduct has been the talk of the colleges! No wonder that the university senate has been compelled to take official notice of such a scandal. Oh, that devilish woman!

And the most dreadful part of it all is my own loneliness. Here I sit in a commonplace English bow-window looking out upon a commonplace English street, with its garish 'busses and its lounging policemen, and behind me there hangs a shadow which is out of all keeping with the age and place. In the home of knowledge I am weighed down and tortured by a power of which science knows nothing. No magistrate would listen to me. No paper would discuss my case. No doctor would believe my symptoms. My own most intimate friends would only look upon it as a sign of brain derangement. I am out of all touch with my kind. Oh, that devilish woman! Let her have a care! She may push me too far. When the law cannot help a man he may take a law for himself.

She met me in the High Street yesterday evening and spoke to me. It was as well for her, perhaps, that it was not between the hedges of a lonely country road. She asked me with her cold smile whether I had been chastened yet. I did not deign to answer her. "We must try another turn of the screw," said she. Have a care, my lady, have a care! I had her at my mercy once. Perhaps another chance may come.

April 28th. — The suspension of my lectureship has had the effect also of taking away her means of annoying me, and so I have enjoyed two blessed days of peace. After all, there is no reason to despair. Sympathy pours in to me from all sides, and every one agrees that it is my devotion to science and the arduous nature of my researches which have shaken my nervous system. I have had the kindest message from the council, advising me to travel abroad, and expressing the confident hope that I may be able to resume all my duties by the beginning of the summer term. Nothing could be more flattering than their allusions to my career and to my services to the university. It is only in misfortune that one can test one's own popularity. This creature may weary of tormenting me, and then all may yet be well. May God grant it!

April 29th. — Our sleepy little town has had a small sensation. The only knowledge of crime which we ever have is when a rowdy undergraduate breaks a few lamps, or comes to blows with a policeman. Last night, however, there was an attempt made to break into the branch of the Bank of England, and we are all in a flutter in consequence.

Parkinson the manager is an intimate friend of mine, and I found him very much excited when I walked round there after breakfast. Had the thieves broken into the counting-house they would still have had the safes to reckon with, so that the defense was considerably stronger than the attack. Indeed the latter does not appear to have ever been very formidable. Two of the lower windows have marks as if a chisel or some such instrument had been pushed under them to force them open. The police should have a good clue, for the woodwork had been done with green paint only the day before, and from the smears it is evident that some of it has found its way on to the criminal's hands or clothes.

4.30 P.M. — Ah, that accursed woman! That thrice-accursed woman! Never mind! She shall not beat me! No, she shall not! But oh, the she-devil! She has taken my professorship; now she would take my honour. Is there nothing I can do against her, nothing save — ah, but hard pushed as I am I cannot bring myself to think of that!

It was about an hour ago that I went into my bedroom and was brushing my hair before the glass when suddenly my eyes lit upon something which left me so sick and cold that I sat down upon the edge of the bed and began to cry. It is many a long year since I shed tears, but all my nerve was gone, and I could but sob and sob in impotent grief and anger. There was my house jacket, the coat I usually wear after dinner, hanging on its peg by the wardrobe, with the right sleeve thickly crusted from wrist to elbow with daubs of green paint.

So this was what she meant by another turn of the screw! She had made a public imbecile of me. Now she would brand me as a criminal. This time she has failed. But how about the next? I dare not think of it — and of Agatha, and my poor old mother! I wish that I were dead!

Yes, this is the other turn of the screw. And this is also what she meant, no doubt, when she said that I had not realized yet the power she has over me. I look back at my account of my conversation with her, and I see how she declared that with a slight exertion of her will her subject would be conscious, and with a stronger one unconscious. Last night I was unconscious. I could have sworn that I slept soundly in my bed without so much as a dream. And yet those stains tell me that I dressed, made my way out, attempted to open the bank windows, and returned. Was I observed? It is possible that some one saw me do it and followed me home! Ah, what a hell my life has become! I have no peace, no rest. But my patience is nearing its end.

10 P.M.—I have cleaned my coat with turpentine. I do not think that any one could have seen me. It was with my screwdriver that I made the marks. I found it all crusted with paint, and I have cleaned it. My head aches as if it would burst, and I have taken five grains of antipyrene. If it were not for Agatha I should have taken fifty and had an end of it.

May 3rd. — Three quiet days. This hell-fiend is like a cat with a mouse. She lets me loose only to pounce upon me again. I am never so frightened as when everything is still. My physical state is deplorable—perpetual hiccough and ptosis of the left eyelid. I have heard from the Mardens that they will be back the day after to-morrow. I do not know whether I am glad or sorry. They were safe in London. Once here they may be drawn into the miserable network in which I am myself struggling. And I must tell them of it. I cannot marry Agatha so long as I know that I am not responsible for my own actions. Yes, I must tell them, even if it brings everything to an end between us.

To-night is the university ball, and I must go. God knows I never felt less in the humour for festivity, but I must not have it said that I am unfit to appear in public. If I am seen there and have speech with some of the elders of the university it will go a long way towards showing them that it would be unjust to take my chair away from me.

11 P.M.—I have been to the ball. Charles Sadler and I went together, but I have come away before him. I shall wait up for him, however, for indeed I fear to go to sleep these nights. He is a cheery, practical fellow, and a chat with him will steady my nerves. On the whole, the evening was a great success. I talked to every one who has influence, and I think that I made them realize that my chair is not vacant quite yet. The creature was at the ball—unable to dance, of course, but sitting with Mrs. Wilson. Again and again her eyes rested upon me. They were almost the last things I saw before I left the room. Once as I sat sideways to her I watched her and saw that her gaze was following some one else. It was Sadler, who was dancing at the time with the second Miss Thurston. To judge by her expression it is well for him that he is not in her grip as I am. He does not know

the escape he has had. I think I hear his step in the street now, and I will go down and let him in. If he will—

May 4th. — Why did I break off in this way last night? I never went down-stairs after all—at least I have no recollection of doing so. But, on the other hand, I cannot remember going to bed. One of my hands is greatly swollen this morning, and yet I have no remembrance of injuring it yesterday. Otherwise I am feeling all the better for last night's festivity. But I cannot understand how it is that I did not meet Charles Sadler when I so fully intended to do so. Is it possible—my God, it is only too probable! Has she been leading me some devil's chance again? I will go down to Sadler and ask him.

MIDDAY. — The thing has come to a crisis. My life is not worth living. But if I am to die then she shall come also. I will not leave her behind to drive some other man mad as she has me. No, I have come to the limit of my endurance. She has made me as desperate and dangerous a man as walks the earth. God knows I have never had the heart to hurt a fly, and yet if I had my hands now upon that woman she should never leave this room alive. I shall see her this very day, and she shall learn what she has to expect from me.

I went to Sadler and found him to my surprise in bed. As I entered he sat up and turned a face towards me which sickened me as I looked at it.

"Why, Sadler, what has happened?" I cried, but my heart turned cold as I said it.

"Gilroy," he answered, mumbling with his swollen lips, "I have for some weeks been under the impression that you are a madman. Now I know it, and that you are a dangerous one as well. If it were not that I am unwilling to make a scandal in the college you would now be in the hands of the police."

"Do you mean—?" I cried.

"I mean that as I opened the door last night you rushed out upon me, struck me with both your fists in the face, knocked me down, kicked me furiously on the side, and left me lying almost unconscious in the street. Look at your own hand bearing witness against you."

Yes, there it was, puffed up with sponge-like knuckles as after some terrific blow. What could I do? Though he put me down as a madman I must tell him all. I sat by his bed and went over all my troubles from the beginning. I poured them out with quivering hands and burning words which might have carried conviction to the most sceptical.

"She hates you and she hates me," I cried. "She revenged herself last night on both of us at once. She saw me leave the ball and she must have seen you also. She knew how long it would take you to reach home. Then she had but to use her wicked will. Ah, your bruised face is a small thing beside my bruised soul!"

He was struck by my story. That was evident. "Yes, yes, she watched me out of the room," he muttered. "She is capable of it. But is it possible that she has really reduced you to this? What do you intend to do?"

"To stop it," I cried. "I am perfectly desperate. I shall give her fair warning to-day, and the next time will be the last."

"Do nothing rash," said he.

"Rash!" I cried. "The only rash thing is that I should postpone it another hour." With that I rushed to my room. And here I am on the eve of what may be the great crisis of my life. I shall start at once. I have gained one thing to-day, for I have made one man at least realize the truth of this monstrous experience of mine. And, if the worst should happen, this diary remains as a proof of the goad that has driven me.

EVENING. — When I came to Wilson's I was shown up, and found that he was sitting with Miss Penelosa. For half an hour I had to endure his fussy talk about his recent research into the exact nature of the spiritualistic rap, while the creature and I sat in silence looking across the room at each other. I read a sinister amusement in her eyes, and she must have seen hatred and menace in mine. I had almost despaired of having speech with her when he was called from the room and we were left for a few minutes together.

"Well, Professor Gilroy — or is it Mr. Gilroy?" said she, with that bitter smile of hers, "how is your friend Mr. Charles Sadler after the ball?"

"You fiend!" I cried, "you have come to the end of your tricks now. I will have no more of them. Listen to what I say." — I strode across and shook her roughly by the shoulder. "As sure as there is a God in heaven I swear that if you try another of your devilries upon me I will have your life for it. Come what may, I will have your life. I have come to the end of what a man can endure."

"Accounts are not quite settled between us," said she, with a passion that equalled my own. "I can love and I can hate. You had your choice. You chose to spurn the first, now you must test the other. It will take a little more to break your spirit, I see, but broken it shall be. Miss Marden comes back to-morrow as I understand."

"What has that to do with you?" I cried. "It is a pollution that you should dare even to think of her. If I thought that you would harm her — "

She was frightened I could see, though she tried to brazen it out. She read the black thought in my mind and cowered away from me.

"She is fortunate in having such a champion," said she. "He actually dares to threaten a lonely woman. I must really congratulate Miss Marden upon her protector."

The words were bitter, but the voice and manner were more acid still.

"There is no use talking," said I. "I only came here to tell you — and to tell you most solemnly — that your next outrage upon me will be your last." With that, as I heard Wilson's step upon the stairs, I walked from the room.

Ay, she may look venomous and deadly, but for all that she is beginning to see now that she has as much to fear from me as I can have from her. Murder! It has an ugly sound. But you don't talk of murdering a snake or of murdering a tiger. Let her have a care now.

May 5th. — I met Agatha and her mother at the station at eleven o'clock. She is looking so bright, so happy, so beautiful. And she was so overjoyed to see me. What have I done to deserve such love! I went back home with them and we lunched together. All the troubles seem in a moment to have been shredded back from my life. She tells me that I am looking pale, and worried, and ill. The dear child puts it down to my loneliness and the perfunctory attentions of a housekeeper. I pray that she may never know the truth! May the shadow, if shadow there must be, lie ever black across my life and leave hers in the sunshine! I have just come back from them, feeling a new man.

With her by my side I think that I could show a bold face to anything which life might send.

5 P.M.—Now let me try to be accurate. Let me try to say exactly how it occurred. It is fresh in my mind and I can set it down correctly, though it is not likely that the time will ever come when I shall forget the doings of to-day.

I had returned from the Mardens after lunch, and was cutting some microscopic sections in my freezing microtome, when in an instant I lost consciousness in the sudden hateful fashion which has become only too familiar to me of late.

When my senses came back to me I was sitting in a small chamber very different from the one in which I had been working. It was cosy and bright, with chintz-covered settees, coloured hangings, and a thousand pretty little trifles upon the wall. A small ornamental clock ticked in front of me, and the hands pointed to half-past three. It was all quite familiar to me, and yet I stared about for a moment in a half-dazed way until my eyes fell upon a cabinet photograph of myself upon the top of the piano. At the other side stood one of Mrs. Marden. Then, of course, I remembered where I was. It was Agatha's boudoir.

But how came I there, and what did I want? A horrible sinking came to my heart. Had I been sent here on some devilish errand? Had that errand already been done? Surely it must, otherwise why should I be allowed to come back to consciousness? Oh, the agony of that moment! What had I done! I sprang to my feet in my despair, and as I did so a small glass bottle fell from my knees on to the carpet.

It was unbroken and I picked it up. Outside was written "Sulphuric Acid. Fort." When I drew the round glass stopper a thick fume rose slowly up and a pungent choking smell pervaded the room. I recognized it as one which I kept for chemical testing in my chambers. But why had I brought a bottle of vitriol into Agatha's chamber? Was it not this thick reeking liquid with which jealous women had been known to mar the beauty of their rivals! My heart stood still as I held the bottle to the light. Thank God, it was full! No mischief had been done as yet. But had Agatha come in a minute sooner, was it not certain that the hellish parasite within me would have dashed the stuff on to her —ah! it will not bear to be thought of. But it must have been for that. Why else should I have brought it? At the thought of what

I might have done my worn nerves broke down and I sat shivering and twitching, the pitiable wreck of a man. It was the sound of Agatha's voice and the rustle of her dress which restored me. I looked up and saw her blue eyes, so full of tenderness and pity, gazing down at me.

"We must take you away to the country, Austin," she said, "you want rest and quiet. You look wretchedly ill."

"Oh, it is nothing," said I, trying to smile. "It was only a momentary weakness. I am all right again now."

"I am so sorry to keep you waiting. Poor boy, you must have been here for quite half an hour. The vicar was in the drawing-room, and as I knew that you did not care for him I thought it better that Jane should show you up here. I thought the man would never go."

"Thank God he stayed! Thank God he stayed!" I cried hysterically.

"Why, what is the matter with you, Austin?" she asked, holding my arm as I staggered up from the chair. "Why are you glad that the vicar stayed? And what is this little bottle in your hand?"

"Nothing," I cried, thrusting it into my pocket. "But I must go. I have something important to do."

"How stern you look, Austin. I have never seen your face like that. You are angry?"

"Yes, I am angry."

"But not with me?"

"No, no, my darling. You would not understand."

"But you have not told me why you came."

"I came to ask you whether you would always love me—no matter what I did or what shadow might fall on my name. Would you believe in me and trust me however black appearances might be against me?"

"You know that I would, Austin."

"Yes, I know that you would. What I do I shall do for you. I am driven to it. There is no other way out, my darling!" I kissed her and rushed from the room.

The time for indecision was at an end. As long as the creature threatened my own prospects and my honour there might be a question as to what I should do. But now when Agatha—my innocent Agatha—was endangered, my duty lay before me like a turnpike-road. I had no weapon, but I never paused for that. What weapon should I need when I felt every muscle quivering with the strength of a frenzied man? I ran through the streets, so set upon what I had to do that I was only dimly conscious of the faces of friends whom I met — dimly conscious also that Professor Wilson met me, running with equal precipitance in the opposite direction. Breathless but resolute I reached the house and rang the bell. A white-cheeked maid opened the door, and turned whiter yet when she saw the face that looked in at her.

"Show me up at once to Miss Penelosa," I demanded.

"Sir," she gasped, "Miss Penelosa died this afternoon at half-past three."

The Winning Shot

"The Winning Shot" is undoubtedly the rarest item in this collection, and is probably the very rarest piece of published Doyle. This editor knows of only four copies in existence, and it has never been reprinted until now.

It was originally published in London by John Dicks in a publication entitled AN ACTOR'S DUEL AND THE WINNING SHOT *"by Conan Doyle." This curious little paperback is actually the John Dicks publishers' catalogue for 1894, combined with the two short stories named in the title so that it might have a popular appeal and be sold on the newsstands. "An Actor's Duel," despite some evidence that it was once sold, or at least offered, to* BLACKWOOD'S *magazine, this editor is willing to swear was not written by Doyle. It is an insipid, rambling, pointless, overwritten tale about an actor's on-stage revenge upon the colleague who ruined his daughter. It is not at all in Doyle's style. And it would not be by any means the only time that his name was put on someone else's story by an unscrupulous publisher.*

"The Winning Shot," on the other hand, is prime Conan Doyle. One wonders where a third-rate publisher such as Dicks got it, for, if it is not Doyle's best, it is forcefully written and clearly belongs to the phase of paired sexual compulsion and supernaturalism of which THE PARASITE *is such a supreme example. The device of having the story told in the first person by a young lady is not unique, either. Once before, in a comedy tale called "Our Derby Sweepstakes" (1882), he had done the same, with equal credibility. Doyle was always extending himself, with seeming effortlessness, to new experiments in storytelling, and they almost always were successful.*

"CAUTION. — The public are hereby cautioned against the man calling himself Octavius Gaster. He is to be recognized by his great height, his flaxen hair, and by a deep scar upon his left cheek, extending from the eye to the angle of the mouth. His predilection for bright colours — green neckties, and the like — may help to identify him. A slight foreign accent is to be detected in his speech. This man is beyond the reach of the law, but is more dangerous than a mad dog. Shun him as you would shun the pestilence that walketh at noonday. Any communication as to his whereabouts will be thankfully acknowledged by A. C. U., Lincoln's Inn, London."

This is a copy of an advertisement which may have been noticed by many readers in the columns of the London morning papers during the early part of the present year. It has, I believe, excited considerable curiosity in certain quarters, and many guesses have been hazarded as to the identity of Octavius Gaster and the nature of the charge brought against him. When I state that the "caution" has been inserted by my elder brother, Arthur Cooper Underwood, barrister-at-law, upon my representations, it will be acknowledged that I am the most fitting person to enter upon an authentic explanation.

Hitherto the horror and vagueness of my suspicion, combined with my grief at the loss of my poor darling on the very eve of our wedding, have prevented me from revealing the events of last August to anyone save my brother. Now, however, looking back, I can fit in many little facts almost unnoticed at the time, which form a chain of evidence that, though worthless in a court of law, may yet have some effect upon the mind of the public. I shall therefore relate, without exaggeration or prejudice, all that occurred from the day upon which this man, Octavius Gaster, entered Toynby Hall up to the great rifle competition. I know that many people will always ridicule the supernatural, or what our poor intellects choose to regard as supernatural, and that the fact of my being a woman will be thought to weaken my evidence. I can only plead that I have never been weak-minded or impressionable, and that other people formed the same opinion of Octavius Gaster that I did. Now to the story.

It was at Colonel Pillar's place at Roborough, in the pleasant county of Devon, that we spent our autumn holidays. For some months I had been engaged to his eldest son Charley, and it was hoped that the marriage might take place before the termination of the Long Vacation. Charley was considered "safe" for his degree, and in any case was rich enough to be practically independent, while I was by no means penniless. The old Colonel was delighted at the prospect of the match, and so was my mother; so that, look what way we would, there seemed to be no cloud above our horizon. It was no wonder, then, that that August was a happy one. Even the most miserable of mankind would have laid his woes aside under the genial influence of the merry household at Toynby Hall.

There was Lieutenant Daseby, or "Jack," as he was invariably called, fresh home from Japan in Her Majesty's ship *Shark,* who was on the same interesting footing with Fanny Pillar, Charley's sister, as Charley was with me, so that we were able to lend each other a certain moral support.

Then there was Harry, Charley's younger brother, and Trevor, his bosom friend at Cambridge.

Finally, there was my mother, dearest of old ladies, beaming at us through her gold-rimmed spectacles, anxiously smoothing every little difficulty in the way of the two young couples, and never weary of detailing to them her own doubts, and fears, and perplexities when that gay young blood, Mr. Nicholas Underwood, came a-wooing into the provinces, and forswore Crockford's and Tattersall's for the sake of the country parson's daughter.

I must not, however, forget the gallant old warrior who was our host; with his time-honoured jokes, and his gout, and his harmless affectation of ferocity.

"I don't know what's come over the governor lately," Charley used to say. "He has never cursed the Liberal Administration since you've been here, Lottie; and my belief is that unless he has a good blow-off, that Irish question will get into his system and finish him."

Perhaps in the privacy of his own apartment the veteran used to make up for his self-abnegation during the day. He seemed to have taken a special fancy to me, which he showed in a hundred little attentions.

"You're a good lass," he remarked one evening, in a very port-winey whisper. "Charley's a lucky dog, egad! and has more discrimination than I thought. Mark my words, Miss Underwood, you'll find that young gentleman isn't such a fool as he looks!"

With which equivocal compliment the Colonel solemnly covered his face with his handkerchief, and went off into the land of dreams.

How well I remember the day that was the commencement of all our miseries! Dinner was over, and we were in the drawing-room, with the windows open to admit the balmy southern breeze. My mother was sitting in the corner, engaged on a piece of fancy-work, and occasionally putting forth some truism which the dear old soul believed to be an entirely original remark, and founded exclusively upon her own individual experiences. Fanny and the young Lieutenant were billing and cooing upon the sofa, while Charley paced restlessly about the room. I was sitting by the window, gazing out dreamily at the great wilderness of Dartmoor, which stretched away to the horizon, ruddy and glowing in the light of the sinking sun, save where some rugged tor stood out in bold relief against the scarlet background.

"I say," remarked Charley, coming over to join me at the window, "it seems a positive shame to waste an evening like this."

"Confound the evening!" said Jack Daseby. "You're always victimizing yourself to the weather. Fan and I aren't going to move off this sofa — are we, Fan?"

That young lady announced her intention of remaining by nestling among the cushions, and glancing defiantly at her brother.

"Spooning is a demoralizing thing, isn't it, Lottie?" said Charley, appealing laughingly to me.

"Shockingly so," I answered.

"Why, I can remember Daseby here when he was as active a young fellow as any in Devon; and just look at him now! Fanny, Fanny, you've got a lot to answer for!"

"Never mind him, my dear," said my mother, from the corner. "Still, my experience has always shown me that moderation is an excellent thing for young people. Poor dear Nicholas used to think so, too. He would never go to bed of a night until he had jumped the length of the hearthrug. I often told him it was dangerous; but he would do it, until one night he fell on the fender and snapped the muscle of his leg, which made him limp till the day of his death, for Doctor Pearson mistook it for a fracture of the bone, and put him in splints, which had the effect of stiffening his knee. They did say that the doctor was almost out of his mind at the time from anxiety, brought on by his younger daughter swallowing a halfpenny, and that that was what caused him to make the mistake."

My mother had a curious way of drifting along in her conversation, and occasionally rushing off at a tangent, which made it rather difficult to remember her original proposition. On this occasion Charley had, however, stowed it away in his mind as likely to admit of immediate application.

"An excellent thing, as you say, Mrs. Underwood," he remarked; "and we have not been out to-day. Look here, Lottie, we have an hour of daylight left. Suppose we go down and have a try for a trout, if your mamma does not object."

"Put something round your throat, dear," said my mother, feeling that she had been out-manoeuvred.

"All right, dear," I answered; "I'll just run up and put on my hat."

"And we'll have a walk back in the gloaming," said Charley, as I made for the door.

When I came down, I found my lover waiting impatiently with his fishing-basket in the hall. We crossed the lawn together, and passed the open drawing-room windows, where three mischievous faces were looking out at us.

"Spooning is a terribly demoralizing thing," remarked Jack, reflectively staring up at the clouds.

"Shocking," said Fan; and all three laughed until they woke the sleeping Colonel and we could hear them endeavouring to explain the joke to that ill-used veteran, who apparently obstinately refused to appreciate it.

We passed down the winding lane together, and through the little wooden gate which opens on to the Tavistock Road. Charley paused for a moment after we had emerged, and seemed irresolute which way to turn. Had we but known it, our fate depended upon that trivial question.

"Shall we go down to the river, dear?" he said, "or shall we try one of the brooks upon the moor?"

"Whichever you like," I answered.

"Well, I vote that we cross the moor. We'll have a longer walk back that way," he added, looking down lovingly at the little white-shawled figure beside him.

The brook in question runs through a most desolate part of the country. By the path it is several miles from Toynby Hall; but we were both young and active, and struck out across the moor, regardless of rocks and furze-bushes. Not a living creature did we meet upon our solitary walk, save a few scraggy Devonshire sheep, who looked at us wistfully, and followed us for some distance, as if curious as to what could possibly have induced us to trespass upon their domains. It was almost dark before we reached the little stream, which comes gurgling down through a precipitous glen, and meanders away to help to form the Plymouth "leat." Above us towered two great columns of rock, between which the water trickled to form a deep, still pool at the bottom. This pool had always been a favourite spot of Charley's, and was a pretty cheerful place by day; but now, with the rising moon reflected upon its glassy waters, and throwing dark shadows from the overhanging rocks, it seemed anything rather than the haunt of a pleasure-seeker.

"I don't think, darling, that I'll fish, after all," said Charley, as we sat down together on a mossy bank. "It's a dismal sort of place, isn't it?"

"Very!" said I, shuddering.

"We'll just have a rest, and then we will walk back by the pathway. You're shivering. You're not cold, are you?"

"No," said I, trying to keep up my courage; "I'm not cold, but I'm rather frightened, though it's very silly of me."

"By Jove!" said my lover, "I can't wonder at it, for I feel a bit depressed myself. The noise that water makes is like the gurgling in the throat of a dying man."

"Don't, Charley; you frighten me!"

"Come, dear, we mustn't get the blues," he said, with a laugh, trying to reassure me. "Let's run away from this charnal-house place, and — Look! — see! — good gracious! What is that?"

Charley had staggered back, and was gazing upwards with a

pallid face. I followed the direction of his eyes, and could scarcely suppress a scream.

I have already mentioned that the pool by which we were standing lay at the foot of a rough mound of rocks. On the top of this mound, about sixty feet above our heads, a tall, dark figure was standing, peering down, apparently, into the rugged hollow in which we were. The moon was just topping the ridge behind, and the gaunt, angular outlines of the stranger stood out hard and clear against its silvery radiance.

There was something ghastly in the sudden and silent appearance of this solitary wanderer, especially when coupled with the weird nature of the scene. I clung to my lover in speechless terror, and glared up at the dark figure above us.

"Hullo, you sir!" cried Charley, passing from fear into anger, as Englishmen generally do. "Who are you, and what the devil are you doing?"

"Oh, I thought it! — I thought it!" said the man who was overlooking us, and disappeared from the top of the hill.

We heard him scrambling about among the loose stones, and in another moment he emerged upon the banks of the brook and stood facing us. Weird as his appearance had been when we first caught sight of him, the impression was intensified rather than removed by a closer acquaintance. The moon shining full upon him revealed a long, thin face of ghastly pallor, the effect being increased by its contrast with the flaring green necktie which he wore. A scar upon his cheek had healed badly and caused a nasty pucker at the side of his mouth, which gave his whole countenance a most distorted expression, more particularly when he smiled. The knapsack on his back and stout staff in his hand announced him to be a tourist, while the easy grace with which he raised his hat on perceiving the presence of a lady showed that he could lay claim to the *savoir faire* of a man of the world. There was something in his angular proportions and bloodless face which, taken in conjunction with the black cloak which fluttered from his shoulders, irresistibly reminded me of the blood-sucking species of bat which Jack Daseby had brought from Japan upon his previous voyage, and which was the bugbear of the servants' hall at Toynby.

"Excuse my intrusion," he said, with a slightly foreign lisp, which imparted a peculiar beauty to his voice. "I should have had to sleep on the moor had I not had the good fortune to fall in with you."

"Confound it, man!" said Charley; "why couldn't you shout out, or give us some warning? You quite frightened Miss Underwood when you suddenly appeared up there."

The stranger once more raised his hat as he apologized to me for having given me such a start.

"I am a gentleman from Sweden," he continued, in that peculiar intonation of his, "and am viewing this beautiful land of yours. Allow me to introduce myself as Doctor Octavius Gaster. Perhaps you could tell me where I may sleep, and how I can get from this place, which is truly of great size?"

"You're very lucky in falling in with us," said Charley. "It is no easy matter to find your way upon the moor."

"That can I well believe," remarked our new acquaintance.

"Strangers have been found dead on it before now," continued Charley. "They lose themselves, and then wander in a circle until they fall from fatigue."

"Ha, ha!" laughed the Swede; "it is not I, who have drifted in an open boat from Cape Blanco to Canary, that will starve upon an English moor. But how may I turn to seek an inn?"

"Look here!" said Charley, whose interest was excited by the stranger's allusion, and who was at all times the most open-hearted of men. "There's not an inn for many a mile round; and I dare say you have had a long day's walk already. Come home with us, and my father, the Colonel, will be delighted to see you, and find you a spare bed."

"For this great kindness how can I thank you?" returned the traveller. "Truly, when I return to Sweden, I shall have strange stories to tell of the English and their hospitality!"

"Nonsense!" said Charley. "Come, we will start at once, for Miss Underwood is cold. Wrap the shawl well round your neck, Lottie, and we will be home in no time."

We stumbled along in silence, keeping as far as we could to the rugged pathway, sometimes losing it as a cloud drifted over the face of the moon, and then regaining it further on with the return of the light. The stranger seemed buried in thought, but once or twice I had the impression that he was looking hard at me through the darkness as we strode along together.

"So," said Charley, at last breaking the silence, "you drifted about in an open boat, did you?"

"Ah, yes," answered the stranger; "many strange sights have I seen, and many perils undergone, but none worse than that. It is, however, too sad a subject for a lady's ears. She has been frightened once to-night."

"Oh, you needn't be afraid of frightening me now," said I, as I leaned on Charley's arm.

"Indeed, there is but little to tell, and yet it is sorrowful. A friend of mine, Karl Osgood, of Upsala, and myself started on a trading venture. Few white men had been among the wandering Moors at Cape Blanco, but nevertheless we went, and for some months lived well, selling this and that, and gathering much ivory and gold. 'Tis a strange country, where is neither wood nor stone, so that the huts are made from the weeds of the sea. At last, just as we had what we thought was a sufficiency, the Moors conspired to kill us, and came down against us in the night. Short was our warning, but we fled to the beach, launched a canoe, and put out to sea, leaving everything behind. The Moors chased us, but lost us in the darkness; and when day dawned the land was out of sight. There was no country where we could hope for food nearer than Canary, and for that we made. I reached it alive, though very weak and mad; but poor Karl died the day before we sighted the islands. I gave him warning! I cannot blame myself in the matter. I said, 'Karl, the strength that you might gain by eating them would be more than made up for by the blood that you would lose!' He laughed at my words, caught the knife from my belt, cut them off, and eat them, and he died."

"Eat what?" asked Charley.

"His ears," said the stranger.

We both looked round at him in horror. There was no suspicion of a smile or joke upon his ghastly face.

"He was what you call headstrong," he continued; "but he should have known better than to do a thing like that. Had he but used his will he would have lived as I did."

"And you think a man's will can prevent him from feeling hungry?" said Charley.

"What can it not do?" returned Octavius Gaster, and relapsed into a silence which was not broken until our arrival in Toynby Hall.

Considerable alarm had been caused by our non-appearance, and Jack Daseby was just setting off with Charley's friend Trevor in search of us. They were delighted, therefore, when we marched in upon them, and considerably astonished at the appearance of our companion.

"Where the deuce did you pick up that second-hand corpse?" asked Jack, drawing Charley aside into the smoking-room.

"Shut up, man; he'll hear you," growled Charley. "He's a Swedish doctor on a tour, and a deuced good fellow. He went in an open boat from What's-its-name to another place. I've offered him a bed for the night."

"Well, all I can say is," remarked Jack, "that his face will never be his fortune."

"Ha, ha! Very good—very good!" laughed the subject of the remark, walking calmly into the room, to the complete discomfiture of the sailor. "No; it will never, as you say in this country, be my fortune."

And he grinned until the hideous gash across the angle of his mouth made him look more like the reflection in a broken mirror than anything else.

"Come up-stairs and have a wash. I can lend you a pair of slippers," said Charley, and hurried the visitor out of the room to put an end to a somewhat embarrassing situation.

Colonel Pillar was the soul of hospitality, and welcomed Doctor Gaster as effusively as if he had been an old friend of the family.

"Egad, sir," he said, "the place is your own, and as long as you care to stop you are very welcome. We're pretty quiet down here, and a visitor is an acquisition."

My mother was a little more distant.

"A very well-informed young man, Lottie," she remarked to me; "but I wish he would wink his eyes more. I don't like to see people who never wink their eyes. Still, my dear, my life has taught me one great lesson, and that is that a man's looks are of very little importance compared with his actions." With which brand new and eminently original remark, my mother kissed me and left me to my meditations.

Whatever Doctor Octavius Gaster might be physically, he was certainly a social success. By next day he had so completely installed himself as a member of the household that the Colonel would not hear of his departure. He astonished everybody by the extent and variety of his knowledge. He could tell the veteran considerably more about the Crimea than he knew himself; he gave the sailor information about the coast of Japan, and even tackled my athletic lover upon the subject of rowing, discoursing about levers of the first order, and fixed points and fulcra, until the unhappy Cantab was fain to drop the subject. Yet all this was done so modestly, and even deferentially, that no one could possibly feel offended at being beaten upon their own ground. There was a quiet power about everything he said and did which was very striking.

I remember one example of this, which impressed us all at the time. Trevor had a remarkably savage bulldog, which, however fond of its master, fiercely resented any liberties from the rest of us. The animal was, it may be imagined, rather unpopular, but as it was the pride of the student's heart, it was agreed not to banish it entirely, but to lock it up in the stable and give it a wide berth. From the first it seemed to have taken a decided aversion to our visitor, and showed every fang in its head whenever he approached it. On the second day of his visit we were passing the stable in a body, when the growls of the creature inside arrested Doctor Gaster's attention.

"Ha!" he said. "There is that dog of yours, Mr. Trevor, is it not?"

"Yes; that's Towzer," assented Trevor.

"He is a bulldog, I think—what they call the national animal of England on the Continent?"

"Pure bred," said the student, proudly.

"They are ugly animals—very ugly! Would you come into the stable and unchain him, that I may see him to advantage? It is a pity to keep an animal so powerful and full of life in captivity."

"He's rather a nipper," said Trevor, with a mischievous expression in his eye; "but I suppose you are not afraid of a dog?"

"Afraid? No; why should I be afraid?"

The mischievous look on Trevor's face increased as he opened the stable door. I heard Charley mutter something to him about its being past a joke; but the other's answer was drowned by the hollow growling from inside. The rest of us retreated to a respectable distance, while Octavius Gaster stood in the open doorway with a look of mild curiosity upon his pallid face.

"And those," he said, "that I see so bright and red in the darkness — are those his eyes?"

"Those are they," said the student, as he stooped down and unbuckled the strap.

"Come here!" said Octavius Gaster.

The growling of the dog suddenly subsided into a long whimper, and, instead of making the furious rush that we expected, he rustled among the straw as if trying to huddle into a corner.

"What the deuce is the matter with him?" exclaimed his perplexed owner.

"Come here!" repeated Gaster, in sharp, metallic accents, with an indescribable air of command in them — "come here!"

To our astonishment, the dog trotted out and stood at his side, but looking as unlike the usually pugnacious Towzer as it is possible to conceive. His ears were drooping, his tail limp, and he altogether presented the very picture of canine humiliation.

"A very fine dog, but singularly quiet," remarked the Swede, as he stroked him down. "Now, sir, go back!"

The brute turned and slunk back into its corner. We heard the rattling of its chain as it was being fastened, and next moment Trevor came out of the stable door with blood dripping from his finger.

"Confound the beast!" he said. "I don't know what can have come over him. I've had him three years, and he never bit me before."

I fancy — I cannot say it for certain — but I fancy that there was a spasmodic twitching of the cicatrix upon our visitor's face, which betokened an inclination to laugh. Looking back, I think that it was from that moment that I began to have a strange, indefinable fear and dislike of the man.

Week followed week, and the day fixed for my marriage began to draw near. Octavius Gaster was still a guest at Toynby Hall, and, indeed, had so ingratiated himself with the proprietor that any hint at departure was laughed to scorn by that worthy soldier. "Here you've come, sir, and here you'll stay – you shall, by Jove!" Whereat Octavius would smile and shrug his shoulders, and mutter something about the attractions of Devon, which would put the Colonel in a good humour for the whole day afterwards.

My darling and I were too much engrossed with each other to pay very much attention to the traveller's occupations. We used to come upon him sometimes in our rambles through the woods, sitting reading in the most lonely situations. He always placed the book in his pocket when he saw us approaching. I remember on one occasion, however, that we stumbled upon him so suddenly that the volume was still lying open before him.

"Ah, Gaster!" said Charley. "Studying, as usual? What an old bookworm you are! What's the book! Ah, a foreign language! Swedish, I suppose?"

"No, it is not Swedish," said Gaster; "it is Arabic."

"You don't mean to say you know Arabic?"

"Oh, very well – very well indeed!"

"And what's it about?" I asked, turning over the leaves of the musty old volume.

"Nothing that would interest one so young and fair as yourself, Miss Underwood," he answered, looking at me in a way which had become habitual to him of late. "It treats of the days when mind was stronger than what you call matter; when great spirits lived that were able to exist without these coarse bodies of ours, and could mould all things to their so powerful wills."

"Oh, I see! A kind of ghost story," said Charley. "Well, adieu! We won't keep you from your studies."

We left him sitting in the little glen still absorbed in his mystical treatise. It must have been imagination which induced me, on turning suddenly round half an hour later, to think that I saw his familiar figure glide rapidly behind a tree. I mentioned it to Charley at the time, but he laughed my idea to scorn.

I alluded just now to a peculiar manner which this man Gaster had of looking at me. His eyes seemed to lose their usual steely expression when he did so, and soften into something which might be almost called caressing. They seemed to influence me strangely, for I could always tell, without looking at him, when his gaze was fixed upon me. Sometimes I fancied that this idea was simply due to a disordered nervous system or morbid imagination, but my mother dispelled that delusion from my mind.

"Do you know," she said, coming into my bedroom one night, and carefully shutting the door behind her, "if the idea was not so utterly preposterous, Lottie, I should say that the doctor was madly in love with you."

"Nonsense, 'ma!" said I, nearly dropping my candle in my consternation at the thought.

"I really think so, Lottie," continued my mother. "He's got a way of looking which is very like that of your poor dear father, Nicholas, before we were married. Something of this sort, you know." And the old lady cast an utterly heartbroken glance at the bed-post.

"Now, go to bed," said I, "and don't have such funny ideas. Why, poor Doctor Gaster knows that I am engaged as well as you do."

"Time will show," said the old lady, as she left the room. And I went to bed with the words still ringing in my ears.

Certainly, it is a strange thing that on that very night a thrill which I had come to know well ran through me, and awakened me from my slumbers. I stole softly to the window, and peered out through the bars of the Venetian blinds, and there was the gaunt, vampire-like figure of our Swedish visitor standing upon the gravel walk, and apparently gazing up at my window. It may have been that he detected the movement of the blind, for, lighting a cigarette, he began pacing up and down the avenue. I noticed that at breakfast next morning he went out of his way to explain the fact that he had been restless during the night, and had steadied his nerves by a short stroll and a smoke.

After all, when I came to consider it calmly, the aversion which I had against the man and my distrust of him were founded on very scanty grounds. A man might have a strange face, and be fond of curious literature, and even look approvingly at an engaged young lady, without being a very dangerous member of society. I say this to show that even up to that point I was perfectly unbiassed and free from prejudice in my opinion of Octavius Gaster.

"I say," remarked Lieutenant Daseby, one morning, "what do you think of having a picnic to-day?"

"Capital!" ejaculated everybody.

"You see, they are talking of commissioning the old *Shark* soon, and Trevor here will have to go back to the mill. We may as well compress as much fun as we can into the time."

"What is it that you call nicpic?" asked Doctor Gaster.

"It's another of our English institutions for you to study," said Charley. "It's our version of a *fête champêtre.*"

"Ah, I see! That will be very jolly!" acquiesced the Swede.

"There are half a dozen places we might go to," continued the Lieutenant. "There's the Lover's Leap, or Black Tor, or Beer Ferris Abbey."

"That's the best," said Charley. "Nothing like ruins for a picnic."

"Well, the Abbey be it. How far is it?"

"Six miles," said Trevor.

"Seven by the road," remarked the Colonel, with military exactness. "Mrs. Underwood and I shall stay at home, and the rest of you can fit into the waggonette. "You'll all have to chaperon each other."

I need hardly say that this motion was carried also without a division.

"Well," said Charley, "I'll order the trap to be round in half an hour, so you'd better all make the best of your time. We'll want salmon, and salad, and hard-boiled eggs, and liquor, and any number of things. I'll look after the liquor department. What will you do, Lottie?"

"I'll take charge of the china," I said.

"I'll bring the fish," said Daseby.

"And I the vegetables," added Fan.

"What will you do, Gaster?" asked Charley.

"Truly," said the Swede, in his strange, musical accents, "but little is left for me to do. I can, however, wait upon the ladies, and I can make what you call a salad."

"You'll be more popular in the latter capacity than in the former," said I, laughingly.

"Ah, you say so?" he said, turning sharp round upon me, and flushing up to his flaxen hair. "Yes. Ha, ha! Very good!"

And with a discordant laugh, he strode out of the room.

"I say, Lottie," remonstrated my lover, "you've hurt the fellow's feelings."

"I'm sure I didn't mean to," I answered. "If you like, I'll go after him and tell him so."

"Oh, leave him alone," said Daseby. "A man with a mug like that has no right to be so touchy. He'll come round right enough."

It was true that I had not had the slightest intention of offending Gaster; still, I felt pained at having annoyed him. After I had stowed away the knives and plates into a hamper, I found that the others were still busy at their various departments. The moment seemed a favourable one for apologizing for my thoughtless remark; so, without saying anything to anyone, I slipped away and ran down the corridor in the direction of our visitor's room. I suppose I must have tripped along very lightly, or it may have been the rich thick matting of Toynby Hall. Certain it is that Mr. Gaster seemed unconscious of my approach. His door was open, and as I came up to it, and caught sight of him inside, there was something so strange in his appearance that I paused, literally petrified for the moment with astonishment.

He had in his hand a small slip from a newspaper which he was reading, and which seemed to afford him considerable amusement. There was something horrible, too, in this mirth of his, for, though he writhed his body about, as if with laughter, no sound was emitted from his lips. His face, which was half turned towards me, wore an expression upon it which I had never seen on it before. I can only describe it as one of savage exultation.

Just as I was recovering myself sufficiently to step forward and knock at the door, he suddenly, with a last convulsive spasm of merriment, dashed down the piece of paper upon the table, and hurried out by the other door of his room, which led through the billiard-room to the hall. I heard his steps dying away in the distance, and peeped once more into his room. What could be the joke that had moved this stern man to mirth? Surely some masterpiece of humour!

Was there ever a woman whose principles were strong enough to overcome her curiosity? Looking cautiously round to make sure that the passage was empty, I slipped into the room, and

examined the paper which he had been reading. It was a cutting
from an English journal, and had evidently been long carried
about and frequently perused, for it was almost illegible in
places. There was, however, as far as I could see, very little to
provoke laughter in its contents. It ran, as well as I can remember,
in this way: —

"SUDDEN DEATH IN THE DOCKS. — The master of the barque-
rigged steamer *Olga,* from Tromsberg, was found lying dead in
his cabin on Wednesday afternoon. Deceased was, it seems, of a
violent disposition, and had had frequent altercations with the
surgeon of the vessel. On this particular day he had been more
than usually offensive, declaring that the surgeon was a necro-
mancer and worshipper of the devil. The latter retired on deck to
avoid further persecution. Shortly afterwards the steward had
occasion to enter the cabin, and found the captain lying across
the table quite dead. Death is attributed to heart disease,
accelerated by excessive passion. An inquest will be held to-day."

And this was the paragraph which this strange man had
regarded as the height of humour! I hurried down-stairs,
astonishment not unmixed with repugnance, predominating in
my mind. So just was I, however, that the dark inference which
has so often occurred to me since never for one moment crossed
my mind. I looked upon him as a curious and repulsive enigma —
nothing more.

When I met him at the picnic, all remembrance of my unfortunate speech seemed to have vanished from his mind. He made
himself as agreeable as usual, and his salad was pronounced a
chef-d'oeuvre, while his quaint little Swedish songs and his tales
of all climes and countries alternately thrilled and amused us. It
was after luncheon, however, that the conversation turned upon
a subject which seemed to have special charms for his daring
mind.

I forget who it was that broached the question of the supernatural. I think it was Trevor, by some story of a hoax which he
had perpetrated at Cambridge. The story seemed to have a
strange effect upon Octavius Gaster, who tossed his long arms
about in an impassioned invective as he ridiculed those who
dared to doubt about the existence of the unseen.

"Tell me," he said, standing up in his excitement, "which among you has ever known what you call an instinct to fail. The wild bird has an instinct, which tells it of the solitary rock upon the so boundless sea on which it may lay its egg, and is it disappointed? The swallow turns to the south when the winter is coming, and has its instinct ever led it astray? And shall this instinct which tells us of the unknown spirits around us, and which pervades every untaught child and every race so savage, be wrong? I say never!"

"Go it, Gaster!" cried Charley.

"Take your wind, and have another spell," said the sailor.

"No, never!" repeated the Swede, disregarding our amusement. "We can see that matter exists apart from mind, then why should not mind exist apart from matter?"

"Give it up," said Daseby.

"Have we not proofs of it?" continued Gaster, his grey eyes gleaming with excitement. "Who that has read Steinberg's book upon spirits, or that by the eminent American, Madame Crowe, can doubt it? Did not Gustav von Spee meet his brother Leopold in the streets of Strasburg, the same brother having been drowned three months before in the Pacific? Did not Home, the spiritualist, in open daylight, float above the housetops of Paris? Who has not heard the voices of the dead around him? I myself — "

"Well, what of yourself?" asked half a dozen of us, in a breath.

"Bah! It matters nothing," he said, passing his hand over his forehead, and evidently controlling himself with difficulty. "Truly, our talk is too sad for such an occasion."

And, in spite of all our efforts, we were unable to extract from Gaster any relation of his own experiences of the supernatural.

It was a merry day. Our approaching dissolution seemed to cause each one to contribute his utmost to the general amusement. It was settled that, after the coming rifle match, Jack was to return to his ship and Trevor to his University. As to Charley and myself, we were to settle down into a staid, respectable couple.

The match was one of our principal topics of conversation. Shooting had always been a hobby of Charley's, and he was the Captain of the Roborough company of Devon volunteers, which boasted some of the crack shots of the county. The match was to be against a picked team of regulars from Plymouth, and as they were no despicable opponents, the issue was considered doubtful. Charley had evidently set his heart on winning, and descanted long and loudly on the chances.

"The range is only a mile from Toynby Hall," he said, "and we'll drive over, and you shall see the fun. You'll bring me luck, Lottie," he whispered — "I know you will."

Oh, my poor, lost darling, to think of the luck that I brought you!

There was one dark cloud to mar the brightness of that happy day. I could not hide from myself any longer the fact that my mother's suspicions were correct, and that Octavius Gaster loved me. Throughout the whole of the excursion his attentions had been most assiduous, and his eyes hardly ever wandered away from me. There was a manner, too, in all that he said, which spoke louder than words. I was on thorns lest Charley should perceive it, for I knew his fiery temper; but the thought of such treachery never entered the honest heart of my lover. He did once look up with mild surprise when the Swede insisted on relieving me of a fern which I was carrying; but the expression soon faded away into a smile at what he regarded as Gaster's effusive good nature. My own only feeling in the matter was pity for the unfortunate foreigner, and sorrow that I should have been the means of rendering him unhappy. I thought of the torture it must be for a wild, fierce spirit like his to have a passion gnawing at his heart which honour and pride would alike prevent him from ever expressing in words. Alas, I had not counted upon the utter recklessness and want of principle of the man; but it was not long before I was undeceived.

There was a little arbour at the bottom of the garden, over-grown with honeysuckle and ivy, which had long been a favourite haunt of Charley and myself. It was doubly dear to us from the fact that it was here on the occasion of my former visit, that words of love had first passed between us. After dinner on the day following the picnic I sauntered down to this little summer-house, as was my custom. Here I used to wait until Charley, having finished his cigar with the other gentlemen, would come down and join me. On that particular evening he seemed to be longer away than usual. I waited impatiently for his coming, going to the door every now and then to see if there were any signs of his approach. I had just sat down again after one of those fruitless excursions, when I heard the tread of a male foot upon the gravel, and a figure emerged from among the bushes. I sprang up with a glad smile, which changed to an expression of bewilderment, and even fear, when I saw the gaunt, pallid face of Octavius Gaster peering in at me. There was certainly something about his actions which would have inspired distrust in the mind of anyone in my position. Instead of greeting me, he looked up and down the garden, as if to make sure that we were entirely alone. He then stealthily entered the arbour, and seated himself upon a chair, in such a position that he was between me and the doorway.

"Do not be afraid," he said, as he noticed my scared expression. "There is nothing to fear. I do but come that I may have talk with you."

"Have you seen Mr. Pillar?" I asked, trying hard to seem at my ease.

"Ha! Have I seen your Charley?" he answered, with a sneer upon the last words. "Are you, then, so anxious that he come? Can no one speak to thee but Charley, little one?"

"Mr. Gaster," I said, "you are forgetting yourself."

"It is Charley, Charley, ever Charley!" continued the Swede, disregarding my interruption. "Yes, I have seen Charley. I have told him that you wait upon the bank of the river, and he has gone thither upon the wings of love."

"Why have you told him this lie?" I asked, still trying not to lose my self-control.

"That I might see you; that I might speak to you. Do you, then, love him so? Cannot the thought of glory, and riches, and power, above all that the mind can conceive, win you from this first maiden fancy of yours? Fly with me, Charlotte, and all this, and more, shall be yours! Come!"

And he stretched his long arms out in passionate entreaty. Even at that moment the thought flashed through my mind of how like they were to the tentacles of some poisonous insect.

"You insult me, sir!" I cried, rising to my feet. "You shall pay heavily for this treatment of an unprotected girl!"

"Ah, you say it," he cried, "but you mean it not! In your heart so tender there is pity left for the most miserable of men. Nay, you shall not pass me — you shall hear me first!"

"Let me go, sir!"

"Nay; you shall not go until you tell me if nothing that I can do may win your love!"

"How dare you speak so?" I almost screamed, losing all my fear in my indignation. "You, who are the guest of my future husband! Let me tell you, once for all, that I had no feelings towards you before save one of repugnance and contempt, which you have now converted into positive hatred!"

"And is it so?" he gasped, tottering backwards towards the doorway, and putting his hand up to his throat as if he found a difficulty in uttering the words. "And has my love won hatred in return? Ha!" he continued, advancing his face within a foot of mine as I cowered away from his glassy eyes. "I know it now. It is this—it is this!" And he struck the horrible cicatrix on his face with his clenched hand. "Maids love not such faces as this! I am not smooth, and brown, and curly like this Charley—this brainless schoolboy—this human brute, who cares but for his sport and his—"

"Let me pass!" I cried, rushing at the door.

"No; you shall not go—you shall not!" he hissed, pushing me backwards.

I struggled furiously to escape from his grasp. His long arms seemed to clasp me like bars of steel. I felt my strength going, and was making one last, despairing effort to shake myself loose, when some irresistible power from behind tore my persecutor away from me, and hurled him backwards on to the gravel walk. Looking up, I saw Charley's towering figure and square shoulders in the doorway.

"My poor darling!" he said, catching me in his arms. "Sit here—here in the angle. There is no danger now. I shall be with you in a minute."

"Don't, Charley, don't!" I murmured, as he turned to leave me.

But he was deaf to my entreaties, and strode out of the arbour. I could not see either him or his opponent from the position in which he had placed me, but I heard every word that was spoken.

"You villain!" said a voice that I could hardly recognize as my lover's. "So this is why you put me on a wrong scent?"

"That is why," answered the foreigner, in a tone of easy indifference.

"And this is how you repay our hospitality, you infernal scoundrel!"

"Yes; we amuse ourselves in your so beautiful summer-house."

"We! You are still on my ground, and my guest, and I would wish to keep my hands from you; but, by heavens —" Charley was speaking very low and in gasps now.

"Why do you swear? What is it, then?" asked the languid voice of Octavius Gaster.

"If you dare to couple Miss Underwood's name with this business, and insinuate that —"

"Insinuate? I insinuate nothing. What I say I say plain for all the world to hear. I say that this so chaste maiden did herself ask —"

I heard the sound of a heavy blow, and a great rattling of the gravel. I was too weak to rise from where I lay, and could only clasp my hands together and utter a faint scream.

"You cur!" said Charley. "Say as much again, and I'll stop your mouth for all eternity!"

There was a silence, and then I heard Gaster speaking in a husky, strange voice.

"You have struck me!" he said. "You have drawn my blood!"

"Yes; I'll strike you again if you show your cursed face within these grounds. Don't look at me so! You don't suppose your hankey-pankey tricks can frighten me?"

An indefinable dread came over me as my lover spoke. I staggered to my feet, and looked out at them, leaning against the doorway for support. Charley was standing erect and defiant, with his young head in the air, like one who glories in the cause for which he battles. Octavius Gaster was opposite to him, surveying him with pinched lips and a baleful look in his cruel eyes. The blood was running freely from a deep gash on his lip, and spotting the front of his green necktie and white waistcoat. He perceived me the instant I emerged from the arbour.

"Ha, ha!" he cried, with a demoniacal burst of laughter. "She comes! The bride! She comes! Room for the bride! Oh, happy pair, happy pair!"

And, with another fiendish burst of merriment, he turned and disappeared over the crumbling wall of the garden with such rapidity that he was gone before we had realized what it was that he was about to do.

"Oh, Charley," I said, as my lover came back to my side, "you've hurt him!"

"Hurt him! I should hope I have! Come, darling, you are frightened and tired. He did not injure you, did he?"

"No; but I feel rather faint and sick."

"Come, we'll walk slowly to the house together. The rascal! It was cunningly and deliberately planned, too. He told me he had seen you down by the river, and I was going down when I met young Stokes, the keeper's son, coming back from fishing, and he told me that there was nobody there. Somehow, when Stokes said that, a thousand little things flashed into my mind at once, and I became in a moment so convinced of Gaster's villainy, that I ran as hard as I could to the arbour."

"Charley," I said, clinging to my lover's arm, "I fear he will injure you in some way. Did you see the look in his eyes before he leaped the wall?"

"Pshaw!" said Charley. "All these foreigners have a way of scowling and glaring when they are angry, but it never comes to much."

"Still, I am afraid of him," said I, mournfully, as we went up the steps together, "and I wish you had not struck him."

"So do I," Charley answered, "for he was our guest, you know, in spite of his rascality. However, it's done now, and it can't be helped, as the cook says in 'Pickwick,' and really it was more than flesh and blood could stand."

I must run rapidly over the events of the next few days. For me, at least, it was a period of absolute happiness. With Gaster's departure a cloud seemed to be lifted off my soul, and a depression which had weighed upon the whole household completely disappeared. Once more I was the light-hearted girl that I had been before the foreigner's arrival. Even the Colonel forgot to mourn over his absence, owing to the all-absorbing interest in the coming competition in which his son was engaged. It was our main subject of conversation, and bets were freely offered by the gentlemen on the success of the Roborough team, though no one was unprincipled enough to seem to support their antagonists by taking them. Jack Daseby ran down to Plymouth, and "made a book on the event" with some officers of the Marines, which he did in such an extraordinary way that we reckoned that in case of Roborough winning, he would lose seventeen shillings; while, should the other contingency occur, he would be involved in hopeless liabilities.

Charley and I had tacitly agreed not to mention the name of Gaster, nor to allude in any way to what had passed. On the morning after our scene in the garden, Charley had sent a servant up to the Swede's room with instructions to pack up any things he might find there, and leave them at the nearest inn. It was found, however, that all Gaster's effects had been already removed, though how and when was a perfect mystery to the servants.

I know of few more attractive spots than the shooting-range at Roborough. The glen in which it is situated is about half a mile long and perfectly level, so that the targets were able to range from two to seven hundred yards, the further ones simply showing as square white dots against the green of the rising hills behind. The glen itself is part of the great moor, and its sides, sloping gradually up, lose themselves in the vast rugged expanse. Its symmetrical character suggested to the imaginative mind that some giant of old had made an excavation in the moor with a titanic cheese-scoop, but that a single trial had convinced him of the utter worthlessness of the soil. He might even be imagined to have dropped the despised sample at the mouth of the cutting which he had made, for there was a considerable elevation there, from which you looked down on the long, straight glen. It was upon this rising ground that the platform was prepared from which the riflemen were to fire, and thither we bent our steps on that eventful afternoon.

Our opponents had arrived there before us, bringing with them a considerable number of naval and military officers, while a long line of nondescript vehicles showed that many of the good citizens of Plymouth had seized the opportunity of giving their wives and families an outing on the moor. An enclosure for ladies and distinguished guests had been erected on the top of the hill, which, with the marquee and refreshment tents, made the scene a lively one. The country people had turned out in force, and were excitedly staking their half-crowns upon their local champions, which were as enthusiastically taken up by the admirers of the regulars.

Through all this scene of bustle and confusion we were safely conveyed by Charley, aided by Jack and Trevor, who finally deposited us in a sort of rudimentary grand stand, from which we could look round at our ease on all that was going on. We were soon, however, so absorbed in the glorious view, that we became utterly unconscious of the betting, and pushing, and chaff of the crowd in front of us. Away to the south we could see the blue smoke of Plymouth curling up into the calm summer air, while beyond that was the great sea stretching away to the horizon, dark and vast, save where some petulant wave dashed it with a streak of foam, as if rebelling against the great peacefulness of nature. From the Eddystone to the Start the long rugged line of Devonshire coast lay like a map before us. I was still lost in admiration when Charley's voice broke half-reproachfully on my ear.

"Why, Lottie," he said, "you don't seem to take a bit of interest in it!"

"Oh, yes, I do, dear," I answered. "But the scenery is so pretty, and the sea is always a weakness of mine. Come and sit here, and tell me all about the match, and how we are to know whether you are winning or losing."

"I've just been explaining it," answered Charley. "But I'll go over it again."

"Do, like a darling," said I; and settled myself down to mark, learn, and inwardly digest.

"Well," said Charley, "there are ten men on each side. We shoot alternately; first one of our fellows, then one of them, and so on—you understand?"

"Yes; I understand that."

"First we fire at the two hundred yards' range—those are the targets nearest of all. We fire five shots each at those; then we fire five shots at the ones at five hundred yards—those middle ones; and then we finish up by firing at the seven hundred yards' range —you see the targets far over there on the side of the hill. Whoever makes most points wins. Do you grasp it now?"

"Oh, yes; that's very simple," I said.

"Do you know what a bull's-eye is?" asked my lover.

"Some sort of sweetmeat, isn't it?" I hazarded.

Charley seemed amazed at the extent of my ignorance. "That's the bull's-eye," he said—"that dark spot in the centre of the target. If you hit that, it counts five. There is another ring, which you can't see, drawn round that, and if you get inside of it, it is called a 'centre,' and counts four. Outside that, again, is called an 'outer,' and only gives you three. You can tell where the shot has hit, for the marker puts out a coloured disc, and covers the place."

"Oh, I understand it all now," said I, enthusiastically. "I'll tell you what I'll do, Charley. I'll mark the score on a bit of paper every shot that is fired, and then I'll always know how Roborough is getting on."

"You can't do better," he laughed, as he strode off to get his men together, for a warning bell signified that the contest was about to begin. There was a great waving of flags and shouting before the ground could be got clear, and then I saw a little cluster of red-coats lying upon the greensward, while a similar group, in grey, took up their position to the left of them.

"Pang!" went a rifle-shot, and the blue smoke came curling up from the grass. Fanny shrieked, while I gave a cry of delight, for I saw the white disc go up, which proclaimed a "bull," and the shot had been fired by one of the Roborough men. My elation was, however, promptly checked by the answering shot, which put down five to the credit of the regulars. The next was also a "bull," which was speedily cancelled by another. At the end of the competition at the short range each side had scored forty-nine out of a possible fifty, and the question of supremacy was as undecided as ever.

"It's getting exciting," said Charley, lounging over the stand. "We begin shooting at the five hundred yards in a few minutes."

"Oh, Charley," cried Fanny, in high excitement, "don't you go and miss, whatever you do!"

"I won't if I can help it," responded Charley, cheerfully.

"You made a 'bull' every time just now," I said.

"Yes; but it's not so easy when you've got your sights up. However, we'll do our best, and we can't do more. They've got some terribly good long-range men among them. Come over here, Lottie, for a moment."

"What is it, Charley?" I asked, as he led me away from the others. I could see by the look in his face that something was troubling him.

"It's that fellow!" growled my lover. "What the deuce does he want to come here for? I hoped we had seen the last of him!"

"What fellow!" I gasped, with a vague apprehension at my heart.

"Why, that infernal Swedish fellow, Gaster!"

I followed the direction of Charley's glance, and there, sure enough, standing on a little knoll close to the place where the riflemen were lying, was the tall, angular figure of the foreigner. He seemed utterly unconscious of the sensation which his singular appearance and hideous countenance excited among the burly farmers around him, but was craning his long neck about, this way and that, as if in search of somebody. As we watched him, his eye suddenly rested upon us, and it seemed to me that, even at that distance, I could see a spasm of hatred and triumph pass over his livid features. A strange foreboding came over me, and I seized my lover's hand in both my own.

"Oh, Charley," I cried, "don't — don't go back to the shooting! Say you are ill — make some excuse, and come away!"

"Nonsense, lass!" said he, laughing heartily at my terror. "Why, what in the world are you afraid of?"

"Of him!" I answered.

"Don't be so silly, dear. One would think he was a demi-god to hear the way in which you talk of him. But there, that's the bell, and I must be off."

"Well, promise, at least, that you will not go near him," I cried, following Charley.

"All right — all right!" said he.

And I had to be content with that small concession.

The contest at the five hundred yards' range was also a close and exciting one. Roborough led by a couple of points for some time, until a series of "bulls" by one of the crack marksmen of their opponents turned the tables upon them. At the end it was found that the volunteers were three points to the bad — a result which was hailed by cheers from the Plymouth contingent, and by long faces and black looks among the dwellers on the moor.

During the whole of this competition, Octavius Gaster had remained perfectly still and motionless upon the top of the knoll on which he had originally taken up his position. It seemed to me that he knew little of what was going on, for his face was turned away from the marksmen, and he appeared to be gazing abstractedly into the distance. Once I caught sight of his profile, and thought that his lips were moving rapidly, as if in prayer, or it may have been the shimmer of the hot air of the almost Indian summer which deceived me. It was, however, my impression at the time.

And now came the competition at the longest range of all, which was to decide the match. The Roborough men settled down steadily to their task of making up the lost ground, while the regulars seemed determined not to throw away a chance by over-confidence. As shot after shot was fired, the excitement of the spectators became so great that they crowded round the marksmen, cheering enthusiastically at every "bull." We ourselves were so far affected by the general contagion, that we left our harbour of refuge, and submitted meekly to the pushing and rough ways of the mob, in order to obtain a nearer view of the champions and their doings.

The military stood at seventeen when the volunteers were at sixteen, and great was the despondency of the rustics. Things looked brighter, however, when the two sides tied at twenty-four, and brighter still when the steady shooting of the local team raised their score to thirty-two against thirty of their opponents. There were still, however, the three points which had been lost at the last range to be made up for. Slowly the score rose, and desperate were the efforts of both parties to pull off the victory. Finally, a thrill ran through the crowd when it was known that the last red-coat had fired, while one volunteer was still left, and that the soldiers were leading by four points.

Even *our* unsportsman-like minds were worked into a state of all-absorbing excitement by the nature of the crisis which now presented itself. If the last representative of our little town could but hit the bull's-eye, the match was won. The silver cup, the glory, the money of our adherents, all depended upon that single shot.

The reader will imagine that my interest was by no means lessened when, by dint of craning my neck and standing on tiptoe, I caught sight of my Charley coolly shoving a cartridge into his rifle, and realized that it was upon his skill that the honour of Roborough depended. It was this, I think, which lent me strength to push my way so vigorously through the crowd, that I found myself almost in the first row, and commanding an excellent view of the proceedings.

There were two gigantic farmers on each side of me, and while we were waiting for the decisive shot to be fired, I could not help listening to the conversation, which they carried on in broad Devon, over my head.

"Mun's a rare ugly 'un," said one.

"He is that," cordially assented the other.

"See to mun's een?"

"Eh, Jock; see to mun's moo', rayther! Blessed if he bean't foamin' like Farmer Watson's dog — t' bull pup whot died mad o' the hydropathics."

I turned round to see the favoured object of these flattering comments, and my eyes fell full upon Doctor Octavius Gaster, whose presence I had entirely forgotten in my excitement. His face was turned towards me, but he evidently did not see me, for his eyes were bent with unswerving persistence upon a point midway, apparently, between the distant targets and himself. I have never seen anything to compare with the extraordinary concentration of that stare, which had the effect of making his eyeballs appear gorged and prominent, while the pupils were contracted to the finest possible point. Perspiration was running freely down his long, cadaverous face, and, as the farmer had remarked, there were some traces of foam at the corners of his mouth. The jaw was locked, as if with some fierce effort of the will which demanded all the energy of his soul. To my dying day that hideous countenance shall never fade from my remembrance nor cease to haunt me in my dreams. I shuddered, and turned away my head in the vain hope that perhaps the honest farmer might be right, and mental disease be the cause of all the vagaries of this extraordinary man.

A great stillness fell upon the whole crowd as Charley, having loaded his rifle, snapped up the breech cheerily, and proceeded to lie down in his appointed place.

"That's right, Mr. Charles, sir — that's right!" I heard old McIntosh, the volunteer sergeant, whisper as I passed. "A cool head and a steady hand, that's what does the trick, sir!"

My lover smiled round at the grey-headed soldier as he lay down upon the grass, and then proceeded to look along the sight of his rifle amid a silence in which the faint rustling of the breeze among the blades of grass was distinctly audible. For more than a minute he hung upon his aim. His finger seemed to press the trigger, and every eye was fixed upon the distant target, when suddenly, instead of firing, the rifleman staggered up to his knees, leaving his weapon upon the ground. To the surprise of everyone, his face was deadly pale, and perspiration was standing on his brow.

"I say, McIntosh," he said, in a strange, gasping voice, "is there anybody standing between that target and me?"

"Between, sir? No, not a soul, sir," answered the astonished sergeant.

"There, man, there!" cried Charley, with fierce energy, seizing him by the arm, and pointing in the direction of the target. "Don't you see him there, standing right in the line of fire?"

"There's no one there!" shouted half a dozen voices.

"No one there? Well, it must have been my imagination," said Charley, passing his hand slowly over his forehead. "Yet I could have sworn — Here, give me the rifle!"

He lay down again, and having settled himself into position, raised his weapon slowly to his eye. He had hardly looked along the barrel before he sprang up again with a loud cry.

"There!" he cried; "I tell you I see it! A man dressed in volunteer uniform, and very like myself — the image of myself. Is this a conspiracy?" he continued, turning fiercely on the crowd. "Do you tell me none of you see a man resembling myself walking from that target, and not two hundred yards from me as I speak?"

I should have flown to Charley's side had I not known how he hated feminine interference, and anything approaching to a scene. I could only listen silently to his strange, wild words.

"I protest against this!" said an officer, coming forward. "This gentleman must really either take his shot, or we shall remove our men off the field and claim the victory."

"But I'll shoot him!" gasped poor Charley.

"Humbug!" "Rubbish!" "Shoot him, then!" growled half a score of masculine voices.

"The fact is," lisped one of the military men in front of me to another, "the young fellow's nerves aren't quite equal to the occasion, and he feels it, and is trying to back out."

The imbecile young lieutenant little knew at this point how a feminine hand was longing to stretch forth and deal him a sounding box on the ears.

"It's Martell's three-star brandy, that's what it is," whispered the other. "The 'devils,' don't you know. I've had 'em myself, and know a case when I see it."

This remark was too recondite for my understanding, or the speaker would have run the same risk as his predecessor.

"Well, are you going to shoot or not?" cried several voices.

"Yes, I'll shoot," groaned Charley—"I'll shoot him through! It's murder—sheer murder!"

I shall never forget the haggard look which he cast round at the crowd.

"I'm aiming through him, McIntosh," he murmured, as he lay down on the grass, and raised the gun for the third time to his shoulder.

There was one moment of suspense, a spurt of flame, the crack of a rifle, and a cheer which echoed across the moor, and might have been heard in the distant village.

"Well done, lad—well done!" shouted a hundred honest Devonshire voices, as the little white disc came out from behind the marker's shield and obliterated the dark "bull" for the moment, proclaiming that the match was won.

"Well done, lad! It's Maister Pillar, of Toynby Hall. Here, let's gie mun a lift, carry mun home, for the honour of Roborough. Come on, lads! There mun is on the grass. Wake up, Sergeant McIntosh. What be the matter with thee? Eh? What?"

A deadly stillness came over the crowd, and then a low, incredulous murmur, changing to one of pity, with whispers of "Leave her alone, poor lass—leave her to hersel'!"—and then there was silence again, save for the moaning of a woman, and her short, quick cries of despair.

For, reader, my Charley, my beautiful, brave Charley, was lying cold and dead upon the ground, with the rifle still clenched in his stiffening fingers.

I heard words of sympathy. I heard Lieutenant Daseby's voice, broken with grief, begging me to control my sorrow, and felt his hand, as he gently raised me from my poor boy's body. This I can remember, and nothing more, until my recovery from my illness, when I found myself in the sick-room at Toynby Hall, and learned that three restless, delirious weeks had passed since that terrible day.

Stay!—do I remember nothing else? Sometimes I think I do.

Sometimes I think I can recall a lucid interval in the midst of my wanderings. I seem to have a dim recollection of seeing my good nurse go out of the room—of seeing a gaunt, bloodless face peering in through the half-open window, and of hearing a voice which said, "I have dealt with thy so beautiful lover, and I have yet to deal with thee!" The words come back to me with a familiar ring, as if they had sounded in my ears before, and yet it may have been but a dream.

"And this is all!" you say. "It is for this that a hysterical woman hunts down a harmless *savant* in the advertisement columns of the newspapers! On this shallow evidence she hints at crimes of the most monstrous description!"

Well, I cannot expect that these things should strike you as they strike me. I can but say that if I were upon a bridge with Octavius Gaster standing at one end, and the most merciless tiger that ever prowled in an Indian jungle at the other, I should fly to the wild beast for protection. For me, my life is broken and blasted. I care not how soon it may end, but if my words shall keep this man out of one honest household, I have not written in vain.

Within a fortnight after writing this narrative, my poor daughter disappeared. All search has failed to find her. A porter at the railway station has deposed to having seen a young lady resembling her description get into a first-class carriage with a tall, thin gentleman. It is, however, too ridiculous to suppose that she can have eloped after her recent grief, and without my having had any suspicions. The detectives are, however, working out the clue.

—EMILY UNDERWOOD.

The Brazilian Cat

In 1898, Doyle began a new series for the STRAND — *a group of twelve tales, unrelated except for their shared interest in "the grotesque and the terrible." They ran for a year and were finally published, along with others, as the* ROUND THE FIRE STORIES *in 1908. These moody tales have long been particular favorites among Conan Doyle aficionados. Of them all, "The Brazilian Cat" is the most conventional, with the fewest supernatural overtones, and the most satisfying in terms of its protagonist's reliance upon his own resources.*

With important exceptions — notably the resurrection of Sherlock Holmes and forays into science fiction — ROUND THE FIRE *was Doyle's last major fiction project. The outbreak of the Boer War in 1899 changed the direction of his writing forever, and for the final thirty years of his life he devoted himself primarily to nonfiction and to playwrighting. Having established himself as the greatest writer of popular fiction since Dickens, he abandoned his position as quickly as he had won it.*

IT is hard luck on a young fellow to have expensive tastes, great expectations, aristocratic connections, but no actual money in his pocket, and no profession by which he may earn any. The fact was that my father, a good, sanguine, easy-going man, had such confidence in the wealth and benevolence of his bachelor elder brother, Lord Southerton, that he took it for granted that I, his only son, would never be called upon to earn a living for myself. He imagined that if there were not a vacancy for me on the great Southerton Estates, at least there would be found some post in that diplomatic service which still remains the special preserve of our privileged classes. He died too early to realize how false his calculations had been. Neither my uncle nor the State took the slightest notice of me, or showed any interest in my career. An occasional brace of pheasants, or basket of hares, was all that ever reached me to remind me that I was heir to Otwell House and one of the richest estates in the country. In the meantime, I found myself a bachelor and man about town, living in a suite of apartments in Grosvenor Mansions, with no occupations save that of pigeon-shooting and polo-playing at Hurlingham. Month by month I realized that it was more and more difficult to get the brokers to renew my bills, or to cash any further post-obits upon an unentailed property. Ruin lay right across my path, and every day I saw it clearer, nearer, and more absolutely unavoidable.

What made me feel my own poverty the more was that, apart from the great wealth of Lord Southerton, all my other relations were fairly well-to-do. The nearest of these was Everard King, my father's nephew and my own first cousin, who had spent an adventurous life in Brazil, and had now returned to this country to settle down upon his fortune. We never knew how he made his money, but he appeared to have plenty of it, for he bought the estate of Greylands, near Clipton-on-the-Marsh, in Suffolk. For the first year of his residence in England he took no more notice of me than my miserly uncle; but at last one summer morning, to my very great relief and joy, I received a letter asking me to come down that very day and spend a short visit at Greylands Court. I was expecting a rather long visit to Bank-ruptcy Court at the time, and this interruption seemed almost providential. If I could only get on terms with this unknown relative of mine, I might pull through yet. For the family credit he could not let me go entirely to the wall. I ordered my valet to pack my valise, and I set off the same evening for Clipton-on-the-Marsh.

After changing trains at Ipswich, a little local train deposited me at a small, deserted station lying amidst a rolling grassy country, with a sluggish and winding river curving in and out amidst the valleys, between high, silted banks, which showed that we were within reach of the tide. No carriage was awaiting me (I found afterwards that my telegram had been delayed), so I hired a dog-cart at the local inn. The driver, an excellent fellow, was full of my relative's praises, and I learned from him that Mr. Everard King was already a name to conjure with in that part of the country. He had entertained the school-children, he had thrown his grounds open to visitors, he had subscribed to charities—in short, his benevolence had been so universal that my driver could only account for it on the supposition that he had Parliamentary ambitions.

My attention was drawn away from my driver's panegyric by the appearance of a very beautiful bird which settled on a telegraph-post beside the road. At first I thought that it was a jay, but it was larger, with a brighter plumage. The driver accounted for its presence at once by saying that it belonged to the very man whom we were about to visit. It seems that the acclimatization of foreign creatures was one of his hobbies, and that he had brought with him from Brazil a number of birds and beasts which he was endeavouring to rear in England. When once we had passed the gates of Greylands Park we had ample evidence of this taste of his. Some small spotted deer, a curious wild pig known, I believe, as a peccary, a gorgeously feathered oriole, some sort of armadillo, and a singular lumbering intoed beast like a very fat badger, were among the creatures which I observed as we drove along the winding avenue.

Mr. Everard King, my unknown cousin, was standing in person upon the steps of his house, for he had seen us in the distance, and guessed that it was I. His appearance was very homely and benevolent, short and stout, forty-five years old perhaps, with a round, good-humoured face, burned brown with the tropical sun, and shot with a thousand wrinkles. He wore white linen clothes, in true planter style, with a cigar between his lips, and a large Panama hat upon the back of his head. It was such a figure as one associates with a verandaed bungalow, and it looked curiously out of place in front of this broad, stone English mansion, with its solid wings and its Palladio pillars over the doorway.

"My dear!" he cried, glancing over his shoulder; "my dear, here is our guest! Welcome, welcome to Greylands! I am delighted to make your acquaintance, Cousin Marshall, and I take it as a great compliment that you should honour this sleepy little country place with your presence."

Nothing could be more hearty than his manner, and he set me at my ease in an instant. But it needed all his cordiality to atone for the frigidity and even rudeness of his wife, a tall, haggard woman, who came forward at his summons. She was, I believe, of Brazilian extraction, though she spoke excellent English, and I excused her manners on the score of her ignorance of our customs. She did not attempt to conceal, however, either then or afterwards, that I was no very welcome visitor at Greylands Court. Her actual words were, as a rule, courteous, but she was the possessor of a pair of particularly expressive dark eyes, and I read in them very clearly from the first that she heartily wished me back in London once more.

However, my debts were too pressing and my designs upon my wealthy relative were too vital for me to allow them to be upset by the ill-temper of his wife, so I disregarded her coldness and reciprocated the extreme cordiality of his welcome. No pains had been spared by him to make me comfortable. My room was a charming one. He implored me to tell him anything which could add to my happiness. It was on the tip of my tongue to inform him that a blank cheque would materially help towards that end, but I felt that it might be premature in the present state of our acquaintance. The dinner was excellent, and as we sat together afterwards over his excellent Havanas and coffee, which latter he told me was specially prepared upon his own plantation, it seemed to me that all my driver's eulogies were justified, and that I had never met a more large-hearted and hospitable man.

But, in spite of his cheery good nature, he was a man with a strong will and a fiery temper of his own. Of this I had an example upon the following morning. The curious aversion which Mrs. Everard King had conceived towards me was so strong, that her manner at breakfast was almost offensive. But her meaning became unmistakable when her husband had quitted the room.

"The best train in the day is at twelve fifteen," said she.

"But I was not thinking of going to-day," I answered, frankly — perhaps even defiantly, for I was determined not to be driven out by this woman.

"Oh, if it rests with you——" said she, and stopped, with a most insolent expression in her eyes.

"I am sure," I answered, "that Mr. Everard King would tell me if I were outstaying my welcome."

"What's this? What's this?" said a voice, and there he was in the room. He had overheard my last words, and a glance at our faces had told him the rest. In an instant his chubby, cheery face set into an expression of absolute ferocity.

"Might I trouble you to walk outside, Marshall?" said he. (I may mention that my own name is Marshall King.)

He closed the door behind me, and then, for an instant, I heard him talking in a low voice of concentrated passion to his wife. This gross breach of hospitality had evidently hit him upon his tenderest point. I am no eavesdropper, so I walked out on to the lawn. Presently I heard a hurried step behind me, and there was the lady, her face pale with excitement, and her eyes red with tears.

"My husband has asked me to apologize to you, Mr. Marshall King," said she, standing with downcast eyes before me.

"Please do not say another word, Mrs. King."

Her dark eyes suddenly blazed out at me.

"You fool!" she hissed, with frantic vehemence, and turning on her heel swept back to the house.

The insult was so outrageous, so insufferable, that I could only stand staring after her in bewilderment. I was still there when my host joined me. He was his cheery, chubby self once more.

"I hope that my wife has apologized for her foolish remarks?" said he.

"Oh, yes — yes, certainly."

He put his hand through my arm and walked with me up and down the lawn.

"You must not take it seriously," said he. "It would grieve me inexpressibly if you curtailed your visit by one hour. The fact is — there is no reason why there should be any concealment between relatives — that my poor, dear wife is incredibly jealous. She hates that anyone — male or female — should for an instant come between us. Her ideal is a desert island and an eternal *tête-à-tête*. That gives you the clue to her actions, which are, I confess, upon this particular point, not very far removed from mania. Tell me that you will think no more of it."

"No, no; certainly not."

"Then light this cigar and come round with me and see my little menagerie."

The whole forenoon was occupied by this inspection, which included all the birds, beasts, and even reptiles which he had imported. Some were free, some in cages, a few actually in the house. He spoke with enthusiasm of his successes and his failures, his births and his deaths, and he would cry out in his delight, like a schoolboy, when, as we walked, some gaudy bird would flutter up from the grass, or some curious beast slink into the cover. Finally he led me down a corridor which extended from one wing of the house. At the end of this there was a heavy door with a sliding shutter in it, and beside it there projected from the wall an iron handle attached to a wheel and a drum. A line of stout bars extended across the passage.

"I am about to show you the jewel of my collection," said he. "There is only one other specimen in Europe, now that the Rotterdam cub is dead. It is a Brazilian cat."

"But how does that differ from any other cat?"

"You will soon see that," said he, laughing. "Will you kindly draw that shutter and look through?"

I did so, and found that I was gazing into a large, empty room, with stone flags, and small, barred windows upon the farther wall.

In the centre of this room, lying in the middle of a golden patch of sunlight, there was stretched a huge creature, as large as a tiger, but as black and sleek as ebony. It was simply a very enormous and very well-kept black cat, and it cuddled up and basked in that yellow pool of light exactly as a cat would do. It was so graceful, so sinewy, and so gently and smoothly diabolical, that I could not take my eyes from the opening.

"Isn't he splendid?" said my host, enthusiastically.

"Glorious! I never saw such a noble creature."

"Some people call it a black puma, but really it is not a puma at all. That fellow is nearly eleven feet from tail to tip. Four years ago he was a little ball of black fluff with two yellow eyes staring out of it. He was sold me as a new-born cub up in the wild country at the head waters of the Rio Negro. They speared his mother to death after she had killed a dozen of them."

"They are ferocious, then?"

"The most absolutely treacherous and bloodthirsty creatures upon earth. You talk about a Brazilian cat to an up-country Indian, and see him get the jumps. They prefer humans to game. This fellow has never tasted living blood yet, but when he does he will be a terror. At present he won't stand anyone but me in his den. Even Baldwin, the groom, dare not go near him. As to me, I am his mother and father in one."

As he spoke he suddenly, to my astonishment, opened the door and slipped in, closing it instantly behind him. At the sound of his voice the huge, lithe creature rose, yawned, and rubbed its round, black head affectionately against his side, while he patted and fondled it.

"Now, Tommy, into your cage!" said he.

The monstrous cat walked over to one side of the room and coiled itself up under a grating. Everard King came out, and taking the iron handle which I have mentioned, he began to turn it. As he did so the line of bars in the corridor began to pass through a slot in the wall and closed up the front of this grating, so as to make an effective cage. When it was in position he opened the door once more and invited me into the room, which was heavy with the pungent, musty smell peculiar to the great carnivora.

"That's how we work it," said he. "We give him the run of the room for exercise, and then at night we put him in his cage. You can let him out by turning the handle from the passage, or you can, as you have seen, coop him up in the same way. No, no, you should not do that!"

I had put my hand between the bars to pat the glossy, heaving flank. He pulled it back, with a serious face.

"I assure you that he is not safe. Don't imagine that because I can take liberties with him anyone else can. He is very exclusive in his friends — aren't you, Tommy? Ah, he hears his lunch coming to him! Don't you, boy?"

A step sounded in the stone-flagged passage, and the creature had sprung to his feet, and was pacing up and down the narrow cage, his yellow eyes gleaming, and his scarlet tongue rippling and quivering over the white line of his jagged teeth. A groom entered with a coarse joint upon a tray, and thrust it through the bars to him. He pounced lightly upon it, carried it off to the corner, and there, holding it between his paws, tore and wrenched at it, raising his bloody muzzle every now and then to look at us. It was a malignant and yet fascinating sight.

"You can't wonder that I am fond of him, can you?" said my host, as we left the room, "especially when you consider that I have had the rearing of him. It was no joke bringing him over from the centre of South America; but here he is safe and sound — and, as I have said, far the most perfect specimen in Europe. The people at the Zoo are dying to have him, but I really can't part with him. Now, I think that I have inflicted my hobby upon you long enough, so we cannot do better than follow Tommy's example, and go to our lunch."

My South American relative was so engrossed by his grounds and their curious occupants, that I hardly gave him credit at first for having any interests outside them. That he had some, and pressing ones, was soon borne in upon me by the number of telegrams which he received. They arrived at all hours, and were always opened by him with the utmost eagerness and anxiety upon his face. Sometimes I imagined that it must be the turf, and sometimes the Stock Exchange, but certainly he had some very urgent business going forwards which was not transacted upon the Downs of Suffolk. During the six days of my visit he had never fewer than three or four telegrams a day, and sometimes as many as seven or eight.

I had occupied these six days so well, that by the end of them I had succeeded in getting upon the most cordial terms with my cousin. Every night we had sat up late in the billiard-room, he telling me the most extraordinary stories of his adventures in America — stories so desperate and reckless, that I could hardly associate them with the brown little, chubby man before me. In return, I ventured upon some of my own reminiscences of London life, which interested him so much that he vowed he would come up to Grosvenor Mansions and stay with me. He was anxious to see the faster side of City life, and certainly, though I say it, he could not have chosen a more competent guide. It was not until the last day of my visit that I ventured to approach that which was on my mind. I told him frankly about my pecuniary difficulties and my impending ruin, and I asked his advice — though I hoped for something more solid. He listened attentively, puffing hard at his cigar.

"But surely," said he, "you are the heir of our relative, Lord Southerton?"

"I have every reason to believe so, but he would never make me any allowance."

"No, no, I have heard of his miserly ways. My poor Marshall, your position has been a very hard one. By the way, have you heard any news of Lord Southerton's health lately?"

"He has always been in a critical condition ever since my childhood."

"Exactly—a creaking hinge, if ever there was one. Your inheritance may be a long way off. Dear me, how awkwardly situated you are!"

"I had some hopes, sir, that you, knowing all the facts, might be inclined to advance——"

"Don't say another word, my dear boy," he cried, with the utmost cordiality; "we shall talk it over to-night, and I give you my word that whatever is in my power shall be done."

I was not sorry that my visit was drawing to a close, for it is unpleasant to feel that there is one person in the house who eagerly desires your departure. Mrs. King's sallow face and forbidding eyes had become more and more hateful to me. She was no longer actively rude—her fear of her husband prevented her—but she pushed her insane jealousy to the extent of ignoring me, never addressing me, and in every way making my stay at Greylands as uncomfortable as she could. So offensive was her manner during that last day, that I should certainly have left had it not been for that interview with my host in the evening which would, I hoped, retrieve my broken fortunes.

It was very late when it occurred, for my relative, who had been receiving even more telegrams than usual during the day, went off to his study after dinner, and only emerged when the household had retired to bed. I heard him go round locking the doors, as his custom was of a night, and finally he joined me in the billiard-room. His stout figure was wrapped in a dressing-gown, and he wore a pair of red Turkish slippers without any heels. Settling down into an arm-chair, he brewed himself a glass of grog, in which I could not help noticing that the whisky considerably predominated over the water.

"My word!" said he, "what a night!"

It was, indeed. The wind was howling and screaming round the house, and the latticed windows rattled and shook as if they were coming in. The glow of the yellow lamps and the flavour of our cigars seemed the brighter and more fragrant for the contrast.

"Now, my boy," said my host, "we have the house and the night to ourselves. Let me have an idea of how your affairs stand, and I will see what can be done to set them in order. I wish to hear every detail."

Thus encouraged, I entered into a long exposition, in which all my tradesmen and creditors, from my landlord to my valet, figured in turn. I had notes in my pocket-book, and I marshalled my facts, and gave, I flatter myself, a very business-like statement of my own unbusiness-like ways and lamentable position. I was depressed, however, to notice that my companion's eyes were vacant and his attention elsewhere. When he did occasionally throw out a remark, it was so entirely perfunctory and pointless, that I was sure he had not in the least followed my remarks. Every now and then he roused himself and put on some show of interest, asking me to repeat or to explain more fully, but it was always to sink once more into the same brown study. At last he rose and threw the end of his cigar into the grate.

"I'll tell you what, my boy," said he. "I never had a head for figures, so you will excuse me. You must jot it all down upon paper, and let me have a note of the amount. I'll understand it when I see it in black and white."

The proposal was encouraging. I promised to do so.

"And now it's time we were in bed. By Jove, there's one o'clock striking in the hall."

The tinging of the chiming clock broke through the deep roar of the gale. The wind was sweeping past with the rush of a great river.

"I must see my cat before I go to bed," said my host. "A high wind excites him. Will you come?"

"Certainly," said I.

"Then tread softly and don't speak, for everyone is asleep."

We passed quietly down the lamp-lit, Persian-rugged hall, and through the door at the farther end. All was dark in the stone corridor, but a stable lantern hung on a hook, and my host took it down and lit it. There was no grating visible in the passage, so I knew that the beast was in its cage.

"Come in!" said my relative, and opened the door.

A deep growling as we entered showed that the storm had really excited the creature. In the flickering light of the lantern, we saw it, a huge black mass, coiled in the corner of its den and throwing a squat, uncouth shadow upon the whitewashed wall. Its tail switched angrily among the straw.

"Poor Tommy is not in the best of tempers," said Everard King, holding up the lantern and looking in at him. "What a black devil he looks, doesn't he? I must give him a little supper to put him in a better humour. Would you mind holding the lantern for a moment?"

I took it from his hand and he stepped to the door.

"His larder is just outside here," said he. "You will excuse me for an instant, won't you?" He passed out, and the door shut with a sharp metallic click behind him.

That hard crisp sound made my heart stand still. A sudden wave of terror passed over me. A vague perception of some monstrous treachery turned me cold. I sprang to the door, but there was no handle upon the inner side.

"Here!" I cried. "Let me out!"

"All right! Don't make a row!" said my host from the passage. "You've got the light all right."

"Yes, but I don't care about being locked in alone like this."

"Don't you?" I heard his hearty, chuckling laugh. "You won't be alone long."

"Let me out, sir!" I repeated, angrily. "I tell you I don't allow practical jokes of this sort."

"Practical is the word," said he, with another hateful chuckle. And then suddenly I heard, amidst the roar of the storm, the creak and whine of the winch-handle turning, and the rattle of the grating as it passed through the slot. Great God, he was letting loose the Brazilian cat!

In the light of the lantern I saw the bars sliding slowly before me. Already there was an opening a foot wide at the farther end. With a scream I seized the last bar with my hands and pulled with the strength of a madman. I *was* a madman with rage and horror. For a minute or more I held the thing motionless. I knew that he was straining with all his force upon the handle, and that the leverage was sure to overcome me. I gave inch by inch, my feet sliding along the stones, and all the time I begged and prayed this inhuman monster to save me from this horrible death. I conjured him by his kinship. I reminded him that I was his guest; I begged to know what harm I had ever done him. His only answers were the tugs and jerks upon the handle, each of which, in spite of all my struggles, pulled another bar through the opening. Clinging and clutching, I was dragged across the whole front of the cage, until at last, with aching wrists and lacerated fingers, I gave up the hopeless struggle. The grating clanged back as I released it, and an instant later I heard the shuffle of the Turkish slippers in the passage, and the slam of the distant door. Then everything was silent.

The creature had never moved during this time. He lay still in the corner, and his tail had ceased switching. This apparition of a man adhering to his bars and dragged screaming across him had apparently filled him with amazement. I saw his great eyes staring steadily at me. I had dropped the lantern when I seized the bars, but it still burned upon the floor, and I made a movement to grasp it, with some idea that its light might protect me. But the instant I moved, the beast gave a deep and menacing growl. I stopped and stood still, quivering with fear in every limb. The cat (if one may call so fearful a creature by so homely a name) was not more than ten feet from me. The eyes glimmered like two discs of phosphorus in the darkness. They appalled and yet fascinated me. I could not take my own eyes from them. Nature plays strange tricks with us at such moments of intensity, and those glimmering lights waxed and waned with a steady rise and fall. Sometimes they seemed to be tiny points of extreme brilliancy—little electric sparks in the black obscurity—then they would widen and widen until all that corner of the room was filled with their shifting and sinister light. And then suddenly they went out altogether.

The beast had closed its eyes. I do not know whether there may be any truth in the old idea of the dominance of the human gaze, or whether the huge cat was simply drowsy, but the fact remains that, far from showing any symptom of attacking me, it simply rested its sleek, black head upon its huge forepaws and seemed to sleep. I stood, fearing to move lest I should rouse it into malignant life once more. But at least I was able to think clearly now that the baleful eyes were off me. Here I was shut up for the night with the ferocious beast. My own instincts, to say nothing of the words of the plausible villain who laid this trap for me, warned me that the animal was as savage as its master. How could I stave it off until morning? The door was hopeless, and so were the narrow, barred windows. There was no shelter anywhere in the bare, stone-flagged room. To cry for assistance was absurd. I knew that this den was an outhouse, and that the corridor which connected it with the house was at least a hundred feet long. Besides, with that gale thundering outside, my cries were not likely to be heard. I had only my own courage and my own wits to trust to.

And then, with a fresh wave of horror, my eyes fell upon the lantern. The candle had burned low, and was already beginning to gutter. In ten minutes it would be out. I had only ten minutes then in which to do something, for I felt that if I were once left in the dark with that fearful beast I should be incapable of action. The very thought of it paralyzed me. I cast my despairing eyes round this chamber of death, and they rested upon one spot which seemed to promise I will not say safety, but less immediate danger than the open floor.

I have said that the cage had a top as well as a front, and this top was left standing when the front was wound through the slot in the wall. It consisted of bars at a few inches' interval, with stout wire netting between, and it rested upon a strong stanchion at each end. It stood now as a great barred canopy over the crouching figure in the corner. The space between this iron shelf and the roof may have been from two to three feet. If I could only get up there, squeezed in between bars and ceiling, I should have only one vulnerable side. I should be safe from below, from behind, and from each side. Only on the open face of it could I be attacked. There, it is true, I had no protection whatever; but, at least, I should be out of the brute's path when he began to pace about his den. He would have to come out of his way to reach me. It was now or never, for if once the light were out it would be impossible. With a gulp in my throat I sprang up, seized the iron edge of the top, and swung myself panting on to it. I writhed in face downwards, and found myself looking straight into the terrible eyes and yawning jaws of the cat. Its fetid breath came up into my face like the steam from some foul pot.

It appeared, however, to be rather curious than angry. With a sleek ripple of its long, black back it rose, stretched itself, and then rearing itself on its hind legs, with one fore paw against the wall, it raised the other, and drew its claws across the wire meshes beneath me. One sharp, white hook tore through my

trousers — for I may mention that I was still in evening dress —
and dug a furrow in my knee. It was not meant as an attack, but
rather as an experiment, for upon my giving a sharp cry of pain
he dropped down again, and springing lightly out into the room,
he began walking swiftly round it, looking up every now and
again in my direction. For my part I shuffled backwards until I
lay with my back against the wall, screwing myself into the
smallest space possible. The farther I got the more difficult it was
for him to attack me.

He seemed more excited now that he had begun to move
about, and he ran swiftly and noiselessly round and round the
den, passing continually underneath the iron couch upon which
I lay. It was wonderful to see so great a bulk passing like a
shadow, with hardly the softest thudding of velvety pads. The
candle was burning low — so low that I could hardly see the
creature. And then, with a last flare and splutter, it went out
altogether. I was alone with the cat in the dark!

It helps one to face a danger when one knows that one has
done all that possibly can be done. There is nothing for it then
but to quietly await the result. In this case, there was no chance
of safety anywhere except at the precise spot where I was. I
stretched myself out, therefore, and lay silently, almost breath-
lessly, hoping that the beast might forget my presence if I did
nothing to remind him. I reckoned that it must already be two
o'clock. At four it would be full dawn. I had not more than two
hours to wait for daylight.

Outside, the storm was still raging, and the rain lashed
continually against the little windows. Inside, the poisonous and
fetid air was overpowering. I could neither hear nor see the cat. I
tried to think about other things — but only one had power
enough to draw my mind from my terrible position. That was
the contemplation of my cousin's villainy, his unparalleled
hypocrisy, his malignant hatred of me. Beneath that cheerful
face there lurked the spirit of a mediaeval assassin. And as I
thought of it, I saw more clearly how cunningly the thing had
been arranged. He had apparently gone to bed with the others.
No doubt he had his witnesses to prove it. Then, unknown to
them, he had slipped down, had lured me into this den, and
abandoned me. His story would be so simple. He had left me to
finish my cigar in the billiard-room. I had gone down on my own

account to have a last look at the cat. I had entered the room without observing that the cage was opened, and I had been caught. How could such a crime be brought home to him? Suspicion, perhaps — but proof, never!

How slowly those dreadful two hours went by! Once I heard a low, rasping sound, which I took to be the creature licking its own fur. Several times those greenish eyes gleamed at me through the darkness, but never in a fixed stare, and my hopes grew stronger that my presence had been forgotten or ignored. At last the least faint glimmer of light came through the windows — I first dimly saw them as two grey squares upon the black wall, then grey turned to white, and I could see my terrible companion once more. And he, alas, could see me!

It was evident to me at once that he was in a much more dangerous and aggressive mood than when I had seen him last. The cold of the morning had irritated him, and he was hungry as well. With a continual growl he paced swiftly up and down the side of the room which was farthest from my refuge, his whiskers bristling angrily, and his tail switching and lashing. As he turned at the corners his savage eyes always looked upwards at me with a dreadful menace. I knew then that he meant to kill me. Yet I found myself even at that moment admiring the sinuous grace of the devilish thing, its long, undulating, rippling movements, the gloss of its beautiful flanks, the vivid, palpitating scarlet of the glistening tongue which hung from the jet-black muzzle. And all the time that deep, threatening growl was rising and rising in an unbroken crescendo. I knew that the crisis was at hand.

It was a miserable hour to meet such a death — so cold, so comfortless, shivering in my light dress clothes upon this gridiron of torment upon which I was stretched. I tried to brace myself to it, to raise my soul above it, and at the same time, with the lucidity which comes to a perfectly desperate man, I cast round for some possible means of escape. One thing was clear to me. If that front of the cage was only back in its position once more, I could find a sure refuge behind it. Could I possibly pull it back? I hardly dared to move for fear of bringing the creature upon me. Slowly, very slowly, I put my hand forward until it grasped the edge of the front, the final bar which protruded through the wall. To my surprise it came quite easily to my jerk. Of course the difficulty of drawing it out arose from the fact that I was clinging to it. I pulled again, and three inches of it came through. It ran apparently on wheels. I pulled again . . . and then the cat sprang!

It was so quick, so sudden, that I never saw it happen. I simply heard the savage snarl, and an instant afterwards the blazing yellow eyes, the flattened black head with its red tongue and flashing teeth, were within reach of me. The impact of the creature shook the bars upon which I lay, until I thought (as far as I could think of anything at such a moment) that they were coming down. The cat swayed there for an instant, the head and front paws quite close to me, the hind paws clawing to find a grip upon the edge of the grating. I heard the claws rasping as they clung to the wire netting, and the breath of the beast made me sick. But its bound has been miscalculated. It could not retain its position. Slowly, grinning with rage and scratching madly at the bars, it swung backwards and dropped heavily upon the floor. With a growl it instantly faced round to me and crouched for another spring.

I knew that the next few moments would decide my fate. The creature had learned by experience. It would not miscalculate again. I must act promptly, fearlessly, if I were to have a chance for life. In an instant I had formed my plan. Pulling off my dress-coat, I threw it down over the head of the beast. At the same moment I dropped over the edge, seized the end of the front grating, and pulled it frantically out of the wall.

It came more easily than I could have expected. I rushed across the room, bearing it with me; but, as I rushed, the accident of my position put me upon the outer side. Had it been the other way, I might have come off scatheless. As it was, there was a moment's pause as I stopped it and tried to pass in through the opening which I had left. That moment was enough to give time to the creature to toss off the coat with which I had blinded him and to spring upon me. I hurled myself through the gap and pulled the rails to behind me, but he seized my leg before I could entirely withdraw it. One stroke of that huge paw tore off my calf as a shaving of wood curls off before a plane. The next moment, bleeding and fainting, I was lying among the foul straw with a line of friendly bars between me and the creature which ramped so frantically against them.

Too wounded to move, and too faint to be conscious of fear, I could only lie, more dead than alive, and watch it. It pressed its broad, black chest against the bars and angled for me with its crooked paws as I have seen a kitten do before a mouse-trap. It ripped my clothes, but, stretch as it would, it could not quite reach me. I have heard of the curious numbing effect produced by wounds from the great carnivora, and now I was destined to experience it, for I had lost all sense of personality, and was as interested in the cat's failure or success as if it were some game which I was watching. And then gradually my mind drifted away into strange, vague dreams, always with that black face and red tongue coming back into them, and so I lost myself in the nirvana of delirium, the blessed relief of those who are too sorely tried.

Tracing the course of events afterwards, I conclude that I must have been insensible for about two hours. What roused me to consciousness once more was that sharp metallic click which had been the precursor of my terrible experience. It was the shooting back of the spring lock. Then, before my senses were clear enough to entirely apprehend what they saw, I was aware of the round, benevolent face of my cousin peering in through the opened door. What he saw evidently amazed him. There was the cat crouching on the floor. I was stretched upon my back in my shirt-sleeves within the cage, my trousers torn to ribbons, and a great pool of blood all round me. I can see his amazed face now, with the morning sunlight upon it. He peered at me, and peered again. Then he closed the door behind him, and advanced to the cage to see if I were really dead.

I cannot undertake to say what happened. I was not in a fit state to witness or to chronicle such events. I can only say that I was suddenly conscious that his face was away from me—that he was looking towards the animal.

"Good old Tommy!" he cried. "Good old Tommy!"

Then he came nearer the bars, with his back still towards me.

"Down, you stupid beast!" he roared. "Down, sir! Don't you know your master?"

Suddenly even in my bemuddled brain a remembrance came of those words of his when he had said that the taste of blood would turn the cat into a fiend. My blood had done it, but he was to pay the price.

"Get away!" he screamed. "Get away, you devil! Baldwin! Baldwin! Oh, my God!"

And then I heard him fall, and rise, and fall again, with a sound like the ripping of sacking. His screams grew fainter until they were lost in the worrying snarl. And then, after I thought that he was dead, I saw, as in a nightmare, a blinded, tattered, blood-soaked figure running wildly round the room—and that was the last glimpse which I had of him before I fainted once again.

I was many months in my recovery—in fact, I cannot say that I have ever recovered, for to the end of my days I shall carry a stick as a sign of my night with a Brazilian cat. Baldwin, the groom, and the other servants could not tell what had occurred when, drawn by the death cries of their master, they found me behind the bars, and his remains—or what they afterwards discovered to be his remains—in the clutch of the creature which he had reared. They stalled him off with hot irons, and afterwards shot him through the loophole of the door before they could finally extricate me. I was carried to my bedroom, and there, under the roof of my would-be murderer, I remained between life and death for several weeks. They had sent for a surgeon from Clipton and a nurse from London, and in a month I was able to be carried to the station, and so conveyed back once more to Grosvenor Mansions.

I have one remembrance of that illness, which might have been part of the ever-changing panorama conjured up by a delirious brain were it not so definitely fixed in my memory. One night when the nurse was absent, the door of my chamber opened, and a tall woman in blackest mourning slipped into the room. She came across to me, and as she bent her sallow face I saw by the faint gleam of the night-light that it was the Brazilian woman whom my cousin had married. She stared intently into my face, and her expression was more kindly than I had ever seen it.

"Are you conscious?" she asked.

I feebly nodded—for I was still very weak.

"Well, then, I only wished to say to you that you have yourself to blame. Did I not do all I could for you? From the beginning I tried to drive you from the house. By every means, short of betraying my husband, I tried to save you from him. I knew that he had a reason for bringing you here. I knew that he would never let you get away again. No one knew him as I knew him, who had suffered from him so often. I did not dare to tell you all this. He would have killed me. But I did my best for you. As things have turned out, you have been the best friend that I ever had. You have set me free, and I fancied that nothing but death would do that. I am sorry if you are hurt, but I cannot reproach myself. I told you that you were a fool—and a fool you have been." She crept out of the room, the bitter, singular woman, and I was never destined to see her again. With what remained from her husband's property she went back to her native land, and I have heard that she afterwards took the veil at Pernambuco.

It was not until I had been back in London for some time that the doctors pronounced me to be well enough to do business. It was not a very welcome permission to me, for I feared that it would be the signal for an inrush of creditors; but it was Summers, my lawyer, who first took advantage of it.

"I am very glad to see that your lordship is so much better," said he. "I have been waiting a long time to offer my congratulations."

"What do you mean, Summers? This is no time for joking."

"I mean what I say," he answered. "You have been Lord Southerton for the last six weeks, but we feared that it would retard your recovery if you were to learn it."

Lord Southerton! One of the richest peers in England! I could not believe my ears. And then suddenly I thought of the time which had elapsed, and how it coincided with my injuries.

"Then Lord Southerton must have died about the same time that I was hurt?"

"His death occurred upon that very day." Summers looked hard at me as I spoke, and I am convinced—for he was a very shrewd fellow—that he had guessed the true state of the case. He paused for a moment as if awaiting a confidence from me, but I could not see what was to be gained by exposing such a family scandal.

"Yes, a very curious coincidence," he continued, with the same knowing look. "Of course, you are aware that your cousin Everard King was the next heir to the estates. Now, if it had been you instead of him who had been torn to pieces by this tiger, or whatever it was, then of course he would have been Lord Southerton at the present moment."

"No doubt," said I.

"And he took such an interest in it," said Summers. "I happen to know that the late Lord Southerton's valet was in his pay, and that he used to have telegrams from him every few hours to tell him how he was getting on. That would be about the time when you were down there. Was it not strange that he should wish to be so well informed, since he knew that he was not the direct heir?"

"Very strange," said I. "And now, Summers, if you will bring me my bills and a new cheque-book, we will begin to get things into order."